HER OWN DEVICES

A novel or two

GUERNICA WORLD EDITIONS 79

GEOFFREY DUTTON

HER OWN DEVICES

A novel or two

GUERNICA
World
EDITIONS

TORONTO—CHICAGO—BUFFALO—LANCASTER (U.K.)

2024

Guernica Editions Founder: Antonio D'Alfonso

Michael Mirolla, editor
Cover and interior design: Errol F. Richardson

Guernica Editions Inc.
1241 Marble Rock Rd., Gananoque (ON), Canada K7G 2V4
2250 Military Road, Tonawanda, N.Y. 14150-6000 U.S.A.
www.guernicaeditions.com

Distributors:
Independent Publishers Group (IPG)
600 North Pulaski Road, Chicago IL 60624
University of Toronto Press Distribution (UTP)
5201 Dufferin Street, Toronto (ON), Canada M3H 5T8

First edition.
Printed in Canada.

Legal Deposit—Third Quarter
Library of Congress Catalog Card Number: 2023952487
Library and Archives Canada Cataloguing in Publication
Title: Her own devices : a novel or two / Geoffrey Dutton.
Names: Dutton, Geoffrey, 1944- author.
Series: Guernica world editions (Series) ; 79.
Description: Series statement: Guernica world editions ; 79
Identifiers: Canadiana (print) 20230620167 | Canadiana (ebook) 20230620426 | ISBN
9781771838986
(softcover) | ISBN 9781771838993 (EPUB)
Subjects: LCGFT: Novels.
Classification: LCC PS3604.U89 H37 2024 | DDC 813/.6—dc23

To my characters, who deserved better fates

About Being in This Writer's Book

THIS IS ANNA BURMEISTER, but some of you might know me by another name. We'll get to that. And as much as I didn't want to, here I am introducing a novel someone I don't know wrote about me. In fact, it's the second one he put me in, as I recently found out. Let me tell you, being fictionalized is strange. Just hope it never happens to you, because you'll have a lot of explaining to do if anyone ever finds out.

I've never told anyone about the time when I could have prevented a foolish act that led to a tragedy, and I'm not about to spill those beans now. But after living with the consequences for five years I moved on so I thought until my Vati emailed me from Basel telling me about a novel he read, a political thriller, set right here in Piraeus back in 2015. He billed it as a bunch of young radicals carry out a harebrained plot to dispatch a head of state. It was pretty far-fetched, he said, but there was this Swiss expat anarchist character calling herself Katrina who really reminded him of me. Not that his public-spirited daughter would ever get involved in an international political conspiracy.

Not that he knew, but Katrina was my alias back then! I had to see what Daddy meant. So I bought the eBook and opened it after putting my son to bed. Good night! Right there in the first chapter, that woman in the middle of that big protest demo had to be me. The next one told how I met Mahmoud in the café. It prickled my flesh. Most everything I read was true, down to my neighborhood, flat, appearance, politics, and how I talked my way into those guys' secret team.

I thumbed to the end to see if it told what happened in Turkey—and freaked. Put it down and never read the rest. Couldn't bear to relive all that tension and grief. But I'd seen enough to kickstart Gizzard-Brain. That's what I call the nagging voice in my head that pops up to tell me what a fool I am. *Get a grip*, I heard. *It's only a novel.*

Only a novel? It's my life, dammit! Give me a break! Were you on holiday when all that went down?

The ending drove home what I already knew—that most of my misery is due to a man, but not in the way you're probably thinking. It isn't what he did to me; it's what I did to him that eats at me. That brave, kind, handsome father of our child who loved and protected me, the man who would be raising him with me if not for my stupidity. He would graciously call what befell him kismet. I call it criminal negligence, and the bitter finality of watching him die keeps me under his spell. How would you handle that, Mizz Gizzard-Brain?

But it boils my blood to think I was under surveillance the whole time. All my intimate secrets—even my freaking diary—are in there. Who could have come up with all that? I had to know, so I tracked down the book's website. It's full of intimate details about our ill-fated operation but doesn't say how the author knew about them.

The site had a contact form. I had to know what was going on, so I wrote: This is your Katrina. Who are you and why did you invade my privacy?

Next day someone named Max responded. Said he worked for the publisher and had edited the book. He wrote: And who might you be? What's your real name? Where did you grow up? How old are you?

So I told him I'm Anna Burmeister from Basel. I've lived in Piraeus for six or seven years and, if you must know, I'm more or less 29, so now you come clean.

And he did. We must have exchanged a dozen messages that got stranger and stranger. Max said the writer swore he'd made everything up, any resemblance is coincidental, etc. But this is too much coincidence, I insisted, and he had to agree. Thought the writer must have been channeling me somehow—remote viewing and all that. Said he never believed in clairvoyance but since the writer didn't know me and had never visited Greece, what else could it have been?

Maybe a literary hit job that might blow up in my face. Given what we were up to at the time, that guy's exposé could be a death warrant.

Not only that, Max said the writer now wants me to "participate" in another book. Forget it, I almost auto-replied before that voice in my head said: *Think about it. Wouldn't you like him to shadow you for a while and write it up? Wouldn't cost anything and might enhance your brand.*

Brand? No soap. Notoriety from some freaking tell-all is the last thing I want, even if I got paid for it.

Gizzard-Brain didn't buy it. *Suit yourself, but who wouldn't like an unobtrusive, non-judgmental biographer to chronicle their life and times in a book of life lessons to pass on?*

Sounds a lot like a memoir. Why would I want to outsource anything so intimate?

Like I said, you'll get to know yourself from a fresh perspective. Free therapeutic insights.

Seemed like one of those offers you can't refuse. Look, this writer shadowed me behind my back once and could channel me again whether I want it or not. So I told Max I'd do it as long as I had editorial control. He wrote back telling me it doesn't work that way. As a character, I don't get to edit text, but I can use what it says to edit my life.

He made it sound like self-help. Do I really want a life coach I'll never meet? Even for free?

Max thought so: In my opinion, you're good at hatching big plans but don't always think through consequences and end up jumping to conclusions without a parachute.

Before I could ask what that's supposed to mean, he wrote: Look. This project *is* the parachute. The writer said he feels bad about what he put you through. He guarantees you'll come out better than when you started this time, and I won't let him kick dirt in your face. Me and my red pencil.

I don't know, I wrote. Swear to Dickens or whomever you believe in?

Swear, he said. Not only that, if you tell me at any point that it's too much pressure, I'll reject the manuscript. But that would be a shame, because you are an inspiring woman with greatness in you, and now's your chance to shine your light.

Imagine my surprise that anyone could think that of me. Like he said, all my adult life I've been throwing myself into situations without thinking twice and coming out bitter and bruised from kicking myself. It's time I ejected myself from all that and collect some back pay.

But it's not as if I have a choice. Let's see what happens. I gotta go.

PART ONE

Anxious Activist

As sure as my name was Mahmoud Al Ramadi, this cannot be Paradise, this shimmering haze lodged somewhere between Heaven and Earth. Is it from the mists of Heaven I hear a multitude of chanting voices blending together, droning on constantly, swelling at hours of devotion? I see Earth's curve as if wrapped in gauze, as impenetrable as it is translucent.

For a long time I despaired of my wretched condition, but once I stopped pitying myself I found I could slip through the mists by focusing on places I knew in life. At first the haze disoriented me, but after many failed attempts I willed myself home to Mosul. Our street is almost unrecognizable after the battle to eject Daesh turned it into a wasteland. A strange family was squatting in the remains of our house. The garden where I buried my parents as gunfire echoed through the streets is overgrown. I had hoped to find my younger brother there, but no luck. So I visited the house in Ramadi where my mother's sister Sheba lives along with daughter Jena. They seemed to be getting by but not very well. Sadly, Akhmed was not with them. I fear he was killed or conscripted to fight for Daesh.

If I fail to find him, I hope we'll eventually meet in Paradise, Allah willing. Where I find myself now is very strange and lonely, a plane I have all to myself. Perhaps this is perdition and I am doomed to isolation for eternity.

How many other departed souls are sentenced to solitary confinement and for what reasons? Though I suffered in life, I must have transgressed somehow. Was it disobeying my father, Allah rest his soul? Or because I shot dead that Islamic State fighter in Tal Abyad? It was war, and I was defending our unit. Or, in Piraeus, when I used that blowgun disguised as a walking-stick to dispatch two hooligans who were attacking Katrina? Or in Turkey, when I used it against a despot who corrupted high office while claiming to do God's work? Should that not count as defense of the faith? If those who have taken lives are barred from Paradise, there must be a multitude of very frustrated martyrs and many more relieved virgin angels.

I thought not of virgins as we slipped into Turkey to train for the mission or when we infiltrated the crowd gathering in the courtyard of the mosque to witness their leader pontificate. Nervously arming my weapon. Though I trusted the poison's potency, what I couldn't know was what type of protection my target wore under his suit. And so I aimed high to strike his neck. All the darts I'd fashioned arced a little differently. The one I loaded had flown most true but was among the heaviest, and I was positioned near the limit of its range.

A commotion in the crowd forced me to act. Knowing that I would have no second chance, I inhaled deeply, took aim, puffed out my dart, and lowered my tube as my target winced and reached for his shoulder. As murmurs surged through the crowd, I twisted my tube's handgrip back on and sat in a cold sweat. In my peripheral vision, Katrina in her headscarf edged closer with a poison dart, under orders to permanently silence me before being captured and interrogated. How terrible for her that moment must have been.

Praise Allah, neither of these fates took us and we escaped in a panicked stampede for the exits. Unsatisfied, the angel of death followed us to arrange an accident for me that night, and the dart's poison has no antidote. At least I passed in private, in bed with Katrina, and received a decent burial. The pain was terrible, but it was over in three days. Hers could last a lifetime. How fair is that?

I must know her fate. But now, the chanting rises, calling me to prayer.

Chapter One

You never know who your friends are until you need them, yet even then you still might not know. But that's okay.

PICTURE YOURSELF IN NOT-SO-PICTURESQUE Piraeus, Greece, Athens' neglected port city. Follow your phone to the Keratsini district, brimming with civic-mindedness and civil unrest. Now, step up to the front door of a certain two-story stuccoed house on a side street there. Knock as long as you might, but no one would answer. A peek through the tattered shades of the front windows at the dusty detritus within would confirm that the building cowering between residences triple its size was sadly neglected. Despite its proximity to Dimokratias Boulevard, the commercial core of the district, nobody seemed to want to live there.

In fact, several persons of interest live here, in the rear units. One's a kid who lives with his mom and never knew his father, who, it seems, is not out of the picture. But let's not get ahead of ourselves.

Originally, that little house had one spacious flat per floor, but somewhere along the way its rent-seeking owner had ineptly renovated, sealing doors to split each unit into two and jerry-rigging kitchens and bathrooms for the front ones. So lacking in charm and amenity were those slapdash digs that his anticipated rents never materialized, and for lack of resources he stopped trying.

Unaware of the owner's financial bind, a nosey resident across the street became suspicious when she noticed people who did not seem to be tradesmen entering the alley to the left of the house with housewares and furniture.

Fearing the little tenement have been taken over by squatters, of which Greater Athens seemingly had an infinite supply, the neighbor complained to the police, who contacted the owner. Not true, he told them. Two women had taken up residence as legitimate lessees. Having researched the building and found it was slated to be confiscated for unpaid taxes, they had sought him out and proposed to improve the place in exchange for paying off his tax arrears. It was an offer the owner couldn't refuse, especially after the women intimated that, if they couldn't come to terms, word of the unoccupied building would soon reach homeless immigrants.

The women, Anna and Penelope, had met at a protest rally several months before and discovered both were in need of housing. Penelope settled in the upstairs unit. She was taller, with dark narrow-set eyes, an afro-bush of henna-hued hair, and an outgoing personality to match her full figure.

While Penelope was a native Athenian, her downstairs housemate was a Swiss implant who had lost her luggage in Athens en route from Lagos to Zürich seven years earlier, only to find her calling there as an activist opposing Greece's financial austerity measures. After settling into a commune that she came to feel wasn't for her, she chanced upon Penelope, who was looking for someone to share a house with.

Anna was slim and blue-eyed, with honey-blond hair that clung to her neck and inched down her brow to curl over wire-rim spectacles resting on cheeks that dimpled when she smiled. Someone had suggested that she looked like a younger, cuter version of the politician Elizabeth Warren, and upon looking up the American senator's pictures and platforms Anna was sufficiently flattered to agree. "Not bad for a liberal," she'd responded. Both were closely-cropped blonds with similar eyewear perched on short noses who doggedly took on the high and mighty with equivocal success.

Penelope, a graphics artist and teacher, garishly repainted every vertical surface in her two-room flat except for a side of the kitchen she called her "doodle wall." Three meters below, Anna painted cabinets white and refinished floors and woodwork in austere Swiss style.

The two accessed their two-room flats, with their sunny kitchens and decent bathrooms, via the cramped alleyway. In the rear was a door with a stout latch opening into a cramped vestibule with two newly painted doors. The soothing saffron one straight ahead led to Anna's kitchen, and the red, green, and purple one to the side secured a stairway to Penelope's flat. It was within that gaudy entryway that they typically communicated face-to-face, frequently at first and then less so once they had established themselves and went about their respective lives that tended not to intersect.

The women christened their liberated lair the Winter Palace, commemorating the Bolshevik storming of the Czar's in St. Petersburg in 1920. Truth be told, neither one was a Bolshevik and didn't enjoy being politically pigeonholed. The more extroverted Penelope was of the socialist persuasion. She had worked to bring the leftist SYRIZA Coalition to power, which promptly disillusioned her by meekly succumbing to Eurocratic demands for economic austerity. Her party's betrayal moved Penelope to undertake direct action. Confronting power sometimes requires putting one's body where one's mouth is, which she did. But her experience in detention after a short-lived occupation of the Finance Ministry dampened her militancy and eventually bred complications with her downstairs neighbor.

Anna self-identified as an anarchist of the communitarian sort who left bomb-throwing to others. A student of the theory and practice of collective self-reliance, she emulated the American refusenik Thoreau, the Russian anarchist Kropotkin, and Lithuanian-American firebrand Emma Goldman. She'd also studied the work of American philosopher Murray Bookchin and his more notorious disciple, imprisoned Kurdish separatist Abdullah Öcalan. All but one had done hard time for their beliefs, a badge of honor that Anna felt she could do without.

Anna's revolutionary ambition was to some extent self-limiting, as she congenitally shunned notoriety, preferring to shine her light from the shadows. Texting and blogging from behind her saffron door, she called attention to threats to civil society and suggested participatory alternatives. And in real life, she pitched in to transform a defunded branch library in Keratsini into a community center and took part in street actions. The most eventful one was the anticlimactic siege of the Finance Ministry at which Penelope was busted. Anna eluded capture that day by occupying the backfield as a medic. Her turn at the barricades was yet to come, and when, in another country, it did, it upended her life.

But even before that, Anna's activist lifestyle had begun to unravel. She'd been polishing her passable Greek online under the byline "Katrina," on a blog she called *Greece for All*, dedicated to making peace between political tribes. Despite her sensible suggestions for how left and right might unite to confront their common oppressors, her posts came to be roundly trolled. Leftist support vaporized when rightists vilified her for pointing out that some of the same blood runs in nationalists' veins as in those of the swarthy immigrants they despise for not being Greek. *We're all mongrels*, she had written after looking up the noun's Greek translation. *Get over it.* They didn't take her advice, and the ensuing flames forced her to liquidate the post.

Life was never the same for her after that, especially when one of her critics upped the ante. Endearingly addressed to one Katrina Kunt, an anonymous poison pen letter arrived that threatened grave injury. Concerned that her identity and location might be compromised, Anna upgraded her door latch and carried a canister of pepper spray, which only made her feel she was under house arrest.

Fortuitously, her Austrian activist friend Andreas called to ask her to board his house guest, a young Iraqi code-named Peter, for a few days. Andreas didn't explain beyond saying his house had become unsafe. Aware that Andreas had been keeping a low profile lately, Anna didn't press for details. Happy enough to house a needy immigrant, if not a potential protector, she replied: "Sure, how long?"

"Just for a few days," Andreas said. "Until the weather clears up. He's a recently-arrived refugee fleeing tragic circumstances. Very polite, no trouble at all, really, but being here illegally, he needs to avoid contact with authorities."

Andreas was right about Peter being polite, but had neglected to mention how fit and handsome he was—broad-shouldered and athletic, with a trim black beard and alert brown eyes. She was equally taken by his aura of calm determination. To do what, he didn't say and she knew better than to ask. The same for his real name; like Andreas and herself, most of the radical expats she knew assumed some sort of *nom de guerre*. Nonetheless, Anna felt a need to know.

Peter bunked on her kitchen floor for just two nights before Andreas absconded with him to occupy a new flat, but by then Anna was captivated. Reaching out, she texted invitations to get together, fielding a campaign to capture his heart. And when at last he came to her, her expressed need, persistence, and possibly her cooking, overcame what little remained of his defenses, not to mention his virginity.

But the object of her affection was also in the embrace of Andreas's secretive comrades, who were dubious of her agenda, unwilling to share theirs, and didn't fancy having a girlfriend hanging around. Regardless, on the cheeky presumption that whatever they were up to should include her, she proceeded to demonstrate to them worthiness and warrior qualities that came to include some she didn't know she possessed.

Impetuously, and over the objections of half its members, she wormed her way into a shadowy political conspiracy. It was a rash decision that would transport her and Mahmoud, the man formerly known as Peter, to foreign shores and then blow her back alone to radically rearrange her life's furnishings. Among other life lessons, the experience taught her to consider unexpected consequences, the foremost of which was bearing a fatherless child.

#

Three of the conspirators slipped across the Aegean to topple a tyrant and nearly succeeded. After making their getaway, the Turkish one called George decided to remain in his homeland. Mahmoud, the Iraqi, made peace with Allah before succumbing to poison, for which the Swiss miss who loved him blamed herself and George. She returned to Greece alone to reassemble the shards of her life into a form that would include the one she soon learned she carried in her womb.

To come to terms with her bleak situation, she wrote home for money and volunteered her services at a street clinic that had a part-time obstetrician, booking appointments and filing paperwork. There she encountered other recent and prospective mothers whom she sought to befriend, vaguely hoping to establish a daycare collective. She especially liked Cassie, a practical woman with a decent husband living nearby, herself expecting twins, who taught Anna to make apple-rose-hip-ginger tea to allay morning sickness. But Anna still missed her wake-up shots of espresso.

Despite making new friends, Anna's sense of isolation abided as her belly swelled. After marking time for two trimesters, she decided to retreat to her home country in pursuit of superior sanitation, community support, and a Swiss passport for her passenger.

The day before her departure she took a sentimental journey on three buses to the other end of Piraeus, a seaside neighborhood called Piraiki, to pay her respects to the father of her unborn child. Guided by the street map on her phone, Anna alighted from a 904 bus on a broad boulevard that circumscribed the coast. Across it, a phalanx of upscale apartment blocks reflected an unforgiving sun. She leaned upon a low wrought-iron fence running along the promenade, surveying a field of jagged limestone boulders sloping down to lapping seawater. Somewhere down there, drenched and queasy, Mahmoud had smuggled himself ashore to start a new life under a new name. She counted the months since; just half a life-changing year ago.

With a glance up and down the roadway, she boosted herself over the fence and scrabbled down to the water's edge. She sat for a while on the smoothest boulder she could find and shut her eyes to the sun, trying to visualize Mahmoud emerging from the sea, disinherited, displaced, disoriented, just hours before they first encountered one another. Soon she slid from her perch to gather stones that she piled into a cairn that rose to her knees. Kissing her hand and laying it on its capstone, she murmured "Rest in peace. Wish us luck" before breathlessly clambering up to the promenade and boarding a bus back to the Winter Palace to pack up her worries and send herself on a journey to beget the rest of her life.

Chapter Two

ANNA'S ROUTE TO HER fatherland and motherhood started with a bus and a ferryboat ride to Bari in Italy, where she boarded the first of three trains that would carry her to Basel after another sunrise. She'd intended to use the time meditating on life changes but spent most of it sleeping off her exertions.

She was shaken awake when her train lurched to a halt at the Swiss border. It stayed put for a long time for passport check, and when it finally started rolling her window displayed a panorama of a small group of travelers who had been ejected from the carriages, minded by fatigue-clad border guards sporting side arms. A young girl clung to the folds of a detainee's dress, a pretty woman in a headscarf who was, like herself, obviously pregnant with no mate apparent. As the scene slid past, Anna turned from the window and blotted her eyes with her sleeve.

Clacking up the Alps, buffeted by up- and downdrafts, Anna ruminated on the stranded mother and child. Imagining that soon they would be forced into hiding or the confines of rude refugee camps, she drew no satisfaction at her own privilege to travel at will almost anywhere.

Three and a half hours later, her train squealed to a stop inside the cavernous Zürich Hauptbanhof. Pealing church bells from across the Limmat signaled she had barely enough time to satisfy her craving for an ice cream cone before boarding her train to Basel.

As Swiss timetables dictated, precisely one hour and twelve minutes hence, she staggered stiff and weary into the expectant arms of her *Mutti und Vatter*, who kissed her three times each and eyeballed her belly before escorting her to a tram. Home was a little yellow row house a catapult-toss across the Rhein to the University where her mother was an archivist. Anna arrived to find her father had commandeered her garret bedroom for his office equipment leasing business, forcing her to bunk in the guest room, which was fine by her.

"I'm okay," she said through hooded eyes as Mutti bedded her down. "It's what I want. Please don't judge me until you've heard the whole story."

But of course she couldn't tell it whole. Most of what happened after meeting Mahmoud last fall would have to go; where they went, what they did, how he died. Yes, she'd tell her folks they went to Turkey, she thought before sleep claimed her. But on holiday, not to ambush its leader.

The late summer weather being splendid, she walked the quays along the Rhein and shopped with her mother at thrift shops for baby clothes and other paraphernalia of motherhood. During their time together Anna unwound the story she'd polished to elide everything her family didn't need to know: How a couple of Turks they knew had invited her and her Iraqi boyfriend for a holiday excursion to Turkey. She and the refugee from Mosul had only been together for a couple of months when a wayward motorist struck him after stepping off a city bus in Izmir.

She described his dancing eyes and chiseled face, steadfast yet gentle demeanor, how he had lost his parents and brother to ISIS and had to flee his country, dashing his dream of becoming an environmental engineer. All true. But to tell the whole truth of their ill-fated clandestine exploit would both break her parents' hearts and convince them she'd gone mad

Nor, to her relief, was that necessary. Beyond wanting to know more about the father, all that they seemed to care about was the health of their daughter and their unborn *Enkelkind*, and placed her under the care of an obstetrician. Freethinkers that they were and had raised her to be, her parents held no brief against Islam or premarital sex, but did ask about her Turkish comrades. Fairly truthfully, she spoke of the men as political dissidents holed up in Piraeus. Just how dissident and what they were doing in Turkey exceeded anyone's need to know.

Basking in the garden and snuggling in bed, Anna abided cramps and cravings, such as for schnitzel and coffee and cigarettes, as her mom administered herbal compresses and teas. And so it went, until one night late in August when, as the clock in the parlor cuckooed eleven, her water broke. Rushed by anxious parents to the closest medical center, six hours later, pretty much on her own, Anna gave birth to a Virgo like herself, who—as she'd predicted, having foregone ultrasound—featured male genitalia. And when baby Ramadi, the patronymic she's chosen for him, squalled for half an hour after delivery, Anna had to agree when her mutti said: "Perhaps he cries for his vati." And again, when her vati smiled and said: "He doesn't look too Swiss."

During her months in Basel, Anna got to know, appreciate, and rely upon her parents again, enjoying being pampered and prepped. But no sooner than Ramadi had adjusted to his welcoming environment and put on a kilo or two, Anna felt Greece tugging at her sleeve.

Her mother had gone back to cataloging old tomes across the river. Vati mostly sequestered himself upstairs or was off appeasing some customer. Overconfident that she'd gotten the hang of motherhood after about as much coaching as she could stand, Anna's cozy flat beckoned. And so, at six weeks, ignoring her mother's pleas to wait until he was weaned, Anna booked a flight to Athens on Vati's bank card, with a return ticket as flight insurance.

All but oblivious to the toothy Alps slipping under her wings, Anna thumbed through a book for new parents her mom had slipped her as if it were a sex manual, but found no special instructions for single moms. Lulled by throbbing engines, her snuggling baby placidly abided, alternately sleeping, burbling, drooling, and kicking Anna's gut insecurities about her local support system. It didn't come to much; her upstairs neighbor Penelope might help out in a pinch, but she kept an erratic schedule and, while somewhat matronly, wasn't at all motherly. With few friends to count on to cushion her landing, perhaps her decision to return was not so wise. Stretching past the horizon were two decades of child rearing that she didn't want to fly through solo.

Outside the terminal, Athens enveloped them in a humid pall of fumes. She was remembering arriving here from Izmir late last year, exiting this same portal into crisper air, traipsing after a Turkish gentleman with suit, tie, and a business agenda in Athens who was greeted by a liveried man holding a placard. The rapport they struck up on their flight from Izmir had given her a sorely needed lift. Upon hearing Anna describe herself as a community organizer, he'd offered to pay her to evangelize the communitarian social media platform his company hoped to launch in Athens. Thinking gainful employment would be useful, Anna said she would entertain the proposition, vague as it was.

In the liveried man's limousine they had exchanged phone numbers before bidding each other Turkish goodbyes at his hotel, where he tipped the driver and Anna gave directions to the Winter Palace before cushioning into black leather to enjoy her ride. She remembered being overcome by nausea en route, and had assumed it was carsickness, but soon learned the truth: she was baking a baby, like it or not.

No placard greeted her today. The long ride home by metro and bus seemed endless, with Ramadi fidgeting and her upstart inner critic scolding her for not having a plan. But upon letting herself in, her critic backed off as she flung open windows, activated a fan to circulate the humid air, stripped them both down, and offered mother's milk. Rejecting refreshment, Ramadi squalled. In desperation, she fetched a basin to tickle him with a sponge bath. The caress of tepid water seemed to soothe him, and after being toweled and bundled he acceded to nurse. The notion of wetting herself in the shower appealed, but thinking that the relief she sought was more than skin-deep, she placed a phone call instead.

It was to her fellow émigré Andreas, by now her oldest friend in their adopted city. Tumult in Greece had drawn them separately to Athens to join the people's rebellion against financial austerity and fascist tendencies. Both had settled in gritty Keratsini, on the western flank of Piraeus, hard hit by recession, a short haul from cargo docks where freighters, not cruise ships, disgorge their contents, at least when longshoremen weren't on strike. Crossing paths at popular protests and community projects engendered mutual respect, leading to camaraderie and that risky mission to Turkey that didn't end well. Both had responded to that blow by deactivating, Andreas to focus on perfecting his tonsorial skills, and Anna to cope with upcoming constraints on her lifestyle.

"Salut, Katrina," the Austrian said upon picking up, still unable to stop using the moniker she'd abandoned last winter. Likewise, no one here called him Jurgen, the Christian name he'd abandoned along with his homeland and religion. Always the rebel, he had kept the signature ponytail of his student days, even though as a hairdresser he could have better advertised his craft.

"You're back!" he said. "With child? Boy or girl? How is baby? How are you?"

Her *Switzerdeutsch* accent playing off his *Wienerisch*, she serially replied, "Yes, yes, boy, doing well, developing heatstroke."

"I see."

"And when he's in a good mood, Ramadi's adorable. He can already turn over all by himself."

"Ah, a patronymic."

"You could say that. 'Mahmoud Junior' just didn't feel right, so Ramadi Burmeister it is."

"Lovely! So who does he mostly resemble?"

"I'll let you decide. Can we come over to chill awhile? Maybe you can help me figure out what to do with him."

"Um, in what way?"

"Well, for starters, he'll need male role models."

"Like me? I'm hardly standard issue."

"Nonsense, Andreas. You are a natural-born leader as well as queer, if that's what you mean. You are also the most caring person I know."

He sighed. "And likely the most neurotic. Anyway, I haven't been leading anything recently, just snipping and slaving at the salon. But he's welcome to hang out here if you need me to mind him now and then."

"Thanks. Perhaps in a year or so. Can't quite picture you administering formula."

"By then you might have a boyfriend. You meet the nicest people at street demonstrations."

"Were I going to any, infant at my breast. So how has hooking up with activists worked for you?"

"I've had better luck at bars, but let's not go there," he said. "You both must be *worn out*. Bring the boy over to my place and chill out with our *Klimaanlaga Maschine*. I'll look after him while you take a cold shower."

"Thanks. Cool air and water sounds attractive. See you in an hour. Is Kosta around?"

"Ja, we're both here in the shop with customers. Business picked up while you were away."

"That's great. Any of your new clients attractive single men?"

"They're *all* attractive when we're done with them. Most are single but probably wouldn't swing with you, sorry to say."

"Story of my life. See you soon with Ramadi. Be ready to gush."

\#

Drowsing at Anna's bosom, Ramadi's first exposure to the Radically Chic hair salon didn't register, but she registered pleasure at finding both hairdressers engaged with customers. Off to the side, another lounged in a form-fitting ultraviolet jumpsuit that chicly complemented the orange seat cushions, and a disheveled, improbably platinum mane that fairly defied taming. The wall behind the androgynous individual featured cheaply framed monochrome head shots of suave stars from Hollywood's golden age, some autographed. All had inspirational hair.

At their entrance, Andreas holstered his hair dryer and Kosta laid down his shears to gingerly hug Anna and her snuggling infant. She'd seen a lot less of Kosta since he broke up with Andreas and moved in with Thomás, one of their customers. The split had depressed Andreas, who had only himself to blame for his handsome lover's change of heart. Anna had wanted to speak up for Andreas, but due to their unmentionable project, both their lips were sealed.

It was a truly difficult time for all of them. While Kosta was confined to a hellish provincial lockup on trumped-up charges, Andreas had a fling with an ex-partner from Austria. Reigniting that old flame conveniently provided Andreas cover as he struggled to salvage the conspiracy after its mastermind George was detained. Convinced his flat was under surveillance, Andreas enticed first love Ivan to rent them a condo on his company's tab. They moved in, along with Mahmoud and Kaan, another comrade. It was fun while it lasted.

For all of his efforts, Andreas suffered blowback. Given the circumstances, Kosta understood the infidelity, but rightly felt abandoned. His meagre reward for gallantly driving off the nationalist thug stomping Andreas at a protest in Syntagma Square was a six-month sentence punctuated only by a phone call and one lousy letter.

Andreas had excused his inattentiveness by maintaining he'd been consumed with "managing" a "delicate operation" he wasn't at liberty to describe. Hardly mollified, but thankful that Andreas had kept his salon on life support while he was in stir, Kosta kept Andreas on and ceded the upstairs flat they had cohabited, minus most of his mid-century furniture.

To fill the void in his home decor, Andreas scoured thrift stores for bargains: a beige sofa-bed, a red-velveted Victorian rocker, a typesetter's tray on an orange crate for a coffee table, a nest of oriental tea tables, and retrieved from a sidewalk, a squishy leather ottoman. Kosta had left behind the teak bedroom set when he decamped for Thomás' flat. Grateful for that, as well as for having a steady gig with flex time and an easy commute, Andreas reluctantly accepted their new normal, and in that socially-distanced mode the ex-lovers appeared to amicably coexist.

Ramadi stirred, making alarming hiccupping noises. Anna grabbed a towel from the counter in case of an eruption, but what came out were oddly sedate cooing sounds. "He makes this funny noise like a pigeon when he's hungry," she said. "I should take him upstairs."

Kosta flourished his blow dryer in a grand salute to his client, who exited a new man, leaving behind a tip and a pecked cheek. Sweeping clots of hair into a corner, he announced: "Marcos, my love, come hither and be served." The epicene diva in waiting slid into Kosta's swivel chair, chucking Ramadi's chin on his way.

As Kosta took up the challenge, Andreas excused himself and told Anna to follow him through a door into a storage room, a rough but generous space dimly lit by two small windows. Cardboard boxes, paint cans, bottles of hair care products, and a laundry basket heaped with towels occupied rude wooden shelves along the front wall. A rag mop stuck into a roller-bucket canted against a washer-dryer next to a water closet. On the back wall, Andreas's old English bicycle hung from a hook like a fish skeleton. Neither he nor any of his activist acquaintances owned a car, but one of them had a vintage red Vespa that had devolved into a communal possession.

Anna had once tried to persuade Andreas to toss down a carpet over its broad boards and furnish the room as a meeting space. But after Kosta had been unjustly convicted for his act of bravery in Syntagma Square, Andreas suspected police agents were keeping an eye on the premises, making setting up a conference room for radicals there problematic. Anna had agreed, but now was thinking that the room, outfitted with scaled-down furniture, would make a dandy daycare center and made a mental note to bring it up with the management.

Unlocking a stout wooden door, Andreas led them up a dim stairway to a kitchen with soothing lavender walls flooded with afternoon light. A jungle of ferns, Ficus, Schefflera, and a spreading avocado tree basked in its southern exposure, obscuring the air conditioner wheezing in a window. Taking a seat at the table, Anna opened her shirt to nurse Ramadi while Andreas started water for tea, asking if an herbal infusion would suit her.

"What I'd really like is a hit of espresso, but I can't have that yet," she said, caressing Ramadi's black-rimmed brow as his lips smacked at an aureole. "But sure, mint is good. And who by the way is that alluring creature downstairs?"

"Oh that's just Marcos, Marcos Hexadecimos—not his real name, I'm sure—being his normal outrageous self. He cuts *quite* a figure, doesn't he? You should see him in action at the big flea market peddling vintage clothing. Straight ladies from the suburbs simply *adore* him."

When Ramadi came up for air, Anna wiped away drool and buttoned up. Accepting a mug of mint tea, she took a sip and asked Andreas what he'd been up to that didn't involve littering the floor with hair. "I've been away for like three months. What did I miss?"

Rubbing his chin, Andreas said: "Well, even though the SYRIZA coalition has close to an absolute majority, it's been dragged rightward by coalition partner ANEL. PM Tsipras isn't standing up to foreign creditors as he'd pledged to and the coalition seems to be unraveling. Furthermore, the government is practically giving away the Port of Piraeus to Chinese conglomerates, and of course the dockworkers union is hopping mad."

"No surprise. What about the neofascists? The Golden Dawn Party lost a bunch of seats, as I recall. Are they still making immigrants' lives miserable?"

"Ja, they're back to basics, whipping up hatred of foreigners at torch-lit rallies and harassing them and vandalizing their shops. But the new Hellenic Solution Party may yet outdo them. Their so-called solution to immigration is to build a wall."

She chuckled. "Let's see … How many islands does Greece have?"

"… And to restore the death penalty."

"Right. Which the EU prohibits. Good luck with that."

"In short," he said with a toss of his sandy ponytail, "no rest for the oppressed."

Conversation lulled. Tea was sipped. Ramadi slept at Anna's bosom. "This calls for a photo," Andreas said, taking up his phone. He held it up to her. "Say *Käse*."

"Hold on," she said. She straightened up and turned Ramadi to display his slumbering face.

His phone clicked. "There you go. Share this when you put out a birth announcement."

Blue eyes crinkling, Anna said, chortling: "That's a good one. Sure, blog it. Post it on Facebook. Send it to newspapers. Let the creeps like the ones who targeted me know they have a potential hostage situation. Hope you weren't serious."

"Sorry. Are you *still* worried about blowback from when we took them out? It's been almost a year, and they would be after Mahmoud, not you."

"Whom they won't find. But I'm the one who set the trap for the thugs he blew away, and my name might've lived on."

She gazed down at her son and caressed his brow. "I could still be in someone's crosshairs. Can't believe I ever let myself to do such a thing."

He drained his mug. "But they *threatened* your life. The police wouldn't have protected you. What were you supposed to *do*?"

"Go back to where I came from, like they told me to do. Would've saved me a pile of grief."

His gaze fell on the baby. "I suppose it might have. But look, now you have a new beginning. Something to live for."

"It's a lot to get used to and struggle through. You wouldn't know."

Andreas studied his teacup without replying. Anna yawned with extended arms and let them drop. "Time for that shower. Can I put Ramadi down on your bed for you to watch over while I refresh?"

"Can do, I guess, but what if he wakes up and makes noise?"

"Poke his belly, tickle his feet, make a funny face. If that doesn't work, pick him up, bring him to your chest, and try burping him. You'll get the hang of it."

Anna deposited Ramadi onto a pillow as one would a jewel-encrusted crown, bunched the coverlet around him, and slipped into the bathroom. Andreas tentatively took a seat next to the little prince. He thought he recalled hearing that babies should be put down on their backs. Or was it their stomachs? With a sigh, he rolled Ramadi over to lie on his side and gazed at him, wondering what he was in for.

Chapter Three

Teleportation isn't easy, I must say. It takes a lot out of what's left of me to will myself anywhere, and then I can see dimly but hear nothing there. Perhaps with practice sound will come. But, each time I visit a place I see things a little more clearly and can hold on for a little longer. Until recently all I've been able do is visit extended family, and then only if they haven't moved. As in learning to ride a unicycle, it takes concentration and practice to keep oriented. After many failed attempts I managed to visit Piraeus long enough to learn that Katrina still occupies her little house and now has a boy who looks old enough to be our child. The last time we made love was the night before I passed. That was close to five years ago, if Aunt Sheba's Calendar is up to date. I praise Allah for allowing me to visit with my son, even if he cannot know me. And I would love to know what Katrina tells him of me. Please let it exclude how I died.

─

THAT UNSEASONABLY WARM OCTOBER day was the first, but hardly the last time Anna leaned on good old Andreas to mind the boy, but mainly after the lad had found his footing. She tried to minimize the inconvenience, rewarding Andreas with bottles of wine, home-cooked meals, and Swiss cheek kisses. She went on to stash a playpen and stroller in his salon's storage room. Andreas said he didn't mind keeping the items, envisioning the playpen a handy restraint, but drew the line at strolling.

Fortunately for him, Andreas was spared heavy lifting thanks to Anna's preschool initiative. Even when Ramadi was in utero, Anna had a mind to confederate a clutch of mothers as a daycare collective. Besides Cassie, she'd managed to corral two adventuresome moms, Doris and Katia, who favored multiculturally schooling their offspring. Doris dropped out when her son entered kindergarten, soon replaced by a pleasant Persian woman named Daria whose daughter Yasmin was part of Anna's target population. Four moms and five kids was good enough, they all agreed, and began taking turns hosting their charges.

For years, Anna had advocated for anarchist alternatives to top-down governance. Unsurprisingly, she saw to it that their daycare collective had no articles of incorporation, no by-laws, no insurance policy, no money changing hands, no paper trail, and no fixed address. She dubbed the fugitive preschool Kinder Cloud, and the name stuck. It drifted from house to house on a rotating basis, generally with one or more moms, aunts, or grandmas as schoolmarms-without-portfolio. As they dwelled in various quarters of Piraeus, logistics were cumbersome. Regardless, the kids seemed to thrive on the chaos and the moms enjoyed controlling the curriculum, each in her own special way.

All the shuffling around didn't seem to faze Ramadi. By the time he could walk without stabilization, he had gained five kilos, and six more by age four. By then he was displaying what Anna of course considered above-average agility, intelligence, and linguistic facility. She taught him to call her *Mutti* in Swiss German, *Mamá* in Greek, as appropriate, and his absent father *Vatter* and *Pateroúlis*, respectively, but became uneasy when he called Andreas Pateroúlis, although not as alarmed as Andreas. So, she told the boy to call Andreas *Onkle* as a sign of respect, saying *Herr Andreas* didn't sound quite right. As he rather liked the lad, Andreas didn't object to the honorific and it stuck.

At home, at daycare, and in places in between, Ramadi's command of both German and Greek steadily arced toward fluency. Anna's concern that he would speak in a hopeless polyglot jumble proved moot. Somehow the right brain connections were being made and he seemed to take his cue from whatever tongue was currently on tap, possibly including gay Greek patois at the hair salon. English and Swiss-German could wait, she had decided, until his memory banks sufficed to meet his conversational needs.

#

Even exposed to his chums and their mums, Ramadi rarely got sick. The few times he did, TLC and other palliatives were sufficient for his immune system to bounce back. But then came a nasty sore throat and a persistent cough that worried Anna enough to take him to urgent care.

It was almost the Vernal Equinox and the air was warm, dry, and turbulent. Spring's signature tulip gardens, baby animals, and Easter pastels notwithstanding, that most optimistic of seasons doesn't always come calling with a smile on its face. Nor was there one on Anna's as she auto-piloted Ramadi along a blustery Piraeus sidewalk en route to the free clinic. Oblivious to the plastic bag fluttering just above them and the dervish of leaves swirling above the gutter that delighted the boy, she worried that the recent spate of what the Health Ministry had dubbed "a mild transitory outbreak of late-season flu," might be neither.

At the next intersection, a fierce gust of wind flipped back the hood of the boy's black sweatshirt marked *Property of Nobody* in bold white letters to flutter his unshorn locks. The blast also blew away Anna's musings to deposit her in the moment. Thrust off balance, she clasped a spindly shade tree with one hand and clamped her beret with the other as her open fatigue jacket slapped at her torso. A baseball cap scudded by, tracing an erratic course that the young man pursuing it vainly mimicked. Invisible tendrils of air frolicked through the street, banging shutters, pinning newspapers to lampposts, and piling debris into doorways, peppering it with grains of African sand.

Tugging at her outerwear was *Livas*—known to her compatriots as *Foehn*, to the French as *Mistral*, and to Californians as *Santa Ana*—one of the insistent, pestilent airstreams that barrel down mountainsides, often marking changes of season. *Livas*, one of several sub-deities commanded by wind-god Aeolus, was said by ancient Athenians to be responsible for southwest winds like this one, which yesterday he had gathered from dusty Libyan peaks and today propelled down the leeward slopes of the Peloponissos to harass the metropole on its way to aerate the fields of Thessaly.

Her fretting disrupted, she remembered the boy whose hand she'd let go to steady her beret, hoping he hadn't been airlifted down the block. She found him planted behind her, rakishly canting into the gale, hood billowing, arms outstretched, burbling engines noises, a black windsock of hair fluttering in his slipstream.

"Ground control to Jay-Jay," she announced, "turn around and fly us down the block."

His motor stopped its purr. "Where we going?"

She had told him but he'd been half asleep. "To see the doctor. Your cough isn't getting better. He can give you medicine."

He stamped a tiny Adidas on the pavement. "No, Mutti"— cough—"No medicine"—cough—"Let's go home!"

She sighed, took hold of an outstretched wing and rotated his fuselage northward. Livas obliged, propelling them up the sidewalk, the boy's protestations unavailing. When they turned onto a sheltering cross street, he asked, "Mutti, does medsin taste bad," his chest rumbling. She squeezed his diminutive hand, hoping his condition was nothing serious.

"Not at all, Ramadi. It might taste … like cherries, or grapes maybe. Sweet, like you, love."

Their destination, the medical clinic Anna had frequented while expecting, materialized around the next corner, its wind-damaged glass door currently dressed in cardboard and surgical tape. That the doctor was out came as no surprise. Having volunteered there, Anna understood that finding one was hit or miss. Since their last wellness visit, a new nurse practitioner in headscarf and scrubs had come on board. Fatma, according to her name tag, greeted them and solicited the boy's symptoms in Greek accented unlike Anna's. At the mention of a sore throat, from a jar she extracted a tongue depressor she gyrated above the boy's head, spiraling it toward his puckered mouth.

"Open please, boy. Airplane coming in to land now."

Having recently been an airplane himself, he obligingly opened his hangar door for it to glide in. After peering down his throat as he stoically quivered in mom's lap, she stabbed in a cotton swab and deftly corked it into a tube before he finished flinching. "You brave boy," she said, appreciating the lack of complaints.

Nurse Fatma unclipped a thermometer from Ramadi's thumb to tell Anna he was close enough to normal. Applying a stethoscope to his chest, she instructed "Breathe, boy. Again. Cough please." Still holding the nipple to his chest, she planted the earpieces on him. "Here, you listen yourself," and to mom: "Might be virus, probably not flu, but we check for strep. Does boy have spring allergies?" Not that she knew of, Anna said.

Fatma scribbled on a pad and handed over two pages. "Go get these at apotek. First to relieve congestion, other to soothe troat. Get linden-blossom tea, give him morning and before bed." She swiveled to a desk cluttered with file folders and cleared away enough of them to locate a keyboard and open a form on the office computer. "We make record for visit. Name please, first you, then boy."

"We've come here before. In fact, I used to volunteer here. Last name is Burmeister. I'm Anna, he's Ramadi."

As the nurse hunted and pecked to locate the boy's file, Anna said, "Thanks so much. See, Ramadi, that didn't hurt. You'll feel better soon. Now thank the nice lady."

"Tank you nize lady," the boy hoarsely said, and received a non-medicinal lollipop in return.

"Nice lady name Fatma," the nurse said in stilted Greek. "I am from Turkey. Where you from?"

Anna wasn't about to let that connection pass unremarked. "No kidding? What a fascinating country! Just been there once but would love to go back. I'm Swiss, but I've lived here for, like, six years. Ramadi's baba was from Iraq."

"I see. You marry him?"

Anna cast her eyes on the pink and grey floor tiles. "Never had the chance," she said. "He passed away before Ramadi was born. Worst day of my life."

"I am sorry. How bad for you. May Allah keep him. So that's why boy has Iraqi name."

"Yes, it was Mahmoud's last name, same as his home town."

"We let you know about troat culture. Call anytime. Let me know how boy does. Here is number." She handed Anna one of the clinic's business cards.

"Thanks so much. I'd like to stay in touch. Do you live here in Piraeus?"

"We wanted to, but no find place here. We live up in Exarcheia in a house with many refugees."

"I'm not surprised. People there go out of their way to shield them. You like living there?"

Fatma gave an affirmative Turkish head-shake. "Evet. People are very kind there."

Anna slipped her phone from her back pocket. "So, do you have email or phone where I can contact you?"

"*Evet*, gmail on cellphone and clinic computer."

By the time mother and child took their leave, Ramadi had finished his lollipop, Anna had learned that Fatma was also a single mom with an eleven-year-old daughter named Irmak, and the two had exchanged phone numbers and email addresses.

"*Güle güle*," Anna said on their way out, a farewell pleasantry she'd picked up in Turkey. Not fully comprehended was Fatma's Turkish reply, "*Allahaısmarladık; seninle tanışmak çok güzel*": Go with Allah; it was very lovely to meet you.

To foil Livas, in the vestibule Anna stuffed her beret in her shoulder bag and withdrew a ceremonial headscarf given to her in Turkey. She draped it over her head and tied it under her chin, but out in the street the demigod seemed to be taking a break. She took advantage of the relative calm to escort Brave Boy first to a pharmacy for the prescribed potions, and then on to a café she frequented some blocks away to refresh him with promised ice cream and her with some well-earned coffee.

I search like a hunting dog pursuing its prey. But just as a scent lingers after a body leaves the scene, she could have come and gone. Is that what drew me to this café, where Andreas took me the day after my landfall? She just showed up and invited herself to sit with us. Neither is here now, but something tells me to wait a while. The clock on the wall shows 10:50, but what day—what year, even, is it?

Amazing. At 10:52 there she is coming in, holding our son's hand. He seems to be coughing, not that I can hear it. His eyes and hair are dark like mine. He is a beautiful child, I must say, please Allah. Were I able, I would weep tears of joy.

The *Choris Onoma Kafeneío*, aka No Name Café, had been Anna's hangout for years. Commonly referred to as Nobody's, it was the source of the *Property of Nobody* sweatshirt Ramadi wore that day. An anarchist collective had transformed the carcass of a defunct hardware store into a sizable convivial gathering place and kept it running for eight years. A shifting miscellany of local artwork graced its tan walls, spottily illuminated from the decorative tin ceiling that some nihilist had painted black. Spanning the frontage was a plate glass window diagonally cracked in one corner, a magnet for posters for concerts, film festivals, and community affairs that regularly had to be scraped off to keep from completely blocking the view. Inside the repurposed room, customers reposed at tables and chairs of assorted styles and vintage. An art deco display case housing inviting confections near the entrance fronted a surprisingly efficient kitchen improvised from a former stockroom.

Anna knew some of the people behind the enterprise, envisioned as an anti-Starbucks by an anarchist collective of shifting composition as members dropped out and others shuttled aboard. The founders had stipulated from the outset that membership would be at-will and that the establishment should not trumpet its politics or disparage anyone else's. Any profits would be equally distributed and tithed to help those in need. They had intended their alternative eatery to be a melting pot in which people of all races, creeds, and persuasions could peaceably commingle, and it had been reasonably successful at that.

A couple of the regulars nodded greetings as Anna and son entered. Of the five unoccupied tables, she chose one by the window to distract Ramadi from his discomfort by observing passers-by, few of whom paused to drop euros into the paper cup beside the homeless man crouching out front.

The morose young server (who had inexplicably dubbed himself Phaeton, after the Greek demigod who plunged to his death after ineptly piloting Zeus's sun carriage) took Anna's order for coffee and ice cream. When he returned with it, to soothe Ramadi's cough, Anna administered a spoonful of chest medicine followed by one of chocolate ice cream, and again with the throat medicine.

"See, Ramadi," Anna said, "that wasn't so bad. I'll bet you feel better already"—and took his nodding "Umph, mmph" as confirmation.

At a table near the back two men were passionately discussing something in Greek, their voices rising and falling. Anna pricked up her ears to get the gist of what sounded like a political argument, an uncommon event within these nonpartisan walls.

"They shouldn't be bringing those Arabs from the islands to camps here," she overheard a mustachioed middle-aged man saying. His white dress shirt was open at the neck, revealing a showy gold chain complemented by brown chest hair. "Too many get out and overrun the city. We don't need more people here who can't support themselves. Our bums should be Greek bums."

The man's interlocutor, a younger curly-headed man in a black turtleneck with a brass hoop in his left ear, replied: "I get it, man, but you know Italy gets all these refugees from Africa. They bring most of them to the mainland and help them get settled. Sure, some people resent it, but for the migrants it beats being sent back home after risking their lives and fortunes to escape from badass rulers, invaders, and brutal conflicts. Prisoners of war get treated better than that."

The older man waggled an index finger. "Look. Greece has seventeen percent unemployment, the highest in Europe. Shouldn't we be getting Greeks back to work instead of trying to be every foreign infiltrator's best friend?"

Anna didn't like where this was going and hoped it would stay civil. Attending to their sharpening words, she hadn't noticed Ramadi wandering over to inspect the food counter, but caught sight of him as he approached the men's table. She bit her lip as the older man regarded Ramadi and said: "What do you want, kid? I bet you're one of them. Are you begging?"

Definitely sure she didn't like where this was going, Anna rose from her chair as the man said: "I got nothing for you, kid, so scram your immigrant ass out of here."

Ramadi got the hint. Tears welling, he ran back to Anna. She took him in her arms, glaring at his tormenter across the room. The outburst attracted the attention of the café's democratically designated shift coordinator Chris, a bearded man with a black man-bun. Chris stormed over to read the riot act to the self-proclaimed patriot. Such behavior was out of bounds here, he was informed and then instructed to quit the premises and apologize to the boy and his mother on his way out. In solidarity, the man in the turtleneck arose with drawn mouth to press his knuckles on the tabletop.

The ousted customer shoved his chair aside and stalked to the front. Taking notice of Anna's headscarf, he said with a snarl: "Go back where you came from, Muslim *pórni*, and take your brat with you!" Heads swiveled, ceasing their chatter and preoccupation with their phones.

Their accuser was middle-aged and heavy-set with a rounded midriff. A broom of a reddish mustache drooped over his upper lip. A matching fringe of hair hemmed his scalp, symbolizing to Anna how his nativism circumscribed his worldview. Though she feared people like him, his presumptive insult enraged her. With Ramadi still in her arms, she spoke with unaccustomed ferocity. "You assume I'm from the Middle East. I'm not. I'm Swiss and proud of it."

The man stiffened as she continued with the line that had incented Nationalist trolls when she'd blogged it. "So, are you a hundred percent Greek? Your DNA could be part Turkish, Armenian, Bulgarian, or who knows, even Arab. So, apologize for looking down your Greek nose at me and for terrorizing my son, please."

He pulled back his shoulders, assuming a military posture that only served to accentuate his gut. Fists on hips, he replied, "Whatever. Look, Greece is broke. Foreigners keep piling in. They're ruining the country. We have to put our foot down."

"How?"

"Send them back to whatever country they were last in. Or shoo them north and let the traitorous Macedonians take care of them."

She shifted Ramadi to her thigh to regard his accuser. "Greeks, Macedonians, immigrants, refugees, we all have problems. We should cooperate to solve them instead of scapegoating."

"I'll cooperate with whoever I want," he said. "Especially Greeks who want to remove this plague of immigrants and foreign meddlers like you."

Chris had followed the self-proclaimed patriot and had witnessed the exchange. Clamping his hand on the man's shoulder, he reiterated his ultimatum. "Didn't I tell you to leave? Stop hassling this woman and her son and get out!"

The man spun around with smoldering eyes, grabbed his accuser's wrist, and shook off his hand. "Don't you dare touch me," he said, "or

I swear you'll regret it! I'm a police officer and would be happy to haul you in for assault."

Chris took a step back, colliding with Phaeton, standing with a knot of people who'd gathered in solidarity. Clasping Chris's shoulder, Phaeton said with a nod to those gathering behind them, "Try to take him, *astynomikós*, and you'll have to take us all."

Several customers rose to attention. Sniffling, Ramadi buried his face in Anna's bosom. "Come on, Ramadi, let's get out of here," she said, fishing a ten-euro note from her pocket and smacking it on the table. "Here, Chris. This should cover our food and indignity." She swept up her handbag and, still cosseting Ramadi, stalked away.

Someone kindly opened the door for them to leave. Outside, she lowered Ramadi to the sidewalk and through the window saw the men still facing off. Shaken, but relieved not to be followed out, she dropped some coins into the homeless man's paper cup and took her son's hand. Buffeted by Livas, they crossed the boulevard to slope up the sidewalk toward home.

Glancing over her shoulder, tugging Ramadi through four endless blocks, clutching his hand as if he would waft away, Anna recalled tangling with extreme nationalists who'd stalked her and threatened her life five years before. Like those misanthropes, the mustachioed man might be capable of hateful acts beyond his swaggering words. She and her comrades had managed to terminate that threat, but not the prospect of retribution. Even now, this or another antipathetic extremist with privy to her past could be an envoy of the angel of death.

~

I don't understand what happened here but it alarms me. Why did this bald man yell at our son? Then, when she was comforting the frightened boy, more words were exchanged. I never saw this man before but I want to punch his jaw. I know his type and pray that he knows nothing of her past, but there is no way to fix that. I can't stand not being able to hear what went on or if she and the boy are in trouble. This is torture.

Chapter Four

ANNA MARCHED UPHILL IN double time as Ramadi galloped alongside, panting for relief. Safely home, she soothed his gullet with herbal tea with honey and lit incense as a way to neutralize the nationalist's miasmatic effluence. Under its influence, she whipped up some crumbed macaroni and cheese with cut-up vegetables, and after supper told Ramadi to study his Greek myths while she washed and swept up.

In mid-sweep, her phone blared its *le Marseillaise* ringtone. The caller ID said ORHAN DEMIRCI. She picked up to hear a throaty voice say: "*Merhaba*, Anna. *Nasilsiniz? Ben* Orhan Demirci. Do you remember me and *belki* some Turkish?"

She knew some Turkish pleasantries, like "greetings" and "how are you" but not that *belki* meant "maybe." But she readily recalled the Turkish telecom owner who'd chatted her up flying home from Izmir five years ago, whom she'd assumed had forgotten her after sympathetically sending her home in his airport limousine, saying it was the least he could do.

And until now, that was the most he could do, as his prospective platform—at which he'd offered her a marketing position—had failed to materialize along with her hopes for gainful employment. But here he was, saying he was in Athens to finalize his deal with a Greek telecom to host his social media service, entreating her to be his guest at lunch the following day to discuss bringing her on board.

"Thank you, Mr. Demirci," she said, "but please remind me what your software does. It's been quite a while."

"Sure, Anna. We call it Altogether. It's a social network. Like others, it lets people collect into groups, be they for business, governance, social interaction, connecting family members, etcetera. Unlike others, there are no ads, tracking or monetizing user data, and users control how they interact with each person in a group and who can see what they post. All interactions are encrypted for privacy and transactions are secured by a blockchain."

Whatever that is. Such tech was beyond her ken. The closest she'd come to a social network platform was the community blog she'd long ago abandoned to Nationalist trolls, nothing like this beast. But recalling his chivalry, flattered he'd remembered her, feeling pinched, and figuring she had nothing to lose but quality time and sleep, she agreed to meet for lunch and then tossed in bed for what seemed like half the night.

Semi-sleepless, she rose with the sun, stripped down, showered, and tried to tame her unruly locks, wishing she'd visited *Radically Chic* for a do. With a sigh, she dithered over her workaday flea market wardrobe to assemble an outfit she hoped would pass for business casual, trying to recall if it was Thoreau who had advised readers to beware of enterprises that require new clothes.

A faint *Are you sure you're up to this?* whispered in her ear. *You know how you hate calling attention to yourself. Do you really want to be out there pitching this thing?*

I know, I know, Anna silently challenged her inner critic. *You have a better idea? If not, shut up.*

As you wish. Just saying think before you leap.

Appreciating that her sink-or-swim approach to life had too often left her gasping for breath, Anna decided to seek counsel from a trusted denizen of the digital demimonde, hoping he would be well disposed. Trying not to come across like a needy ignoramus, she limned her prospective gig in broad strokes to her hacker friend, suggesting it was something he might want to know more about.

To her vague articulations, the reclusive skeptic of all things corporate predictably replied "not enough data." What got him off the fence was her mention of a free lunch downtown—which he insisted be taken at his favorite eatery. "Tell him to meet us at the East Asia on Apollonos. Best Chinese food in the city."

\#

After dropping off Ramadi for lessons at Cassie's, Anna hurried back home to make herself presentable and texted her hacker to meet her at the Piraeus Metro station. Of course, he was late, but at least the subway ran on time.

Exiting the metro, Livas or one of his fellow blowhard deities welcomed them to downtown Athens by tangling Anna's homemade hairdo and resisting her progress. To shield herself, she traipsed behind her stout companion who weighed in at almost 100 kilos, giving him a body mass statistic he carried with pride. That pride extended to other statistics whose formulae he bent to his purposes. Not an actuary or a quant, he specialized in mining well-connected people's data when they weren't looking, searching for evidence of public and private malfeasance. And despite his oversized estimation of his algorithmic acumen, the hacker tended to boast of it only to himself, assuming that most mortals were incapable of appreciating the subtlety and elegance of his code and spycraft.

When and why he had dubbed himself Ottovio, Anna didn't know and hadn't asked, having learned not to pry into his affairs. Mostly they interacted at a distance, as their social networks intersected only around the person who'd introduced them, Andreas. Like the Austrian and herself at the time, he went only by a forename not bestowed at birth. It was not an uncommon strategy for radicals in Athens— especially expats—for flying under the authorities' radar. But while Ottovio was a native son, he too encrypted his name along with his phone, workstation, wallet, and home address.

He and his mystery girlfriend "Beatrice"—also a geek, she'd gathered—cohabited somewhere on the far side of Dimokritias Boulevard. And though he kept that location undisclosed, Ottovio made himself accessible in other ways. He had reconditioned the cast-off phone she carried, tweaking it for maximum privacy (one of his moneymaking sidelines), and rarely rebuffed her when she leaned on him for tech support. But as retiring as he was, Ottovio was certainly capable of sociability and even conviviality, and especially so when a free lunch—toward which they were running late—beckoned.

"Don't worry," Anna said, "Demirci won't be on time. A Turkish friend told me they like to arrive late to gatherings so as to make a grand entrance."

"I don't care about that," Ottovio said as he huffed against the wind. "I forgot to make a reservation and this place fills up fast at lunchtime. Plus I'm hungry."

As they plodded toward their destination, she expanded upon what she knew of Orhan Demirci's company, Olympos InterConnect.

"It provides internet access to cities across Anatolia plus forums and exchanges for its users."

"Okay, but lots of ISPs do that."

It was their secure and somewhat anarchic social network called *Altogether* that got her attention, she explained. Demirci touted it as a godsend to users who were sick of online surveillance. Ottovio said he dimly recalled her telling him about the thing ages ago but had dismissed it as vaporware.

And vaporware it remained until the other day, when Demirci had finally cut a deal with a Greek internet provider after nearly five years of wheedling Turkish bureaucrats for export permits and courting potential partners who kept succumbing to Greece's unhinged economy.

Anna felt gratitude for Ottovio's testy presence, for without his know-how she couldn't hope to understand what she was supposed to peddle, judge its worthiness, or discern if she was being treated to a snow job along with lunch. Despite misgivings about working with what he termed "the dark side," Ottovio had consented to advise her, because if the thing took off in Greece, he said, he should know something about how it worked, what it could be used for, and how hackable it might be.

They had just turned onto narrow Apollonos Street, overrun with office workers in shirtsleeves on midday breaks, its sidewalk barely accommodating Ottovio's wide body. "It's at the end of the block," Anna's windbreak called back as he chuffed along.

They arrived at a poster-plastered façade with dusty circular windows and a fading marquee proclaiming it East Asia Restaurant. Its humble appearance belied its four-star cuisine, the Greek geek maintained, likening it to an exquisite dumpling in a nondescript wrapper, a pearl hidden in an oyster's drab shell, a fortune cookie come true. Eating there for free was worth the long ride downtown, no matter how things might go.

Anna wasn't thinking Pu-Pu Platter. She had dressed for success in pinstriped black slacks and a frilly white top accented by her prized lapis earrings. Her more casual companion was stuffed into a black t-shirt decorated with an acute triangle with sides and angles labeled a, b, c and *I Love my Wife but Oh Euclid lettered* in white. Beatrice had given it to him for Pi Day, he'd revealed, and it still gives him the giggles.

Voices approached from behind. They turned to see Demirci rounding the corner accompanied by a slender man in jeans and a white shirt open at the collar, a shockwave of blond hair streaming past his temples, projecting a nonchalant optimism through yellow-tinted glasses. Demirci in a suit sans necktie looked as Anna remembered him; of medium build with thinning black hair, now streaked with gray, and a jovial hail-fellow manner.

"Anna!" he exclaimed with a double peck of her cheeks. "It is good to see you … and your friend." Anna made a show of holding the door as the men filed into the eatery's van-sized vestibule that kept the queue of customers out from underfoot. Currently, only two parties occupied the airlock and they were soon seated.

Within that isolation booth handshakes were exchanged accompanied by introductions in English, the foursome's only common tongue out of six—ten, if you count computer languages— at their disposal. Demirci introduced the blond, an Estonian tech wizard by the name of Marten Piperal, as his CTO, whom he'd lured to Olympus Interconnect to propagate Estonia's advanced digital infrastructure across the breadth of Anatolia and now beyond. In turn, Anna identified Ottovio as her go-to IT guy and a network security wizard, "security" being somewhat of a misnomer given his proclivity for penetrating databases.

The headwaiter beckoned them to a circular table for four. Anna sat between Orhan and Marten, across from her friend, who as soon as menus were slapped down regaled them with a rundown of his favorites. "Must have their hot-and-sour soup and scallion pancakes," he proclaimed, further extolling local inventions such as Hunan-style Octopus and The Onion Explodes The Pork to chuckles of amusement.

Chit-chat over appetizers ensued until Anna cleared her throat to ask: "So, Orhan, are you really ready to deploy Altogether in Athens now?"

Demirci dabbed at his mouth and laid down his napkin. "Technically, yes. We have set up servers and have gotten them to operate on our partner's network, a hosting company called Prótos. Administratively, no. Because we're a Turkish company, Prótos needs approval from the Greek government to operate the service here. Greece hasn't acted on our application, saying they need approval from Brussels for obscure reasons. The situation is quite silly, because our open-source platform comes from Estonia, a member of the EU."

"Anything you can do about it?" Anna asked, dunking a Crab Rangoon into duck sauce.

"In a few days I'm sending Marten here to Brussels to work things out. Besides being a computer scientist, he's also served his country as a diplomat. I'm sure he will be successful."

"Assuming there's a rational reason for the delay," Marten said. "If they worry about data breaches, once I demonstrate how secure the system is, they should come around."

Ottovio turned to the Estonian. "Secure is pretty strong claim these days. How can you be sure?"

"The platform, called X-Road—spoken 'crossroad'—is state-of-the-art. It's been running in Estonia smoothly for a decade and hasn't been compromised for the last eight of those years. Data is decentralized and all traffic is encrypted. Nobody can view data without the owner's permission. Everyone's data includes metadata identifying the users who have seen it. Data integrity is assured by blockchain. I could go on."

Spearing a potsticker, Ottovio said, "I remember hearing about it. Has good reputation. Did not know it was exported. Are tech docs available for it?"

"Be prepared to spend a lot of time in the code repository. We have hundreds of pages of docs plus how-to videos. What do you hope to learn?"

"Usability. Capability. Security. I like to know how software works before I tell people to use it," Ottovio replied and popped the crescent of dough into his mouth.

"We can demo it for our friends at the office," Orhan said, and turned to Anna. "I'd like to hear your ideas of how the platform might be used here."

She licked, pursed, and then parted her lips. "We have a housing shortage. No, it's a crisis. And yet, there are many unoccupied buildings across the city. Some are owned by absentee landlords who may owe taxes, and some the city may have taken over. Say a group of Altogether users focusing on housing identified an unoccupied building. They could pester its owner and the city to let them fix it up, buying or bartering for tools and materials on Altogether. I can tell you from personal experience that it can be done."

"You could set up a bulletin board with some type of payment system for that," Orhan replied. "As in my country, probably many such properties exist. Whether city officials would grant access to property data is another matter."

"Property records are public data," Ottovio said. "If they hold back, we can find ways to get at them."

"I'm so glad we don't have such problems in my country," Marten said. "We have a national cadastre that any citizen can browse to determine who owns what land, their taxes, and so forth."

"Tell me about it," Ottovio said, probably thinking of how arduous cracking databases to identify connections between Greek public figures, assorted influencers, and known criminals had been.

Attacking his platter of crispy fish with lobster sauce, Orhan asked: "Anna, have you other ideas?"

Anna laid down her chopsticks. "Let me see if I understood what Marten said. You can filter out people from seeing stuff in your data and they can do the same. Is that right?"

"Yes," Marten said, "down to paragraphs, images, comments, and so on. Permissions are that fine-grained. You can also let them in, one at a time or in groups. Groups can have blogs and private forums. Web sites too."

"So one problem people here—including me—have is anonymous trolls disrupting discussions, flaming us, defacing blogs. On Altogether, would we know who they are or just who they say they are?"

Tenting his fingers, Marten replied, "Estonians have universal digital identity cards, good for all government and private transactions. They can even be used as passports. Users can go by avatars, but the system knows who they are. Here it's different because only designated authorities can legally access Greek ID card records. So, while you won't know the real identity of a troll, you can flag them on a five-point scale, where one issues a mild objection and five blocks that user from your feed. Your sanction will apply to all that user's avatars. Good enough?"

Anna sighed. "At least that's something."

"You can view anyone's profile—name, picture, and all their aliases, plus anything else they choose to disclose, such as their bio, photo album, email, blog or commercial site. We don't permit links to their Facebook, Twitter, Instagram or other social media accounts."

"Why not? You see those sharing buttons all over the web."

"Because when you click them, personal data is harvested and monetized. We never do that. What happens on Altogether stays on Altogether. We are a network of communities completely focused on what we can do together."

"So how do you support platform?" Ottovio asked. "Subscriptions? Advertising?

"No ads for ordinary users, but there's an exchange where people can buy, sell, and barter for a small premium. Prótos offers commercial accounts for businesses, government agencies, and nonprofits for a fee, and levies modest fees for bulletin boards, blogs, and storefronts."

"So, Ottovio," Anna said, "does this setup compute for you?"

"Promising. Has potential to disrupt business-as-usual. Just your thing."

Gazing down at her lap, Anna said, "All this sounds fabulous, but I'm an immigrant without many resources … and have responsibilities. So, if I may be so bold, what's in it for me if I help you out?"

Orhan lowered a forkful of fish. "You will be a paid consultant. Bill us for whatever hours you put in recruiting users or other things we might ask you to do. Does twenty-five euros per hour seem reasonable?"

Anna let that penetrate a furrowed brow. "Make it forty and you've got a deal."

"How about thirty-five, then? Would that cover your expenses?"

The furrows gave way to dimples. "Deal. When can I start?"

"As soon as you like. We can set you up on our private network so you can get to know the environment. You have a computer, I assume. Not everything you might need to do works on a mobile device."

Anna averred that she had a three-year-old Apple laptop that Marten said should be fine if her browsers are up to date.

"So plan to visit Prótos' office to meet people you will work with and handle paperwork," Demirci said.

"I'd love that," she said, glancing at Ottovio. "Can Ottovio come too? I may need a translator who speaks geek."

Orhan's eyes fell on Marten, who returned a discreet nod. "Since it seems you will be consulting him anyway, perhaps we should formalize that relationship."

"How so?" Ottovio asked, dabbing brown sauce from his shirt.

"Why not sign him up as a regular user?" Marten said. He turned to Ottovio. "Explore Altogether. Try to hack it. In the unlikely event you find a vulnerability you'll get a cash reward."

Orhan nodded gravely. Ottovio made a show of stroking his beard before telling them he would be happy to help Anna get started.

Plates were cleared, teapot drained, and fortune cookies distributed. Anna giggled and announced hers: "I cannot help you. I am only a cookie."

"That's okay," Ottovio said. "Mine says: 'Ignore previous fortune'."

Chuckling, Orhan tucked a credit card into the wallet on the table as phones were flourished to synchronize a visit to Prótos.

Just saying, a small voice cautioned Anna. *Here you go again, playing a part in a script you haven't read. But don't let that stop you.*

Don't worry, Gizzard-Brain, Anna silently replied. *It won't.*

#

Sliding past a whir of shrubbery and kaleidoscoping graffitied walls on a Piraeus-bound M1 train, Anna nudged Ottovio to ask: "Do you think this thing has legs? At least the technology part?"

"Given where it's coming from, it has to be solid," Ottovio said. "Crossroad works in real world. Runs Marten's country. Survives Russian attacks."

"So they say. So, is Altogether the same as Crossroad?"

"No. Adds a bunch of services to Crossroad platform. Is basically front end for a federation of user communities."

"Not sure what that means, but in my book federation is the wave of the future."

A bell chimed and a soft female voice announced *Moschato Station*. The doors slid open, passengers shuffled out, and a carful of new ones battled in. As the train picked up speed, Anna fended off a standee's wayward shopping bag to ask her traveling companion: "So what did you make of these guys?"

"I'm sure Marten knows his stuff inside out. But once he goes away the Prótos people will be running things. Let's hope they know what they're doing. Orhan's okay, but may have hidden agenda. Seems to know what he's getting into. But do you?"

"So far, I think. Just be a sheepdog and try to herd people into online communities. Maybe try to persuade them to advertise in local media like newspapers, or even here." She pointed to the billboards lining their carriage. "But I need a pitch. Something that promises a better way of connecting to community. No idea how to frame that."

"What it gives you is control of data and privacy and different ways to do things together. So maybe you say, 'Had it with social media companies stealing and selling your data? Harassed by trolls? Give them all the boot. Join Altogether to find and build community on a platform that gives you total control of who can see your data.' Something like that."

"Now you're talking. But that's a little abstract. I think we need to personalize it. Like with ads or videos featuring real people who tried Altogether, made connections, got stuff done, and never looked back."

"If you can find any. Kind of chicken-egg problem."

"Well then, I'll be the chicken and you can be my first egg."

Stroking his beard, Ottovio replied, "If you mean to hatch an ad with me in it, you need to call my lawyer first."

"So who's your lawyer?"

"Don't have one. Another chicken-egg problem."

Mellow tones from above announced their approach to Port of Piraeus terminal, end of the line. Their journey to Keratsini was half over, but Anna's was just beginning.

Chapter Five

EVEN AT FOUR, RAMADI knew his food. He knew Anna's Swiss concoctions that she sometimes laced with African ingredients she'd fancied, like yams, which Ramadi found acceptable when mashed with butter and milk. He chowed down Greek food at tavernas and at food stalls at the Saturday bazaar, charming vendors to pilot sporkfuls of moussaka or—to Anna's alarm—chunks of doner impaled on knife-point into his expectant hangar. He'd scarfed up Middle Eastern delicacies at the homes of immigrant moms staffing his fly-by-night preschool. And, although he generally turned up his nose at tomato-based cuisine, he was always up for pizza.

Ramadi's favorite pizzeria of the three or so he'd dined at was a hole in the wall on Dimokritias Boulevard with three stools at the front and a counter half-way back. It was, of course, Greek pizza, but a plain slice is a plain slice. All that generally differs is the dough. Ramadi preferred his on the crispy side, and the establishment obliged.

Irrespective of Ramadi's endorsement, the Golden House of Pizza wasn't Anna's favorite pizza parlor. Its pies were edible enough but off-odors, possibly augmented by the sweaty guy behind the counter, raised suspicions. Pushing open the glass door, she noted that two of the stools by the window were occupied by a couple of men. The younger of the two seemed taller but thinner, with hollow cheeks framing pouty lips and a thicket of black curls. The older one's penetrating gaze prickled her forearms as she recalled her unpleasant interaction with him at No Name Café. *Displeased to meet you again*, she stopped herself from telling the petulant nationalist.

His eyes flickered on her and lingered on Ramadi. Before she could look away, from behind a blank smile came the unexpected words "Beautiful boy. You must be very proud of him," confounding her conception of him. She wondered if he'd forgotten their rancid encounter the other day or hadn't recognized her without her headscarf.

"Umm, thanks. He is and I am," was all she could or cared to say. The two men exchanged glances as she turned her back to place her order, a small plain and a Greek salad, adding "to go" as Ramadi sought her hand.

The owner boxed a pie from his warming oven, took a container of salad from his cooler and handed them over. Exchanging ten euros for the food, she said "That should be about right. Keep the change." She pivoted, avoiding eye contact with the men, telling Ramadi "It's too hot in here. Let's have this at home," Without a farewell, she barged out with him listlessly tailing after, his urban eating adventure cut short.

#

Peering after them, the man with the rufous mustache asked, "You know them?"

"They come around now and then," the counterman replied. Why?"

"Dunno. Something about her rings a bell. She live around here?"

"Probably. Why else would she keep coming in?"

Scowling, the customer replied, "For the pizza, asshole. Think it's because of your tight abs and buns?"

Clenching his fists, the shopkeeper spat back, "Watch your mouth, pal. You're asking for it."

"Fuck off," the man growled. "You want trouble, I can show you some."

A jerk of his thick neck sent his curly companion out the door. He got up from his stool, pulled a business card from his pocket, and slapped it on the counter. "Special Investigations Unit. Looking for a dame who looks like her. Got a cold case for which she could be a hot lead. What can you tell me about her?"

"I told you what I know. She comes in sometimes."

The plainclothesman's eyes swept over the array of cold dishes in the compartment under the counter. "See those wilted greens and slimy mushrooms? Would be a shame if a health inspector walked in here. You sure that's all you can tell me?"

After thoughtfully wiping his hands on his apron, the counterman said, "I might be able to help. What's it worth to me?"

"Next time you see her, tell her you deliver for free. Offer a nice special, delivery only. I'll pay double for whatever she gets. Call me when she orders and I'll come and deliver it personally for free. Greece will thank you for your service. What did you say your name was?"

"I didn't. Stavros. What's yours?"

He dealt a twenty-euro note on top of his card. "The card has my name and personal number. Use it. Call me next time you see her."

Stavros blankly nodded and slid aside the blue-and-brown bank note to read the business card. Next to the force's shield was *Vassilios Laskaris, Police Investigations Warden, Hellenic Police, Piraeus Municipality* and below that a phone number. As the officer turned to leave, Stavros clipped the bank note and card together and placed them in the back of his cash drawer.

Laskaris let himself out to the sidewalk without a parting salutation. Stavros watched as he stood in front of the shop looking up and down the block until his silent associate rejoined him and they walked together down the avenue.

#

Anna's pace was brisk, but she still lagged behind Ramadi, skipping ahead with pie on the brain.

"Hold up, young son," she said, wanting to keep him in sight. "Stay with me." Ramadi paused, taking the opportunity to creep up on a knot of pigeons contesting a ragged morsel of pita bread.

When Anna reached Young Son, he hopped off the curb to skirt a mellowing heap of trash bags. She glanced behind her for approaching cars and noticed a man standing at the end of the block looking their way. Squinting, she made him as the younger, curly-headed man from the pizzeria. When her gaze turned him away to slip around the corner, she hastened her pace uphill with backward glances. Though the voyeur hadn't reappeared, she decided to take evasive action. At the next corner she intercepted Ramadi's wrist. "Let's go this way, Love. We'll get a sweet from the *pantopoleío* for dessert."

They emerged from the sweet store with two diamonds of baklava in her pizza carton and the unsavory image of the tall stranger still in her mind. Striding along the three blocks home, Anna palpitated at every male blip that appeared on her radar. In her kitchen, Anna mechanically set out plates of pizza, recalling being shadowed on the street a half-decade ago. Her life was on the line then and she was on high alert, and now wondered if it still could be. Trying to shake it off, she sat down across from Ramadi, who'd half eaten his slice, and hoisted hers to wordlessly chow down. When Ramadi declined seconds and went to rummage through his toy hamper, she finished hers and put the remainder in cold storage, wondering what the dude who'd shadowed her was about. Was he undercover police, a vengeful nationalist hooligan, or just a creep? Surely he was one or another, if not all, a person of disinterest to be avoided at all costs.

She noticed their forgotten salad in its flip-top foam box. Upon inspection, it lacked edibility, with soggy, yellowing lettuce, limp, watery cucumbers, and wrinkled cherry tomatoes. She wedged it into the fridge, intending to have a discussion with the pizza guy about salmonella.

"Here, Ramadi," she said, serving up baklava. "Let's have dessert on the bed. Your favorite TV show is on." It was an American animated series from the 90s called *Jay-Jay the Jet Plane* dubbed into Greek, immortally syndicated on a children's channel. Ahead of its time, the cute blue jet with a boyish face and both human and mechanical friends foreshadowed drones. As they watched, chewing pastry and licking fingers, she wondered if Ramadi's thing for airplanes could have come from flying home at the tender age of six weeks and if he might become a pilot someday.

After absorbing a half-hour of the little jet's heroic deeds on behalf of its fellow flyers, the junior airman's eyes grew heavy. Anna switched off the tube and sleepwalked him to bed, wishing she had a drone like Jay-Jay to take on creepy men. Ramadi would love that.

As things would come to pass, it wasn't that crazy an idea.

\#

In the morning they breakfasted on Anna's Central European version of ramen with little dumplings replacing noodles, another comfort food Ramadi had come to enjoy. Eager to get him to Cassie's place for preschool four bus stops away, she laced his sneakers and threw a digital thermometer into his backpack for Cassie to teach the kiddies about temperature.

Policing up the kitchen, she ran into the sad little box of salad and pondered whether to take it back. It was probably safe to return there at this hour, she reasoned, and that guy needs to know he's selling poison.

When she arrived there, the Golden House of Pizza wasn't open yet, but Anna could see the owner inside doing paperwork on the counter. He looked up with arching eyebrows when she rapped on the door, bit his lower lip, and took his time coming around to crack the door.

"Hello. Can I help you?"

"It won't take long," she replied, manifesting his takeout box. "Can we come in?"

He nodded and ushered them past him. "Nice to see you. How did you like your food?"

"I'd give the pizza an eight, mostly cuz we ate it cold, and the salad zero. Take a look at this." She popped open the container. "I dare you to take a bite."

"I know," he said, abjectly. "My cold case doesn't chill like it used to. I was planning to get bags of ice for it before opening the shop. Sorry. I hope you didn't eat any of it."

"Not that festering mess. I just thought you should know before a customer keels over."

He accepted the container and dumped it in a bin. Digging in his pocket, he said, "Here, I give you your money back."

"Keep it," she said, raising a hand. "It'll cost you to get it fixed."

He smiled. "That's decent of you. Tell you what. Next time you want pizza, it's on the house. I'll even deliver for free."

Her opinion of him started to stray. She had assumed he was anti-foreigner, if not worse, but here he was making a kind offer. Not a trace of insincerity or distain. She slipped one of his business cards from a tray on the counter.

"Thanks. Maybe I'll give you a call. My son loves your pizza."

"Nice well-mannered boy," Stavros called after them. "Bring him in anytime."

He re-locked the door and went back behind the counter. From the back of his till he fished out the cop's card, still clipped to the twenty-euro bill. He pocketed the bank note to pay for ice and stared at the card for several beats before putting it back, almost wishing she wouldn't call.

Chapter Six

Anna's impatience for Altogether to launch its social network coupled with ambivalence over what to do with it left her thinking she should think about something else, and that something else was her dwindling bank account. To rectify that, a few weeks before Ramadi turned five to scattered applause, she landed a second job. Part-time, of course. Not an easy or well-paying job, but at least it was in her neighborhood and might put her in front of a lot of people. Motherly duties and general introversion had made socially connecting harder than it used to be, but waitressing at the Taverna Omphalos could help change that.

It was through Cassie that the waitressing job had come. An acquaintance quitting to get married to a man in the provinces was looking for a reliable replacement. Anna thought it over. Serving lunch three or four shifts a week would be tiring and a challenge, but also a learning experience. The mundane prospect of serving drinks and platters to its unruly patrons struck her not as a cross to bear but as being given a scholarship for a degree in networking. She took the Taverna's meager stipend as a challenge to charm her customers to chit-chat about themselves, something she believed everybody save introverts like herself loves if not lives to do. She hoped to ferret out her customers' walks of life, social attitudes, ambitions, and opinions about present conditions and then steer the more responsive ones toward community projects—hopefully via Altogether in its time.

At first, the regulars politely acknowledged Anna's pleasantries as she plied their tables, accepting her compliments on their splendid personal appearance with credulous smiles or indifferent nods. When her customer engagement efforts flagged, she tried propagandizing. Diners began finding folded-up photocopies of flyers and broadsides in their napkin trays appealing for solidarity in support for rent strikes, food banks, and charities serving the destitute. Whenever she noticed a patron perusing one, she seized the moment to gloss its content. Her attention to these matters was not lost on Damon, the manager, who regularly chided her to keep up with orders, not buying her explanation that this was her special way of soliciting extra courses.

In the evenings, after supper and playtime, she logged on to Altogether, now close to becoming a thing, according to her supervisor Irene, the marketing director at Prótos. Irene had set her up with a free account on its network and a login to Altogether, currently a house mostly devoid of furniture. A cheery go-getter who dressed for success, Irene was full of big ideas, few of which came in sizes Anna felt she could deploy. She liked using terms that came in pairs, like Buyer Persona, List Segmentation, and Lookalike Audience, and contractions like B2B and B2C, KPI, CTR, CPI, and SEO. Anna asked Irene how she might get the word out about Altogether in ordinary language.

"You email your friends, don't you?" Irene asked.

"Sure. But not all of them and not a lot."

"Collect your addresses and start sending e-blasts to them about Altogether, like cool things they can do with it. I can set you up to do it with click tracking."

Anna hadn't yet found any cool things because there was hardly anyone to do them with on the network, but let that slide. Hesitant to become a spammer, she said: "Not all of my contacts are into the same sorts of things. Each one might use Altogether differently. I might turn them off with one-size-fits-all announcements."

"Well, you could segment your list and send several different pitches to subsets of contacts."

Anna had neglected to inform Irene that her "list" contained at most 40 people, including some who seemed to have moved away or were keeping their heads down. "What about your lists?" she asked. "Doesn't Prótos have a lot of users I could reach out to?"

Irene allowed that she'd been working on that, but had shifted her focus to corporate accounts. She wanted to go head-to-head with a US-based corporate in-mail platform that centralized workers' interactions under a social media façade. It was a workplace model she dismissed as "surveillance capitalism," another neologism for Anna to digest. "It's rather totalitarian," Irene explained. "Every word that employees type funnels into a database that managers can sift through. Workers know they lack privacy, and that stifles creativity." What makes Altogether different and better, she asserted, was that users could control who sees any given piece of their data, as individuals, within a company, and between ones that have linked themselves together.

"I see," Anna said, trying to sound intelligent. "Organizations can federate to help them interoperate." Yet another term of art she'd picked up.

"Exactly. Think of a city government. Each department is an island of automation that Altogether could link to one another. And then to other cities in the region. All data on citizens, employees, and facilities could be harmonized to weed out inconsistencies and give a complete picture of government operations—taxes, property records, auto registrations, school assignments, and much more."

Anna thought about that and decided it needed a bigger think. Thanking Irene, she rang off. All this talk of bureaucratic efficiency was making her nervous. As an anarchist, the idea of assisting central authorities to better conduct business as usual did not sit well.

But might not Altogether also help political dissidents from across the political spectrum to somehow work together or at least come to understandings? That activist dream, after all, was what had drawn her to the platform when she and Demirci had first chatted about it 20,000 feet over the Aegean. Political factions tend to self-describe according to what distinguishes them ideologically, but most of their reticence to work together boiled down to a lack of trust, she felt. While she didn't expect squabbling leftists to unite into one big happy family, if some would hear her out, a few might be persuaded to shuffle aboard Altogether and once there get to know one another.

Over several evenings she put together a broadside illustrated with a network diagram and screen shots cribbed from Irene's PR collateral. On her next day off from the Taverna, armed with propaganda she barely understood, she and Ramadi paid a visit to Exarcheia, the radical, semi-autonomous enclave in the middle of Athens where Nurse Fatma had said she lived. Just the place.

#

Leafy but littered Exarchion Square, a short hike from the Omonoia Metro, oozed Anna's kind of freedom and Ramadi's sense of play. Storefronts, walls, alleys and alcoves along every street they trod rioted with vibrant street art, sprawling murals, and ballooning graffiti espousing *liberté, fraternité, égalité* and death to pigs, as did some of the t-shirts residents sported. Gawking, they meandered down random streets until thoroughly disoriented, requiring Anna to turn on her GPS to make their way to their destination.

Bourgeois media mouthpieces liked to call the breakaway autonomous neighborhood Anarchia, but serious community building took place here. The compact, quasi-triangular district abutting Athens Polytechnic and home to Greece's largest archeological museum was a defiant redoubt of self-determination almost within spitting distance of the ministries lining Syntagma Square. The powers that be had largely left the district to its own devices, perhaps to catalog whatever organisms this political petri dish incubated. Within its confines, refugees were welcomed and accommodated in "liberated" buildings.

Also liberated was an entire block the city had heedlessly razed only to replace it with a parking lot. In response, angry neighborhood residents had transformed the concrete wasteland into an urban oasis, a leafy commons they dubbed Parko Navarinou, which, its liberators asserted, "breathes, plays, creates and dreams, as if alive." And alive it was, much of the time.

At the northern end of the park they found a children's play area. Anna had come there hoping to strike up conversations with parents and talk up her flyer while their kids did their thing. They arrived around midday to find people sitting on benches and walls lunching on take-out and, for the most part, childless. At the playground, just two children frolicked, a girl of perhaps three and a boy about Ramadi's size. He was apparently connected to a man with Fu Manchu facial hair slouching on a bench reading a newspaper, who didn't look particularly approachable. So she said hi to a woman in Muslim garb, presumably the girl's mom. To Anna's dismay, the "Marhabaan" she received in return was followed by pleasantries in Arabic to which Anna could only smile and nod.

By then another youngster had entered the field, sporting denim coveralls and a mane of red hair, trailed by a youngish woman with auburn bangs in jeans and a posterized Bob Marley t-shirt. Her charge scampered over to a rickety climbing gym improvised from plastic piping and proceeded to fearlessly ascend to its quivering top tier.

Anna stepped forward with a solicitous "Look at him go! Aren't you worried he might fall?" correctly guessing the child was a boy. Ramadi overheard, and, crying out "I save him," hauled himself skyward. As the boys clambered and teetered, the women, hands above heads, squinted into a smog-tinted sky at their silhouettes.

"Don't worry, he's pretty agile," the new mom said. "Your boy seems at home up there too. Pleased to meet you. I'm Imogene. That's Viktor. Haven't seen you before. Do you live in Exarcheia?"

To Imogene's amusement Anna admitted to being a tourist from Kerastini, and went on to confess her intention to do a little networking while she was here that she would be more than happy to talk about. As the boys clambered about, Anna learned that Viktor was six and home-schooled, and hubby Michael was a housepainter, currently whitewashing a new housing complex over in Analipsi. Viktor seemed quite happy to have Ramadi's company and shepherded him over to a swing set. The women trailed after and found themselves standing side by side propelling a pair of pendulums, sometimes applying a little english to liven things up.

Anna cleared her throat. "I came up here to drum up interest a new social network that could really bring communitarian types together," she said, leaning in. "But as I don't know anyone around here who might be interested, do you mind if I start with you?"

Imogene let her son's vehicle come and go without a push. "Sure. Not that I need another social network, but what is it?"

"It's a platform called Altogether about to be launched here. It was developed in Estonia, and in fact, Estonia runs on it. I think it has real potential for managing and coordinating all sorts of community projects, so I signed up to recruit beta users, as they call them. Does that answer your question?"

"Sort of. Tell me more."

Letting Ramadi decelerate, Anna flourished one of her flyers, with its bullet points, acronyms, and diagrams, and ticked off highlights of the private virtuous network, as she'd decided to call it.

"I suppose it could have some use here," a bemused Imogene said, "but I don't have time to fuss with it."

"I hear you," Anna said, giving Ramadi a vigorous push that made the superstructure shudder and him squeal. "Who doesn't have their fill of online media? But I bet people here who make things like this wonderful park happen could make good use something like this."

"Of course," Imogene said. "Don't let me discourage you. Why don't you talk to people at OpenBox, where there's a lot going on? I know some committee members. You can tell them I sent you."

Anna knew of the place—a pivotal anarchist institution featuring a bar on the ground floor, meeting rooms and a free medical clinic in the basement, and an open-air cinema atop. A collective had built it up into a go-to watering hole that featured community forums, radical and classic films, and raving rock concerts. It was one of many little anarchies in the district that to Anna proved that building participatory democracy was possible, at least when the state tolerated it. She considered Exarcheia something like a little Rojava—the Syrian Kurdish enclave whose besieged residents had somehow forged a radically democratic non-state under wartime conditions.

Imogene said she wanted to pack it in, and they stepped away to let the boys taxi in. Sneakers scudded on sand. Contact information and vague intentions for a future playdate in the park were exchanged, and mothers and sons set off in diametric directions. Imogene pointed Anna down Andrea Metaxa Street, which she said would take her directly to Exarchion Square and OpenBox.

Anna guided Ramadi past walls and shutters decorated with militant street art, bulbous graffiti, and geological layers of posters, at one point gingerly stepping around a blotch on the sidewalk that might have been dried blood. The urban legend that police stayed out of Exarcheia wasn't really true, she knew, but their rude intrusions were infrequent. Even at night Exarcheia was generally pretty peaceable. For sure, angry people lived there, but at least they weren't angry at each other.

Chapter Seven

When Anna inquired about Imogene's acquaintances at OpenBox, a patron directed Anna to Lukas, a gangly guy in his twenties with a wispy goatee who helped schedule movies and other events in the theater under the stars out back. Telling her that that the people she's asked after were not present, he said, "You can come back tonight. We're showing the Costa-Gavras film Z at nine."

Begging off, saying it was well past her son's bedtime and possibly hers, she asked where the folks she was looking for might be. Lukas wasn't sure but offered to pass on a message. At that, she described her virtuous network and how it might lubricate the collective's affairs and handed him some flyers.

"It won't help to talk just with these folks," Lucas said. "We have a rotating steering committee, and when suggestions like this pop up, it meets to discuss them. At some point a vote is taken and it needs to be unanimous." He consulted a whiteboard mounted behind the bar. "There's a meeting next week. Do you want to be on the agenda?"

"Guess so, if that's what it takes," she said, rolling her eyes at the painted tin ceiling. "Where and when, then?"

The council was set to convene the following Tuesday upstairs at OpenBox at 7 PM. She would go last, if there was time. A movie needed to run at nine. As that would keep her out at least until ten, she would need a babysitter.

"Salut Andreas," she crooned in into her phone on their way home. "Got any plans for Tuesday evening? I need to run up to Exarcheia for a meeting and am hoping you wouldn't mind hanging out with Ramadi for a couple hours. I'll fix us a nice supper. How does that sound?"

After a show of consulting his calendar, Andreas assented to be the adult in the room, but only on the condition that she cook Wiener Schnitzel *à la Oma*. He arrived for the occasion with one of his famous salads, this one of yellow beet, corn, sweet onion, and fennel, which Ramadi eyed suspiciously. The in-house food critic demolished his cutlet but skimped on his salad, holding out for ice cream. Forgoing dessert, with a hugs to both, Anna donned her field jacket and set her beret. "Wish me luck," she said. "I have a feeling this is gonna be a hard sell."

"Don't go, Mutti" Ramadi , clutching her leg.

She grasped his shoulders and bussed his brow. "I'll be home soon, love. Have fun with Onkle Andreas and do what he says."

"Tell them there's a lot of support for this thing in Piraeus," Andreas called after her. "All the capitalist social media are messing with us one way or another. They can own this."

"As much as any of us can own these companies. Which I'm pretty sure they'll point out."

To distract Ramadi from his sense of abandonment, Andreas shepherded him to Anna's reading chair and boosted him onto his lap. Remembering that he'd been meaning to have a talk with Anna about the boy's provenance, he proceeded to tell him a story—essentially a true one framed as an allegory with real names spoken backwards.

"There once was a very righteous and brave man called, umm, Doumam. So brave he was that he put himself in danger to help people he did not even know. He wasn't royal but he carried himself like a prince."

Ramadi giggled. "How can a man carry himself?"

"Good question. It means he stood tall and unafraid and was strong but kind. Anyway, there was a bad king across the sea who was very cruel and became ever so furious when any of his subjects spoke ill of him that he put them in jail. He had built a great palace with a thousand rooms just for him and his royal family and made his people, who already were poor, pay for it. King Pez—for that was his name— was quite unpopular, to say the least."

He continued as Ramadi eagerly listened. "Doumam had visited his kingdom and saw how unhappy its people were. He wished to help them, but how? In his travels, Doumam came across one of the king's subjects, a man named … Egroeg. Egroeg was being hunted by the king's soldiers and was angry."

"Why he was angry?"

"He hated King Pez for his selfish and cruel ways. He had been accused of telling people to revolt and overthrow the king. This was true, and Egroeg had to run for his life. But he still wished for a kingdom without a king. And when he got to know Doumam, it turned out that Doumam had the same dream."

What did they dream, Ramadi wanted to know.

For a world without kings, Andreas told him. Kings are greedy and their greediness causes wars. He went on: "Then they met, umm, Anirtak, a good witch who hated all kings who told them she would help them slay King Pez. And she did. She prepared poison for the men to carry across the sea to give to the king. But, by then Anirtak and Doumam had fallen in love, and Anirtak insisted on going with them. The three of them crossed the stormy ocean in a tiny boat to the shores of Pez's Kingdom, which was called Yekrut. Egroeg took them to a city where King Pez was making a royal visit. Disguising themselves, Doumam and Anirtak joined the crowd that had assembled and waited for King Pez to make his royal entrance …" His voice trailed off.

"And then?" Ramadi asked, searching Andreas's faraway eyes.

And then, words eluding him, Andreas lowered him to the floor. "I'll finish the story next time I see you. It's your bedtime now."

"Finish it now, Onkle!" demanded the expectant, wide-awake child.

Andreas sadly realized that, like so many fairy tales he had grown up with, the ending wasn't suitable for small children, especially this one. He could not bear to tell Ramadi that King Pez survived Anirtak's poison, but after a tragic, preventable accident, Doumam did not.

His narrative bind turned to self-castigation for starting a tale he couldn't finish. His fruitless search for an anodyne ending was interrupted by a welcome ringtone. It was Anna, checking in, regretting to inform him that she was only now about to meet the committee, and thus might be a bit late. Whatever it takes, he replied, and petitioned her to bid Ramadi good night and tell him it was time for bed, which with a bit of wheedling she managed to pull off.

Ramadi dutifully disrobed, fetched his sleepwear from behind his pillow, and waited to be tucked in. Andreas drew the sheet over him and tickled a protruding foot before stealing into the kitchen to clean up, still puzzling over how to end his grim fable.

It pleases me to see Andreas minding the boy, telling him a story, I think. He seems to have affection for our son, whose name I still do not know. Is it Swiss? Greek? We weren't married, so his last name must be hers, but I hope he's not Mahmoud the Second.

Perhaps it is written somewhere I can see, but changing viewpoints isn't easy. I've gotten better at it but still lurch around as if inebriated. I move toward the sleeping boy but overshoot to his little backpack sitting on the floor. On its flap, I see a piece of white tape with writing on it, perhaps a name tag. In this feeble light all I can read is "AMADI B." Could that be Ramadi, my surname, plus her last initial? If that is so, I couldn't be happier.

A creaking sound from the next room drew Andreas from the kitchen to find Ramadi had flopped onto his back. As he turned to leave, he heard the boy mutter something like "Papi," and stood there listening until, noticing he was hugging himself, he let his arms fall and returned to the kitchen to wash dishes.

#

Anna arrived home at half-past ten to find an immaculate kitchen and Andreas on his back dozing on her bed, lightly snoring. She sat beside him and pecked his forehead. "Sorry for the late hour. They made me wait until they had solved all of Exarcheia's problems."

She tugged him upright by the arms and conducted him into the kitchen to unload her frustrations as she prepared tea.

Andreas yawned. "Like what problems?"

"Oh, like who to invite to speak at the next film festival, and whether a band that wanted to play there might have a bourgeois attitude. The one meaningful item on their agenda was how to prod the city to remove unsanitary trash that's been piling up."

"Hmm. What were they like, this committee?"

"There were six of them, three men and three women, in a room over the bar with thumping music. It gave me a headache.

They did too. They were businesslike, but still I felt patronized for not being from there."

She brought him tea and sat across from him. "So anyway, when my turn finally came I think I made a pretty decent presentation. I told them how Altogether could streamline making decisions like they had just labored over for an hour and a half. How all the neighborhood initiatives could know what each other is doing and share resources. And how private it is."

He lemoned his tea and spooned out a seed. "What did they say to that?"

"I got cross-examined about the two private companies behind Altogether. One said, 'You want us to trust our affairs to unaccountable monopoly capitalists?'"

"Something you expected, as I recall. Did you point out that some of them use Facebook and Twitter and such?"

"Yes, actually, but the answer I got was that they don't use social media to conduct the collective's business or make decisions, just for fundraising, announcements and broadsides, and assorted gossip. Almost like cops, they grilled me—Who I was working for, what they were after?"

"Did anyone stand up for you?"

"Well Imogene said she would put in a good word for me. Don't know if she ever did, though."

"Who's Imogene?"

"A mom I met at a playground up there last week. Has a well-behaved little boy. She's a local, but not part of the collective. Anyway, once I was on the defensive things just got worse."

"I'm so sorry."

"So I leave with one saying, 'We get the picture. We'll think about it and let you know if we want to learn more.'"

Andreas shook his head. "So now what?"

She leaned over her mug, propped on her palms. "Maybe I should hang it up. Everybody seems to think their communications are doing just fine without this thing."

"Fine or not, lots of people spend or waste lots of time on social media. Asking them to try a new kind could feel like overload. Burnout 2.0."

"Ja, I guess. Especially when the point is to get work done instead of escaping it. Look, it's been a long day and I need to chill. Thanks for tending Ramadi. Was he any problem?"

"Not at all. I told him a story and put him to bed with just a bit of fuss that your call overcame, thank you."

"What was the story?"

"Oh, just a fable I made up as I went along. Sort of an origin story about a bad king who got what he deserved."

"Real life should be as gratifying," she said. "But what do you mean, origin story? Whose?"

"Ramadi's. Except I didn't make it about him or use real names."

"Think I know who the bad king is. Are you crazy?"

"Take it easy. I couldn't get past the point where they were about to attack the king. I can leave it at that or make something up if he bullies me into finishing it."

"Well think hard. I don't want him to know how it ended. Even as a fairy tale."

"You know, he'll want to know more about his father and what happened to him at some point. Have you given that any thought?"

"I'll go to my grave before I tell him or anyone about our mission. Nobody needs to know, especially Ramadi."

"Okay, but doesn't he already know that Mahmoud died? Maybe not how, but where?"

"Sure he does. I didn't want him to get the idea he'll ever come back."

"So what did you tell him?"

"That his father got hit by a car getting of a bus."

"Did you say where?"

"In Turkey. It just came out when Ramadi bolted out of a bus before me. Wanted to caution him from ever doing it again."

"And how did he take it?"

"He got quiet and scrunched his eyes, like when something puzzles him. He wanted to know more. So I told him that he came from Iraq but had to leave. He fought bravely in a war then went on to Turkey, where I met him while on holiday."

Andreas tilted back, stroking his stubbly chin. "I'm sure he'll want more details. Maybe say you asked him for directions, found you both spoke English, and ended up talking the rest of the afternoon. He wanted to get to Greece, was working to save up money to pay for it. You found him handsome and gentle and sensed he liked you. So you invited him to your pension and spent a few wonderful days together until that bu … car hit him."

"I picked him up, just like that? Seems kind of casual."

"Well, say he was working in some shop and had nowhere to sleep but there. It would be just like you to offer to share your space."

"Which is basically what I did the night he arrived here. And speaking of stories, better come up with a happy ending for yours."

Andreas yawned again and stretched his arms. "I suppose something like 'and then the good witch put a spell on the bad king that made him good and she and the brave knight married and lived happily ever after.'"

"Talk about an anticlimax." She sighed, got up, and retrieved his salad bowl from the drainboard. "Thanks for everything. Talk with you soon."

He kissed her cheeks, stuffed the bowl in his rucksack, and turned to leave, but stopped himself. "Maybe it was because of my story, but when I checked up on Ramadi he mumbled 'Papi' in his sleep. He never calls me Papi. Made me shiver."

"Funny. That's what I call Mahmoud to him."

"Well, now that I think of it, Mahmoud came to mind the other night in bed, out of the blue."

"What were you thinking?"

"Nothing I can recall. I just felt sorry for him, really sorry, which of course led to remorse and insomnia."

She hugged him and sighed into his ear. "Tell me about it."

After Andreas left to pedal home his rusty steed, Anna closed the light and crept past Ramadi to the bathroom. She emerged in her nightgown to fluff her pillows and collapse onto male-scented sheets, and became wistful. Shake it off, she told herself, rolling onto her side, shutting her eyes, waiting for Mahmoud's afterimage to dissipate. Soon her restive mind rewound, ticking off the minutes of her meeting that led nowhere, suborning sleep. She sat up to have herself a career talk.

Was it even possible to rescue people from the thrall of social media with yet more of it? Yes, Altogether was different from other brands because it was adaptable and private and users are in charge. But would people use it to solve problems, organize for change, or just go on making change someone else's problem?

Maybe those Exarcheian apparatchiks had a point. What would be gained by disrupting their processes, tedious as they might be? Tomorrow, she told herself, she would decide whether to stay with Altogether or not. Staying would mean a lot of time spent struggling to build online communities and a paycheck. Leaving, looking for another job and a lot of solitary downtime. Wrapped in her dilemma, she settled down to drift away, only to start wondering how things might be different, had he lived.

PART TWO

Trafficking Cop

A tour guide without tourists, that's me. All I can do here is revisit familiar places where I can't hear anything, save for the never-ending astral chorus from above. Scenes I surveil appear as silent movies in the muted colors of old postcards. I am free to approach the screen but not to penetrate it to where life is being lived.

Now—for it is always now, just as in pre-afterlife—I visit her flat in Piraeus. It is dark and they are sleeping in the room where we first made love. There is Ramadi, my son. Look at him! Strong, healthy, full of life! Though asleep he seems to speak, perhaps in a dream. I remember the words of the poet: "Love itself describes its own perfection. Be speechless and listen." I do, but no words come to my ears.

And look at Katrina, curled up. Now she stirs to embrace herself. Or is it me? Why did I never tell her I loved her when I could? I tell it now, in case she hears. I also tell her what happened to me was not her fault. It was mine and George's. I was careless, but he was callous to charge her with executing me if I couldn't escape. Preparing the instrument that sealed my fate was not her intention. How full of sorrow she must have been as she made it ready.

Now I visit Andreas. He too is in bed, alone, reading a book. It is in German. He looks up, his eyes sweep the room as if sensing a buzzing fly, then flit back to his open page. Soon he closes it and rubs the point of his chin in thought. Such a good man. He took upon himself to keep us together, house and feed us and drive us to organize a new mission after George was arrested and his plan collapsed. How he managed to free George before they could deport him I will never know. Had he not succeeded, George would be rotting in a Turkish prison and my bones would not be rotting in a Turkish necropolis.

As Andreas shuts the light and slides under his comforter I find myself drawn to the taverna, where Katrina and I told him of our love and she became our comrade against his better judgment. The hour is late and it is almost empty. A tipsy young couple sit at one table staring into their empty glasses. At another table a thin man with hollow cheeks sits alone. He downs a milky liquid, Arak or Ouzo perhaps, lowers his glass, and looks upward, and when he does his dark eyes project coldness. The same revulsion I felt for the nationalists who threatened Katrina comes over me. Whether he is like them or not, I sense he is bad news.

Chapter Eight

FOR HIS IMMINENT FIFTH birthday Ramadi told Anna he would like pizza and cake and an airplane and certain of his preschool pals in attendance. That would be awkward, Anna explained, as Daria, the mother of Yasmin, the girl he wished to exclude, had volunteered her four-room flat for the festivities. Ramadi considered Yasmin a bit of a show-off who went on and on about the clothes she wore and the clothes she wanted next. The garments came from a resale shop where her mom worked part time, which gave her the pick of the litter at a significant discount; he himself sported such venerable threads. After explaining why dissing classmates was bad politics, Anna managed to persuade him to make it an open invitation.

Anna had assigned herself the pizza detail and volunteered to bake a cake, but on second thought visited the old lady at the little *artopoieío* on Dimokratias Boulevard and put in a order for a blue-and-white checkerboard of a birthday cake decorated with a blue fondant airplane and lettered in Greek, *Charoúmena Genéthlia Ramadi*. Then she trucked down to her son's favored Golden House of Pizza to order the entrée.

Noticing her warily regarding his cramped establishment from outside his door, the Golden House's owner waved her in with a hairy arm. Through a plastered-on grin he asked, "Hello, how have you been? It's good to see you. How is the boy?" And remarked on the weather, which hadn't changed for a week.

To his unexpected pleasantry all Anna could muster was "We're good, thank you." Taking a sidelong glance to assure herself they were alone, she noticed a cooler hugging the wall. "Oooh, I see you have a new cold case. Good for you."

"Why, yes," he said as proudly as if it were a Mercedes Benz. "The cooler came from a corner store that went out of business. I got it for almost nothing. And it has lots of very fresh salad, just for you. Want to take some home?"

"Next time, promise. I'm not here to eat. I came in to order pizza for a kid's party. Next Sunday afternoon."

Pen wavering over pad, Stavros said "Okay. How many kids? How many adults?"

"Best case, six of each. Three large should do it. Two plain, one spinach, mushrooms, and olives. Eight pieces each."

"Okay. Where to?"

"I'll pick up."

He was staring out the shop window. "We do free delivery. You sure you don't want?"

"It's a little out of the way, like two bus rides. I have to go there anyway. But thanks for the offer."

Stavros let his pen fall. He gazed out to the street, hands hovering above the counter, kneading his knuckles.

"You okay?" Anna asked.

Hands still clasped, he said: "I cannot do this, nice lady."

"Do what? I don't understand. You can't make pizza for me?"

"I tell you. Hold on please." He straightened up and retreated to paddle a pie from his oven, slid it onto his cutting board, and slashed at it with his cutter disk. Averting his eyes, he said: "I was asked to keep eye on you. By policeman you saw here, say you might have something to do with old crime."

Anna took that in. "Is … that … so?"

He returned to the counter, opened his cash drawer, and fished out a business card. "He leave his card. It say he is Warden."

Her brow furrowed. "I see. Whatever that is. Did he say what he wanted with me?"

"Some unsolved crime. Maybe you were witness, I don't know. Anyway, I have no use for police. They walk in, think I owe them a slice and a Coke. This one wanted to deliver your pizza. He give me a hard time. Don't want him give you hard time too."

A good ten seconds ticked by before Anna replied. "I can't tell you how much I love you for that. You didn't have to tell me."

Pinning the card under an index finger, she asked: "May I copy it, please? It would mean a lot."

Stavros shrugged. "Sure, lady, but be careful with it."

A click on her phone ingested Police Warden Vassilios Laskaris' card into her photo gallery. "Don't worry. I'm not going to call him. He'll never know I saw this. My only goal is to keep away from him. I hope you will help."

Stavros nodded. She offered her hand. "You are very kind. See you next Sunday around one."

He took and gingerly shook it. "Okay. What name I put on order?"

"Make it out to Katri ... um, Katniss." And with a sly wink added: "And don't tell that warden, okay?"

Smiling through his eyes, Stavros nodded. "Okay, Sunday." After she left, he studied Laskaris' card before returning it to the back of his drawer. "Whatever that's about, I don't need to know."

#

Sitting on the bus going to pick up Ramadi, Anna fretted over the pizza chef's awkward revelation and fingered a message to Ottovio asking to get together at her place to check police records. As an inducement, she texted again, promising homemade fish stew with dumplings that she pulled from her freezer when they got home.

When Ottovio arrived, Ramadi took note of the black laptop computer he plopped down at the kitchen table that dwarfed his mom's brushed silver one. He hovered nearby, watching them huddling at it after supper, sensing that the glyphs its screen displayed meant something worth knowing.

I wish I could smell the food she got from the taverna. It's good to see Ottovio. He really hasn't changed but for flecks of grey in that big curly beard. They huddle at his computer staring at lines of text.

Anna displayed Laskaris's business card. "Can you tell if this guy is known to the police?"

Ottovio shoved a thumb drive into his infernal machine. "This copy of the Hellenic Police's criminal database is a little old, but let's assume he is old news to them."

Ramadi announced he felt cold and crawled into Anna's lap. Saying she felt chilled too, she wrapped him in her arms and checked the windows, but all were shut.

Ottovio opened an application, then a file, stubby fingers flying inscrutably. Ramadi followed his actions with interest, understandably unaware of the extreme efforts he'd undertaken to liberate a three-gigabyte relational database from a Hellenic Police file server.

⁓

I think I know what they are doing. After Katrina and I told him we were lovers, Andreas asked Ottovio to look her up in his police file to see if she had a record. Now she shows Ottovio card for someone. Seems to be policeman. Why would policeman be in that database of criminals?

⁓

"Okay, we search by name," Ottovio said as he typed a query. A few seconds later he informed her that Vassilios Laskaris came to their attention after an incident seven years back involving excessive force in an altercation with a shopkeeper for which he was held partly responsible and fined but not sentenced. Nothing about being deputized as a warden. That was pretty much it, he said, allowing that things may have changed since he last pilfered the database.

Laskaris's record included a home address, somewhere down by the docks in the adjacent Perama district, a known Golden Dawn Party stronghold. Anna typed it into her address book along with the phone number and title.

"What exactly is a warden?" she asked.

They're supernumeraries with limited authority, he maintained. When not directing traffic or serving papers, they prowl around rounding up tips for police. Wardens come and go. Maybe he still is, maybe not.

"'We can check," she said. "Call police. What's the closest station to here?"

"Would be the one over in Nikaia, just north of here." He activated his wi-fi and searched anonymously. "This," he said, pointing to the bottom of the screen. She took down its address and phone number, saying she would call from a pay station tomorrow. Ramadi intently studied the web page until Ottovio closed the laptop. Noticing the boy's interest, he said: "Can do a lot with this machine. Maybe you be hacker someday, have even better one."

"Hacker," the boy cheerily responded, seizing upon a new word.

Ottovio had brought a tub of pistachio ice cream, a new flavor for the boy. Anna divvied it up and handed bowls around. Ramadi sniffed and prodded it like a cat dubious about a new kitty concoction, tasted it, and proceeded to tuck it in, leaving the nuts behind. When Anna asked him why, he opened wide to display one stuck where a baby tooth had gone missing. She fished it out, hoping his teeth would come in straight and his overbite would take care of itself.

I remember sitting at that table with her and Kaan after Andreas, worried about the police, took us to board with her. It was the second time I had seen Katrina. We talked politics far into the night. The next day, Andreas found us a new flat. And what a grand one, paid for by his new old flame, Ivan. Soon Katrina joined us, also fearing persecution. We bonded by fleeing danger and then flew into it.

For closely guarded reasons involving Stavros' words, "something to do with old crime," rather than calling the Nikaia police station from her own phone, the next morning found Anna at a Western Union storefront heavily used by locals for money orders and foreigners to transmit remittances. She stood in a listless line clutching spare change to drop into one of the few functional pay phones in the area. Awaiting her turn afforded her time to consider what to say to whomever answers the phone at police stations.

Upon attaining the outworn wall phone, she wiped off the receiver with her bandanna, dialed the number Ottovio had given her, and deposited coins as instructed.

Eventually, a crisp female voice announced "Hellenic Police Nikaia Station, Desk Sergeant Cristopoulos speaking. What can I do for you?"

Anna could hear raised voices and percussive sounds in the background. "Um, I called to see if you could help me find one of your officers, but it sounds like a lot is going on there. Should I call another time?"

"No, it's fine. This is normal. Who are you looking for?"

"Police Investigations Warden Vassilios Laskaris. He gave me his card but I lost it. Do you know him?"

"No, I don't. Wardens don't spend a lot of time here. Let me look him up. Spell last name please."

Anna spelled and then hummed the Marseillaise while the Desk Sergeant searched.

"He's not on our list," Cristopoulos told her after the second chorus. "Perhaps he works out of another precinct. I'll give you over to Central Records. They *should* have a complete list."

A couple of coins later, Anna had her answer. No one had heard of Laskaris. Whoever he was, he wasn't a cop.

She called the Greek geek to impart that news and suggested a quick rendezvous.

#

Friday was a day off for Anna at the Taverna Omphalos ('Navel of the World') but there she was, leveraging her employee discount to treat Ramadi and Ottovio. Today the boy's sights were set not on pizza but on crispy chicken tenders and French fries, which he was told he could have if he ate his peas. Last to order was Ottovio, whose menu selections would likely have sufficed for the three of them.

Nodding toward Ramadi, currently absorbed in jousting fork against knife, Anna shifted languages. "Let's talk in English, if you don't mind. Some things he shouldn't hear." Ottovio returned a nod.

"So, the cops say Laskaris isn't one of their wardens. If he is, he's under deep cover and nobody's talking."

Ottovio stroked his beard. "Well, if he's not, what's his game? Maybe that cold case he mentioned is double murder by poison dart. He called you witness, not suspect, you said."

She shifted in her seat and lowered her voice. "Well, that's what the pizza guy said he heard from Laskaris. But he might suspect I was more than a witness."

"Well, you did set up the ambush, but how would he know that?"

"Either of the two thugs could have described me to someone before he died. Maybe even Laskaris. But even if he's not after revenge, he spooks me."

As their server dished out their fare, she said: "You know, maybe Laskaris fingered me in the No Name. We argued. I mentioned I was Swiss. It could have rung a bell with him. Maybe not then but by the time we ran into each other at the pizza place."

More absorbed in his souvlaki than her hypothetical, Ottovio didn't reply. Anna poured catsup on Ramadi's plate and dabbed yogurt sauce on her falafel. "Whoever he is," she said, "he's definitely Golden Dawn. Same bad attitude as the troll who wanted my blood simply because my post offended his Greekness."

Ottovio liberated a chunk of lamb from its skewer. "Nationalists still haven't gotten over the Ottoman Empire and tend to nurse grudges. But why would they wait years to come after you?"

"Dunno. A few days after those two expired we slipped into Turkey. I was there almost a month. Maybe they thought I was gone for good and only recently suspected I was still around."

"Who you mean, they? The two guys Mahmoud blew away were already dead."

"No, Laskaris and his creepy buddy who tried to follow us home."

"Goal!" Ramadi cried out. On his plate he had formed a U with three French fries and was batting peas into it with his knife.

"Eat some more footballs," Anna instructed, "so you will grow up strong and be a star striker."

"Wanna be airplane pilot," Ramadi said. "Spaceman too."

"Okay, then eat your space helmets," Ottovio said.

"Anyway," Anna said, going back to English, "if he's not a cop, he forged that business card, right? Maybe his identity is forged too. He could be somebody else entirely."

Ottovio scratched his chin, dribbling crumbs from his beard. "Hmm. If so, why pick a real person's name? Seems risky."

"Well, maybe that person is no longer with us. You know how to raise the dead. How many zombies have you signed up on Altogether?"

"Maybe a dozen. Come from death notices in newspapers. Figured it would make your numbers look better."

"Not that they'll participate, but I appreciate your efforts. Since you're so good at that, maybe you can find an obituary for this guy."

Ottovio wielded his phone. "Easy enough."

Anna finished her falafel, spooned some peas into Ramadi's hangar, and was attacking her salad when Ottovio gave a little chuckle. "Good thinking. The Laskaris from Perama with a police record died over two years ago."

"No shit? So, someone is pretending to be him pretending to be a cop?"

"Possibly. Lemme finish reading the obit."

Shortly he looked up, no longer smirking. "He was 67 when he died. At the end it says: 'He is survived by Iris Laskaris, loving wife of 46 years, and one son, Vassilios Laskaris II.' Could be your guy."

"Aha! So maybe he's not a zombie. Does it say where his disreputable son lives?"

"No data. Maybe in his mom's basement."

She laughed. "Funny, but somehow I doubt that. So what's his game? What does he want from me?"

"Well, he's not a cop so can't arrest you and he's not a zombie after your brain. Revenge maybe?"

#

Saturday came, and with it another opportunity for Anna to serve and schmooze customers. Tables at the Taverna Omphalos spilled from its folding glass front onto the sidewalk along teeming Dimokratias Boulevard. It was a popular watering hole with a menu of standard fare served up from a fairly decent kitchen. This was only Anna's second week of serving, but already she had come to recognize some of her diners and they her.

Today her tables were inside. Her shift was yet to get busy, allowing her time to ruminate on Altogether and whether to keep stumping for it. On the plus side, she had just received her first paycheck after invoicing Prótos for 20 billable hours. Even after the government's cut, it was a considerable chunk of change compared to the less than two hundred euros she took home from the Taverna last week, tips included. Money had never particularly attracted her, but she had a child to raise, dammit, responsibilities. Her nest egg—wages, hazard pay, and hush money from her stint in West Africa—was about to hatch and fly away.

Given that the alternative seemed to be penury, then and there she resolved to stick it out. That would mean getting better acquainted with the system and to Irene's gung-ho supervision. Currently she seemed to be in Irene's good graces, thanks to a recent uptick of sign-ups, a salutary trend that Anna was happy to let her boss attribute to her marginal evangelizing efforts, not to Ottovio raising the dead. Although his zombies couldn't animate Altogether, Anna greatly appreciated the geek's obsessive attention to detail in her behalf, though suspected he might have unannounced plans for them.

Her reverie ended when Damon the manager tugged at her arm and pointed to a customer at one of her stations. She grabbed a menu and ran it over to a man absorbed in his phone. When he accepted the menu without looking up, Anna's Adam's apple did a little dance up and down her throat. She hastened back to the service window, back turned to her customer, a lanky unshaven forty-ish man with a mop of curly black hair.

The fine hair on Anna's arms tingled. *It's Laskaris's buddy, the creep who shadowed me from the pizzeria! What if he recognizes me?*

Desperately seeking anonymity, she deposited her eyeglasses in her shirt pocket, pulled her frilly waitress cap down over her forehead, and waltzed to his table to trill "May I take your order?"

This time he did look up, his face betraying no recognition, either because she was too incognito or out of context. "I'm not sure what I want. You have suggestion?"

"Well," she said in her best Greek, "the special today is grilled octopus and pilaf. Comes with salad. People really like it. We might be out of it soon. See it over at that table." As his gaze followed her finger, she shifted position toward his back.

"Okay, I'll have that," he said, eyes returning to his phone. "Oh, and a double Ouzo with two ice cubes in it."

"Right away," she said as she fled.

She told the barkeep to fix the drink and bus it to table nine if he would; she needed to run to the bathroom. Instead, she ran to the kitchen, whisked off her cap and apron, grabbed her handbag from its hiding place, and opened the back door, shouting to the chef, "Just pinned up an order for table nine. I'm terribly nauseous. Tell Damon that I went to the clinic. I'll check in later."

She bolted through the door, unsure where to go. Halfway to the next intersection her frantic pace slowed and then stopped. She turned back toward the taverna and sat on a concrete wall festooned with graffiti with her back to a rubble-filled lot to consider the situation. Presently, she donned her glasses, shook out her headscarf, draped and knotted it primly under her chin, and, now more curious than fearful, waited.

Chapter Nine

For fifteen minutes Anna sat on the concrete wall, fingers interlocked, rhythmically rubbing her thumbs, until the curly-headed man emerged onto the taverna's patio. He was as thin as she had remembered, but taller, with that stooped bearing that tall men fall into from peering down at the world. After briefly stabbing and stroking his phone, he put it in a back pocket, glanced in her direction, again betraying no recognition, and sauntered down the sidewalk away from her. She arose and followed him, using as cover an older woman lugging a shopping bag.

Stopping short a few dozen paces down the boulevard, Anna's human shield laid down her burden to answer her phone. Coming up against her, Anna clutched the woman's shoulder to steady her, apologizing for the misstep. The woman amiably dismissed the incident and attended to her call.

By then, the thin man had stopped to unlock a black sedan. Before opening the door, he glanced her way. Anna shrank behind her shopper and sucked in a breath as he walked back toward her with his lips curled like Mona Lisa.

Anna nervously watched the man extract something from his pocket and approach a boy of seven or eight squatting on the pavement. The boy, crisply attired in khakis and a button-down shirt, was petting a little brown dog tethered to a street sign in front of a nail salon. The man squatted down to pet the dog and chat up the child, neither of whom seemed to mind his sudden attention.

More curious than fearful, Anna edged curbside to watch. She couldn't overhear them, but observed the man offering the boy some sort of bon-bon. The dog expectantly watched as the small human, not he, received it. The boy tentatively unwrapped, licked, and then sucked on the treat as the man continued to converse and patted the dog, who started licking his hand. When the man batted its muzzle away, taking this to be a game of kiss-the-fingers, the dog kept at it and his lanky playmate obliged.

Their fun went on for a minute or two, until the boy dropped an arm to the sidewalk to brace himself. The man grasped his shoulders to steady him, then tugged him to his feet and proceeded to shuffle him down the sidewalk, much as a child would walk a doll to its next exciting appointment. The boy neither protested nor struggled. His feet, she observed with mounting dismay, barely seemed to work.

Gaping after them, Anna felt for her phone, raised it, took a photograph, and followed. Scant seconds later the man was sliding the boy's flaccid frame onto his car's rear seat, a moment that Anna also managed to capture. As she drew closer the man jumped in and started his car. Anna grabbed a shot as it nosed onto the boulevard, and then, oblivious to passing cars, jumped off the curb to snap several photos before traffic obliterated the vehicle.

Just then she heard barking. The little dog was noisily straining against his leash at a well-appointed woman in a blue and yellow sheath hastily exiting a salon blowing on maroon fingernails. High heels click-clacking, she rushed to the tethered dog, who rose on its haunches to scrabble at her dress. She batted him off and scanned the sidewalk with apprehensive eyes.

Anna jogged back to her, panting. "The boy who was here was just kidnapped!" she said, seconded by the dog's yips. "I saw the whole thing. Was he your son?"

Now as agitated as her pet, the woman cried, "It cannot be! What did you see?"

Anna gulped some air and rattled off the sordid sequence of events as the woman's hands came to her face and then fell away, balling into fists.

Glowering, she berated Anna. "You could have screamed, shouted for police!" she wailed, tears streaking her mascara. "In the salon, he was sitting behind me and then he was gone. Oh Sami! I've lost my Sami! How could you let it happen?"

"Maybe I should have yelled, but by the time I realized what was going on, he was almost at his car. But I have photos. Look!"

Instead of looking at Anna's phone, she was punching in 112 on hers, then shouting at the dispatcher loudly enough to gather passersby. "They are coming," she said after clicking off.

"See, I have evidence," Anna said, scrolling through her photos.

The first two images showed the pair walking away and the boy being lifted into the car. They were a bit blurry and didn't show faces. The two of the getaway were crisper. Both captured the sedan's license plate.

"You must give those to the police," the woman said.

"Soon as they get here. Hope it's soon."

A knot of murmuring spectators collected around them as the dog sniffed at their shoes. "Please go about your business and leave us alone," Anna told them, surprised at her assertiveness. "There's nothing you can do."

One by one, the onlookers broke off as the mom waved them away and turned to Anna, head cocked. "I hear a siren. Don't go anywhere."

"Of course not," Anna said, wondering who this lady was and whether to divulge that she's been following the same man who'd pursued her not long ago. In the distance a siren warbled a minor sixth. As it crescendoed, Anna could think of places she'd much rather be.

#

She spent the rest of her shift at a table in the back of the taverna with the victim's mother, Damon the manager, and two Hellenic Police officers, the younger one uniformed, the older in a grey suit and loosened blue tie. His lapel bore a name tag reading *Lt. A. Nicolaides, Inspector*. The plainclothesman, trimmer than his rumpled suit, was clean-shaven with close-cropped black hair, and had searching brown eyes set above a hawkish beak. While pleasant enough, nothing about his grave demeanor assuaged Anna's apprehensions.

Eschewing pleasantries, the inspector took a seat with Damon and the women as his subordinate silently stood by with a notebook. In turn patting her eyes and wringing her handkerchief, the victim's mother identified herself as Fotini Evangelatos and her son Sami, seven, as residents of Piraiki. When Nicolaides turned to Anna, she tersely identified herself and recounted what she'd witnessed before shoving her phone across the table and urging him to track down that car now, please, to Fotini's nodding approval. Faintly glowering, he perused her photos and then used his to place a call. Handing back her phone, he said that they will consult motor vehicle records, broadcast a bulletin, and visit his address in short order.

"Don't let them go in shooting, please," Fotini said, almost rising from her seat. "Oh, Sami!"

"We would never do that, Mrs. Evangelatos," the detective said. "Sami is how old?"

"He's seven, inspector."

"So why did you leave a seven-year-old unattended?"

Fotini bristled. "Sami was with me in the salon. I didn't notice when he slipped out. Maybe he was worried that someone would steal Hercules."

"Your dog, I take it," Nicolaides said. Sniffling, Fotini nodded and turned away.

Before Nicolaides could ask how old the dog was, Damon spoke up to affirm that the suspect had eaten at table nine and left within the past hour. Anna had been waiting on him, he added, and had abruptly fled the premises after taking his order, citing a sudden illness. Kneading her hands, Anna confirmed Damon's version of events, except to say: "I hadn't gotten sick, sir, just terrorized by the sight of him."

Asking Anna to "call me Antonio," the inspector inquired why was that. Under his investigatory gaze she related being followed by him one afternoon about a week ago while walking home.

"Was he alone?" Antonio wanted to know.

"There was nobody with him at the time," she somewhat truthfully replied, wanting to leave the menacing Laskaris and his fake credentials out of the picture. "When he saw me notice him down at the street corner as we walked up the hill, he ducked away."

"You said 'we.' So you were not alone?"

"No, I was with my four-year-old son."

"Why were you out?"

"We were on our way home after shopping," she responded, eliding the pizza guy for the same reason.

"Can you think of any reason he might have been following you? Had you ever met or exchanged words?"

As Anna struggled betwixt yes and no, Fotini said: "I'll bet he was after your son!"

Those seven words sent Anna's gaze sailing upward to somewhere below the ceiling fixtures, where it rested for several beats and a shiver. "I never considered that," she murmured. Her eyes drifted down to Fotini. "I just assumed he was stalking me."

Can Katrina sense my presence here? This is the second time something strange has drawn me to this taverna. First that unpleasant man getting drunk, and now here she is talking to policemen. Who's that woman with her? She looks like she has money but she's sad. Was there was a crime? Whatever happened, I don't like it. I project love to comfort them. They may not receive it, but it's all I can do.

Nicolaides took another tack. "So, today, you fled at the sight of him, but then waited outside to follow him, is that right?" he asked, not waiting for an answer. "If you were so afraid of him, why did you do that?"

Noticing her fingers drumming the table, Anna lowered her hands to her lap. "I panicked. Wanted to put distance between us. But outside, it hit me that he hadn't seemed to recognize me. Curiosity got the better of me, I guess, and decided to tail him, maybe get a look at his car. But I never expected he would do something like that."

Nicolaides wouldn't let go. "You knew he had a car, then?"

"How could I?" Anna replied as a rivulet of moisture trickled down her torso. "But if he had one, I wanted to see it."

"So you just …"

Anna stiffened, gripping the sides of her chair. "Look, he snatched a child. I saw it. I told you what I know. I showed you the car. Now please go find Sami."

"Yes, please!" Fotini said. "There's no time to waste!"

"Don't worry, we will!" Nicolaides, said and tilted his chin to Anna. "Consider yourself a key witness. If we prosecute this guy, you'll need to give a deposition, this time under oath—the truth, the whole truth, and nothing but."

"No problem," Anna said, desperately wanting the interrogation to end, which shortly it did, as "Never on Sunday" pealed from Nicolaides' phone. "Yes it is," he said. "Any news? ... Where?" ... "Right away." He pocketed his phone and told them he had to go but there might be good news. "We'll be in touch soon," he told Fotini as he stood up and signaled his partner to follow him.

Damon arose and tucked his chair. "I'm so sorry. Both of you, stay as long as you like. Anna, take the rest of the day off. Appetizers are on the house." He retreated to the kitchen.

Anna reclined in her chair and let out a breath through pursed lips, making her wish she still smoked. Her eyes sought the ceiling as Fotini blotted hers. They sat in silence until some dishes clattering into a washtub made Fotini jump.

"Are you okay?" Anna asked. "Do you have anyone to come home to?"

"Yes, Ilias, my husband. He's on his way home. Have you?"

Anna shook her head. "But soon I have to get my boy from a friend's house. Can I get you something to eat before I leave?"

"Thanks, no. I have your number. Whatever happens, you'll be the first to know. I can't tell you how much what you did means to me."

"I wish I could have done more, Fotini. Take care getting home and let's hope for the best."

While she did hold out hope, something told Anna that this wasn't going to end well.

#

The next day, Sunday, belonged to Ramadi and his eagerly anticipated fifth birthday party. Anna too had something to celebrate; Fotini had called that morning relating that her son had been recovered and was safe, thanks to Anna's snapshots. Police had pulled over his abductor's car somewhere in Nikaia, where they took him into custody and Sami to a hospital. There, doctors declared the boy unharmed, at least as far as his body was concerned. Both women found the police's performance uncharacteristically efficient. Maybe they just got lucky, Fotini said.

The happy news helped Anna to enjoy the party at Daria's. All but four slices of Stavros' pizza were wolfed down and the cake with the blue fondant figurine of Jay-Jay the Jet Plane was a big hit, especially with the birthday boy. Ramadi extinguished its five candles in one go to a discordant rendition of *Xronia Polla*, the Greek birthday song that makes "Happy birthday to you, happy birthday to you ..." seem rather lame:

May you grow old and have white hair,
give to everyone the light of knowledge,
and may all say here is a wise person

Andreas had asked them to drop by after the party for tea and snacks. He too had a gift for the boy. They munched popcorn as Ramadi wrestled open a brown box big enough for him to hide in, which of course he later did. Peering under a pulled-up flap his features blossomed as he beheld the handlebars of a little blue bicycle with training wheels and a clown's horn, a pint-sized water bottle clipped to its frame. Andreas went over to help him lift it out, but Ramadi had already implemented a strategy of toppling the box and then heaving it upside-down, not considering that the bike would also be.

Righting the box, Andreas said: "If it's too big for your flat, I can keep it downstairs. I rearranged my living room to let him make a circuit."

Awestruck, Anna grinned, applauded, and then embraced his shoulders to bus his cheeks. "This is super! Ramadi, give a big thank-you to Onkle Andreas."

"Tank you Onkle. I love it!" he said, mounting his riding machine.

"*Vielen Danke, Onkle,*" seconded Anna and blew a kiss.

The adults eloped to the kitchen to converse as Ramadi cranked his gleaming handlebars left to wobble anti-clockwise about the parlor. Over mugs of Ceylon tea, Anna afforded Andreas a three-minute synopsis of her recent adventures, from being followed home from a pizzeria to witnessing the stalker commit a kidnapping to a police interrogation and the child's rescue within the hour.

Andreas was spellbound. "That's incredible," he said, sipping tepid tea. He too marveled over how quickly the police had responded.

"Fotini was told a cop spotted the car after a bulletin went out. When he pulled it over the boy was still in the back seat. They took him to hospital and his parents brought him home same day."

"I'm still amazed. Was he okay after that? I mean, the drug, the trauma."

"Don't know about side effects, but Fotini thinks he slept through the whole thing and woke up in hospital. Maybe that counts as trauma."

"What about the kidnapper?"

"Just what Fotini told me. Date, time, name, location. Name is Theodoros Servopoulos, Greek citizen. They picked him up in Nikaia."

Petting his chin like a cat, Andreas wondered aloud what the miscreant might have had in mind for that kid.

"It's pretty clear he did it for ransom, pederasty, or both, don't you think?"

"Ugh. Hope it was ransom, but if you do that it helps to know your victim's name, address, and next of kin. Seems like this fellow didn't, so ugh again. Anyway, now you're a local hero. How does it feel?"

"Not great. Speaking of ugh, now I'm a crime witness. Detective told me to expect to make a statement, maybe testify. As if that's not enough exposure, Fotini said a reporter called her about the kidnapping. I hope she didn't drop my name."

Andreas seemed puzzled. He asked what she was afraid of.

"I need to keep out of the media. Laskaris still stalks the land and I bet he's tied up with this. He's after me for something. If he finds out who furnished evidence, who knows what he'd do?"

He was caressing his chin again. "Not much, maybe. He must be running scared, or should be once he finds out where his buddy is."

"Hopefully too scared to bother with me," she said, as arrhythmic thuds of falling objects issued from the next room. They rushed in to find books scattered across the floor and Ramadi harmlessly pinned under his bicycle, sleepily murmuring "Airplane crash."

#

Shafts of waning sunlight fragmented the streets of Piraeus into jagged silhouettes, casting darkness on the plants guarding Andreas's kitchen windows and on two occupants tucking in slices of birthday pizza. Anna wiped her hands and got up to put a blanket over Ramadi, curled up on Andreas's day bed sleeping off his big day.

"Would it be too much trouble," she asked, "if we stayed over—just in case?"

"In case of what?"

"In case someone bangs on my door in the middle of the night."

"And who might that be?"

"I dunno. The police, a crime reporter, maybe even Laskaris, whoever might want a piece of me, now that I'm a person of interest."

"I doubt that, but sure," Andreas said atop a nonchalant shrug, "if you don't mind sleeping next to me."

She followed him into his chambers with its queen bed, and sat on its pale yellow comforter as he entered the bathroom, admiring the Danish Modern furnishings Kosta had chosen for it and the way the Wedgwood mauve walls complemented the teakwood. From above a double-wide chest of drawers a dusty mirror reflected her concerns.

Andreas exited from the bathroom in baggy hemp pajamas bearing a garment. "You can use this bathrobe. You'll find a nightshirt in a basket in there."

She accepted the crimson robe with navy blue piping and took her turn in the loo, remembering Mahmoud telling her he had slept in this bed with Andreas one night when he and George had to lay low. Now she was on the run, but was it away from or towards something? The bathroom mirror wasn't telling.

It's been quite a day, she heard from within. *Now take comfort in Andreas, who's always been there for you.*

Placing her spectacles on the shelf under the deadpan mirror, Anna wordlessly agreed.

She shed her clothing slowly, remembering a similar scene at her place back then—Mahmoud exiting her bathroom in striped pajamas she had bought for him before shyly joining her in bed, only to shed them along with his virginity. She found the saffron nightshirt embroidered with green vines, slipped into it, and returned to the bedroom to circle around the bed and ease under the comforter.

Andreas lay upon his back vignetted by his reading lamp, hands folded upon the coverlet. She fluffed her pillow and turned to him. Propping herself on her forearm, she said, "You know, I've never been in bed with a gay man. Have you ever slept with a woman?"

Gazing at the ceiling, Andreas stroked his stubbly chin. "Oh yes, before I came to Greece. I was eighteen and at college. Three girls, in fact …"

"I never thought of you that way. Did anything ever develop, other than swelling?"

Still studying the ceiling, Andreas said, "Two of them quickly lost interest. The third one, Angela, lasted a couple of months."

"What made it end?"

Eyes still averted, Andreas said, "Sex felt, well, awkward. We talked about it. I told her I felt ambivalent. Angela understood, said she herself wanted to try it with a woman and suggested we go to an LGBQ Alliance meeting to help sort things out."

"And did it?"

"I would say so. Angela paired off with a woman we met and I ended up falling in love with one of the panelists. That was Ivan. We just clicked."

"Ja, such a handsome guy. Too bad it didn't work out when you got together again here."

He turned to her. "We'd never had a chance to live together until his company transferred him to Athens. His showing up seemed a godsend. Kosta was serving his sentence and I was stressed out trying to salvage our benighted operation. George had just been arrested and I thought I might be next."

"And so you convinced Ivan to lease that fancy condo on his company's tab. Must've made you happy."

"Sure it did, and not just because I was with Ivan. It also pleased me to shelter Mahmoud and Kaan."

"And then me, taking refuge from a berserk nationalist. Nice happy family."

"Ja … until Ivan was transferred to Turkey and you all followed. Nothing was the same after that."

"That's for sure. So, did the separation break you two up?"

"That and the stress of shielding him from knowing what we were up to. And my guilt."

"For?"

"For using Ivan that way. On top of exploiting his generosity, we sent Kaan to live with him in Bursa—ostensibly as his translator, but actually scouting out logistics for our mission. Even though Ivan never knew, I worried he would get dragged into it. And then, when he flew back to visit me, I was so preoccupied with it that he said hey, this isn't fun anymore. I was in no position to disagree, and so we called it off."

"But he'd already walked out on you. That wasn't your fault."

"Nor was it his. He had to relocate for work. Also, Kosta was languishing in prison and I had ignored him. And sure enough, after his release he walked out, too. It was all my own damn fault."

She squeezed his shoulder, seeking his elusive eyes. "I'm sorry. I hope you find what you're looking for. You deserve to be loved."

"I'm not sure what I'm looking for. I've sort of given up looking."

He turned off his lamp and they lay side by side in the darkness. Her hand found his.

"Me too," she said, "in case you hadn't noticed."

Chapter Ten

UNWILLINGLY SUMMONED FROM SLEEP by thump and clatter, Anna jumped from bed to find Ramadi astride his wheeled steed making clumsy figure-eights around the parlor and the kitchen table. Instructing him to dismount, she retreated past a stirring Andreas to throw on her clothes in the bathroom. Little transpired during the awkward few moments that they spent in the kitchen. Several thank-you's, a three-point kiss, and a pat on Ramadi's head sent mother and child on their way.

With no time to waste, she arrived winded from hustling Ramadi's bike uphill. In a jiffy she had changed his clothes, set out bowls of muesli with OJ on the side. Not pausing to clean up or even brew coffee, she shuffled Ramadi out the door, down the hill, and on and off two buses to Daria's flat, today's Kinder Cloud home page.

A goodbye hug and a half-hour reverse commute found Anna and her Greek geek huddling over a table at the No Name Café discussing technical matters over postponed coffee.

"The Ravani cakes here are among the best," Ottovio said between forkfuls.

Anna peered into her cappuccino as if reading tea leaves. "So all it takes is an app?" she said, not entirely clear on the concept of phone spoofing.

"That and wi-fi. I can install app."

"And the person receiving the text can't tell where it really came from?"

"No. Neither can cell provider or police if done right."

"Can the person reply to the text?"

"Sure, to the spoofed number, whoever that is."

"But I can already send anonymous texts. You set that up, remember?"

"Encrypted, not anonymous. Spoofing is anonymous, not encrypted.

"I see. So maybe I should get that app. I wish I could see Laskaris's reaction when he gets a text saying someone's onto his sordid game."

Anna watched him scrape up besotted crumbs of cake, gratified that he didn't lick the plate. "Explain please," he said after sucking his fingers. "What is big picture?"

She brought him up to date on the kidnapping and her part in thwarting it, and that she worried that Laskaris might connect her with his buddy's capture and try to exact vengeance. Her bright idea was to hound him with untraceable messages she was sure would raise a sweat.

Ottovio drained his espresso and tipped back in his chair. "Depends what you expect to happen, what you want him to do."

"Be gone," she replied upon reflection. "Move away or be too paranoid to make a move."

It was Ottovio's considered opinion that if she wanted to put the heat on Mr. Laskaris, use real heat. "Tell police. Call from pay phone or post anonymous letter. Let them check him out to see if he also likes boys. You leave no fingerprints, unless on letter."

"I dunno. They might ignore or dismiss or suppress it. You know how they bumble."

"Look. They have Servopoulos in jail. Probably his phone with contact list …"

"Which could be encrypted," she said. "But suppose they get in and find a number for Laskaris. Why would they think it's special?"

"Wouldn't, unless you tip them off."

"What am I supposed to say? That I saw them together once eating pizza?"

"That's enough to make Laskaris a person of interest. Could be a business partner."

"So what's his role? Disposing the kids Servopoulos snatches?"

"Good guess. They probably don't run an orphanage. Tell cops to follow the money."

"Like from selling kids?"

"Or nasty pictures of them. Maybe both."

"You mean making porn to sell to pederasts?"

"Sure. Biggest business on dark web. Big problem in Greece they say."

She thunked down her mug, raising a small tsunami of foam. "Well, fuck those fucking fuckers. This has to end!" Her proclamation turned nearby heads to see her eyes blazing with indignation. Her son could be next.

Just then, her phone chimed the first two bars of the Marseilles. She picked it up. The caller ID read NICOLAIDES A.

She let the anthem sound again. "It's the cop who grilled me. Should I answer?"

"What's to lose?" he asked, twisting his curly beard and tilting back in his chair. "You can tell him about Laskaris right now and be done with it."

Her nose wrinkled as if he'd passed gas. "Dunno. What Laskaris might do still scares me." She punched the phone, put it to her ear, and bade a tentative hello.

"This is Detective Antonio Nicolaides from the Hellenic Police. How are you today, Anna?"

Their conversation did not last very long. "He wants me to go to his station house to swear a statement," she said. "They've indicted Servopoulos for kidnapping and I'm the prime witness. He wants me to bring my phone."

Ottovio heaved down in his chair. "I didn't hear you mention Laskaris."

"Felt wrong. He was all business. Let him track down Laskaris. That's his job, isn't it?"

"Whatever. Why the phone?"

"He wants my pictures of the kidnapping."

"Don't hand over your phone. They could copy all your stuff. Put them on a flash drive."

"Guess I should. I'll pick one up."

She found one at the chain pharmacy on her way home. That evening she emailed the photos to herself, copied them from her laptop, and in the morning set out for Nikaia with the flash drive, still reluctant to expose the fake cop to the real one. She didn't trust Nicolaides, at least not yet.

#

Besides being a pain to get to, Anna did not relish visiting a police station in Nikaia, a hub of Greek nationalism that child abductor Theodoros Servopoulos and thugs notorious for victimizing foreigners called home. She assumed some of the police there—perhaps including Nicolaides—if not card-carrying Golden Dawn party members, functioned as silent partners. But, having obliged herself, she bit the bullet and had arranged to come at two, early enough to perform a monologue before picking up Ramadi at Daria's flat.

After two bus rides and a ten-block walk, with a shiver of disgust she dolefully plodded up to the entrance and picked her way through a squad of police motorcycles to enter the grim lobby of the squat yellow building. In its foyer, decorated with work rules, wanted posters, and grim Christian icons, she was surprised to find Sami's mom primly sitting on a bench, attired, coiffured, and accessorized as for a job interview. Fotini rose to hug her, saying how good it was to see her and how happy she was about Servopoulos's indictment. When Anna asked how Sami was doing, Fotini claimed that he seemed okay, but had stopped asking to go to the playground they frequented.

Their conversation was interrupted by a female officer with several chevrons on her sleeve. Referring to a clipboard she carried, she asked: "Is one of you Anna Burmeister?"

When Anna signified, the sergeant politely requested her to follow, and escorted Anna to a windowless interrogation room permanently suffused with stale sweat. Inside, a woman with half-glasses sitting at a stenograph bade a perfunctory *chairetó* and told her to take a chair behind a table. As Anna settled into the perp seat, Detective Nicolaides entered. "Good day Miss Burmeister," he said and, before Anna could reply, as if reading from a manual for witnesses, proceeded to instruct her how to depose herself.

She was to tell the whole truth by recounting everything she could remember about the kidnapping, starting with what she was doing at the time, and would do so under penalty of perjury. *I'm just saying what happened*, Anna told herself, wondering if they could hear her heart thumping too.

She nodded, an oath was sworn, Antonio left the room, and Anna recited her account of the kidnapping to the muted thumps of stenograph keys, choosing her words with care and inflecting them to impress the microphone she assumed was listening in.

Anna indeed spoke the truth, but not the whole truth. Just as when she was grilled at the Taverna, she elided Laskaris. She still wanted him out of the picture in case he knew what went down five years ago. Maybe he didn't, but why tempt fate?

Half an hour later, her memory flushed, she surrendered four snapshots to a pot-bellied technician who, after asking for her phone, reluctantly accepted her flash drive. Shortly he handed it back and the lady officer delivered her to the foyer and said she was free to go. Anna asked if Fotini was still inside and was told she hadn't yet left. She stepped outside and waited by the parked motorcycles watching cops come and go, wishing she had a cigarette, and then willing the wish away. She hadn't decided to share her concerns about Laskaris to Fotini when she saw her come out the door.

They shared the gist of their statements and agreed it had gone about as well as recounting a nightmare could, but much harder to forget. Anna said she'd love to keep talking but had to pick up her son in Drapetsona, to which Fotini obligingly responded by offering to drive her there, not very far out of her way.

Traffic congestion provided ample time to get better acquainted. Ensconced in the Audi's white leather, Anna couldn't chase Laskaris out of her mind. *He was there when Servopoulos followed us. He might be after me.*

So, are you going to let that shut you up? Quoth Gizzard-Brain. *You don't have to tell Fotini he might know your past. If he's a criminal, expose him and get him out of circulation.*

For once acquiescing to an inner admonition, Anna opened up.

"There's more to this than Servopoulos," she told Fotini. "He seems to have a partner."

"Oh," Fotini said, edging the Audi onto the sidewalk around a fender-bender that had attracted a crowd.

Anna told her of encountering the kidnapper and his unpleasant associate, what the pizza guy had told her about Laskaris, and that he was a pretend cop. Though admitting it was only guilt by association, she told Fotini she was pretty sure Laskaris enabled Servopoulos's sordid trade somehow, and what did she think. Fotini failed to respond. Figuring she'd struck a nerve, Anna let it go.

It came out along the way that Fotini was married to one Ilias Evangelatos, some sort of banker downtown, more or less happily as best Anna could judge. They owned a flat in one of the white high-rises with ocean views that line the scenic bluffs of Piraiki, south of the cruise ship and ferry terminals, and usually summered on one of the less-developed islands. Their apartment block may well have been in sight of the rocky cove where, Anna reflected, a little over five years ago Mahmoud had made landfall. Had they been on their balcony, the couple could have seen him scramble up the embankment to make his wary, weary way downtown, and likely would have concluded from his appearance that he didn't belong and was up to no good.

Wistfully recalling visiting that little cove a year later to pay him her respects before heading to Basel to give birth to their child, Anna sniffled. Fotini asked if anything was wrong.

"I'm okay," Anna said and wiped her eyes. "Just remembering being in your neighborhood with my boyfriend."

"Well, I'm not all right," Fotini said. "Having to spill my guts to a typist in a dank interrogation room got me down. The detective and that policewoman could have at least sympathized."

The Audi sloped down to Daria's building brimming with sisterly outrage at the cops' cool indifference, both to Fotini's anguish and to Anna's gutsy intervention. Sensing that Fotini could use some moral support, Anna invited her up to Daria's apartment to meet the assembled moms. Upstairs they found Daria, Katia, Cassie, and a handful of kiddies happy to be collected. In honor of her unexpected guest, Daria produced glasses of mint tea and rose-scented baklava.

As the moms sipped at the table, Fotini's plaintive story got their full attention, as did Anna's account of her creepy encounters with Servopoulos and his obnoxious buddy. When Anna said they'd targeted her kid too, a nod went around the table. Katia recounted how a neighbor's teenage daughter had gone out to the store and never came back. Cassie remembered seeing a chilling report on child trafficking on Alpha TV she said drove home the terrifying scale of the problem. All agreed that something like what Fotini experienced could happen to any of them.

They would remember this impromptu tea party as prompting the founding of the Children's Protective League of Greater Athens, along with a motto for it: *No child a slave to lust and greed.* Like their Kinder Cloud, no constitution, bylaws, or fixed location would be necessary, just urgent determination to make city streets safe for women and children and, for starters, recruiting additional members.

For all her zeal for doing something, Fotini was the odd woman out. Her family's comfortable circumstances set her apart from the circle of hardworking moms sharing Daria's tea. But there she was, expressing solidarity, offering to reach out to women in her orbit and chip in to make their league a reality and a feminist force for change. Every mother of a young child has a dog in this fight, she told them. They all need to know.

Anna was all for widening their circle. To multiply their numbers and impact she suggested creating an online community on this new social network called Altogether. When Fotini wanted to know why not Facebook, which she already used, Anna came down on its mercenary tactics and lack of ethics. She proceeded to pitch Altogether's benefits, such as fine-tuning how users interact, privately and publicly, away from surveillance, masters of their data's destiny.

Her nebulous proposition incited both interest ("sounds cool") and doubts ("seems complicated"). To satisfy the two doubters, Anna dug out one of her Altogether PR flyers and gave them her elevator pitch. Seeing no strenuous objections, hoping for better luck than in Exarcheia, Anna put it up for a vote: five in favor to one opposed. Consensus was only gained after Anna promised to manage and moderate the forum.

Now elected lead geek, that evening again found Anna consulting her long-suffering IT guy.

\#

When Anna phoned him to summarize her deposition and her suspicion that Laskaris was Servopoulos' partner in crime, Ottovio said: "Maybe we should make a honeypot."

Her anxiety about what Laskaris might know about that takedown half a decade ago seemed to raise the hacker's hackles. He told her he wanted to expose Laskaris's game, and go on from there to unmask other shady predators on society. As only a developer or a marketer would say, whatever it took to entrap him needed to "scale," which Anna took to mean "generalize." He had a mind, he said, to develop a legitimate business as a forensic hacker, a virtual private dick, solving, perhaps even preventing, crimes, hopefully improving on *Minority Report.*

"Anyway," she said, "what's a Honeypot?"

"A promise of something irresistibly sweet," he replied, "found only on a website you control."

"So when they come and touch it, it sticks to their fingers?"

"More or less."

The only live link to Laskaris was the phone number Anna had scarfed up at the Golden House of Pizza that she hadn't mentioned to the police. "What if," he said, "we spoof a text message to that number enticing him to check out a super-delish discounted trove of kiddie porn? As soon as he takes a look, the site's cookies, beacons, and scripts would start tracking his every hop around the web, kinda like Google and Facebook."

"What would the text message say?"

"Not sure. Needs code words that pornographers use."

"You're familiar with them?"

Hardly, he conceded, but a few visits to some of the seedier districts of the dark web might divulge and decode some terms of pornographers' art.

"Suppose," she said, "someone else visits your porn palace. How would you know it's him?"

"Only tell URL to him and instruct search bots to stay away."

After a moment of dead air she said, "Okay, suppose this works. You text him and he shows up. What's he gonna see?"

"Show face shots of cute random kids. Promise lurid details for a price. Log his activity. Get IP address. Find its location. Follow his movements around web and then submit data anonymously to police."

"You're losing me. Sounds risky and complicated. I think I have a better idea."

She proceeded to hypothesize how Altogether might leverage

(another of Irene's buzzwords) the nascent Children's Protective League of Greater Athens. Suppose their website featured a picture of Laskaris, requesting information about him, maybe headlined YOUR CHILDREN ARE NOT SAFE. It should have a form and a phone number to receive tips."

"So far, you got nothing on him," Ottovio said. "Might open the door for a libel suit, maybe get you fired."

"There is that. But look. He's clearly an associate of an indicted kidnapper, probably a co-conspirator. Despises immigrants and goes around impersonating a police officer."

"That's a start. But a new website isn't going to attract many eyeballs. You need marketing."

"Suppose it took the form of a Wanted Poster that people could print and post around town?"

"Needs a mug shot. Got one?"

Alas not, she said, but she knew an artist who might render a facsimile of his belligerent likeness from her description.

"If that's what you want to do, then go for it," Ottovio replied, saying he would shelve his honeypot and follow her lead, because her interest in putting these guys out of action was personal, while his was more a matter of professional pride.

"Appreciate that, really do," she said. "Sorry to spoil your fun, but it sounded like a lot of work."

He sighed. "Ask me why I do stuff for you."

"Always assumed it was your joy of forensics, and a big heart. You tell me."

"More like guilt than heart ... because that turkey shoot I instrumented for you back then didn't go well. So let me help you net these creeps and keep you out of trouble."

"Thanks, Ottovio. You're very kind. I'll pay you for your time."

"No need. Just expenses. It'll help me polish my skills. But, if Laskaris ever runs into a broadside implying guilt by association he might have a few choice words for the hotline operator."

She hadn't thought of that, Anna said with a shiver unnoticed on the other end, and asked if he might have an old phone lying around she could use to preserve anonymity.

Another sigh came over the line. "All right. I have a prepaid burner I can drop off. Please return when this is over."

"That's great, Ottovio. Many thanks. Oh, can you set its caller ID to 'CPLGA'?"

"Excuse me?"

"Stands for Children's Protective League of Greater Athens. Not a clever acronym, but so be it. Let's hope we hear good tips and kind voices."

#

One Wanted Poster does not a website make, but it seemed as good a way as any to start, Anna mused as she and Ramadi downed her hurriedly-prepared supper of mac and cheese. Trying to imagine its content as she distractedly cleaned up, Anna considered how to approach her artistic housemate. Then she instructed Ramadi to make ready for bed while she ran upstairs to talk to Penelope.

To Ramadi's ken, their upstairs neighbor was a jolly earth mother hailing from another planet who pounded up and down the stairs with little social intercourse. He'd not been told that, before his time, the two women had drifted apart, chiefly at Anna's instigation.

Anna's reluctance to engage Penelope followed her bleak return from Turkey, when Andreas had related a curious factoid from Ottovio's newly burgled download of that Hellenic Police database. Amongst records for detainees and convicts in its maze of tables, one might encounter assorted persons of interest who have come to the cops' attention, such as political organizers. Anna knew that it listed her as such a potential miscreant, identified both by her real name and her screen name, Katrina. While her profile didn't allege any criminal or subversive activities, her record had been updated during the mission to Turkey to note she'd traveled to Switzerland.

She hadn't, of course, and Penelope had been the only person to whom Anna had given that cover story before slipping into Turkey with Mahmoud and George.

The next time she saw Penelope, Anna mentioned what she'd learned and asked if she had any idea how the police came to know her whereabouts. Penelope shrugged it off, but when Anna pointed out that nobody else knew her itinerary, she broke down and fessed up. Yes, she'd admitted, she had passed on that detail as an unwilling informant. Unwilling because, after she'd been arrested for destroying government property at the Finance Ministry occupation, a cop on her case told her she could either feed them occasional information or do hard time. Through tears of contrition, Penelope insisted everything she'd forwarded to the cops was either vague or innocuous. Anna had accepted her apology and her pledge to mind her own business, but kept her own council after that.

Despite or because of all that, Anna felt she could count on her neighbor for small favors, such as the one she was about to request. At the top of the stairway she rapped on Penelope's door, and was pleasantly ushered in. Apologizing for not being in touch more frequently, she gushed over Penelope's gaily decorated space, complimented her on losing weight, breezed through Ramadi's latest achievements, and asked how she'd been doing. Still teaching graphic design at the community college, she replied, and now had part-time work decorating a website.

Anna explained that she was in need of a sketch from Penelope's practiced hand of someone she'd recently encountered. "He's an unsavory character who's connected to a recent kidnapping in our neighborhood. You can imagine how I feel about such creeps."

"Sure, but why do you need a sketch? Why not go to the police? They specialize in portraits of perps."

"I would," Anna said with a knowing wink, "but *confidentially*, he claims he's a police warden. True or not, going to the cops feels risky. So I want to put up posters to warn the community he's on the loose."

Seeming to catch Anna's drift, Penelope replied, "I see. So if someone sees him, what are they supposed to do?"

"Call a hotline to report to us when, where, what he was doing."

"Wait—who is 'us'?"

Anna described the League's mission and motto, and that it was just getting rolling, and might she like to sign on as a charter member? As expected, Penelope replied she wasn't sure it made sense for her, but she'd be happy to try her hand at a portraying the predator. When Anna offered to pay her, Penelope said she wouldn't hear of it, grabbed her sketchbook and graphites, and they traipsed down to Anna's kitchen.

They sat at the table with mugs of tea and Penelope's artist's arsenal. Anna began by describing Laskaris's most prominent features, his broad, reddish mustache and diminishing head hair, as the artist asked about the shape of his head, prominence of nose and ears, eyebrows, and any distinguishing moles, scars, or other disfigurements. After three sketches didn't do it, Anna removed her spectacles and shut her bleary eyes to better visualize her new nemesis. Penelope tore off another sheet of paper and they began afresh. Twenty minutes and two sketches later, Anna complimented the final rendering, nicely modeled in chiaroscuro, and with a hug thanked Penelope and showed her upstairs.

She sat with a fresh cup of tea contemplating the creepy caricature. It captured his general belligerence pretty well, though perhaps his nose was actually a bit more bulbous. Good enough, she decided. With any luck, another inmate would eventually flatten it for him.

Chapter Eleven

No longer on the fence about Altogether, Anna was now raring to go. And so she did, via Metro to Holargos Station and on to the Prótos office. She used the long ride to polish her pitch to Irene for a League web site, but little persuasion was required. Desperate for content on Altogether, not only did she endorse seating the Children's Protective League of Greater Athens on the platform, she even volunteered resources to instantiate—her word—their anti-trafficking community.

Irene introduced her to a Prótos web designer named Portia, describing her as an ace programmer and a pleasant person. A mom herself, Portia fully endorsed the League's mission and obligingly focused her talents on laying out a home page. By lunchtime she had dummied up a home page that would eventually feature a panel of headlines of stories related to child trafficking and white slavery, marching up the page like a Twitter feed. Under the fold would be links to community groups, anti-trafficking organizations, and other resources. The center spread would display lead stories, such as an account of Sami's kidnapping and Anna's Wanted Poster. In the banner across the top, visitors would find the League's motto, a link to log in, and another to sign up for notifications. Portia seemed to have thought of everything.

"Each Altogether public instance, including yours, is a Wordpress website with special plug-ins," Portia said, "glued together by X-Road, enabling them to share and federate as they will."

Federation was great, Anna said, but maybe not until she got a better sense of the lay of Altogether-land, which Portia said was just fine.

A couple of offices down the hall, after clicking around Portia's prototype, Irene said: "This is great. We'll feature it in our promotions, but it's basically up to you to drive traffic there."

Hopefully not traffickers, thought Anna, and went on to ask how.

Irene expected that the first sign-ups typically would be referrals from members, who should all talk up the site on social media.

She would do that, Anna said, making a mental note to ask Fotini to promote it on Facebook, but told Irene she was also looking for war stories and tips, and was there a way that people could offer them anonymously?

"I would use a contact form. You mentioned you wanted a hotline to receive tips. That's a good idea, but Altogether doesn't support voice messaging."

"That's okay, Irene. I have someone working on that."

Then there was what Portia called the Forum, a gathering place where members could message each other. Marten had described how it worked over lunch, but it took Portia's patient exposition for Anna to get it up and running.

The deeper Anna dug in, the more questions and disquiet came to her. *How do I control access to this thing? Suppose stalkers or perverts or even traffickers tried to sign up?* Someone needed to screen users, moderate comments, and edit posts and pages. She recalled how quickly comments on her short-lived column in that anarchist blog had gotten ugly. While she didn't look forward to recapitulating that, they needed a webmaster, and so be it, she was it.

Anna asked Portia to share her prototype with League members for feedback. Do it yourself, Portia told her. Text the web address to your group so they can register, peruse the prototype, click all the links, and post their reactions to the forum. Once they were happy with it and Irene signed off, it could go public.

Members' reactions to the site ranged from "You did that?" to "Who can comment?" to "Will this get us in trouble?" To which Anna respectively replied: "With a little help from my friends," "Members only," and "Who do you mean by 'us'?" She posted: "We need material. Stories, poems, interviews, artwork. Having trouble getting through to certain authorities? Take it to the forum. Maybe one of us can help."

Content dribbled in. Fotini contributed a stirring welcome message. Portia set up a gallery of photos of missing children from public sources, and helped Anna lay out a broadside featuring Penelope's portrait of Laskaris to grace the home page and walls around town. "This man is a predator," the copy judiciously read, not mentioning any names. "He's a suspected child trafficker who spirits away kidnapped children, perhaps forever. If you see him, let us know. Also, if you know of any missing or abused children, or have been personally touched by a kidnapping, tell us your story by calling +30 693 8573421. Help the Children's Protective League of Greater Athens put a stop to child trafficking. Join us online at prostasía-paidia.entolos.gr. All together we can be strong!"

On launch day, the website glistened and the forum expectantly murmured. Ottovio's prepaid phone was armed and ready. Lauding Anna for her proactive entrepreneurship, Irene agreed to print fifty posters from her advertising budget. If she worried that the League's crusade might garner adverse notoriety for Prótos, Irene didn't say. She may have believed there's no such thing as bad publicity, but did insist on leaving the company's name off the poster.

Whether any of this collateral would lead to actionable intelligence wasn't foremost in Anna's mind when the League went live. Irene featured it as Prótos's New Site of the Week in a peppy let's-save-children press release that several minor media outlets regurgitated. Awed by their spiffy web presence and attendant fanfare, Anna didn't concern herself with consequences of having a public face, save for a dim foreboding that things wouldn't be the same for her after this, not that the course of her life had been all that predictable so far.

#

Just after dawn on launch day, armed with a sheaf of broadsides, a stapling gun, glue stick, and packing tape, Anna roamed local streets and boulevards festooning utility poles, graffitied walls, bus shelters, and shuttered storefronts, starting with the Radically Chic salon and ending with the No Name Café. Hoping that other Leaguers had done the same, she waited for someone to "drop a dime," as American cops used to urge crime-spotters when pay phones were cheap and plentiful.

Within hours of her poster blitz her dedicated phone sounded the first eight bars of the 007 theme (courtesy Ottovio). Caller ID read STAVROS STEFANOP, not anyone she thought she knew. She let voicemail pick up and gave the caller a couple of minutes to leave a message before gingerly retrieving it as if it were a live bomb.

A male voice she could almost place said: "Hello. I see your notice and had to call. I hope this helps. Someone like this man come in my shop couple weeks ago. Talked tough. Said he was cop, wanted me call him if certain lady customer shows up again. That was last I see of him. When she come in again I tell her about it but haven't seen her or her kid lately. I hope they are all right."

Stavros went on to dictate Laskaris's business card as her head nodded. Impressed by the pizza man's common decency, she texted him thanking him for his concern and to call if he sees the man again.

The next message came after supper, also from a familiar voice: "This is Lieutenant Antonio Nicolaides of the Hellenic Police. Would whoever monitors this line please return my call at their earliest convenience? Thank you."

Her jaw clenched. *This can't be good. Either he saw a poster or somebody told him about it and I bet he didn't like it.*

Not wishing to have that conversation, she called Ottovio.

"Would you be willing to call back this detective for me to see what he wants to say?" Anna asked. "He phoned our hotline last night wanting a call back."

"Why don't you?"

"He called me when we were at the café, remember? I don't want him to recognize my voice."

"More data, please."

"Seems unlikely, but he must have seen the wanted poster. Please call him back. Call yourself whatever. Say you're just the operator, ask him what he called to say, promise to pass on his message, and hang up before he starts asking questions."

Following a few pretty pleases, Ottovio consented to serve as her receptionist, just this once.

#

Ottovio rang back twenty minutes later.

"You're right, he's not happy. Said nobody should post such flyers except the police. Something about interfering in an investigation. You can be prosecuted, blah, blah."

"Did he say what he wanted us to do about it?"

"Take them down. Must have seen your Altogether site because he wants the poster content stripped from the home page too."

"Hmm. The poster did have a URL. Did he mention me or Fotini?"

"No names, but he doesn't need to be Sherlock Holmes to deduce one or both of you could be behind it."

"Not good. Maybe he tried to sign up while he was snooping around. Hold on while I check."

She opened her laptop to find an email from Altogether Central. Someone was requesting admission to the group, but it wasn't Antonio. Real name given as Melina Cristopoulos, who gave a Gmail address and requested screen name "Mimi." The optional personal information fields were blank. She said the name sounded familiar but couldn't place it.

"Could be an alias for the cop or a helper. Send her an email as Altogether admin. Chat her up. Get her to say more about herself, like does she have kids or any tips to share. Send me her reply so I can locate her computer from IP address."

Anna rang off and crafted an anodyne message to "Mimi," who replied within the hour. She wrote, I have two children, boy and girl, both in grade school and this sort of thing scares me. Besides the one posted on your website, I haven't heard of any other recent abductions, but I can do research if you like.

Thinking she seemed like the sort of person the group could use, Anna forwarded the message to her Greek geek to sleuth.

His call came swiftly. "They didn't cover their tracks. IP is on a subnet of the Hellenic Police system. Closest location I can find puts it in middle of Nikaia."

"That lovely police station, I bet. I called there looking for Laskaris and I'm sure the name of woman I spoke to was Cristopoulos, a desk sergeant. Nice person."

"Could be very nice, but she's probably following orders. What will you do?"

Anna didn't know, but said it seemed like an offer they couldn't easily refuse. She appreciated that Cristopoulos hadn't tried to cloak her identity, and that rebuffing her request would invite trouble.

Ottovio agreed that there wasn't much choice, but at least Anna controlled the situation.

She thanked him for his service and hung up wondering whether to tell the members about "Mimi." Some might be spooked to know a policewoman was among them, yet others might welcome her help. To sound them out she notified the members that a Hellenic policeman had objected to the Wanted Poster, asked that it be taken down along with what's on our home page. At the end she wrote, "We have a new member, Mimi. Please welcome her. Mimi might or might not self-identify as such, but confidentially, she's a Police Sergeant in Nikaia, so please don't post anything you wouldn't want Hellenic Police to see. Questions/comments?"

In a round robin of opinions and responses to them, no one objected to letting Mimi in, though Daria seemed a bit intimidated. Fotini, welcoming a direct line to her case's investigators, was all for it. Unable to fabricate a plausible reason to refuse Mimi's request, Anna abided with the consensus and welcomed her to the fold. She was learning the ropes of managing social media and public relations, ropes that tended to unravel details that never seemed to end. She wasn't happy with all the geeky minutia that she'd been forced to assimilate, but at least Prótos was paying her tuition.

Chapter Twelve

IT WAS FRIDAY, AND Fridays were when Anna liked to bike to the post office. Her postbox was more or less a security blanket, she liked to say. She'd signed up for it one euro per week when settling in, an acceptable price for obfuscating her street address. On most visits, it disgorged little more than bills, solicitations, and circulars, but occasionally came a letter in German from an older Swiss relative who shunned the electronic kind or, rarely, one in French a pen pal in Cameroon had dispatched weeks ago.

Today's visit marked Ramadi's first big excursion on his little blue bicycle whose training wheels now were largely decorative. Along with his helmet, he could have used an airbag, for his sturdy but unconfident legs had a way of pedaling into immovable objects.

Conveniently, her postbox sat at the boy's eye level. She had given him her secret code to unlock it, which today only took two tries. She watched his tiny fingers twitch the dial, polishing his muscle memory, numeracy, and angular dexterity all at one go. The little safecracker's patience was rewarded when the door clicked open to reveal a small sheaf of envelopes, the fattest of which bore his name. Upon tearing it open, Ramadi found three annotated scenic postcards of Switzerland and, more importantly, a somewhat deformed bar of Lindt milk chocolate, a care packet from his *Oma* in Basel.

"I'll read you what Oma wrote when we get home," Anna said. She handed him his letter and leafed through the rest of her mail. All disposable, save for a card from the post office instructing her to sign for a letter at the counter she assumed wasn't a pleasant portent. Seven minutes of queuing later she was shoving it at a taciturn clerk to wait again as he rummaged through cubbyholes. He wandered back with an envelope bearing a receipt he instructed her to sign. When she saw it had come from Piraeus Municipal Court, she wrinkled her nose, stuffed the letter into her backpack and told Ramadi, currently absorbed in spinning the dials of random postboxes, that it was time to go.

And soon it would be Anna's time to go—downtown to the courthouse near the cruise terminals, subpoenaed to testify in the trial of Theodoros Servopoulos for child abduction ten days hence. It struck her a rather speedy one, given how suspects typically tend to sit in stir for days awaiting arraignment and then weeks for trials.

Who knew what might be wrung from her under oath? The prospect of peeing herself on the witness stand loomed. Why couldn't they just go with her statement and the evidence she'd turned over?

A small voice in her head said: *Because, Love, this is important to you and you need to take a stand.*

That's what I've been doing, dammit. Haven't you noticed?

Yes, indeed. But now it's getting real. Time to up your game.

Thanks for the pep talk. Now go away.

When they got home she shared news of the letter on the League's forum that now included the genial but problematic Desk Sergeant "Mimi." Fotini added that she too had been notified, but felt miffed by not being called to testify, raising a chorus of outrage that the victim's mother was being snubbed. Mimi calmly responded that Fotini's deposition would suffice. As she hadn't witnessed the event, her testimony would have no bearing on the outcome, so why drag her down memory lane for no evidentiary purpose?

Anna tended to agree, she wrote, and suggested that they round up whomever they could to attend the trial in a show of solidarity. When someone suggested they make a point by bringing their children, Mimi again piped up to caution that children under ten weren't generally allowed in court. And while Anna would have loved to pack the courtroom with innocent faces, she appreciated that Mimi needn't have said that if she wanted the moms to learn it the hard way. The policewoman from Nikaia did seem committed to the cause. And even if she were relaying their deliberations up the chain of command, they had nothing to hide. But did Mimi?

#

The Piraeus courthouse is easy to miss even if one knows its whereabouts, especially if one is expecting a neoclassical temple of justice graced by marble statuary. Instead, one finds a drab mid-century curtain-walled office block on busy Gounari Street hemmed in by storefronts selling knock-off fashions, home goods, and discount furniture. Anna stood across the street taking in its monotonous glass façade punctuated by air conditioners protruding like misaligned Lego bricks from upper story windows.

Administrative Court of Piraeus, the signage carved into the lintel proclaimed. With a sigh, Anna hopscotched across the busy street into an arcade supported by graceless concrete columns and headed toward a set of glass doors crammed beside a defunct retail outlet. She tugged open a heavy door and stepped into a dusty spartan lobby partly renovated with pressed wood paneling, with construction debris piled in a corner. Off to one side stood a well-appointed blonde news reporter in a frisky blue dress toting a hand-held mic, accompanied by a gnomish man harnessed to a video camera, accessorized with a lumpy belt that brought to mind suicide bombers.

Wondering what made a creep like Servopoulos a media magnet, she followed a mosaic of footsteps embossed in sawdust into a courtroom that might or might not be the right one, and asked a guard who turned out to be the bailiff if this was the Servopoulos trial. When he affirmed it was, she said she was a witness, so what did she need to do? Sit anywhere back there, he waved, and when your name is called present yourself to be sworn in and take the stand, a mahogany wooden armchair with leatherette cushions perched on a low dais.

Scanning the room, Anna was gratified to find three of her momrades ensconced in the visitors section and took an aisle seat next to Katia. Shortly, the victim's mother drifted in along with an assortment of courthouse idlers and settled in behind Anna. Squeezing Anna's shoulder, Fotini murmured: "Tell it, sister. You got the goods. Stick it to him."

Anna turned halfway and patted her hand. "Thanks. I'll do my best. Let's make it one down, one left to go."

Like the lobby, the windowless courtroom was half-renovated. Meekly circulated by a fan spinning lazily four meters overhead, the air quickly lost any semblance of freshness once doors were shut, the bailiff cried for quiet, and the judge made his practiced entrance.

The judge gaveled for order and a guard escorted in the defendant, clad in prison togs, to present himself.

"Does the defendant wish to change his plea?" the judge asked.

"Still not guilty, Your Honor."

"Then take a seat by your attorney and let's get going," the judge said, glancing at his watch.

Servopoulos slid down next to his lawyer, a short man with black hair streaked with grey hanging down to his collar and oversized eyeglasses framed in clear off-yellow plastic. He wore a shiny steely suit and a tired yellow tie, and was referred to as Counselor Yannatos. That Servopoulos had elected to be tried before a judge rather than jury, his prerogative under law, grated on Anna and company, as no jurors meant no mothers who might press for conviction.

His half-glasses sliding past the crook of his aquiline nose, His Honor, a well-fed gentleman with three chins and a fringe of grey hair orbiting his radiant dome, called the court to session with three thuds of his mallet.

Prosecutor Glezos, a trim, wan man in a rumpled brown suit not enhanced by his purplish paisley tie, paced the floor in squeaky loafers to accuse Servopoulos of kidnapping, displaying the principal evidence, blow-ups of Anna's four photos that clearly showed someone resembling Servopoulos dragging one Sami Evangelatos, seven, to his car, sliding him in like a carpet and driving off.

When his turn came, Counselor Yannatos didn't dispute the evidence but dismissed the alleged motive, brazenly maintaining that his client had actually committed a merciful act to hasten a sick boy to urgent care. He had come upon a boy who was collapsing on the sidewalk and took it upon himself to transport him to the closest hospital. Was that a crime? Far from it. This was a quick-thinking benevolent act on the part of Good Samaritan Theodoros Servopoulos.

When Anna's turn to face the majesty of the law came, she made her way forward, uttered an oath, and stepped up to go on display with legs pressed modestly together. She had dressed as for church, with black trousers and a flowing white silk blouse set off by a cameo brooch, with a burgundy scarf gathered around her neck. As she reminded herself to breathe, Prosecutor Glezos stepped forward.

"The evidence, your honor, shows that an abduction took place. We are here to establish the defendant's motive for his action, and hope that the witness can shed light on it. Would the witness please recount the incident exactly as she observed it?"

Assuming that her account of events would bolster his case, Anna had expected the prosecutor to go easy. Instead, like Lieutenant Detective Nicolaides—whom she had spotted standing off to the side, arms folded—he picked at her story.

"You are a waitress at Taverna Omphalos, is that not right?"

"Yes," Anna replied, chalky hands demurely folded in her lap.

"And did the defendant sit at one of your tables?"

"Yes, he did."

"You failed to serve him and in fact left the premises, did you not?"

Also true, she told the court, sensing her palms nearing dew point.

"The taverna was fairly busy and you were needed there. Why did you leave your post?"

"As my deposition says, sir, I recognized him from a week or so before. He had followed me part way home. It scared me, and when he showed up at the taverna I didn't want him to recognize me."

"And why might he want to pursue you at either time?"

"I was with my son the first time. I suspect he took interest in him. He seemed to be up to no good, because when he saw me looking back at him he ducked away."

"How old is your son?"

"He's five."

"Why were you out?"

"We had just bought pizza and were going home to eat it."

"Had you ever seen the defendant before he followed you?"

"He was at the pizzeria, with … another man. He followed us from there."

"Did either of them speak or indicate anything to you there?"

"The other one complimented my son. The defendant just stared at us. It made me uncomfortable."

"I see. Anyway, you ran from the taverna but remained in the area. And when he left you followed him. Why?"

She unfolded her hands and gripped the chair's leatherette arms. "When I got outside, I felt ashamed for being such a coward and decided to grab a photo of him just in case."

"In case of what, may I ask."

"Well," Anna said, raising her right hand and counting one-two on her fingers, "first he tailed me, and then he showed up at my workplace. I wanted a picture to show police if he ever bothered me again. And when I saw him talking to the boy, something didn't seem quite right, so I stayed put and watched."

Servopoulos snickered something to his counsel. The prosecutor waved a document at her. "Your deposition says nothing about feeling ashamed or wanting to photograph the defendant. Are you making that up?"

"No sir. When I was deposed—if that's a word—I was focused on telling the facts. I just didn't think to say how I was feeling, but that's how I felt."

"Look," Fotini whispered to Katia in the gallery, "they're putting *her* on trial. Disgusting."

"Let's go on," Glezos said. "What did you observe next?"

"Sami was petting a little brown dog leashed to a post. The, umm, defendant squatted next to him and patted the dog and struck up a conversation with Sami that I couldn't hear. He had what looked like a piece of hard candy in his hand. I …"

"And what did he do with that object?"

"He held it out. The dog got interested. Sami grabbed it and put it in his mouth."

"You're sure about that? You're under oath, you know."

"Yessir."

Mothers murmured. "The nerve of him!" one was heard to exclaim. The judge scowled, gavel poised.

"And the boy looked well to you up until then?"

"Yes, but in a minute or two he got wobbly and Servopoulos grabbed his arm and brought him to his feet. Sami's legs were sagging under him. Then Servopoulos walked him down the sidewalk with his arm around his waist."

"Go on, please."

Anna licked her lips. "At his car he opened the rear door and heaved Sami onto the seat."

"Describe the car."

Anna stiffened, veins tracing her neck. "You arrested him in it. It's in the photos I handed over. Why are you badgering me? Aren't I your witness?"

"I'll say!" declared Katia, followed by general murmuring that three thunks of gavel on rosewood and an order to the witness to answer the question cut short.

Anna let go of the armrests and crossed her arms over her chest. "It was black with four doors. A Renault, I believe. Not very new."

Telling Anna that would be all for now, Glezos retired and the defense attorney rose to approach the bench. "You say my client gave the child something to eat," he fairly bellowed. "He did not, and there is no evidence that the boy ate anything, much less some drug!"

"That's what it looked like," she replied, glancing at Glezos sitting slumped, forehead propped on one bent arm. "Didn't the police test Sami's blood for narcotics?"

"There was nothing to analyze because nothing had been given the child," came the reply. "The witness must be mistaken. How could she accuse a man trying to save a child's life of malign intent?" His eloquence exhausted, Yannatos spat out "no further questions" and rejoined his smirking client.

Perhaps sensing that neither Anna's words nor body language seemed to please the court, the prosecutor declared: "No more questions, your honor." The judge directed Anna back to her seat.

"What a farce," Anna said to her mates as Katia gave thumbs up with downturned mouth. Fotini rose to hug her, sniffling "At least you stood up for yourself against those bullies."

Closing arguments came as no surprise. Counselor Yannatos reiterated that Servopoulos had simply acted nobly towards a young stranger who had taken ill. Rather than prosecuting him, the defendant should be applauded, an assertion met by jeers that the judge pounded away.

In his wrap-up, the prosecutor declaimed that Anna's pictures proved that Servopoulos had taken the child and driven away with him, but not necessarily why. Whether or not the defendant had given the boy some substance or what it might have been was immaterial. He must be found guilty of unlawful removal of a minor, even if it was for the best of all possible reasons.

"I want to shoot that prosecutor," Fotini said to nodding heads.

"Or garrote him with that ugly tie," Anna said.

"Such weak tea," Daria said, winding and rewinding an end of her scarf. "I don't trust any of these men."

#

His Honor declared a recess *sine die* to review the case and retired to his chambers. The bailiff stood watch over Servopoulos and the opposing attorneys ambled out together. As she arose to freshen up in the restroom, Anna glumly scowled at the defendant slouching in his chair at the front, languidly chewing gum. In the lavatory, a woman spectator she didn't know patted her shoulder. "You did your best." But another said: "You may have been too oppositional. It could have hurt the case."

Close to tears, Anna said: "This trial is a sham. Look at those lawyers; they're supposed to be adversaries but they act like a team."

As Anna re-entered the lobby the blonde in the frisky blue dress hailed her, audio baton in hand. "Zoe Karaoúli, Alpha TV. I saw you testify. Might you have time for a brief interview?"

Stage fright abraded by indignation, Anna uncharacteristically consented.

Zoe asked for her reactions to the proceedings. Cautioned by her bulbous reflection in the cameraman's lens, Anna told herself to watch her language and proceeded to vent her frustration.

"You call this justice? The police didn't collect and analyze evidence. The prosecution was weak and inept. Servopoulos' alibi was a transparent lie. No concern for that child, my child, any mother's child."

"So what will you do," Zoe asked, "if an innocent verdict comes down?"

"Whatever it takes. The mothers of Athens have had it with child trafficking. We're organizing to force the government to do something about it."

Zoe asked how. Breathlessly, Anna described the League and urged Zoe's viewers to visit protect-children.altogether.gr to learn more, just as the bailiff summoned stragglers back to the yeasty courtroom.

"That's important work you're doing," Zoe said, offering her business card. "I host a weekly TV news magazine called Anazitiseis that covers unsolved crimes. All this month we're focusing on missing children. Please get in touch. We should trade tips."

Anna studied and pocketed the card. Turning her back to the camera, she said: "Thanks. I'd appreciate it if you didn't use my name if you air this interview."

"If you wish, but do you have a card, or at least a phone number?"

"I'll call you. I gotta go," Anna replied, and headed back to the courtroom.

The subliminal part of her mind rebelled. *This woman has a TV show about missing kids. Why didn't you jump at the chance to get on it to plug the League?*

Thanks, but no thanks, Anna thought back. *I've had enough exposure for now.*

#

The judge's verdict was speedy, justice not so. Not guilty of unlawful removal of a minor, pronounced the judge, but guilty of failing to notify authorities about the incident. His penalty, a fine of 250 euros. No supervision or hard time. Servopoulos was free to leave and promptly did, escorted by the bailiff through the rear door as Anna fumed. As Servopoulos passed by, Inspector Nicolaides gave a little nod and grinned through his teeth. It was the first time Anna had seen the detective smile.

She strode from the courtroom through a bustle of bodies in the lobby and caught up to Fotini. "Let's get out of here," she said, "before I puke."

"I want to kill somebody," Fotini said. "Let's go before I do. My car is just outside."

Fotini fled down the steps and across the street to her Audi. Anna followed, and at the car glanced back to see Servopoulos, now dressed in slacks and polo shirt, exit the courthouse and descend to the sidewalk with his phone at his ear. "Go to hell," she muttered, almost failing to notice a silver station wagon bearing down on her from behind. She flattened herself against Fotini's car as the Mercedes 350 rolled to a stop just ahead. Even through tinted windows its driver was unmistakable.

Grinning, Servopoulos opened the passenger door and got in. Anna jumped into the Audi. "Follow that Benz! That's the guy we've been looking for!"

"And then what?" Fotini said. "Chase them down and beat the crap out of them?"

"Please. I really want to see where they go. It's Vassilios Laskaris himself. Might be the key to the whole operation."

Anna raised her phone to the windshield just as a taxi interposed itself. "*Scheisse!*" she exclaimed. "Don't lose them! Let's go."

Fotini jockeyed the Audi away from the curb. "All right, all right, I'm going. Just don't ask me why."

"Because of what they might have done to Sami and wanted Ramadi for," Anna said, eyes drilling through traffic. "I won't let go of this until those guys are behind bars."

Atta girl! her gizzard brain hooted, in a rare show of solidarity. *Keep on rolling!*

Chapter Thirteen

THE TAXI IN FRONT of them peeled off at the next intersection, only for a turning delivery van to take its place. Fotini clenched her teeth and shot ahead to block an unappreciative driver from turning and hustled to the end of the block, where the Benz and the van were waiting for cross-traffic to clear. Anna drummed her fingers on the dashboard as Laskaris moved on and the van's driver hesitantly turned right. "Go!" she said to her reluctant chauffeur as the van was halfway into its turn. "Catch up to them!"

Anna clasped her grab bar and showed her other palm to an oncoming car as Fotini gunned the engine and crossed the intersection to the blare of a horn and caught up to queue at a traffic signal. When the light changed, Fotini followed the Benz right onto broad Akti Miaouli, lined with tony apartment houses facing a promenade overlooking the greasy harbor. Another jog left and then right had them heading northward. "This is the way to Keratsini," Anna said. "These guys better not be my neighbors."

Two more jogs kept their vector intact. "It helps that he's been using turn signals," Anna said. "But I hope it's not for our benefit." Her pallid knuckles gripping the steering wheel indicated Fotini had similar thoughts.

A similar set of moves put the Mercedes on Kiprou, a long, mostly residential street dotted with small shops. Half a kilometer on, without warning, Laskaris pulled to the curb and stopped. Fotini had no choice but drive past and idle illegally at the corner. They turned to see Servopoulos get out and enter a store.

"That's a wine shop," Anna said. "Looks like it's party time. We're in Nikaia. You wouldn't know to look at it, but this is Golden Dawn country. Wouldn't surprise me if they're close to home."

Their vigil ended when Servopoulos returned to the Benz clasping a brown bag. Laskaris rolled past them and ran a red light. As they waited, they watched him turn right three blocks ahead without signaling.

Fotini made the turn at that intersection to find no Mercedes beckoning them on. They crept along for three or four blocks glancing down side streets, almost failing to notice the two men walking toward them with the Mercedes parked beyond. Fotini darted to the curb, whispering "I hope they didn't see us," as if she might be overheard. Laskaris was on his phone and Servopoulos was digging in his pocket as they approached a modest bungalow, its tiled roof shaded by its loftier neighbors. Servopoulos inserted his key into a door as blue as the Greek flag and pushed it open. After it shut, Fotini eased past. "House number is 34," she said. "What street is this?"

"Don't know," Anna said. "So, it looks like our perpetrator lives here."

"Possibly both of them. How long do we sit here? What are we trying to do?"

"Gather evidence. This could be where Servopoulos was heading with Sami when he was pulled over. I really want to know what's inside."

"Or who," Fotini said. "They bought alcohol. I wonder if there's a welcoming committee."

Anna grabbed her phone and opened her door. "Be right back. We need evidence."

Lips pinched, Fotini followed Anna in her mirror as she photographed the Mercedes, then crossed the street to capture the blue door before walking down the block to shoot a street sign posted on a building. She noticed a car, a black sedan, drive past Anna and pull to the curb two cars behind the Audi. Its door opened to disgorge a man in white shirtsleeves and grey trousers who locked his door and crossed the street carrying a brown bag with a bottle peeking out.

Focusing on making out his features, Fotini didn't notice Anna hunched between parked cars, camera raised, as he ambled to the blue door and pushed the buzzer. After he was let in, Fotini sunk into her seat fighting down a wave of disgust. The partygoer was none other than Lieutenant Inspector Antonio Nicolaides.

#

128

Anna sprinted up and jumped into the car, hyperventilating. "Did you see who that was? This is too much! I smelled a rat at the trial but not such a big stinking one."

"I need to digest this," Fotini said. "Let's get out of here and find a coffee shop before you decide to crash their party."

"Not to worry, Fotini," Anna replied with a chuckle and told Fotini to drive around the block to get back to the avenue. She consulted Google. "Turn left here, and take the next left."

They found themselves in a back alley that transected the block. About halfway down, they came upon a cobbled patio on their left to find Laskaris grinding out a cigarette and entering a back door. As Fotini drove past, Anna peered back. "That's the rear door. I wonder what goes through it besides that guy's fat ass."

At the end of the alley Fotini turned left and at Magnisias Street hung a right. At Kiprou Avenue, Anna said she'd just as soon escape enemy territory and suggested retreating to Keratsini for coffee. Fotini eyed her watch. "Just for a while. I need to pick up Sami soon."

Shortly they were on Anna's home turf, cruising down memory lane: past the shop where Fotini was being manicured when Sami got nailed, past the Taverna Omphalos, to which Anna had tendered her resignation, past the Golden House of Pizza, where Stavros had clued her in, and on to the No Name Café, where truth can be spoken.

Ambling down the boulevard, Anna said, "I never thought to ask before. What brought you all the way over here just to get your nails done?"

"Oh, my wonderful Vietnamese manicurist changed jobs and ended up there. I'd never been over here before. It's an intriguing area. So different from where we live."

"For sure. And unlike where we just came from, it's a haven for the *liberté, égalité, fraternité* crowd. It's the next Exarcheia."

Fotini didn't comment.

The Café still sported the Laskaris poster Anna had taped to its window, now strangely irrelevant. Anna ripped it down and ushered Fotini in and to a table, where they shared a French press and poked at squares of the honey cakes Ottovio liked to rave about.

Fotini furtively surveyed the assortment of casually-dressed, generally hirsute customers and turned back, whispering: "So this is an anarchist hangout?"

Anna chuckled. "Run by them as sort of a mini-UN. Even capitalists are welcome here."

She hoisted her brew and puffed off steam at her companion. "Anyway, we have your child's abductor, his friend with a Mercedes-Benz who pretends he's a cop, and an actual cop who hangs out with them in a neighborhood that's crawling with nationalists. What does that add up to?"

"Six-six-six, by Satan's arithmetic."

"And sick, sick, sick. The police, or at least this sterling specimen, are all for pederasty, it seems. Who is there to turn to? Do you feel the helpless rage I do?"

Fotini stabbed at her ravani, and savored some. "At least we have each other and the League, such as it is. All we know is these three guys and where they get together. You have photos. Show me what you got."

What Anna had were street scenes and a video of Nicolaides approaching a small house with a blue door and being let in. His face was seen but briefly in profile. And while whoever ushered him in was obscured, it was solid evidence, as were the timestamped photos showing his car bearing unofficial plates parked there barely an hour after the trial had concluded. "Whatever happens, we've got that on him," Anna said. "Let's see what else we can find out about what goes down there."

"I shudder when I think of the children who might have been taken there," Fotini replied. "Are you suggesting keeping an eye on the house somehow?"

"Not a bad idea. But we would probably be noticed."

"So let's not."

Anna chewed and dabbed her mouth. "Right, but that alley's a perfect spot for a camera that's always on duty."

"If you could. How would that help?"

"Servopoulos was picked up in Nikaia. I'm betting they move kids in and out of there. If we could capture them at it, it would expose all of them."

"Say you get pictures. Then what?"

"Well, isn't there some office that's supposed to investigate police misconduct?"

"I think there is. Let me ask my husband. Ilias has connections downtown."

"Great. I have a geek connection that might help with surveillance."

Neither embracing nor dismissing that idea, Fotini moved on. "At least we have Altogether to rally around, but what can we do with it?"

"Well, what if you contribute a home page article about the kidnapping and that mockery of a trial?"

"I don't know. Giving that deposition was traumatic enough ... But you're right, it should be done and I'm the best one to do it. I'll see. But now I must go get Sami."

"And I Ramadi," Anna said, swigging the last of her latte. "Can you drop me off at Cassie's? While you do your write-up I'll try to find out who owns that house and check in with my IT guy."

Fotini waved a credit card at their server. Anna interceded. "It's cash-only here. Don't worry, I'll take care of it."

"Thanks. I'll pay next time. I'm afraid to carry cash these days." She took Anna's hand. "I really admire you, Anna. You saved Sami and stuck up for us in court. You made us a place to gather online. And all that while working and raising a child on your own. You should be proud of yourself."

"Thanks. Guess I'm proud, but I'd be prouder if those creeps weren't still at large. Or that cop."

"Me too, but there's not much we can do about them," Fotini said, releasing Anna's hand.

"Maybe," Anna said as they filed out. "But we know who they are, we know what they do, and we know where they live. Gotta be a way to stop them."

"And you're gonna do it?"

"No, we are."

#

The next morning again found Anna socializing at the No Name, brunching with her menfolk. When he learned it was on her tab,

Andreas had readily accepted. Ottovio of course did too, but only after insisting on Ramadi's presence without saying why.

Mother and son arrived at eleven, just after Andreas's entrance. They caught up with him at the big round table in back that Ottovio occupied. In front of him sat a box unceremoniously wrapped in Kraft paper.

Andreas ushered in Anna and Ramadi and scraped back chairs for them. "Salut all," he said, pecking Anna's cheek, squeezing Ramadi's neck. "Ottovio! Good to see you. It's been a while. What have you been up to?"

"The usual—fixing up cell phones and mining data. Recently, scoping out Altogether on behalf of our Swiss miss."

Andreas sat down next to Anna, resting a hand on her shoulder. "Keeping her out of trouble, are you, or into it?"

Ottovio shrugged. "Too soon to tell," he replied before turning to Ramadi and greeting the birthday boy.

"*Chairetísmata, Ramadi, xronia polla.*" He handed Ramadi his parcel. "You say you want to be spaceman. Let's see how far this will take you."

Ramadi took eager possession and tore into the thick paper to reveal a Lego kit displaying a suited-up astronaut jetting toward a winged space vehicle bearing American insignia. He wrestled out a cardboard tab and flipped the cover up to behold polyethylene bags of resinous components. Anna intercepted a grabbing hand to squeeze out a thank-you to its benefactor and hustled the boy and his booty to the far side of the table.

Kneeling on a chair, he tore at the first bag he could lay his little hands on, as Ottovio reached for the wordless instruction sheet and unfolded it. "Pictures show how things go together. Like comic book. Do one box, then next. Will go much easier."

As Ramadi perused diagrams, Ottovio asked Anna what prompted the occasion.

"I'll tell you. But first, have you any experience with surveillance cameras?"

Admitting he'd disabled a few, he asked what occasioned her need to know.

"You might have one or know where to get one that can work outside," Anna said, evading the question. She told them to order whatever they fancied, and proceeded to recap her yesterday: the set piece in the courthouse with her contested testimony and lousy verdict, the chase to Nikaia, the rotten cop, none of which seemed to surprise either man.

"A rigged trial and a shady policeman," Andreas said. "Are you saying he's mixed up with them, whatever their game is?"

"If he's not part of it, he profits from it. Why else would he show up right after the trial to party with them? Those guys might be Golden Dawners. Nicolaides too."

"So now you want camera watching this house in Nikaia," Ottovio said.

Anna showed them her street photos. "Here's the house you see the detective visiting. It has a back door on an alley that I think is worth watching. Can you manage that?"

"Possibly feasible," Ottovio said. "You have street address?"

"One I'll never forget. Magnisias 34, Nikaia."

Ottovio woke up his laptop and typed into a map browser.

"Here is house," he said, switching to a street view and navigating up the block, where he virtually turned left and found the alley behind the house. "Alley is between views. Can't see in. Would need place to mount camera." He went back to the map view and toggled its background to show an aerial image. At maximum zoom, he pointed. "I see shadows in alley that might be some kind of pole, maybe streetlamp. But camera would be hard to disguise. Let me think about it."

"I knew you'd get into it," Anna said, smiling until her dimples flared.

"Just saying. We'll see. New kind of hack for me but could pay off."

"Sure. With incriminating evidence."

"Besides that, new way to repurpose some old cell phones sitting around."

He scratched his beard in thought. "Andreas, that old Vespa—if it still runs—can I borrow?"

Andreas agreed to round up the scooter, only to have his duty doubled by Anna petitioning him to round up the house's property record, saying she had no idea how to do that. Nor did he, he hastily acknowledged, but he would ask Evangeline, an estate agent who'd secured him an elegant safe house when he was on the lam.

Ramadi begged for help solving his astronautical puzzle. Ottovio slid over to refer him to the instructions he was ignoring. He picked up a cargo bay door with his stubby fingers and handed it to the boy. "Find this on diagram. Then find what it attaches to."

Ramadi looked at the pictures, picked up a section of fuselage, and snapped it in. "Got it!" he cried. "Tanks, Onkle Ottovio."

"Ever thought of being a teacher, Ottovio?" Anna asked.

"Already am," he replied with a shrug. "Beside him, don't I teach you?"

"For sure, and thanks. So let's teach these creeps what they should have learned in kindergarten."

Chapter Fourteen

THE RED MOTOR SCOOTER was parked outside the Radically Chic Salon with Ramadi parked inside with Andreas. Astride the Vespa, Anna straddled behind Ottovio clutching a miniature Swiss chalet with a circular doorway. Foot poised on starter, he asked Anna what she intended to do with her spy pictures. Her response that she was working on that elicited a shrug, followed by a kick. The old two-stroke engine sputtered to life, and they teetered off to Nikaia trailing a cloud of blue smoke.

Puttering past the abductor's bungalow with the blue door, Anna looked out for the silver Mercedes. Neither it nor Servopoulos' Renault was in sight, boding well. Anna told Ottovio to park on the side street and then to stroll through the alley as casually as possible, eyeballing the environs for a perch for the chalet, and snap pictures of whatever seemed worth documenting.

On their left, about midway down the alley, Anna pointed out the back door where she and Fotini had spied Laskaris smoking, saying: "Let's be quick about this."

Bleak brick walls along the right side were interrupted by a forlorn parcel heaped with bricks and construction debris that Ottovio said he presumed was detritus from an underfunded and probably illegal construction project. Hugging the corner of the lot closest to them, a spindly Ailanthus tree almost four meters tall had sprouted. Ottovio grasped its trunk and then withdrew his hand to inspect his spread-apart fingers. "Maybe eight centimeters across, good enough," he said. "Need something to stand on to mount camera to give bird's-eye view and put out of reach."

Anna cast her eyes across the undeveloped parcel and pointed. "Looks like a milk crate over there. Would that help?"

"Probably. So now we have a tree for the birdie, and," he said, directing her attention to a bulbous street light, "a convenient night light, assuming it works."

"All set," Anna said, fondling the birdhouse, admiring its fit and finish. "You made this?"

"Woodworking's not my thing. A carpenter friend made it. Still needs phone with app to make it sing."

Anna started to exit the alley, taking Ottovio by the hand. "Well, let's go back so you can keep working. This place gives me the creeps."

#

Right around then, Andreas was treating Ramadi to milk and cookies at his kitchen table. As they snacked, Ramadi deconstructed his space shuttle to fix something he found not quite right while Andreas rang up Estate Agent Evangeline Vyros. He began his pitch by plying her with the kind of gossipy small talk expected of him:

"… And did you *know* that the tanning salon on Dimokritias was going under? I *heard* the place will be empty in a month, so you might want to start your marketing engine *now*."

At last remembering why he'd called, he mentioned a friend of his was *interested* in a sweet little property in Nikaia—*why*, in such a place, he wasn't sure—and might want to *tender an offer* to whomever owned it. Could she *please* find the owner's contact information and relay it to him? Were his friend to proceed, she would be the *ideal* go-between.

Evangeline told him it might not be easy. It could be owned by some opaque trust. But she would try, because Andreas is a good man who had brought her business when times were tough.

"Thanks, Evangeline. You're the best. Talk to you later, then. Ciao!"

Ah yes, he mused sitting back, that luxury condo overlooking the shipping harbor that she'd leased to old flame Ivan on his company's tab. He missed sharing the sumptuous master bedroom with Ivan and their stimulating revolutionary roommates Mahmoud and Kaan, discussing details of our operation behind Ivan's back. For two months, that odd-fellow arrangement was almost a second nuclear family for him. But like his first, it had fissioned, scattering everyone. At least he still knew where to find his parents.

His reverie was cut short by Ramadi tugging at his sleeve, petitioning for help attaching flaps to the wings of his otherwise full-fledged model.

Andreas pocketed his phone and referred to instructions. Ramadi's infectious joy as he snapped the last piece into place stirred Andreas to join him in a victory jig, skipping in circles with the boy holding his craft aloft. Their silly little dance, he later reflected, was likely the most spontaneous act he'd allowed himself in years, and how sad was that?

~

The look of concentration on his face as he assembled that flyer reminds me of myself. As a boy I too was fascinated by flight and dreamed of being a helicopter pilot until the occupation turned it to a nightmare. When American storm troopers and gunships went after Sunni rebels, all of us were the enemy. We fled Ramadi the next day, burdening our car with whatever would fit and drove to my uncle's house in Mosul, somehow avoiding aircraft, checkpoints, and IUDs. The swaths of destruction I witnessed erased my aspirations, and I vowed to become a civil engineer to reconstruct our devastated nation. If my boy is to fly airplanes, I pray that it will be in peacetime.

~

Ottovio dropped Anna off at the salon and buzzed off, saying he was close to finishing the code for his bird and to check in the next day. She went upstairs to retrieve Ramadi and thank Andreas for babysitting.

"Not a problem," he said, "and a good excuse for milk and cookies. I suppose you want to hear about the Nikaia house."

"Sure."

"Evangeline couldn't find the property owner of record. But the person who pays the electric bill is one Theodoros Servopoulos, who likely lives there and could be either owner or renter."

"Good to know. I figured he lived there. Thanks for checking."

Anna and Ramadi pedaled home for supper. Around eight came a message via Altogether from Fotini, quite a long one that summarized the depravity of Servopoulos's crime and the injustice of his trial and asked for Anna's reaction. She thanked Fotini, saying that she would take a look and post it to the League's home page.

Finding Fotini's headline, YOUR CHILDREN ARE NOT SAFE, a bit vague, she recast it as PIRAEUS COURT FREES CHILD ABDUCTOR TO STRIKE AGAIN, and went on to anchor the story with a more provocative lede:

> *Outrage swept through the courtroom at the Piraeus Administrative Court last week when a Nikaia man charged with kidnapping a seven-year-old boy in Keratsini was released after pleading innocent. Despite clear evidence of abduction, the magistrate let Theodoros Servopoulos go with only a €250 fine for failing to notify authorities of a medical emergency.*

The article continued with a furtive photo Katia took of the accused smirking in court above Fotini's edited text, and ended with a box reminding readers to report suspicious activity via the hotline. After a quick reread, she saved her draft and fired it off to Irene for comment.

By midmorning, Irene came back with copy edits to Anna's treatment, evincing disgust about the verdict and admiration to Anna for testifying, saying she would blurb the article on the Prótos home page, which, she noted, recently was receiving almost a thousand views a day.

Such exposure would have gratified Anna had the post not identified her as an eyewitness. She flashed on the time when blogging had put her in a nationalist's crosshairs, leading her to take extreme measures and flee the country. The irony of being a fugitive from justice testifying in court on the right side of the law facing a cop on its wrong side did not escape her.

By the time the earth had turned a few degrees she had managed to incorporate Irene's edits, caption the photo, set up tags and categories for the post and post it, both basking in self-satisfaction and chilled by angst. She closed her laptop and then re-opened it, recalling she owed a visit to the League's forum. To the ill-concealed outrage about the trial she found there, she responded:

Read Fotini's account of the trial on the home page. If you see media reports on any related matters, send me links. Try to recruit new members and keep the faith.

She noticed a comment from Mimi, offering regrets for not attending the trial due to having to work, expressing disappointment at the verdict, cheering them on, finishing with: Does anyone have ideas for what we can do next?

As much as Anna wished to respond with *Stop protecting those guys*, she quit the discussion, wondering how much Mimi knew about Nicolaides' extracurricular activities and whether to judge her friend or foe.

Mulling over a cup of tea, Anna decided that the only way to crack that nut was to get to know Mimi woman-to-woman. After considering costs and benefits of cultivating the cop, she sent a private message:

Hi Mimi. Thanks much for your helpful contributions to our forum. I'm hoping to get to know everyone in the group personally Would you like to have lunch or something sometime soon? Anna.

Returning from reading Ramadi to sleep, she found a positive response from Mimi, signing as Melina. While lunch during the week was out, she'd replied, why not bring her son over on Saturday, maybe take their kids to the park. Anna replied that would be great and early afternoon would be perfect. Either that or perfectly awkward.

#

The next day, Ottovio texted to say he had something for her. Suspecting what it was, she asked to meet in a couple of hours for ravani and java on her.

Anna arrived at the café to peck a wooly cheek, asking what was up.

"So here's your bug, m'lady," Ottovio said with ill-concealed pride, handing her a smartphone with a strip of Velcro on its backside. "Sticks to inside of bird box, back camera behind hole. Power pack should last a couple weeks."

"What? No solar roof?"

"Sorry, maybe for 2.0."

She fondled the instrument with an evil grin. "That's awesome. So how does it work?"

"Phone runs custom app. You text it commands. First one tells how often to take pictures. I set interval at ten seconds. Every ten minutes it zips up batch of images and attaches file to email to you, then deletes evidence. Pictures have timestamps. Dispatch interval is parameter you can set."

"Parameter?"

"Number that tells app how to behave. With more time between dispatches, you get fewer emails but they come with more images."

"Sounds like a lot of photos to look through, and most of them may be the same."

"I think of that and put in code to compare new image with last one. If under five percent of pixels change, dispatcher deletes new one. Will save you lot of work."

"Cool. But what if they notice the box, take it down, inspect the phone?"

"Well, if they do, it will show them doing it. If you notice, text phone to dump photos and then tell app to delete itself. End of story, except we lose sixty euros of hardware and Gyro's birdhouse."

"And if I don't?"

"They're still out of luck. Phone data is encrypted."

"Beautiful," she said, turning it around in her hand. "I think you should patent it."

"Don't believe in such nonsense. Don't need it to start selling these gizmos."

Fearing facial recognition and technical difficulties, Anna begged him to install his bird box. He'd figured she wouldn't want to stalk the alley in the dead of night, he said, and had already made arrangements. But first, a tutorial: "Now I send you four texts. Each is command to forward to spy phone. First one is a test that dumps all current pictures to email. Second sets time between pictures, one to sixty seconds. Third sets time between emails, one to sixty minutes. Last one kills my app. Don't mix them up."

She read the messages and giggled. The commands all commenced with SIRI. The last one was SIRI DESTRUCT. Geek humor.

#

Athens' omnipresent smog rendered the sky a paler blue than the Greek flag hanging limply from the terraced apartment house in Tampouria where Anna and Ramadi found themselves that Saturday morning. They were not far from the harbor, their noses noted. Pressing a doorbell with her unclasped hand, she assured Ramadi he would have fun with Melina's kids and herself that it was just a friendly visit, hoping Melina didn't associate her with the Laskaris poster incident.

Apparently not. "I know you!" Melina exclaimed at the door in all earnestness. "You came to my station to depose in the Servopoulos case! Please come in."

Anna managed to produce a broad smile. "Of course! So that's who you are! Good to see you again."

Half a head taller than Anna and with more jutting curves, Melina greeted them warmly. Like Anna's, Melina's hair was blond, but brighter, straighter, and constrained by a pony tail. She too wore jeans, topped by a black t-shirt with the playful warning *I AM GREEK. I CAN NOT KEEP CALM*, which Anna took as a positive sign. Except for travel posters and family photos, her apartment was simply appointed with big-box modern furniture, dominated by a toy-littered faux-leather sectional facing a home cinema bigger than the coffee table sitting between them.

"Do you travel much?" Anna asked, nodding at some travel magazines on the coffee table featuring exotic ports-of-call. "Only in my dreams," Melina said, and summoned son Mikos and daughter Sophia to welcome Anna and her boy with a perfunctory chorus of *chairetó*. Ramadi responded by wielding his space shuttle, popping a toy car from the couch into its bay, and asking if they wanted to help him ferry it to the international space station. Anna had no idea where he'd come up with such a scenario, and based on their quizzical expressions, neither did Mikos or Sophia.

As the children amused and bemused one another in the living room, the moms carried coffee and sweets to the whitewashed balcony overlooking nearly identical ones across the way. Melina expressed regret that husband Stephan, an electrician by trade, was not at hand. Saturdays were never easy on him. She asked if Anna had a partner. No, she replied, downcast. She was the widow of a lovely Iraqi man who had perished in an auto accident without ever having known his dear son.

"How hard that must have been for you and must still be. How do you get along?"

"I and some other moms around town have a co-op preschool that we take turns running, plus I have a part-time job. Two of them, actually, until recently."

"Sounds like a lot to do. What are the jobs?"

"As you must've learned, I worked at a taverna in Keratsini. Now I'm at Prótos, the company that hosts Altogether. Working there's turned me into something of a geek," she said, pinching the rim of her glasses.

Melina smiled. "You've had a lot to handle. I admire you." She dunked a sugar cookie in her coffee and took a bite. "How long have you lived here?"

"Almost six years, after taking a degree in international relations in Geneva and serving with an NGO in Africa," Anna said before deflecting to ask Melina what she had studied.

"I went to the University of Athens but had to drop out when I got pregnant with Mikos. I wanted to study law. Still do, but at least I work in that area. After Sophia was born I trained as a Hellenic Police officer. Earlier this year I got promoted and assigned to the Nikaia precinct."

"I'm impressed," Anna said. "But isn't that dangerous work? That's a pretty tough precinct."

Melina replied that she hardly ever left the station house and wasn't so happy about that. Hers was a desk job—logging calls, booking suspects, filing documents, plus helping to maintain their computer setup. Not terribly stimulating but it beats directing traffic.

"Speaking of computers," Anna asked, "how did you discover the Children's Protective League website?"

Melina's eyes wandered momentarily. "I saw one of your posters changing busses on my way to work," she said. "Child trafficking is hideous to me, so I took down the address and signed up. Only then did I discover that Fotini was involved in the group, and only now that you are too. Small world!"

"Indeed it is," Anna said, remembering that Nicolaides had objected to her posters just before Melina signed up as Mimi, speaking of coincidences.

Anna put down her cup. "So that case is closed now. Are you satisfied with the outcome, Melina?"

"Hardly. There's no justification for what he did. I've seen enough reports to know we have serious problems with child exploitation, and I joined the League in case I could further its mission."

Anna found herself wondering whether Melina had told the truth on the phone that no person named Laskaris was known to her. She was about to ask Melina whether she believed Servopoulos had any partners in crime when a loud thud followed by a squeal issued from behind the sliding doors. They rushed in to find Ramadi on the floor, crying, surrounded by upturned magazines shed by the upended coffee table pinning his legs.

"I told him we don't go up there," Sophia said, pointing to the sofa.

Melina righted the table as Anna picked up the boy. "It hurts!" he howled through sobs, clutching his right wrist.

"I'll get a warm washcloth," Melina said and hastened off. Anna deposited Ramadi on the sofa and asked if anything else hurt, receiving only tears in reply. At least there was no blood.

"I'm so sorry about this," Anna said when Melina returned to wrap the injured wrist. "I'll bet he was flying his plane and tried to take it into orbit." Sophia solemnly nodded from across the room. Mikos had disappeared.

"Don't worry about the furniture," Melina said. "I hope he's not badly hurt. Do you want me to call in paramedics?"

Anna had joined Ramadi on the sofa to slide his head into her lap and blot his tears with a napkin. "Thanks, but please don't. I don't want to expose him to all that commotion."

"I really think he should get medical attention. Do you have anyone who could treat him?"

Anna said she did, wondering whether Melina was trying to get rid of them. Even if she wasn't, the party was over for Ramadi and her as well, she sensed, and that nothing would be gained by bringing up Laskaris. As sympathetic to Anna's cause as Melina seemed to be, she was still a cop, and her allegiance to Nicolaïdes probably trumped sisterhood.

Melina squatted down to hug Ramadi, telling him how brave he was and would feel better soon. Awkwardly grasping Melina's hands at the front door, Anna gave thanks for having them over and again apologized for the incident. Insisting it was not a problem, Melina sent them off with a brave smile.

At street level, Anna told Ramadi they were going to see nice Nurse Fatma, who would make him feel better. She led him down the block toting his improvised jetpack, feeling as unsettled as ever. Sergeant Melina Cristopoulos remained a puzzle box.

Chapter Fifteen

ANNA WOULDN'T NORMALLY BE thrilled to have her phone notify her at 5:30 AM, especially after a night of lovemaking, but suspected this call was special. She rolled away from Andreas and fumbled for her glasses and then her phone. Ottovio had told her to expect to be spammed by morning, and here it was—her first photo essay from Nikaia, sent to an anonymous mailbox by an Android. She would thank him, but not now. Let the poor guy get some well-earned sleep.

As instructed, she saved, unzipped the robot's email attachment, and decrypted it with password SIRI to find four images with date-stamps for filenames, as sharp as their lighting conditions allowed. The first showed a dark alley rendered in orange from the streetlight above. The panes of number 34's back door reflected darkness. Not a car or a creature stirred. The second image, a few minutes newer, captured a portly figure wearing a helmet astride a motorbike waving at the camera. In the next image he was gone, leaving just the caresses of the rosy-fingered dawn on stuccoed walls.

The next batch had but four photos, one of which revealed human activity—a man passing by, walking a dog and smoking a cigarette. All that distinguished the others, she suspected, were shape-shifting shadows as the sun god arced through the heavens. The stop-motion sequences that burdened her inbox six times an hour suggested that her stakeout would be tedious. Thinking less is more, she instructed the robot to slack off, texting it to take a picture every fifteen seconds and email them every fifteen minutes rather ten, hoping her instructions were understood.

She deposited her phone and turned toward slumbering Andreas, wondering if he'd understood her intentions when she'd rung him yesterday afternoon to suggest spending the evening together. And by the time they'd finished their takeout gyros and salad, he'd gotten her drift, offering no objections to extending the visit through morning. And when she proceeded to kiss and unbutton him in his bedroom after putting Ramadi to bed in the parlor, he'd put up only token resistance before getting into it.

So do you understand those intentions, part of her asked the rest of her.

Let's see. Andreas always attracted me, even before I met Mahmoud. But it made no sense—he was gay, had a partner. But they broke up, and then he told me he's bi. So I got curious. He seemed willing enough but a little shy. I enjoyed it, and he seemed to.

Do you want more of this?

Hmm. Sex aside, he's a good man, and seems good for Ramadi too. Soul mate or helpmeet, I Dunno.

So what do you feel you want?

Look, she told her inner interrogator. *I'm as confused as he is. For different reasons, of course. So, abide, if you don't mind.*

As you wish.

Andreas was yawning and stretching his arms. Silence from behind the door where Ramadi slept on the day bed. She reached across the bed to caress a bare shoulder. "Thank you for last night, Andreas. Don't know about you, but I didn't realize how much I needed that."

"I did," he said, letting her roll him over. He picked a strand of hair from his mouth.

"Need it, or realize how much I did?" she asked.

"Hard to say. First you seemed to need it, and then I did. And so it just grew. You know."

"Cute. But surely you felt something besides that. C'mon, you can tell me. I won't bite."

He propped himself on left arm and when his eyes stopped darting, said: "I love you. Love you both. That's easy. But we're both foreigners here, and don't fit in. We've both had issues with the locals. That brings us together—"

"Sure, but forget all that," Anna said. "Can't we try to make the most of what we have? Would you believe me if I told you I'd loved you for a long time?"

"Even when you were with Mahmoud?"

"Even, but that was different. You weren't accessible, I was vulnerable, and he was irresistible."

"And now?"

She sank back, clasping her hands behind her head. "It seems I almost always feel vulnerable. Guess I'm good at covering it up. But we were talking about you, not me. So admit it: you're vulnerable too."

"Yes, to you. And to Ramadi, now that I think of it. And there've been consequences."

"Like what?"

"Um, some clients have been teasing me with shit like balls-in-chains after noticing you two around so often. It shouldn't get to me, but it does."

"Kosta too?"

"No, thanks heaven. Thomás has an ex-wife and a daughter. He understands. But still, he chuckles at the jibes."

"Look, I'm sorry if I've caused you grief. I'm not forcing you to choose. Just follow your heart. Tell them who you care for is none of their damned business."

He turned to face her. "Ja, but trash talk comes with the territory. So does gossip. And gossip has a way of getting around."

"It does. And your reputation takes hits. I get it and I'm sorry for that, but I'm talking about a loving relationship. If they can't handle witnessing one, it's their problem. How many of those guys have one?"

"I wouldn't know, but two couples formed from guys who met at the salon."

"And yours dissolved. I'm sorry for that too, but this is a second chance, if you want. Do you?"

"I do. But I worry whether it's for the right reasons."

Anna rubbed her eyes, recalling her recent self-debate. "I know what you mean. I nag myself too. But having someone upstanding and simpatico who cares for Ramadi, someone he can look up to, means a lot to me."

Andreas started to say something but she wasn't done. "—Someone I can make happy, and someone to build a better world with. So what do you want?"

He slumped back and gazed mutely upward. When she noticed her thumbs twiddling she stopped, just as her phone rang. She ignored it and closed her eyes.

Oh, how this confuses me. I remember worrying about Andreas when we had to sleep together one night. He didn't try to seduce me or anything, but just days later he and Ivan were carrying on in that luxurious flat Ivan rented for us. But Ivan was a good man and I got used to it.

That night she offered herself to me I was nervous too. I remember quoting Rumi—"your task is not to seek for love, but to tear down the barriers within yourself that you have built against it." And, along with my pants, some did come down.

Of course, our closeness made Andreas worry about our mission. Bringing in Katrina would do the team no good, he warned, but it worked out and he got used to it.

And now, here she is by his side. As much as I wish it were me in her arms, I can accept it if that's what they truly want. I think it will be good for my boy too. If he is happy and they are happy, I am happy.

Day is dawning, time for the Fajr Salah prayer.

"I like things the way they are," Andreas said, eyes still focused elsewhere. "I like my work. I like being with and helping you and Ramadi, but I like being alone too. I guess what I want is more of the same."

"Like dropping by for occasional sex?" Her thumbs were gyrating again.

He turned to her and cupped her hand. "Don't say that. But this is about us living together. I'm not opposed, but I'm not there, at least not yet. I just have to let this stew until it's done."

Anna drew a deliberative breath and received an inaudible chiding: *You were about to apologize for using him, weren't you? Maybe you have, but stand up for yourself.*

"How?" Anna unintentionally asked aloud.

Cocking his head, Andreas begged pardon. *"Verzeihung?"*

"Entschuldigung," she said, sniffling back tears. "I'm being needy. Pushy. But that doesn't mean I don't love you."

Andreas kissed her cheek, tasting saline. "All true, I suppose. I just need time. I hope you understand."

She cradled his head in her palms and kissed him, lingering, and gazed into his brown eyes flecked with gold. "Of course. We both have things to think over. Take your time. Let me know by next weekend. Just kidding."

Her hands slipped from his head. She rolled over and reached for her phone to see whose call she'd ignored. It was Melina, whose message asked her to call back within the hour, before she had to be at work. Doesn't sound like a get-well call for Ramadi, she thought, so what now?

#

Andreas excused himself to toss on gym shorts and a politically impertinent t-shirt, and padded through the living room past a sleeping Ramadi to the kitchen in pursuit of breakfast. He had corn flakes in stock that he knew Ramadi would find acceptable, but in his penitent frame of mind, he decided to reboot their day with pancakes, crushing some corn flakes into the batter for extra points.

Anna propped herself up, wondering what Melina needed to know or say at this hour that couldn't wait. Unless it concerned a Nobel Prize, an early morning phone call seldom portends good news. She took up her phone to find more alerts from the birdhouse in Nikaia. Ignoring them, she reluctantly returned the cop's call.

"This is Melina," she heard when the call went through. A bit chilly, Anna thought, given that she could tell who was calling. "Hi Melina, it's Anna. What's up?"

"First, I hope Ramadi didn't break anything. How is he doing?"

"Fortunately, it was just a sprain, now taped up and healing, and how are you this morning?"

"Well enough, except for my wake-up message from my Chief alerting the precinct to expect a Hellenic Police Internal Investigation Unit to show up any day. Is that anything you know about?"

Anna truthfully assured her that she knew not, and asked what it might be about. Perhaps the Servopoulos case, Melina supposed. Such probes happened rarely, she said, and while they usually ended without casualties, they entailed angst and unrewarding busywork.

"I'm sorry about that," Anna said. "Whatever it's about, it sounds like an inconvenience. Might they be looking into … I don't know … irregularities in the case work?" Melina had no opinion, but mentioned that Servopoulos's file had been mysteriously reclassified.

"I might be interviewed," Melina said, "and it could ripple out to the League. I thought you should know in case questions come your way."

The Laskaris poster came to mind. "Thanks for telling me. Any idea when they'll set up their tent?"

"Not really. They ride by night."

Picturing an early-morning police raid on the Nikaia police station, Anna could only suppress a chuckle. "So good luck, and please let me know how it goes. I'll be thinking good thoughts for you."

"Appreciate it, but please don't share them until the department makes a public statement."

Saying "I hear you," Anna wished Melina the best morning she could have and lay back with her eyes closed, wondering if this might be her chance to expose Nicolaides. But even if she could demonstrate his connection to the traffickers, to put them all out of business she would need allies and evidence she had yet to gather.

Her day, she reflected, wasn't starting all that well. But it helped to have Ramadi scamper in and leap onto the bed. "Onkle Andreas says come and have his special pancakes."

#

The rest of the morning was a blur. Saying she had kids to mind, Anna towed Ramadi home as soon as he'd wolfed down his pancakes, leaving Andreas Swiss-kissed to wash up. As they made their way to the Winter Palace, Anna chewed on Melina's news. Her best guess was that, if anyone could shed light on the situation, it would be Fotini. Her husband, she had let on, had connections downtown.

After spending the morning occupying Ramadi, Josef, Yasmin, and Cassie's twin boys Christos and Adám with spelling games and geometric puzzles in her cramped quarters, she took advantage of nap time to check in with Fotini. Following pleasantries, Anna asked her if she'd heard about the alleged probe. The answer was no, but it was good news and high time to shine some sunlight on her botched case. She asked Anna how she knew of it, to which Anna guardedly replied "a source close to the investigation," expecting Fotini to get her drift.

"Might your well-connected husband have made any inquiries downtown?" Anna asked.

"In fact. Ilias did. The day after the trial, he woke up incensed. Instead of going to work, he typed a letter that he hand-delivered downtown, possibly to someone in the Mayor's Office. He didn't pass it by me, but it was likely a litany of my complaints about the matter. That's his style."

"Don't you realize what a pickle this puts us in? Nicolaides will be fit to be tied. I expect he'll pin it on us, so expect blowback."

"Not that I could have stopped Ilias, but perhaps the publicity will keep Nicolaides from retaliating."

"At least until this blows over. But after that all bets are off. These internal investigations just sweep dirt under the carpet, but if by some fluke Nicolaides is disciplined he'll be even angrier. We have to stop these guys."

"And how might we do that?"

Anna considered disclosing her surveillance activity but vetoed the idea. "Well, I suppose Ilias could hire a private eye to stake out the house in Nikaia."

"That's not his style, Anna. Or yours, I suspect. Anyway, the investigation is what it is."

"Such as it is. Let's hope it doesn't blow up in our faces."

Hearing her pre-schoolers bouncing on the bed, Anna signed off. She told her charges to don their shoes for a jaunt to the playground a few blocks up the hill and grabbed her laptop. Sitting on a bench with one eye on the frolickers and the other on her screen, she unzipped twenty batches of spy photos from her inbox into folders. As her index finger stroked through the monotonous lot, her mind was on Nicolaides—what his game was, what the probe might dig up, what he would do after that. The watchbird was her only hope, but if it failed to reveal misdeeds, what then?

A few of the scores of photos she flipped through weren't entirely devoid of life. One large batch showed Laskaris hovering by the doorway in sweats, baggy gym pants girdled over his paunch, cigarette in hand, unaccompanied. In one photo he stared straight at the camera. She hoped he wouldn't investigate, and was relieved when she saw him go inside, grateful not to have to bring her birdie to an untimely end just when it had started to sing.

She scrolled back to scrutinize the sequence. One shot showed Laskaris tossing his butt away, kneeling down. Fifteen seconds later, his right hand was reaching for the doorknob and his left hand held what was clearly a cobblestone. Then he was kneeling down again. The last photo showed him halfway through the door. What was that about?

Realizing she hadn't seen Laskaris going out the door made her think: what if he'd gone out the front door for exercise, doughnuts, or whatever, and returned to find he'd forgotten his keys? It sure looked like he'd retrieved a spare key hidden under a paving stone to let himself in, and then replaced it before going inside.

She coveted that key.

PART THREE

COPING MECHANISMS

I don't gad about like Superman, soaring over the countryside to my next urgent destination. To go anywhere, I need to picture a place I know. Somehow, visualizing it and willing myself to be there is enough to transport me in an instant. That's amazing, but it also means I cannot go any place new. And that means I'll probably never find my brother unless he makes it to a relative.

I'm in Mosul, at the house of my widowed aunt Farida, looking at a tattered photograph of Akhmed and me. I think I'm about 15 with a shadow of a beard and he's ten with gangly arms and legs. It's leaning against a row of books in a curio cabinet with cracked glass. Some of those books are poetry, some written by her husband, uncle Yusef. He was a pretty well-regarded poet. A fundamentalist took exception to some of his lovely lines extolling nature, and a few days before Daesh thugs descended on our house, Yusef's body was found on the street. He'd been on his way to mosque. I hope to see him in Paradise if ever I make it there.

I hope Akhmed is not yet in Paradise. When I arrived home, there was no sign of his body, so he must have been taken alive, but is he still? To save his skin was he forced to assert that this crime was Allah's will? Then, did they drag him away and order him to kill other innocents? I must know if he has survived. If he did, he is probably somewhere I cannot visit.

The bedroom door opens and my cousin Jena comes in. She closes the door, looks about the parlor and hastens into the kitchen where Aunt Farida is. Daesh has left a city of women, with few fathers and sons but many widows and daughters and orphans such as I. Whether it pleased Allah or not, killing one of them in battle gave me pleasure.

Chapter Sixteen

STILL CURSING ILIAS FOR inciting an investigation whose crosshairs could fix on her, Anna turned to fixing supper. Having promised Ramadi shepherd's pie, she got to it while he was in the bedroom launching toys into space. She had just put potatoes up to boil when her phone sounded the Marseillaise. The caller's ID, HELLENIC CHILDREN, didn't ring a bell. She picked up to proffer a tentative hello.

"Hello, is this Anna Burmeister?" a female voice said.

"Yes it is."

"The same Anna Burmeister who testified at the trial of Theodoros Servopoulos?"

Anna affirmed and then asked with whom she had the pleasure of speaking.

"My name is Nikki Troia. I work for The Children's Advocacy Center out of our Piraeus office. We're an NGO that, as our name implies, aids children in distress and their families. I saw your interview at the courthouse and am eager to find out more about what you are doing. Is this a good time?"

Anna glanced into the bedroom. Ramadi had docked his space shuttle and picked up a children's book. He was starting to read Greek.

"Um, sure, but how did you get my phone number?"

"Via a friend of yours. I hope it's all right to be calling."

"I see," Anna said, first flashing on Fotini, then on Melina. "What can I do for you?"

Her caller cheerfully explained that the Hellenic Children's Advocacy Center had been founded over a decade before to help vulnerable and neglected children, aid victims of trafficking, and combat xenophobic and racist hate. Aside from medical assistance, they offered social and legal services to immigrant families, working closely with other children's, women's, and minority welfare organizations in Greece and across Europe.

"I see. Which friend and why me?"

"Your friend asked me not to say, but I'm reaching out to you because you seem to be the leader of a new group interested in protecting children. Something called *prostasía-paidia-dot-gr* online. Am I correct?"

"Guess you could put it that way, but I'm just another mom," Anna said. "I barely know what I'm doing." She sat down at the table, picked up a pencil, and started tapping corners of squares on the checkered tablecloth.

"That's why I'm calling, actually." Saying she'd visited the League's website, it was Nikki's opinion that it looked promising but aside from a slogan, she didn't find much about what the organization does. Anna had to agree.

"So," Nikki said, "if there's anything we can do to help you move ahead, like finding issues to focus on or pointing you to information resources, it might help your group make a unique contribution to what we all care about."

Dead air, save for the pencil taps, ensued before Anna replied: "What would you like us to be doing?"

"That should be up to your group. There are many issues facing children. So far, you seem to have focused on abductions. If that's your main concern, I say go with it."

"And you can help us with that?"

"Absolutely. We monitor wire services, news channels, and radio dispatches for incidents of where children may be at risk. They go into a database and reports come out, reports we can feed you. You can filter them by date, type of incident, location, and source to alert your community."

"That's impressive. Could save us—me, mostly—a ton of work. But turn that around. What would your group do if we came up with any leads?"

It would depend on what sort of thing it was, Nikki replied. Were it a kidnapping, they would notify the appropriate law enforcement unit; were it an abused child, they might contact government child protective services. Were it …

Pencil poised, Anna broke in. "Do the police have units that investigate crimes against children?"

"Some police forces do. Hellenic Police has one, so does Interpol. We have our own search and rescue unit, some forty professionals and trained volunteers equipped with vehicles and canine teams that's on alert day and night. We have a hotline to report missing children. The toll-free number is 1056. You might want to post it on your home page."

"Wow. I guess I have a lot to learn. We set up the League thinking we were on our own, but it looks like you people have it covered. Makes me feel like there's no point to what we're doing."

"Oh, don't say that. We're not the only group in Greece focusing on children's issues. We're one of the oldest and most visible, but we can't do it alone. Children need all the help they can get. Find your niche."

Finding a niche in Nikki's ecosystem felt daunting, but connecting to that world could be just what she needed. Fogged by possibilities, Anna told Nikki that she was glad she called, but now she needed to put food on the table and thanked her for confusing her. Nikki chortled. "Why not meet for lunch to discuss how we might work together?"

Not wanting to rebuff a potential ally, Anna assented. They made an arrangement to meet down at the waterfront two days hence. Anna rang off and got up to pace around the table, silently chanting: What am I doing? What *Am* I doing? What am *I* doing? What am I *Doing*? After three revolutions, an answer came: making supper.

Lying in bed that night, Anna's brain buzzed with unanswerable questions. Who had put Nikki on to her and why? Should her watchbird capture an abduction, should she let Nikki's team handle it? What if they alerted police, tipping off Nicolaides? Then what? What *was* she doing?

You're doing the right thing, something told her. *Let this woman help you.*

Just when sleep's balm had come to soothe her, Ramadi squirmed in next to her aquiver, needing to nestle, whimpering about a bad dream. There he was, playing in a park when he saw a big, big bird circling way above him that flew down and picked him up in its big sharp claws and carried him up and then he woke up. Cuddling and caressing him, telling him it was just a dream that anyone could have and no bird could do such a thing, she wondered if somehow she'd subliminally implanted her obsession in his impressionable mind? Not until he winked into sleep in her arms did she find rest, still not knowing.

#

Saturday dawned smelling of the sea, with overcast skies and a nip in the air that kept Anna bed-bound until Ramadi stirred beside her and begged for breakfast. She reluctantly donned her lotus-flower kimono, and went to mix pancake batter, broil bacon, and set up espresso to wind her clock. Three orthogonal cuts of her chef's knife expertly rendered a navel orange into eight triangular wedges that she reassembled on a saucer, musing over Nikki's account of Greece's flourishing child protection industry. It depressed her to think of how much predation must be happening to make all that rescuing necessary. Dribbling out pancakes, she glanced at Ramadi sucking on a section of orange, giving him a bulbous three-cornered grin. That she might lose him to some two-legged beast now seemed more than a bad dream.

Forcing her mind away from morbid thoughts, she resumed contemplating the League and what it was good for. All the groups Nikki had mentioned were well-established and talking to one another to boot, linked together across Greece and Europe, taking action. That federation of humanitarians was a kind of Altogether writ large, it occurred to her. There should be a sweet spot for us somewhere in that galaxy of do-gooders, but how to home in on it?

Remembering she was occupied, she flipped a flapjack to find its pitted underside burnt umber. She turned the others aside, squirted more oil on the griddle, dolloped new discs, and rescued sizzling strips of bacon from the oven, appreciating the hazards of multitasking.

"See these pancakes, Ramadi?" she said, lowering a plate of overcooked ovals before him, trying to sell them with "They look like the surface of Mars, don't they?"

The boy scrutinized one of the disks and poked it with his fork. "It's brown. Mars is red," he said, before dredging it with cinnamon sugar and elevating it to his mouth. He chewed, and pinched his features. "Does Mars taste like this?"

She didn't know, she replied, never having tasted Mars, and advised him to just eat the more earth-toned disks and leave the darker ones for her to consume.

Ramadi ate with gusto, seemingly having forgotten his nightmare. When they'd had their fill, Anna informed him she had some work to do, but after that they would ride their bikes over to Onkle Andreas for haircuts and how did that sound? She knew Ramadi would get stir-crazy if she didn't get him out of the house and she would go crazy if she didn't see Andreas soon, and wondered how crazy was that.

She asked herself what captivated her. He was tall, slim, reasonably good-looking and personable, but sometimes (understandably) a bit prickly. From knowing him for six years, she'd come to respect him as an idealist capable of motivating people to drop whatever they were doing to stand up for justice, democracy, and the commonweal. He'd treated her with utter compassion after Mahmoud perished by her star-crossed hand. And, despite having been conscripted for day care any number of times, he'd been there for them time and again with only the occasional whimper of protest. Who wouldn't love such a man, no matter his unpredictable sexual preferences? And while she understood that none of his admirable traits need portend mutual happiness here and now or ever after, it might be worth a try.

#

They pedaled over to the hair salon in windbreakers through a misty drizzle to find Kosta honing cutlery and Andreas sweeping the floor. Saturdays tended to be busy, especially when the sun wasn't diverting patrons to the beach, but on this dim day their clients must have collectively decided to sleep in.

"Who wants to do Ramadi?" Anna asked, hoping Maestro Kosta would volunteer, and he accepted the challenge. He pulled out a cushioned plank that normalized the height of young people at some expense to their dignity and set it on the arms of his salon chair. Raising Ramadi by his armpits to giggle into the wall-to-wall mirror, he asked the room: "What'll it be? Razor? Undercut? Pompadour or quiff? Beatle? Slick back? Buzz cut? How about a Mohawk or even an Afro?" Kosta knew his cuts.

Unaccustomed to tonsorial lingo, Ramadi liked the sound of a buzz cut but was overruled. Andreas recommended a curly top with a mid fade, given the boy's natural bushiness, which his mom seconded.

"Then let the styling begin!" Kosta pronounced as he seated, collared, and draped the young fellow and treated him to a 360-degree spin. Andreas selected one of Kosta's mix tapes and popped it into the boom box in the corner. As Barbra Streisand started crooning *My Man*, Anna beckoned him to sit with her in the waiting area.

She would have synced lips with Andreas but for Kosta's observant eyes in the mirror. In lieu, she palmed his knuckles on the arm of his chair and addressed him in German, recounting developments in Nikaia. Ottovio's watchbird had revealed Laskaris letting himself in with a spare key stashed behind the cottage that might come in handy. Andreas cautioned her to avoid that temptation and instead focus on formulating a response plan to the evil she feared.

She told him of Nikki's unsolicited call and of the redoubtable Children's Advocacy Center, describing it as a sort of a mother ship in a fleet of child protectors trawling for victims of traffickers, abusers, and hard times.

"What did she want from you?"

"Said some 'friend' told her about the League and wanted to help. Maybe it was Fotini, but why would they be acquainted? Perhaps Melina knows her professionally."

"Melina?"

"Lady cop in Nikaia. Works with Nicolaides, might be covering for Nicolaides. Joined the League after we posted that mug shot of Laskaris. I try to keep her at arm's length."

"Hmm. Anyway, did Nikki say what this outfit could do for you?"

She opened her phone to their website and scrolled through its array of humanitarian resources and urban outposts, links to kindred organizations, and unlike her dinky one, a hotline staffed by professionals 24/7. Oh, and a search and rescue team that dwarfed most city fire departments.

"So why not call them in when you see something?" he asked, studying a photo of a contingent of yellow-vested rescue workers posing with sniffer dogs and emergency vehicles. "Seems like they could be there in a flash."

"It's complicated. If I alert them, they might call in the cops. And one of those cops might alert the traffickers. Let me think about it."

She pecked his cheek. "You know, I've been meaning to get a haircut too. How about I be your first customer of the day?"

There was no name for Anna's hairstyle, but given how it swept across her forehead to partially cover her left ear, it might be described as Cinnamon Swirl. She'd taken a cue from Elizabeth Warren's I-mean-business hairstyle to project a professional image for Prótos, but now she wanted something zippier, if only to kindle Andreas' desire.

He agreed to do the honors, but what would it be? He ran down some styles she couldn't quite picture, so she scanned the headshots of movie idols lining the wall. She couldn't picture herself as Bette Davis, Claudette Colbert, or Katherine Hepburn. But finding herself attracted to Hedy Lamar's luxuriant tresses, she told him to do it like hers, only shorter and cuter.

After much snipping, combing, tinting, brushing, blowing, and spraying, a new Anna arose from her throne to hug her stylist and give him a big Swiss kiss. Umber highlights streaked the flaxen tresses that curled just below her ears to accentuate her dimples and caress her neck. And while the result wasn't exactly Hedy's look, Andreas declared it his masterpiece, and Kosta, the supervising aesthetician, concurred that the lady was well coiffed.

It was Ramadi's turn to be admired, much of what he did himself, standing on Kosta's cutting board and making faces in the big mirror. Before Kosta had done his thing, Ramadi's hair was fuller in the back and on the sides than on top. Now that was inverted. With his faded sides, tangly top and little duck-ass taper, he looked almost punk, a fitting complement to Anna's frisky new do.

They should be going, she said, and before pedaling off to shop for food, embarrassed the hairdressers with generous tips. To keep up appearances, she zipped and hooded Ramadi and covered herself with a headscarf, and they took leave to dodge raindrops.

#

Zeus had raised the ante from drizzle to noisy splatters by the time they wheeled up to their back door, hungry as hell. Anna returned from consulting the bedroom mirror to see how her 'do did to find Ramadi twisting apart a rope of string cheese and dropping the strands into his upturned mouth like a baby bird feeding itself worms.

She put out tuna fish sandwiches, carrot sticks, and potato crisps, and upon demolishing them she let Ramadi watch his Jay-Jay-the-Jet-Plane videos while she poked around the Internet to get a handle on the child protection racket. Her perusal of the Children's Advocacy Center's exhaustive resources and its links to kindred organizations both impressed and depressed her. Overtaken by sheepishness, she snapped closed her laptop. All those child advocates had been soldiering on for years without any notice or help from her. Given all that concerted activism, what could she possibly achieve with one peeping birdhouse and no action plan?

As was her tendency at such moments, she got up to tread around the table in a cycle of self-doubt. A quarter past her third revolution, it occurred to her: *Dammit, I hold the key to shutting down a criminal conspiracy.* Rather than dwell on her insignificance in the child welfare universe, why not see what its luminaries might do for her? Andreas had it right. Nikki's all-star search and rescue squad might just be the ticket should something sinister go down at the cottage on Magnisias Street. Time to get that team on board.

She stopped pacing. *This is what I am doing. Catching rats and joining forces to dispose of them.*

Chapter Seventeen

*Next to the photo of Akhmed and me outside our house in Mosul
I noticed a letter partly hinged open. It is to Farida. I do not see
who signed it, but I can read the beginning: "Dear Aunt Farida, I
dearly hope you receive this. My love to Jena. I am in a camp near
Şanilurfa and wanted you to know I am all right. I escaped Daesh
when the Americans and Kurds took Raqqa. The town was in
ruins and they told me it was too dangerous to stay or try to reach
Iraq. I was injured and after medics patched me up got a ride to
the Turkish border and will try to work my way west. I hope to—"*

*The rest is below the fold, but this must be a letter from
Akhmed because who else of us would be in Raqqa? Praise Allah,
he is alive! Let me see, the letter is dated close to a year ago
by Farida's wall calendar. So where is he now? He said he was
heading west, but to where?*

Whether they toil inside, outside, above, below, for or against the law,
those who hack computers tend to share certain personality traits and
quirks. Taking manifest pride in their craft and creations, they are
solvers who shamelessly appropriate whatever code seems useful for a
task and meets their standards. Whether or not they hack images, they
are creative artists, some of whom even dub themselves data architects.
The code they construct—the less of it the better, they assert—is
their art. Fenced into cubicles or roaming the wild, they constitute a
collegium of coders with an underlying ethos of learning from others,
self-improvement, and sharing their wares—subject to intellectual
property restrictions most of them resent and occasionally subvert.
They are creatures of the night, and even when their wings have been
corporately clipped, after dark they tend to grow back, not unlike a
vampire's.

Such was Ottovio's tribe. He and his online comrades gathered on forums and encrypted channels to share secrets of algorithms, blockchains, and cybersecurity—their ABC's as it were. When they needed data, it was on the Dark Web for a price or free for the taking by plundering online archives, should the taker have sufficient temerity and skills.

Appropriating data was Ottovio's métier, and he had done so big time, mostly from government servers, eschewing warez hawked by disreputable sources, or as he called them, "Darth Vendors." A persistent disgust of political corruption drove him to amass a rogue's gallery of Greek political actors, corporate enablers, and public servants and, by cataloging and connecting bits of data, typifying their relationships to depict them as a multidimensional graph. That database was not unlike LinkedIn's, except that many of the connections he'd ferreted out in what he called his "Antisocial Network" went unadvertised.

The most succulent fruit of his labor was the Hellenic Police database of suspects, criminals, and informants, and other persons of official interest he'd shown Anna, a treasure trove of unadvertised connections. Using phished credentials, he'd hacked into it several times to download its tables and had even managed to upload some after editing certain entries. But all that it had to say about one Vassilios Laskaris Sr. was that he had been arrested for assault five years ago and subsequently released, only to pass away two years hence of an apparent heart attack. But, over in Nikaia, his checkered name lived on.

Ottovio had taken an interest in the resurrected Vassilios Laskaris, though not to connect to him. He wanted to ID him both to help Anna discern who he really was and to hone his investigatory skills. As all he had on Laskaris was genealogical tidbits about the man's name and his dad's obit, he asked Anna for whatever photos she had of him. She had obliged with a couple from the spycam and Penelope's hand-drawn mug shot, and with them he tried a different tack.

As the photos from the alley had been shot from afar, Laskaris's face was less than crisp. Seeking a sharper image, he cropped the face from three of them. Enlarging and sharpening somewhat improved the man's unphotogenic features, but thinking he could do better, he downloaded open source software for reconstructing images. Once he'd doped out how it worked, he displayed the three fuzzy pictures in separate windows, picked corresponding points on Laskaris's face in each of them, and instructed the program to combine them into a composite. After a little normalizing and sharpening it looked reasonably usable.

Whistling a happy tune, he uploaded his composite to Google over his VPN to search by image. At least all of the dozen or so matches it presented were men, but of differing age and physiognomy. Some of them vaguely resembled his caricature but seemed too old, too young, or clearly not from Greece. So much for Google.

Thinking that Facebook might be his friend, Ottovio whistled the image onto the wall of his fake Facebook account, tagged it *Vassilios Laskaris*, and went to fix himself brunch as he waited for what he called Facebook's Kumbaya algorithm to cough up friend suggestions. Why should he have to do all the work?

Upon checking Facebook several hours later, a friend had indeed been suggested. He clicked through to a page belonging to one Leander Eugenides. His personal info was hidden but at least the page was in Greek and some of its featured photos seemed to have been taken in and around Athens. Other than a receding hairline, Eugenides failed to resemble Laskaris. He looked younger, between thirty and forty, was clean shaven, dressed more casually, and seemed to have difficulty smiling in the few photos that featured him.

Except for one in an eating place that may have been taken by a waiter: Three men were gathered at a table grinning as best they could for the camera. Next to Eugenides sat a jowly man with a fringe of auburn hair and a Nietzschean mustache whose presence must have triggered Facebook's facial recognition algorithm.

Was this Vassilios Laskaris? While none of the three had been tagged, the third man was a ringer for a mugshot he'd seen of "Theodoros the Abductor," as he had come to call Servopoulos. Assuming it was Laskaris sitting next to him, the question then became: Who is Leander Eugenides? Searching the Web disclosed a profile for that name on LinkedIn. To decide if it was the same fellow, Ottovio logged in with his entrepreneurial paramour Beatrice's credentials to discover that Eugenides called himself Shipping Manager at Meteor Import-Export

Ltd in central Athens, a post he'd occupied for about a year after serving in the Greek Navy.

Ottovio would have loved to check out Eugenides' connections, but couldn't without first linking up with him in Beatrice's behalf, so he went back to Facebook. Where were those guys dining? He downloaded the photo and zoomed in. They had mostly finished their food. A bottle of Ouzo sat next to Servopoulos, half empty. Ottovio noticed the reflection of a neon sign in a picture hanging on the wall behind the men. He flipped the image to read the letters, but all he could make out was *erna*, likely implying *Taverna*. Not a lot of help.

He was still puzzling over the photograph when something occurred to him, something so obvious that he gave himself a dope slap. *Look at the metadata, donkey-ass*, the telltale info tucked inside almost every digital photo that documents the camera, lens, aperture, and flash setting that was used to image it, plus date, time, and, if it came from a cellphone, possibly location.

It seemed that the photo of the trio was taken on an iPhone 6 at 1:39 PM this past July 18 at latitude 37.976278, longitude 23.726588. Plugging that into a map transported him to a pedestrian way off Aeolus Street, near Monastiraki Square in central Athens. A red lollipop on the map identified an eatery called *Taverna Kalógeros*—Monks Tavern. Some fan photos of it and the street view clinched it. *That's where they ate, probably souvlaki.*

The eatery was pretty far from Nikaia, he observed. Might it be close to Eugenides's workplace? And when he searched for the address of Meteor Import-Export Ltd., sure enough, it was on Athinaidos, a mere five-minute walk to the taverna. Had this been a business lunch, and what might have been discussed? Might Meteor Import-Export Ltd. dabble in live cargo?

Save that for later, he decided, and dashed off an email to Anna with the photo attached, saying he hoped it would help. Be patient, he wrote. *As Greeks say, one day the unripe grape becomes as sweet as honey.* And how sweet it would be if Eugenides was the connection.

#

Nikki Troia's kid threw up in his stroller just as Anna took her seat across from her at the Rose of Piraeus café. Perhaps it was the spoonfuls of chocolate pudding directly following the strained peas, a juxtaposition that would lead many diners to lay down their spoons. Nikki had invited Anna to meet at the "waterfront" bistro where she took breaks during the week. Situated on a busy street corner a block between the Metro and cruise ship terminals, it was separated from the waterfront by the almost impassable Akti Kallimassioti. And even though throaty ships' horns and honking cars impeded conversation, at least the coffee and pastries were not so bad.

"I like how you fixed your hair since I saw you on TV," Nikki said. "And I liked what you said in your interview even more."

"Thanks. It wasn't my idea. All of a sudden there was this mic in my face and I had to say something. In fact, it wasn't my idea to testify, but as the only live witness I couldn't really refuse."

Giorgios, Nikki's two-year-old, burbled brown bubbles in acknowledgment as Nikki asked about her son. Anna reported that Ramadi was playing at another mom's house not far away, and took the opportunity to digress about their Kinder Cloud by way of burnishing her communitarian credentials. Watching Nikki replacing Giorgio's soiled bib, Anna thought she ought to know more about Nikki's credentials before telling her too much.

She ceased wondering that when Nikki suggested strolling over to the Piraeus branch of the Children's Advocacy Center, just three blocks away.

"Sure, if there's time," Anna said over a blast from a ferry, "but first I want your take on this sordid business. The stats on your site about neglected, abused, and abducted children in Athens and across the country made my heart sink. Even Ramadi seems to have been a target, and he's just five!"

Nikki wanted to know what she meant. Anna related how Servopoulos had followed them not long before he abducted Sami in the same neighborhood.

"I see," Nikki said. "He wanted your son too, the creep. I admire you for exposing him and having the courage to take the witness stand."

"Actually, it wasn't until after I saw him snatch Sami that I understood he was shadowing Ramadi, not me. But after all that, there he is, free as a bird up in Nikaia, exonerated for kidnapping a child in broad daylight, and still at it, no doubt."

"And, after all that, are you afraid of reprisals? I might be."

Vengeance was something Anna didn't want to think about, but the question convinced her that Nikki was the humanitarian she claimed to be and truly wanted to help. Anna decided she might as well open up. "I doubt Servopoulos would make a move on me, not after all that publicity, but he could strike again, and I want to catch him in the act."

"What do you mean?" Nikki asked, leaning forward. "How would you ever know?"

"Don't want to get into the details, but we know where he lives and have placed the house under 24-hour surveillance. If that's where he takes his victims, we'll have evidence in close to real time."

After several seconds, Nikki said: "What do you mean, surveillance? And who is 'we'? Are you working with a detective or the police?"

She was the detective, Anna answered, and was working against, not with, the police. She took a deep breath and, insisting this was strictly confidential, said: "There's this cop who grilled me after I reported the kidnapping, a detective in Nikaia. Seems to be a friend of Servopoulos and his partner."

"Seems how?"

Anna thumbed her phone and showed Nikki her wavering video of Nicolaides entering a front door. "That's where they seem to live, and that's the detective calling on them with a bottle of wine less than an hour after he was tried and released."

"Amazing. What were you doing there?"

"When Sami's mom and I were getting into her car after the trial, we saw Servopoulos's buddy Vassilios Laskaris pick him up. We followed them all the way to Nikaia, to a cottage they seem to share. They bought alcohol on the way, and then the detective shows up to help them to celebrate the acquittal. Three rotten apples, I'd say."

"My goodness!" Nikki said, leaning back. "I don't know what to make of it. Have you told anybody about this?"

"Just a couple of close friends. Suspect those three have some kind if arrangement. That cop's a big cheese in his precinct. If I report what I saw I could get myself into big trouble."

"It does seem a bit circumstantial," Nikki said, "and I understand your reluctance to talk to the police. But we work closely with the police and we've never found evidence of collusion between them and child traffickers."

Anna leaned on the table with crossed arms. "There's always a first time. And since this cop appears to be their pal, we set up a camera behind their back door to capture comings and goings. But so far, nothing to go on."

"A surveillance camera? How did you manage that?"

"It's a hacked cell phone that takes pictures of their back door and sends them by email."

Nikki's lips pursed in thought. "So what will you do if your spying pays off?"

"Not sure, but we would need to move fast. Suppose we see them bringing in a child and told your team. Would they rush to the rescue without calling the cops?"

Nikki leaned back and scratched behind an ear. "Well, in a situation where there's endangerment, we like to have police present when we intervene. We aren't a SWAT team."

"At least, couldn't they show up to bear witness—plus whomever else we could round up—before calling in police?"

Nikki lifted her gaze to the swirls on the plastered ceiling. "And you're afraid that this cop might cover it up?"

"It's worse than that. After someone filed a complaint about the trial, internal affairs opened an investigation of the Nikaia precinct. Whatever that amounts to, it'll probably land me in that cop's crosshairs and maybe the traffickers' too. That's why I need backup."

Nikki sighed and clasped Anna's hands across the table. "It seems like you've gone out of the smoke and into the flame. Of course I want to help, but this is above my pay grade, I'm afraid. I'll tell you what. Let me put you in touch with Peter Mavridis. He's our search and rescue coordinator." She poked at her phone. "Here's his number. I'll tell Peter to expect a call from you."

"Guess that could help," Anna said, typing it in. "Tell him I'd like to consult his wisdom about a possible abduction. But let me tell him the details, please."

"Sure, if that's what you want. But I will tell him you have credible information he should know."

Taking a cue from Giorgios' pudgy legs kicking his stroller, Nikki said: "Sorry, I must go. My husband is expecting us. It was really nice to meet you and I really hope we can help you and your group. Please keep in touch."

They shook hands. Nikki covered up Giorgios and wheeled him away. Anna recharged her French Roast and returned to the table to discreetly panic. Lightning could strike any day and she would be the lightning rod. Maybe she should call it quits. She'd done her duty. She could simply caption her photos and videos of the crooks and the cop and anonymously mail them to Internal Affairs on a flash drive and tell her spy-cam to self-destruct. Wash her hands of the whole fraught affair.

Nursing her newfound detachment, she boarded an uptown bus to retrieve Ramadi. Along the way she inspected her email, consisting of ten new batches of spy photos and Ottovio's message attaching a photo of the traffickers with some balding guy, news she wasn't sure how to use. Poking through her bird's monotonous reels seconded her sense of resignation. But then, if something evil went down unnoticed, how would she ever forgive herself?

Let it be for now. Call Peter Mavridis. Get his take. Then see.

Chapter Eighteen

After I read Akhmed's letter I follow Jena into the kitchen. She joins Farida at the table by the window and hands over her phone. They look at it, chattering excitedly. I move to where I can see the screen. It's a photo of an old car, a rust-spotted powder blue compact sedan parked on a city street. Not particularly interesting if you ask me, but it must mean something to them. Oh, for ears!

The next shot is a selfie of a young man in a tee shirt. He's sitting on the hood of the car looking quite proud. His wavy beard and stringy hair is black. Under his fisherman's cap and tinted glasses his face is disfigured by scars, as if burned. So tragic for such a young man.

He is my brother, seven years older than when Daesh took him! Whatever horrors he has endured, at least he is free and even has a car! Were I corporeal, I would weep.

Jena advances to a photo of the car from behind. It clearly has seen better days. In the background I notice a sign on a building written in Greek. Then Akhmed survives. In Greece, maybe even in Athens!

I take a closer look. I am almost sure that building is the Metro terminal in Piraeus, near the big weekend bazaar where Katrina took me to buy clothes. That is somewhere I can put myself, and now that I know my brother has been there, I surely must.

At Daria's Kinder Cloud classroom all seemed well. Ramadi was eager to display his literary prowess by haltingly orating from his book of Greek myths. Daria's daughter Yasmin seemed a bit pouty, perhaps due to benign neglect. Sensing that she and Ramadi had had enough of each other, Anna loaded up his backpack with his omnipresent space shuttle strapped on as a jetpack and they took off for the bus stop.

Noticing that their bus was passing close to Melina's place, Anna debated checking in. Ever since Melina's unsettling wake-up call the other day, Anna had expected the other shoe to drop, and should it fit Antonio Nicolaides, its heel could very well come down on her. But, should the probe peter out inconclusively, would it bespeak his innocence, incompetence, or corruption? Anna needed to know.

She dialed.

"Oh hi, Anna," Melina said. "Funny you called because I was thinking of calling you. How are things?"

"That's what I wanted to ask you. About the investigation. Any news?"

"Nothing official, but two guys from Internal just spent two days here. They interviewed some officers but aren't done snooping. So far, so good."

"Hope all goes well," Anna replied as cheerily as she could. "What's the mood over there, then?"

"Improving, I'd say, but I still hear gripes around the coffee machine."

"Anything come up about the League or the wanted poster?"

"One of them asked me about the League. I described who we are and our mission. I didn't say anything about you, and nobody asked."

Sensing a cover-up in the making, Anna asked: "Have they asked why the boy wasn't tested for drugs? Could have changed the outcome, you know."

"Not that I know. Anyway, isn't it time to put that behind us? There are plenty of child abusers out there for us to worry about. Each week, there are several incidents across Greater Athens."

"So I understand. But now what? There's a big, bustling child welfare sector out there. What should the League do to make itself relevant?"

"Don't give up. Keep building your network. Post bulletins about missing children on the website. Our files are full of unsolved disappearances."

"So, what do you guys do when a missing child is reported?" Anna asked, wondering why so many remained unsolved.

"It depends on the situation. Unless we're in hot pursuit we'd normally alert media outlets to tell people to call if they see something. Some of the child welfare groups we inform spread the word via phone trees."

"How so?"

"They use it like a chain letter. A calls B, C, D, and E. Each of them has a shortlist of contacts they call, and so forth. It's remarkably efficient."

"Guess that could come handy in a pinch. Thanks." As much as Anna wished to end the call, she couldn't help but ask: "Just one more thing, Melina. Does Nicolaides resent the investigation?"

"Well, we all do, but no harm was done. I heard Inspector Nicolaides say that people don't understand how police work is done, and when they interfere in a case it usually doesn't end well."

Instead of asking "For whom," Anna replied: "I can see what he means. No professional likes to be second-guessed," having done just that.

Now she was being told to move on and mind her own business. But what made it not her business? Kidnappers who'd targeted her child were on the loose, along with a begrudged policeman who knew how to find her.

Clearly, none of that would change unless something was done. With "phone tree" ringing in her ears, she vowed to make this not just *her* business. Time for a call to arms.

#

Nicolaides was flying high and Melina was his flight attendant, Anna groused as she calmed herself with chamomile tea in her kitchen. No matter what came of the internal investigation, she would still be facing a corrupt cop whose comrades would surely close ranks behind him. Keenly aware that her watchbird could shriek at any time, she poured more tea and dialed Nikki's search-and-rescue dog, Peter Mavridis.

"It sounds like what you're up to may be of dubious legality," he said after listening to her brief. Despite his doubts, his voice had an accommodating tone, perhaps due to a salutary briefing from Nikki. "It's very clever and possibly could net valuable evidence, but whether your photos would be admissible in court is something our lawyers would have to look into."

"I hadn't thought of that angle. But suppose we see something and tell you. Your team could spring into action to catch them in the act. Would it matter where the tip came from?"

"I suppose not. But we aren't superheroes who can bound over tall buildings. It takes time to coordinate an operation and ramp it up. Police and EMTs can respond faster than we can. Why not alert them too? Just dial 112. That's what we would likely do if someone urgently called our hotline."

"I see," Anna said as she debated telling Peter about the fly in that ointment. Nicolaides would surely be among the first responders to a crime in progress in Nikaia and his response might be to phone ahead to tell the guys to scram with whatever unfortunate child might be in their care. But then, she realized, they would be on the lam with everyone after them, likely leaving damning evidence at the scene. Still, even if they were caught, Nicolaides would be off the hook and never brought to justice.

She was still thinking it over when Peter asked if she was still on the line. "I would still call you first," she said. "You guys know what to do and I would hope you would set your wheels in motion. Once you've mobilized I'll put in a 112 call."

"So why not do that first?"

Tired of begging the question, Anna came clean. "Well, as I told Nikki, at least one cop up there knows what these guys are up to and hasn't done anything to stop it. They seem to have a nice, cozy arrangement."

"That's a pretty strong accusation, Anna. Do you have evidence?"

"Yes, Peter, I do and expect to have more. Look: I foiled a kidnapping. The guy got let off when he should have gone to jail. The cops don't seem to care, especially this one. The kidnapper stalked my child and could strike again at any time. That's why I need backup."

"Yes, Nikki told me all about the trial. The outcome was a travesty but I have no doubt you saved the child from his fate." He paused.

She heard him take a deep breath and expel it. "All right; if something happens, call me. If it makes sense, I'll activate our team. But you must tell me everything you know about what's going down and be absolutely sure about it."

"Deal. You can call the authorities once you're at the scene. Promise you'll be there?"

"We always keep our promises to children. If you have credible evidence, we'll be there. But it better be the real deal or there will be hell to pay."

#

Ancient Greeks would have blamed the *Anemoi* deity *Notus* for the southerly wind piling up sea foam off Piraiki and gusting ashore, rattling the awnings of Fotini's balcony and disheveling her Sunday papers. The impertinent gusts drove her back inside to read in solitude. Normally on a Sunday afternoon such as this, Ilias would be squirreled away in his man-cave doing whatever Ilias did to optimize their investments, but today he had taken Sami to watch their football team play visitors from Croatia.

Her bleached Versace jeans settled into her Herman Miller lounge chair. She reached to the glass-topped end table for her half-empty box of cigarettes, but the ravel of butts and ashes in the ashtray suggested that she try again later. Eight years had passed since she'd quit the filthy habit, but the trauma of Sami's brush with white slavery and the anticlimactic trial had upended her resolve. She rationalized by telling herself nicotine might help her lose weight, not that her body curved to excess. Ilias smoked too, a pipe. He had always smoked a pipe and had a rack of crusty bowls to prove it. Fotini pictured him born with a pipe clenched in his tiny gums and his baby teeth coming in all yellow.

She flipped through the lifestyle pages, tossed them aside, and was settling in with the Sunday magazine when her phone tingled, obliging her to rise and traipse to the breakfast counter to seize her handbag. Anna was calling. Fotini hoped it wasn't urgent. Not on Sunday.

First came obligatory inquiries into the wellbeing of sons, Anna saying pretty good, he's starting to read, Fotini replying so-so, look at the pressures on third-graders these days before asking what was up. Her tidings were mixed, Anna conceded. Her good news was that the internal investigation of the Nikaia police station had concluded. The bad news was that no fault seemed to have been found.

"I'm not surprised," Fotini said. "You expected exposure or closure?"

"Exposure, yes. Thanks to Ilias' intervention you may have joined me on Nicolaides's shit list. Maybe he should know that."

Fotini glanced down the carpeted hallway to Ilias's den. "I would let you tell him yourself, but he's out with Sami."

"Then why don't you suggest to him that he's stirred the soup enough."

"I will tell him, Anna, but have no control over what he'll do."

With an "Oh, well," Anna went on to new business.

"When I was talking to Mimi today, I asked her what the League could do if we learned of a child in trouble. She suggested setting up a phone tree to alert our supporters. Is that something you know about?"

Fotini said she'd heard of them, though hadn't partaken. It might be worthwhile, but a prime mover was needed and was Anna volunteering?

"Guess it's gotta be me. I can recruit five or six people and tell them to do the same. Anyone hearing bad news should bounce it to me and I'll pass on down the chain, hoping nothing gets garbled."

"Which can easily happen. So why not send a text and ask them to forward it?"

"Maybe, but kinda feels less urgent than a phone call."

"That might go to voicemail. Anyway, would you limit it to our members?"

"Certainly not. We'll need all the help we can get."

"But suppose the news came through TV or radio," Fotini asked. "Should we still make calls?"

"Sure, if it's local. They might've seen something and it'll condition them to be watchful. So, do you know people you could convince to sign up for this?"

A few, Fotini guessed. She asked Anna to message their forum explaining how it's supposed to work.

"Guess I should. Thanks a bunch and don't break the chain. Gotta go now. Enjoy your day."

Fotini laid down her phone and reached for her Parliaments, avoiding eye contact with her ashtray. She lit up, took a drag, and reclined, recalling being in Nikaia after the trial, watching Anna scurry around, furiously snapping pictures, all fired up. And here she is, weeks later, still crusading. What's driving her? What crazy plan is she hatching?

Anna herself was wondering something like that.

Chapter Nineteen

OVER THE NEXT HOUR Anna busied herself trying to graft branches onto what she told prospects was a "tree of life," starting with her momrades. As she couldn't say what she expected from them, it took some cajoling, but four tentatively assented and were told to await instructions that she decided to put off writing in favor of some playtime. The mild weather induced her to suggest a Sunday bike ride to reward Ramadi for patiently amusing himself during her telethon. She bagged snacks, filled water bottles, and told him they would cycle to the sprawling Andreas Papandreou Park, a twenty-minute journey at Ramadi's average velocity, to explore its many avenues and activities.

Ramadi enjoyed touring the grid of pathways demarcating the park's four hectares into blocks, each featuring something different to do—play spaces for kids and pets, a café or two, an arching tensile structure used as a bandstand, lily ponds traversed by footbridges, a giant sundial to circumnavigate to beat the clock, and other arresting amenities.

But it was pigeons that particularly delighted him. Approaching some aimlessly pecking at compacted soil around a park bench, he veered into their midst and attempted to snatch one without success. For better or worse, Anna lamented, pigeons seemed to be his primary connection to the world of nature.

They had looped through most of the pathways and were heading to the main playground when Ramadi skidded up to a huge chessboard, each of its 64 squares a meter across arrayed with oversized chess pieces. Two older men leisurely tugged their remaining pieces around in a friendly battle to the death. Ignoring their slow-motion duel, Ramadi pointed to a nearby tall privet hedge. It had an opening, behind which another hedge could be seen.

"Mutti, what's in there?"

"It's called a labyrinth. Inside is a maze of narrow paths you can get lost in and have to find your way out."

"Lybarin," he said, as in library. "Can we go in?"

"Lab-ee-rinth," she said. "They say inside it are ghosts of explorers who never made it out." She told him about the one Daedalus constructed to imprison a monster called the Minotaur, who ate people who wandered in.

Hip to the myth from his Greek lessons, Ramadi surprised her. "And then Feesis went in and killed it!"

"Yes, *Thee-see-us* did. Very good, Ramadi! So, think you're brave enough to explore it?"

"If you come too," he said, dubiously regarding the hedgerows.

"Tell you what. I'll go in first and be the monster. You be Theseus. Try to find me and if you can tag me, you killed the Minotaur. But ... if I tag you, you'll be my supper."

They laid down their bikes at the entrance. "Count to twenty, Ramadi—I mean Theseus—and then come get me." She slipped into the opening as he recited his numbers. When he stalled at twelve, he scampered in after her.

As the boy warily blundered and backtracked, two men strolled up the footpath. They paused at the chessboard to watch the endgame. One, middle-aged and out-of-shape, was mustachioed with a bald pate that reflected the sun, wore a yellow sport shirt and dark grey trousers. The other, in blue jeans, a tank top, and a fisherman's hat, was taller and younger, clean-shaven, and lacked his companion's paunch.

The former lit a cigarette and took a drag as his companion said: "Been a while. So where's the money you owe me?"

"As you well know, it's been a tough month, but I expect we're about to get busier. Can you wait a week or two?"

"How's that gonna help?"

"Sources tell me police plan to raid squats in Exarcheia. That'll put a lot of talent on the street. All the confusion will make it easy."

"There's plenty of talent out there now. I got mouths to feed. We got a deal, Vassilios, and you got trouble if it breaks."

The heavy-set man brought his cigarette to his lips, drew on it, and tipped it up, middle-finger style. "Stop breaking my ..." he exhaled, just as Ramadi burst from a gap in the maze beyond the chessboard, shrieking "Free!" before Anna emerged to clamp on his arm. "Gotcha, Theseus!"

Letting his sentence hang, he turned his attention toward the labyrinth.

Beyond earshot, the boy said: "Doesn't count! It was outside! Let's do it again!"

"Okay, one more time," Anna said. "Go hide. I'll count to twenty and then come to devour you."

Screaming "No you won't!" Ramadi streaked into the maze. Anna turned her back and counted, "One, two, three, four, five, six, seven … Omigod! That's Laskaris and Nicolaides over there!"

Hoping they hadn't noticed her, Anna bolted into the maze after Ramadi.

Fifteen meters away, Laskaris stubbed out his cigarette and nudged Nicolaides. "You see what I saw? Isn't that the Swiss broad who fingered Theo? I'd love to give her some painful memories," he said, cracking his knuckles.

"Yeah, so would I," the cop said. "But not in a public place."

"No one's gonna see in there."

"Forget about it. Leave them alone for chrissakes or our deal's off. Come on, let's get out of here."

Inside the labyrinth, Anna managed to corner Ramadi and grabbed his arm. "Let's keep still in case the monsters I saw decide to come in."

"You saw monsters?" a wide-eyed Ramadi said.

"Not actual monsters. Just men I want us to stay away from. Now keep quiet."

After counting to a hundred, firmly gripping his wrist, Anna conducted Ramadi out the back way and then around it toward the front side to peer toward the chessboard.

The men seemed to have moved on.

"Remember?" Anna said, trying to explain to the baffled boy. "One of those monsters yelled at you at the No Name Café. There are bad men out there. You have to be careful."

"And that's why kids shouldn't talk to strangers," Ramadi said, having been told that more times than he could remember.

They righted their bikes and pedaled back down the footpath. Spying the men heading toward the exit, she told Ramadi to take a breather. Next to them, a shiny obelisk towered over a concrete circle ten meters across, a Brobdingnagian sundial. They watched two youngsters merrily chasing around the pylon, compressing the hours, causing her to wonder whether someone might decide to chase her.

They pedaled on to the portal. Anna dismounted and walked her bike through the gate to cautiously peer into the parking area. The men weren't in sight, but exiting the lot was a silver Mercedes-Benz wagon she figured she'd seen before.

Her hands tightened on her handle grips as the encounter replayed in her mind. Even though her feet were solidly planted, she felt wobbly.

"How about we drop in on Onkle Andreas?" she said.

He was gazing longingly at a concession stand. "Can I have ice cream, Mutti?"

"Sure, kiddo. But let's go to a store and get enough for all of us. He likes it too."

By the time they were walking their bikes across busy Salominos Boulevard, her trepidation was giving way to antipathy that renewed her resolve. *Okay Inspector Antonio, let's see what you do the next time these guys snatch a kid.*

#

With Ramadi's sincere approval, Anna scored a tub of chocolate gelato to celebrate their safe passage before pedaling up to the Radically Chic Salon. With a key Andreas had kindly given her, she unlatched the rear door and frisked up the back stairs to vigorously rap upon his kitchen door. When no response came forth, she shouted: "We know you're in there! Open the door!"

Shortly the latch turned. An eye peeked out from behind a security chain.

"Salut, Andreas," she said brightly. "Let us in. We've come to inspect your pillows."

The eyebrow she could see arched. "Beg pardon?"

"Your bed pillows," she said, suppressing a giggle. "We've come to check them for tags. If you've torn them off you could be in big trouble."

"Um, I didn't know that," he said through the crack. "Maybe some other time?"

"Oh come on. Let us in. We have delicious gelato and disgusting news to share."

"I suppose so," Andreas said, unchaining the door and ushering them into his cheery jungle of a kitchen. In his crimson bathrobe he seemed not particularly cheery.

Anna flourished her treat, ceremoniously revealing the gelato and handing out spoons. The three of them sat silently communally spooning gelato with Anna unsuccessfully willing the Austrian's eyes to meet hers.

"Ramadi and I biked over to Papandreou Park today," Anna said, breaking the awkward silence, "and guess who was there?"

When Andreas confessed he couldn't, she told of their close encounter with monsters that could have gone much worse.

"Together again. Interesting," Andreas said without further comment. Apologizing for his ragged appearance, he said he'd been napping when they barged in. Anna asked him if he was feeling all right, as he looked a little peaked. Just tired, he told them. For the first time in many moons, he disclosed, he'd gone carousing at a bar with some friends until the cock crowed.

"Such are the wages of sin," he said, and languidly arose. "If you don't mind, I feel chilled and think I should go back to bed. Sorry, but I'm not good company just now."

Anna was about to ask if there was anything she could do when she noticed a fairly large pair of sneakers lying in the corner she didn't recall seeing before. It seemed that Andreas had company. Possibly in bed.

"Sure, I understand," she said, wiping Ramadi's mouth. "Had enough ice cream, love?"

"Can we take it home?" he asked, licking his fingers.

"Go ahead, take it," Andreas said. "Maybe that's what made me feel cold."

"Sure," Anna said. "Pamper yourself with some nice hot tea and take it easy." She capped the container, collected their backpacks, and pecked a cheek. "Hope you feel better soon."

After they decamped, Andreas took her advice and put a kettle up to boil. He steeped a pot of green tea in his cat-shaped teapot, placed it on a tray with a pair of mugs, and carried it through his parlor with its thrift-store furnishings and a toy box shoved into a corner and into his bedroom.

"Sorry about that, Stephan. My friend and her kid stopped by with some ice cream. I had to entertain them."

Stephen blew a smoke ring, snubbed out his cigarette, and sat up effortlessly. Besides a well-sculpted physique, he had Kosta's chiseled good looks, though not his tinted hair or flamboyance. Andreas put down the tea tray.

"Where's *my* treat?" Stephan said, noting an absence of ice cream.

"Gone, I'm afraid. But I made tea for us," Andreas said, offering a mug across the disheveled comforter. He placed his on a nightstand, shook off his bathrobe, and slid under the covers. Blowing across his tea, he tried to remember the last time he'd connected with a stranger at a bar. Stephan was a handsome find, virile and unattached, just what he had wanted, so why was he feeling out of sorts?

#

Anna also fixed a pot of tea upon arriving home and shared it with Ramadi, who had taken a liking to the beverage as a vehicle for honey. While he slurped, she sat, blowing across her mug thinking of Andreas and how he'd likely spent the past evening, reflecting on which of them was more confused about the other. Staring out her window at lengthening shadows on the brick façade across the alley, she thought: *If this is how it's going to be, is it really what I want?*

You want my advice? Enjoy the good times and don't ask for more.

Just so you know, gizzard-brain, I'm done with not asking for more. I've been alone for five non-fucking years. I want somebody to want me, even if he's androgynous.

That sounds desperate, sis. You need to get out more.

Right. As if I can pick up a guy who will love Ramadi as much as he'll love me.

That's what you have now. So cherish him. Accept him. Don't try to force it. Let it happen.

Forcing herself away from her reverie, she decided that, while there was nothing she could do about Andreas, there might be something she could do about Vassilios Laskaris.

Only Facebook knew anything about him; that was just an errant snapshot, but perhaps he'd been featured in her neglected photo stream.

She retrieved her laptop from the bedroom to catch up. She had a lot to look at. Even if only one picture came through every fifteen minutes, that would amount to almost a hundred a day. There could be many more, simply due to random people and vehicles coursing through her bird's-eye view. She refreshed her tea, opened the largest folder, sorted the images by date, and began by inspecting the largest batch.

In that set were twenty shots, mostly taken up by workmen who'd parked their van at the right edge of the scene to unload kitchen appliances destined for a building she couldn't see. The next largest batch featured several teenagers on skateboards and a car ghosting by.

It was the third set that caused her to forget to breathe as she sat transfixed. In dim early morning light, a white cargo van had pulled up and its driver, a darkly clothed man in a black watch cap, opened its back doors. Then he was standing at the rear door of the house. In the next frame he was gone. Two frames later he was backing out, hunched over. Then came Servopoulos, holding the other end of a rolled-up carpet that drooped between them. The next shot captured them sliding the carpet into the van and then standing aside after closing the doors. Two frames later the van is gone and Servopoulos returns to the house.

That was it. There was no clear shot of the driver's face, but she was sure from his stature it wasn't Laskaris. So, who was he?

"Omigod," she said and zoomed into the photo of the men with the carpet arcing down between them. It was a lightweight, utilitarian cotton rug bulging from something rolled up inside it.

She assumed it contained a human, and not a large one judging on how little it sagged, hopefully alive. Where that small person had come from and how long might he or she have been sequestered? How had the victim come in without her camera capturing it? She checked the date: 6:30 AM, two days ago. A perusal of older images revealed no one entering the house. Perhaps the victim had been smuggled in through the front door or had been held for a while. Whatever, that unlucky young person could by now have been whisked far away, perhaps never to see their family again.

Anna exhaled. At last, she had evidence of suspicious activity involving Servopoulos and a furtive driver of a white van, but not Laskaris. Laskaris, who earlier this day was palling around with that sleazy detective with who knows what passing between them. Thankfully they had left them alone, but the encounter had spooked her and maybe Ramadi, who didn't need any more monsters in his nightmares or his days.

Water she'd been boiling in her teakettle hissed and sputtered, almost gone. She refilled it, wondering if her evidence of an apparent crime was also destined to evaporate. Those pictures proved nothing. The images her watchbird had captured could, as at the trial, be explained away. Clearly, it would take better evidence to convict the bastards. They needed to be caught in the act, not after the fact.

Nor would it help to sound an alarm. Why alert her team about an event two days ago involving a victim who was only implied? And were she to post her shots on Altogether, Melina might pass them up the food chain to blow her cover. No point, she dejectedly concluded, in setting those gears in motion.

But something bad must have gone down and she needed to say something to somebody. Not the league, and certainly not Fotini, only to have her hubby spread news of her findings downtown. Perhaps Peter or Nikki, who already knew she was watching a house somewhere. That would show them she had evidence. She would send Peter her pictures, she decided, but not digitally, which would identify her watchbird's location.

She printed out the four most damning frames, looked up the address for Children's Advocacy Center's outpost in Piraeus, and tucked them into an envelope without a return address along with a note.

Dear Peter, she wrote. *These photos were taken two days ago by a surveillance camera. I believe the two men are removing a young abductee inside that rolled-up carpet. The man in back is Servopoulos. The driver and where he took that person is unknown to me. If anything more develops I will let you know, but please keep this confidential for now. Anna*

She sealed the envelope and made ready for bed brimming with newfound resolution. In the morning she would post her package to Peter after dropping off Ramadi and let Ottovio know his invention had borne strange fruit. But what then? What if it captured a drop-off in the middle of the night? How long would it take to get to the scene before the child got whisked away? And no matter how many allies responded, it was she who would make the call and bear the consequences.

So be it. She disrobed and squirmed under her comforter, wishing Mahmoud lay beside her.

~

After watching her work, I think I am starting to understand. All those photos of the same place can only come from a surveillance camera. Where it is and how she got them is a mystery. She lingered over some that showed men hauling a carpet to a truck. The one who stayed behind looks like the man I saw sitting in the taverna who disturbed me. Whatever she is up to, I hope she is not in danger.

Chapter Twenty

FINDING HER PARAMOUR CONSORTING with some hunk following a distressing encounter with a child trafficker consorting with a cop served to fend off sleep. Anna slid from bed, stole to the kitchen, returned with some chamomile tea and flicked on her book light. She rummaged in her nightstand for her journals, notebooks penned in German script going back to when she was sweating it out in Africa.

The one she sought encompassed the year after she'd settled in Piraeus. Ten entries, ranging from exigent to elegiac, telescoped the two months she had with Mahmoud. Hoping to recall how she felt for him then, wondering what would he have made her situation now, she leafed through it and started to read:

> 12 October: That handsome Iraqi man who boards with Andreas called tonight, lost at the wrong bus stop. I brought him home, we sat and talked about ourselves and I put him to bed. Perhaps next time, if there is one, I will take him to bed. He seems quite shy, but resolute, and doesn't say what he's up to with Andreas. Why do I want to know more? Why do I care? Maybe I'm a sucker for attractive, militant, wounded men. Watch out girl.

Her eyes lifted. *Well, I didn't watch out, did I? I wanted him to want me and I went all out. I got my wish when he and I sat with Andreas in the taverna, just after George got hauled off to jail. Andreas had vowed to rescue George's foundering operation and the man himself, and was well over his head. On top of that, he felt blindsided and betrayed when Mahmoud took my hand and told him we wished to marry. We didn't, really, and had never spoken of it. We simply wanted to be together as lovers and comrades, but Andreas was sure it would sow discord and doom their operation. I argued I would be an asset, not a liability. I can forgive myself for my cheek because, as much as any of those guys, I made it work. Wasn't*

Mahmoud's blowgun and its payload my idea? And didn't what we did bend history at least a little bit?

She gazed back down and turned the page.

15 November: M made a new shooter that seems more accurate. Today I almost distilled pure ricin. Something didn't work, so will try again tomorrow. Sex—not that I can complain—and death, abiding in uneasy harmony.

Her eyes lifted to gaze at the daybed where the fruit of their passion slept, shrouded in darkness. Waiting for her eyes to adjust, the ending of the prayer Mahmoud recited every morning came to her:

I ask You for the best the day has to offer, victory, support, light, blessings and guidance; and I seek refuge in You from the evil in it, and the evil to come after it.

And that was how he lived. Had I not sought refuge in Mahmoud from the evil coming after me?

21 November: M said he would—gladly, even—target the nationalist creep who's been threatening to slit my throat. It gave me goosebumps to think he would put his life on the line for me. I'm not sure if I deserve that, but he says I need protection and he needs target practice.

She laid down the journal to sip tepid tea. *To cancel that threat, Mahmoud became a murderer, with me as his accessory. After that, there was no turning back, especially when George decided to head the operation after Andreas sprung him from detention. None of us felt ready, certainly not me, but a week later I was sneaking into Turkey with George and Mahmoud, not for refuge, but to protect it from the evil we came after ...*

1 December: Mission as ready to launch as it will ever be. Working with A to gather relief supplies to take to Chios for refugees, and then bribe a smuggler to ferry us over. Then it will be on to Bursa and destiny. M better shoot straight and get lucky. This really will be do or die.

Her journal slipped to the comforter. She cupped her eyes, contemplating the evil she could have saved him from. When she lifted her palms, phosphenes swarmed on the darkened ceiling like shooting stars that seemed to limn his countenance. She blinked the vision away and read the last entry.

7 Dec: M & I safe at Safiye's flat after the chaotic event. She was very brave. Guess we all were, doing our parts. We'll stay here until things quiet down but what's our exit plan?

Scheisse! M stuck his finger on the dart I left in my handbag. Why didn't I get rid of it? I flushed and sucked the wound and bound it with alcohol. That was late afternoon. He seems okay. Sleeping now. Rubbing my thumbs for luck.

Monday: M woke up sick. Definitely the ricin. Damn me. Damn me. Damn me.

Tuesday: M goes up and down as does his temp and we with it. Fixed him a healing tea Safiye was told about. M took a call from Kaan then watched TV. Now he's praying. Hope someone's listening. Rubbing thumbs again.

The rest of the notebook was blank. She closed it, placed it on the nightstand, and dabbed her eyes with her comforter. *Goddam George made me carry that goddam dart. Next morning, when he didn't wake up, I just lost it. I staggered through the next week like a zombie as Safiye, bless her, arranged the burial.*

She gazed at the daybed and blew a kiss to Ramadi. Not that she ever did or believed she would be heard, she prayed for him to be delivered from evil and herself from her trespasses, and was granted the absolution of sleep.

I remember her writing in that little black book when I lived here. "When I lived," indeed. The mullahs never said almutahar would be an eternity of loneliness with voices droning from afar, like a big party next door to which I am not invited. Now she pauses reading and looks up, right into whatever I see with. I can almost hear her thoughts. It made me smile with whatever I smile with and remember how happy and good for each other we were. I doubt she is so happy now. I know I am not.

All too suddenly Monday happened, and with it a flurry of morning matters to top off a troubled sleep. Heading back home on the bus after depositing Ramadi at Cassie's, remembering she had a date at the café, she jumped off and doubled back. Inside she found her friends sitting at the big round table in back with beverages, Andreas absorbed in his phone and the hacker in his laptop.

She asked server Phaeton for a tall mocha latte and slumped into a chair, eying Andreas. "Hope you feel better. Sorry to intrude yesterday," she said, leaving him to mutely nod and Ottovio to wonder what she meant. She went on to pitch her phone tree, and wouldn't they like to sign on as first responders?

Depositing his mug of tea to stroke his chin, Andreas offered a maybe. "While some of my old leftist friends might resonate with your cause, I really can't say how obliging any of them might be. Same for the salon's clients. From my time as an organizer, I well know how much wheedling it takes to build solidarity. I would need to raise their consciousness about the subject, and before that, mine. All I can say is that I'll give it a try."

Willing as he was to spread urgent word, Andreas remained dubious. He'd just told Ottovio that he considered Anna's war on child trafficking a bit chimeric. Not that he'd ever told her that. What he said now was that, as impressed as he was with her energetic campaign, he felt her strategy was too reactive. In his view, what she and her cohorts also needed to do was to amass examples of how law enforcement has failed to protect children, and press political leaders to confront this societal climate crisis. Document, expose, motivate, mobilize, confront, disrupt were his watchwords, stressing disrupt.

But before he could expound further, her phone was in his face presenting hair-raising scenes of adult delinquency in Nikaia.

"My goodness," he said. "Have you reported this?"

"I sent them to the guy who runs search and rescue operations for Hellenic Children's Advocacy Center. By post. Maybe he can connect it with a missing kid and be on the lookout."

"Why by post? Isn't it more urgent than that?"

"It's old news. I got behind on my viewing. It happened three days ago, and I don't want my photos getting passed around on the net."

"These are good shots," Ottovio said with grim satisfaction. "Even though you can't see the victim, this is first real evidence."

"Correction," Andreas said. "Even though you can't see *there is* a victim. They could just as well be taking out the trash."

"Whatever," Ottovio replied. "Are you sure this NGO guy won't share with police?"

"We have an arrangement," Anna said. "He agreed to hold off until I can catch them bringing somebody into the house. Anyway, he doesn't know where it is."

"Did you tell him about the corrupt cop?"

"Nicolaides? Not by name. Just that there's a policeman who may be complicit. And yesterday proved it."

"What happened yesterday?" Andreas asked before remembering, "Oh yes, the cop and the crook in the park. At least they didn't give you grief."

"True, but I sensed they wanted to, or at least Laskaris did."

"Explain, please," Ottovio said.

Anna reiterated her tale of fear and loathing among the hedgerows. "Pretty much proves that Nicolaides is either a sicko like them or has been bought and paid for."

"Or both," Ottovio said. "So what about that van? Maybe we can ID it. Let's see those photos again."

She panned and zoomed through photos of the carpetbaggers.

"In the last one you can almost make out the license plate," Ottovio said.

He flipped open his computer and told her to pair phone with Bluetooth, and within a minute his machine had ingested the photo sequence.

He opened an image-processing tool. "This app can make dark images bright and crisp up fuzzy ones. So let's see."

Unfortunately, the camera hadn't captured any lettering on the van. Nor was there a clear shot of its driver's face, but he looked shorter than Servopoulos, and under his watch cap eyeglasses glinted.

Ottovio noted that the last shot, grainy and oblique, caught the vehicle creeping away with part of its license plate showing. He zoomed in. The first letter was obscured in shadow. The second one seemed to be K, and the third the number 8 or a capital B. The remaining ones seemed to be digits.

"Looks like 2168 or maybe 2163," Anna said. "But maybe that one is the letter I and that two might be a seven. Hard to say."

"Let me tweak," Ottovio said, and fiddled to improve the image's sharpness. "Looks like it's EKB-2163, possibly EKB-2168."

"You're sure about those letters?" Andreas asked. "Especially that first one?"

"The plate is yellow. Plates for commercial vehicles are yellow and all begin with EK. The following token must be B, not 8, because first three symbols on plates are always letters. The last four tokens are always numeric, so the tag either ends with 2163 or 2168. Q.E.D."

Anna asked Ottovio—who'd never owned a car—how he knew so much about vehicle registration.

"One of my old projects involved tracing contraband shipments."

"Well," Anna said, "glad you're experienced, because that's what we're doing. So now, can you crack into the vehicle registration system to find the owner?"

Shaking his head, he informed them that only police, prosecutors, security agencies, and insurers are privileged to check vehicle records, and he wasn't about to hack the Transport Ministry's system for an arduous one-off.

Pouting unconvincingly, for she was already in his debt, she jotted down the two sequences on a paper napkin, scribbled *Melina* below them, and circled the name. It didn't take long for her to come up with a story for the officer.

Chapter Twenty-One

THAT NIGHT, RAMADI DREAMS. He is playing on a climbing gym in the park and just as he reaches the top a dark hole opens in the sky above him and sucks him in. He finds himself lying in a bed with three creatures with fishy heads peering down at him with unblinking eyes. The bed is in an open box. They stare at him and then move out of sight. The top of the box closes over him and all goes black. He wakes up, palpitating, confused, then relieved that he is not in a box. He has never seen a coffin, but for years the sight of one will make him uneasy.

He has climbed into Anna's bed, jostling her awake, recounting his terror. She hugs and soothes him, suppressing tears, remembering that he dreamt of being carried off by a bird of prey. Sleep blesses the boy in her arms but not her. Her eyes cloud. *It's as if he senses what I'm going through,* she thinks. *It needs to end, one way or another.*

By morning, Ramadi had either forgotten or repressed his dark dream. They consumed scrambled eggs, toast and jam, and when he ran off to amuse himself, she called after him to read his books before opening her laptop and turning to her bulging inbox. For the next ten minutes she unzipped files into new folders, each holding at least a dozen photos, tagged with red dots for persons of interest, green otherwise. Two branches now showed red.

Wondering when her hard drive is going to top off, she inspected images but nothing she revealed more than the odd vehicle, dog walker, or stray reflection. By now, she knows the scene better than her own face, down to missing cobblestones and cracks in whitewashed walls.

Staring at that back door, her mind's eye replayed the carpet-bagging sequence. Was the captive headed to a staging point on an underground railway to servitude? Or was ransom involved? If not, the child's fate could be decided at auction, she shuddered to think, not on a wooden platform in some dusty square, but over the Web.

Overanxious to get Peter's reaction to the photos she's posted the other day, she placed a call. He answered, seemingly in a good mood.

"I sent you surveillance photos of a possible abduction," she said. "Did you get them?"

"Not yet. An abduction?"

"It seems so. Three days ago, but I only saw the pictures yesterday." She described capturing two men making off with a carpet cocooning what seems to be a small body from the back door of a cottage, and asked if he could connect it to any recent abductions.

"Where did this take place?"

"In Nikaia. Have you heard of any recent abductions around there?"

Not specifically, but hold on while I check."

A minute later he told her that over the past month, they had seven reports for all of Athens. None in Nikaia, but many missing children go unreported because parents are afraid to talk to authorities. Also, the alleged victim easily could have lived elsewhere.

Anna rubbed her forehead, and then asked, "So, where might they have taken that victim? What sorts of people do this and why?"

"The child trafficking racket spans the planet," Peter said. "It's up there with drug and arms smuggling." He went on to inform her that kidnappers tend to specialize, choosing victims based on the age, sex, immigration status, and sometimes abilities and attractiveness, opportunistically, depending on what they think customers want.

"They move their pawns around within a country, export them abroad, wholesale them to smugglers, or retail them to their new masters, sometimes called end users. Those two and under tend to go to shady adoption agencies."

"Makes me wonder what they would have done with the Sami," Anna said.

"The boy you saved? There's no telling. If they thought his family had money, they might have demanded ransom. But that's risky, so he might have been sold to work in industry, agriculture, or the sex trade, including child pornography. Sorry, but I need to go. I'll look at your photos, but I still think you should work with the police."

Anna thanked him and let him go. She reflected that it was almost as if what she'd spied had never happened. The chief of the nation's largest child rescue team had told her she should rely on the Hellenic Police she had long mistrusted. Nothing could be done for that bundle in the van, who could be earmarked for peonage at a factory, a farm, a fishing boat, a brothel, or a household wherever. She wondered how much money would change hands along the way, transacted with cash, money orders, and cryptocurrency.

She opened her computer to grimly absorb unreliable statistics of the trade she'd bookmarked. Despite their best efforts, law enforcement agencies and groups like Peter's managed to liberate fewer than ten thousand trafficking victims a year, probably less than one percent. And so much of that hard work was merely remedial, she dejectedly realized; so few of the shadowy procurers, middlemen, pornographers, and auctioneers seemed to get put out of business, unless by their rivals, and few "end users" suffered any consequences.

How might the Nikaia operation fit into to this ghoulish business? As Ottovio would say, no data. Well, on second thought, maybe a little, like that Facebook photo he'd sent the other day of Laskaris and Servopoulos dining with some fellow downtown. What was his name? She found the message in her inbox. The man with receding hair and glasses was Leander Eugenides, billing himself as a shipping manager at Meteor Import-Export Ltd. Could he be their middleman? His job title certainly seemed apt. The firm's office was downtown on Athinaidos Street, but a shipping company must have a warehouse nearby, one that might now and then handle human cargo.

Upon reviewing the abduction scene, she decided there was a resemblance between Eugenides and the driver of that van. Maybe she should pass that on to Peter Mavridis.

Not yet. He isn't going to play detective for me and might hand it over to the police. After all this work she actually had some evidence. Time to see what's up with Leander Eugenides and Meteor Import-Export.

#

Thanks to her interventions and those of Fotini's husband, Anna knew she wasn't on Melina's top ten list of citizen-activists, but she might as well try. Melina greeted her in her warm, guarded fashion to ask how are you, how's Ramadi, what's up. Anna reciprocated, inquiring after her kids, saying we should get them together again—maybe outdoors this time. Avoiding mentioning the internal investigation, Anna went straight to business.

"Ramadi and I were nearly run over on Dimokritias Boulevard yesterday. A van came careening around the corner without stopping just as we were starting to cross. I had to yank him out of the way and we both fell down."

"That sounds terrible. Were either of you injured?"

"Just a scrape on the elbow for me. Ramadi wasn't hurt but it really scared him."

"You can file an accident report, but it won't go anywhere if you can't identify the truck."

"It was a white delivery van with no windows. A Mercedes."

"So we're down to maybe 10,000 vehicles now. Anything else?"

"Well, it had to slow down halfway up the block and I could sort of read its license plate before it moved on."

"And you have it?"

"Think so. Two possible versions. Can you look up the owner so I can yell at him? We could have been killed."

"Some corporation might own it, not the person driving it."

"I know, I know, but I need to put them on notice. Can you dig up that info for me?"

"It's possible, but I shouldn't. We aren't supposed to release vehicle registration data."

"Please, Melina. You would do this if I was calling from an insurance company. I'm not about to go wring someone's neck. I just want them to know how reckless that driver was."

Desk Sergeant Cristopoulos took Anna's plea under advisement. "Give me the number you think you saw and I'll see what I can do. As I said, you can file a report, and I recommend that you do."

Saying she would think about doing that, Anna read off the numbers scrawled on her napkin, thanked Melina, and said she hoped to hear from her.

Anna clicked off wondering what she would do if the van turned out to belong to a leasing agency. But if Eugenides or his company owned it, that would prove his complicity. But then what?

#

She sat with tea in the kitchen that evening intending to update the League's website with human trafficking stories and a blurb about the Children's Advocacy Center. The site needed refreshing and she needed a billable hour or two to stay in Prótos' good graces. Irene was nudging her to turn in a time sheet that Anna didn't want to be entirely fabricated.

Absorbing warmth from her mug, she stared dumbly at her screen, still preoccupied with the cargo van, before forcing herself to search the Net using keywords that made her shiver in disgust. Twenty minutes later she had bookmarked eight articles reporting progress and setbacks in the fight against child abuse, neglect, and abductions across Europe. She picked three to feature on the home page, all in the minus column. To inspire the faithful, she reblogged a hopeful account of several Balkan émigrés recently arrested in Belgium after snatching youngsters in Paris for delivery to unknown customers. A tip had led French police to place a GPS device on their lorry and track it all the way to a safe house in Brugge, where Interpol agents descended to arrest them and rescue their captives.

How clever it was to track the traffickers that way. Wondering if only police were able to do that sort of thing, she put her project aside to check out GPS tracking devices. To her amazement, she found little black boxes for sale all over the Web to anyone who could afford to pay a hundred euros or more plus another ten to twenty a month to subscribe to the data feed. The ads showed maps on cellphones tracking a vehicle's location, updated every fifteen seconds or so, just like her spy camera. Now if only she could home in on that van.

It seemed time for another meeting with the men in her life, this time an expedition downtown with lunch on her.

Chapter Twenty-Two

When Anna told him she wanted them to check out Meteor Import-Export, Ottovio was not averse. He said he would come equipped, whatever that meant, and would gladly be her lunch guest at Monk's Tavern, where the Facebook photo of Laskaris, Servopoulos, and Eugenides had been shot, just a few blocks from the firm's alleged headquarters. No reservations necessary, he said. She also rang up Andreas, who expressed reservations about the utility of the expedition that Anna cancelled by saying food was on her.

Just after noon the trio emerged from the Monastiraki Square Metro station and strolled to Taverna Kalógeros, occupying the entire ground floor of a pediment-laden brownstone building that generously hosted different restaurants on its second and third floors. They entered the dining hall through glass doors sheltered by a portico scattered with unoccupied tables. Ottovio surveyed the room, starkly appointed with boxy white tables and chairs with an Ikea esthetic, and led them to a table up front.

The hacker plopped down his black shoulder bag and scraped in his chair to briefly scan and collapse the bill of fare, predictably ordering lamb souvlaki. Andreas dithered through the menu only to order his staple, a falafel gyro. Economizing, Anna settled on a chicken Caesar salad plus pita wedges and tzatziki for the table.

Ottovio displayed the three Facebook friends on his mobile and pointed to a table.

"See? That's where they sat."

"You say that almost as if you had expected them to be here," Andreas said.

"You never know. People pattern their lives more than they realize."

"People like me," Anna said. "People with kids, responsibilities, and obsessions. Anyway, here's what I want to do if we find that white van: put a tracker on it."

"Another of your dizzy ideas," Andreas said with a flip of his braided ponytail. "Maybe you should track where my gyro is"—just as the waiter materialized to present it. "And is it legal to track a vehicle you don't own?"

"Probably not, but so what," Anna said. "Is it legal to kidnap children in a vehicle whether you own it or not?"

"Cell phone might do the trick," Ottovio said, warming to the idea. "I could modify my code to return GPS readings instead of pictures, but making interactive maps of them is whole other thing."

"Don't need to," Anna said, displaying her newly-minted mastery of the subject. "Let's buy a tracker and let the vendor handle that. They all make maps."

"You find van; I'll find tracker," Ottovio said. "I use Bitcoin. Pay me later. Shouldn't be on your credit card."

Following an unproductive discussion over coffee of the value of illegally acquired intelligence, Anna absorbed the check and they took to the street. A ten-minute saunter brought them to a four-story granite commercial building on Athinaidos Street with a defunct café on one side and a parking lot on the other. They stepped up to peer through its dusty plate glass doorway. Next to it, a column of buttons on a corroded brass escutcheon. The one on the bottom was labelled Μετέωρο Εισαγωγή-Εξαγωγή.

"LinkedIn didn't lie," Ottovio said. "This is Eugenides' company."

"Or the one he claimed to be with," Andreas said. "Do you want to take his word for it?"

"For now. Assume office is on ground floor."

Face pressed to glass, Anna peered into the gloom of the lobby. "There's a door straight ahead and one to the left that's probably a stairway. They're both closed. Anyway, I'm more interested in seeing if there's a rear entrance."

Presumably in the name of a greater Greater Athens, the adjacent building had been demolished to make way for an asphalt parking lot that was half-full. Motioning to her companions to follow, she walked along the side of the building and past a shanty with an attendant dozing in a swivel chair to the back corner, where a solid steel fire door forbade entry. Right next to it, an orange road cone staked out a parking space.

Ottovio inspected the door. With a sly grin, boasting "I can pick lock," he extracted a leather case from his shoulder bag. From it he retrieved a pointy object looking like a cross between a stapler and a handgun. Lock-picking and safecracking, he explained, had been his first stop on the road to geekdom. This peculiar item was a handy tool of the locksmithing trade called a snap gun.

"Opens tumbler locks like this one without key," he said, fondling it, "but takes good technique."

"Breaking and entering might be premature," Anna said after noticing a man in a t-shirt and a backwards baseball cap standing by the attendant's hut eyeballing them. "Someone's watching."

"Okay," Ottovio said, holstering his instrument. "Tool is kind of noisy."

The attendant ambled over to interrogate them. "You have car here?"

"No car," Anna said, pointing over her shoulder. "Where's the white van that usually parks in that corner?"

The man shrugged. "*Poiós xérei?* Must be on delivery somewhere. What's it to you?"

"My shipment is two days late. Came to find out why," Anna said. "They aren't returning calls. When did you last see it?"

"It's usually here when I show up. Sometimes all day. Some days it's out for hours."

"Was it here this morning?"

"*Ochi.* Not today," he said, eyeing each of them in turn as a car turned into the lot. "I'm busy. Please to leave now."

They heeded his suggestion and stalked off as he waved in a car. Halfway to the next corner Anna stopped short. "Hey! Where's Ottovio?"

Andreas pointed to Ottovio standing on the sidewalk with his phone at his face. Ignoring Anna beckoning him to come, he took shots of the abutting buildings.

When Ottovio galumphed across the street, Anna said, "You know, the parking lot guy probably saw you doing that."

"Tourist pictures. Capturing the scenery for later appreciation."

"Suppose he tells somebody about us snooping around?"

"Unlikely. The pot smoke wafting from that shanty tells me he may have forgotten already."

Walking arm-in-arm, Andreas patted Anna's hand and said, "That was brilliant of you to ask about the van. Now we know where to find it. Bravo!

"Thanks," she said, smiling, seeking his eyes. "Well, maybe. There are a whole lot of white vans in this town. It's pretty circumstantial."

"Easy," Ottovio said as they trudged away. "Just come back when it's here and check license plate."

"I'm supposed to keep coming back here hoping it showed up? No, thank you."

"Fine," he replied. "I see good place for a watchbird, across from building. I have new design I'm tinkering with. Will prove van parks there, maybe other things."

"I like it, Ottovio," she said. "Get them coming and going. Thanks so much."

They turned onto a busy shopping street on their way to Monastiraki Metro. Anna disengaged from Andreas to make way for a knot of pedestrians. When she caught up to them, she said, "Maybe I'm jumping to conclusions, but I think it's time to get a tracker."

Neither companion replied, but she could swear she heard someone say: *And then what?*

#

Were a museum to mount an exhibition of hacker artifacts, Ottovio's spy cameras would surely make the cut. His first masqueraded as a cute Tyrolean birdhouse. Its successor was more sleekly utilitarian. To house it, he retrieved a sturdy rectangular one-liter food container from his pantry and sprayed it with aluminum paint. On its bottom, near one end, he excised a square of plastic with a utility knife. He then fashioned a cardboard holster that he epoxied to the bottom of the container, into which he dropped a Nokia smartphone running his apps, its back-facing camera peeking through the opening.

To complete the assembly, he made a second cardboard holster and glued it to the inside of the lid for a battery pack that he cabled to the phone's charging port. After gluing four magnetic discs to the lid and securing them with a strip of duct tape, he snapped it on. Finally, to provide authenticity, he printed out the logo of the municipal electrical authority, glued it to the container's lid, and sprayed it with clear fixative.

He regarded his creation and found it good. From his phone he texted the box SIRI SNAP. Obediently, it took a selfie and emailed it to him as proof of concept.

Satisfied with his handiwork, he shut down the spy phone and rewarded himself by nuking slices of sausage-and-mushroom pizza, musing, *I can get old phones for almost nothing. If I could sell a few of these babies at a hundred euros a pop, I could afford to expand my big machine to eight processors and take Beatrice out for fancy seafood uptown.*

Assuming the more eyeballs the better, he added Andreas to the Watchbird II email distribution list. He texted Anna and Andreas its phone number and a shortlist of commands, advising them to expect incoming messages with attachments four times an hour starting tomorrow morning.

Of course, this would annoy both of them. Andreas wasn't expecting to receive photo-spam and Anna would now be getting a double dose of it, but that's what it would take to keep on top of things. High on spycraft, he was eager to install his new bird. However, as it would be lodged four meters up the side of a building, he needed a ladder, something he didn't have but knew where to find.

#

Under a crescent moon dimly hanging in a murky sky, a battered utility van turned onto Athinaidos Street. Its driver switched off the engine and lights to let it roll to a stop past Meteor Import-Export Ltd. The old Iveco truck belonged to an itinerant cabinetmaker and handyman calling himself Gyro who bunked in it alongside his tools inside the rented garage he called home. At twenty minutes past one, two men emerged from its rear door. Silhouetted in sodium light, Gyro led as they trundled an extension ladder toward the building across the parking lot from Meteor Import-Export. Twenty paces down the wall Ottovio signaled halt and they righted the ladder.

"Up you go," he said.

Gyro ascended the ladder with a satchel slung over his shoulder. "What am I looking for?" he whispered down.

"Between ground and first floor is cast iron plate with bolts. Secures ceiling beam to wall."

Gyro fumbled in the bag and withdrew Ottovio's newest work of hacker art.

"I see it," Gyro said, followed by a slight clang. "Nice mount. Clings like a bastard."

His face pale in the ghostly glow of his phone, Ottovio typed a text with pursed lips and sent it to the spy phone. Half a minute later he said: "A little to left. Can see door but not back wall." He texted again and waited a spell. After examining the next report he made a thumb circle and motioned Gyro down.

They lowered the ladder, trotted it back to the truck, gingerly shoved it in, and clambered aboard. Gyro closed the door and they minced their way over buckets and tools to settle into the cab's tattered seats. After checking his mirrors, Gyro fumbled under the dashboard to retrieve a cigar tube. He popped it open, shook out a bulky cigarette, lit it, and toked deeply before passing it over. Ottovio waved it away. "Too late to do that stuff. Still need to find a gadget to track that van when it shows up."

Gyro exhaled, took another drag, and flicked the flame off the joint. He dropped it into its tube, stashed it away, and removed his watch cap. His long black hair, gathered by a filigreed silver hair-clip, tumbled down to his shoulders. "You have more work to do tonight?" he asked.

Staring out the windshield, Ottovio shrugged. "Need to move this thing along so I can get back to another project." His life thus far had been a succession of projects, many driven by deep antipathy to the oppressive and corrupt machinery of the established order that it pleased him to expose and sometimes disrupt. This project was for a good cause, he told Gyro, and could bring in new revenues.

"Like what?"

"Should be market for these gizmos, plus, if her strategy pays off, can sell pictures of what goes down to media."

"Maybe, but don't you mind her being in your hair? As you said, you have things to do."

"Sure, sometimes. But for now, her project takes priority."

"Why? Is she paying you to put up these cameras?"

"She chips in. What she's doing means something. Not just to her because she's afraid for her kid—nice boy, BTW—but because trafficking is out of hand and cops are letting it happen. She could make a difference."

"Does Beatrice mind you hanging out with her?"

Ottovio turned toward his driver. In the shadowed cab, cleanly shaven with hair pulled back, in profile Gyro looked a bit like Andreas. "Beatrice isn't like that," he said. "She's a free spirit. We parallel-play. Tonight she's off with some guy helping him code his bitcoin mine, so she says. I dunno what they do and don't really care."

"Well, I'm happy to help you help your friend. I'm still grateful that you brought my phone back to life."

"No problem. Appreciate your wheels and knocking together that birdhouse. My skill set doesn't include woodworking. Or truck driving, for that matter."

"My pleasure," Gyro said, turning the key. The truck shivered and rattled as its engine sputtered to life. At the end of the block its lights came on as it turned left to rumble toward Keratsini, the moon and Gyro a little higher.

\#

Gyro pulled over on deserted Dimokritias Boulevard to let Ottovio out. "You know," he said, "I admire you for helping this woman catch traffickers. Anything I can do to help?"

Ottovio scratched his beard, opened his door, and started to step down. "Well, you could drive me and maybe some others to a demo when time comes."

"Sure," Gyro said. "For what, though?"

"A flash mob when they snatch another kid, probably at their house. Could happen anytime. I'll text you when it does. You in?"

"Sounds righteous but kind of stressful."

"As is getting any good thing done. So are you in? Can you be a taxi when I call? You need to be quick about it."

"Can do. Let me know. See you."

They bade farewell and the Iveco rumbled off. Ottovio trudged down a side street and then another to the flat he shared with his girlfriend. Their lovers' nest was perched above an odorous Chinese laundry whose wi-fi unsuspectingly hosted their private virtual network. Their computers, internet, and phones were all encrypted. They never received visitors, preferring to keep their location undisclosed. It was better that way, he told friends by way of apology. Given their marginally legitimate lines of work, privacy trumped conviviality.

It was after 2 AM and the apartment was dark. Beatrice was still out, presumably excavating Bitcoin with her undisclosed client or otherwise engaged with him. He felt his way down to the kitchen, past the curled-up cat that had taken possession of his beanbag chair, flipped the light switch and fired up the teakettle. When it impatiently whistled he poured a mug of black tea, shuffled to a desk chair commanding three wraparound screens powered by four CPUs running Debian, and woke up his console.

Before getting down to business, he ran through his email from the parking lot. Four batches of from one to three photos had come in, one every fifteen minutes. Nothing in the scene had changed but the occasional glimmer of passing headlights. Hoping the van would materialize, he shopped for GPS transponders for most of an hour. Slurping tepid tea, he compared specs, features, maps, prices, terms, and dubious promises of data security, and settled for one that balanced ratings and price and purchased it under an assumed name in care of the laundry downstairs.

Thinking about tracking the van in real time brought to mind wartime footage from drones homing in on moving vehicles before blowing them to smithereens. Not that that was his intention, but wouldn't it be nice to have an eye in the sky to document what Anna expected to take place at that cottage in Nikaia? A drone might cost a bit, but if her scheme panned out it could pay for itself with marketable footage of the event. Pondering the possibilities, he nodded off in his chair until Beatrice returned to prop him up and shuttle him to bed.

Chapter Twenty-Three

CONSTANTLY NAGGED BY EMAIL notifications from her watchbird every fifteen minutes precisely, Anna had turned them off. Unaccustomed to them, Andreas had left his on. And thus, it was he who first glimpsed images of the white van parked by Meteor Import-Export Ltd. that had materialized around daybreak.

His phone had pealed just as he shuffled into his kitchen to prepare breakfast for his guests. He picked it up to find an unexpected email message with suspicious attachments issued from an unknown address. He considered deleting it, but recalling a recent text alert from Ottovio, with a sigh, he unzipped the attached file to find a series of photos of the parking lot on Athinaidos Street. Annoyed, he viewed and quickly deleted each in turn until he spotted a change of scenery. A van had shuttled to the lot's far corner with lights on. In the next one, the lights were off and a silhouetted somebody was letting himself in by the fire door near where they'd stood yesterday.

Assuming Anna had received the photos too, he silenced his whistling teakettle, and poured hot water into a mug with a teabag for himself. He filled another mug with water, scooped in some instant coffee, poured a glass of orange juice for the boy, and bussed the drinks to his sleeping chamber on a tea tray.

"I'm afraid this Nescafé will have to do," he announced. "I keep forgetting to buy real coffee." Ramadi, who had wandered in and tunneled under the covers, emerged to accept the OJ. "Thank you, Onkle Andreas."

"No problem. Better than nothing," Anna said, sliding up and grasping a mug.

He settled beside Anna with his tea. She patted his thigh and let her hand rest there.

"*Danke*," she said.

"For …?" he replied, focusing on his beverage.

She sought his eyes. "For being here, and not just for me. I know it can be difficult for you at times, but knowing you care means a lot."

Andreas sipped his tea and put his mug on the nightstand. His hand found hers and twined fingers. Noticing the display of affection, Ramadi mimicked, touching Anna's thigh, and received a maternal squeeze. She smiled at him as her eyes gathered tears.

"Why do you cry, Mutti?"

"Just because I love you so much, both of you," she said, sniffling. "They're called tears of gratitude."

Ramadi's eyes darted to Andreas and back to her. "You love Onkle more than me," he said, pouting. It could have been a question or a statement, possibly both.

"Oh love," she said, unclasping hands and pulling him to her breast. "Sure, I love Onkle Andreas, and he loves us both, but no one loves you more than I do, believe me."

The boy in her arms shivered. His response was unexpectedly existential.

"Mutti, do bad people want to hurt me?"

Suspecting where that came from, she squeezed him until he yelped. *The abduction dreams, channeling my anxiety. I did this.*

She unwound her arms to wipe her eyes. "Nobody wants to hurt you," she said. "Did you dream that?"

"I don't remember. But why all the muttis tell us never talk to strangers and why did we hide from those men in the park?"

"Those, those men … don't like people from other countries coming here. Remember, how rude one of them was when I took you for ice cream after we saw Nurse Fatma?"

"I think so. Does he want to hurt us?"

"Don't know what he wants, but I didn't want to take any chances in the park. Anyway, that's what mothers do, love," she said, petting his head like a puppy. "Like when we tell you to watch for cars and trucks and busses when crossing streets."

"And scooters and bicycles and skateboards and old ladies with shopping carts," Andreas said. "It comes with living in the city."

"Ooh," Ramadi said, his voice rising about an octave, "Mutti, can I have a scooter?"

"We'll see. They can be tricky to steer around things and stop going downhill."

"Oh, speaking of vehicles," Andreas said, "that white van showed up overnight. In its designated parking spot."

"Same one?" she asked.

"Fits the description. Check your inbox."

She padded down the comforter and onto the floor where her clothes lay, fumbled for her phone, and began stroking and poking. Ramadi crawled to the end of the bed and flopped down, chin propped on hands. Noticing his interest, she said: "Ottovio asked us to check out a spy camera he made. Takes pretty good pictures."

Upon hearing "spy," Ramadi said that was pretty neat and scrambled down to join her. The parade of parking lot views soon paled but the concept incited him to crawl under the bed to play undercover agent. Anna got up and went to sit next to Andreas, feet tapping the floor. "Look," she said, "the van shows up a little after five. It backs in by that road cone. The lights go out. Then someone in dark clothing gets out and goes into the building."

"I saw that," Andreas said. "Can't make out his face, though."

She zoomed in on the figure. "It's murky but doesn't it look a lot like the guy the watchbird captured in the alley? Same watch cap, same van."

Andreas squinted at her screen. "You mean their Facebook friend?"

"Eugenides. Ja, I'm thinking it must be him," she said, and scrolled ahead. "License plate ends in 2163. Bingo." She sprang up, executed a pirouette, and grasped Andreas's shoulders to smooch his cheek. "Wherever he delivers the next shipment, we've got him covered!"

Ramadi wriggled out from his lair to investigate and request food. Andreas suggested they dress up while he fixed breakfast.

They chewed granola with bananas and milk as Andreas boiled eggs and toasted wheat bread. Anna had a mind to continue their earlier conversation, but deferring to Ramadi's presence, pushed the thought onto her to-do list and instead fixed herself another unsatisfying cup of Nescafé.

#

Later that morning came a text from Ottovio featuring a photo of a featureless black box. *This what we got,* he wrote. *Nice unit made in UK. Expect in two days. You owe 150 + shipping.*

Envisioning skulking downtown to crawl under a truck in the middle of the night, Anna texted back: *Many thanks can you install?*

She waited and was about to add *Please???* when he replied OK. *Get app from trackcracker.co.uk & learn to work it,* followed by login credentials and the thing's unique ID.

Dutifully, she downloaded the app and, as instructed, logged on using his creepy password LasKaris007. When asked to register her unit, she typed in its 13-digit serial number, hoping she wouldn't have to do that every time she ran the app. But in the next step she was afforded the opportunity to give her brick a nickname. *jayjay* it would be, in honor of Ramadi's favorite TV character. So, of course that made her Brenda Blue, the old TV series' human aviatrix and queen of the control tower. *Ja,* she thought, I *liked how she took control of those kid planes. Good role model for Ramadi.*

She felt no need to reply when she heard from within: *And for you, one would think.*

Closing the app, she forced herself to triage her neglected photo-stream from Nikaia. A dozen batches yielded nothing interesting, and then nothing at all. The latest collection was from yesterday afternoon. After that, they had just stopped coming. Not good.

Nothing she saw in the last few photos indicated tampering with the spycam. She called tech support to discuss.

"Probably ran out of juice," Ottovio said. "Needs new power pack I don't have."

"*Scheisse!* We need that bird. Anything you can do?"

"Recharge would take at least a day and two late-night trips. Can it wait?"

"Tell you what, get a new pack and I'll pay for it."

"Would take even longer and still need to charge overnight."

"Please give it a try. Something could happen soon that would be heartbreaking to miss."

"Understood, but installing that GPS unit takes priority."

"I'm sorry to keep leaning on you, Ottovio. I also owe you for the GPS thing. It looks perfect. I set up the app and kinda see how it works. In case you are tracking too, I named it jayjay."

"Are those someone's initials?"

"No, it's spelt j-a-y-j-a-y. After an animated airplane Ramadi loves. Anyway, a big hug and a kiss and an invite to dinner downtown for all you've been doing."

"Throw in a bottle of retsina and it's a deal."

"Deal. Thanks for everything."

"No problem. Let's hope this ends soon."

"Ja. And well."

#

Even though she'd fingered the white van, Anna felt a need to close the loop on the fictitious story she'd laid on Officer Melina, whose lack of follow-up did not bode well.

"I'm sorry, but the data is not available," Melina said after keeping Anna on hold for over a minute.

"Even to you?"

"No, to the general public, which unfortunately includes you."

"Hmm. Well, thanks anyway."

"I'm sorry, Anna. But at least you two weren't harmed."

Anna rang off, wondering if Melina had taken the matter to Nicolaides, who might have suggested it was none of her damn business. Worse, had he realized the van belonged to one of his pet criminals, he would now know what she had taken such care to conceal. And so unnecessary, now that she knew where the van lived and was about to shadow it. She could only hope that whatever might have gone wrong, hadn't.

Thinking about what tracking the van would entail multiplied her anxieties. Relieved to be off the hook until jayjay took off, she scrolled through her mental to-do list. She owed Ramadi a playdate. Her thoughts drifted to Nurse Fatma, whose daughter was older than Ramadi but still might be good company and a potential baby-sitter. She was fond of Fatma but hadn't yet socialized outside the clinic. To rectify that, she rang her up to suggest an outing.

"I've had been thinking of you," Fatma said. "Sure, let's get together on Saturday. Why not here in Exarcheia?"

Recalling the people's park in Exarcheia where she'd encountered local residents Imogene and son Viktor, Anna suggested meeting there. Fatma accepted, insisting that they come by her flat for tea and Turkish brunch featuring *börek* pastries. That suited Anna just fine, saying she'd come to love their savory puffy layers in Izmir but had no idea how to assemble them. It was actually easy, Fatma told her, as she would be pleased to demonstrate.

After arranging their playdate, it occurred to Anna that Imogene and Viktor might wish to meet up with them. That day they'd met at Parko Navarinou their kids had gotten along well, and she'd never thanked Imogene for suggesting she introduce Altogether to the powers-that-be at the anarchist hangout, OpenBox, as fruitless as that had turned out to be. And when Anna rang her up, Imogene immediately remembered her and asked how it had gone over there.

"Well, you know anarchists won't be herded, especially by a technology company they never heard of. The collective grilled me and never got back, but Altogether is doing fine without them. Anyway, what have you been up to?"

"Not a lot," Imogene said, adding that she would enjoy seeing them again and the timing was good. Her husband was on a painting job in the outskirts this weekend. She was sure Viktor would enjoy playing with Ramadi again, and looked forward to meeting Anna's Turkish friend. Eleven would be fine.

"Great," Anna said, "It'll be fun to hang out with you in one of the safest parts of the city."

"Usually," Imogene said. "Anyway, see you then."

Anna clicked off, considering the word "usually." Usually, Exarcheian residents managed their own affairs, except when it pleased city officials to intervene, usually with police power. But that didn't happen very often.

Chapter Twenty-Four

ANNA STAYED HOME THE next morning to stew over strategy. Anticipating tracking a kidnapping in real time made her acutely aware of her unreadiness. That van could visit that alley in Nikaia again any day at any hour. When it happened, she would need to sound the alarm, drop everything, and rush to the scene like a volunteer firefighter. This she already knew, but never quite so viscerally.

Unfortunately, she didn't have a fire engine. Nor could her tracker tell her if the van carried a victim or just a carpet. And even if it paid a call, there might be no victim to show for it, certainly not as long as her watchbird remained incommunicado.

But the one watching Meteor Import-Export on Athinaidos Street, a potential port of call, was working fine. And that represented another contingency for which she needed to plan. How were her first responders supposed to know where to go and what to do?

She needed a text message for them to forward verbatim. Attaching pictures of the destination would make it feel real. To mark an assembly point, nothing could beat a conspicuous dot on an online map. It also needed a rousing preamble stressing urgency and solidarity, summoning the faithful to hustle on down. She needed to compose two messages— one routing responders to Nikaia, the other to Central Athens—that she damn well better not mix up when time came.

All that logistical pondering took time. Already it was eleven-thirty. She stretched her arms and got up to fix tea, then opted for espresso. Waiting for her stovetop pot to geyser and gurgle, she dug out her phone to review her list of volunteers.

She counted them. Just six. Feeling a need to know how many other tree dwellers hung from those limbs, she decided to test her emergency broadcast system. To them she wrote: *THIS IS A TEST of the Child Protection League emergency phone tree. Pls fwd this msg to your ppl. Ask them to reply & tell me how many answered. KEEP ON RECRUITING. An actual alert would tell you where to assemble with clear instructions. PLS BE PREPARED TO ACT FAST. You can make a difference.*

She fired it off and sipped her coffee, considering whom else she might enlist. Certainly not Melina. How about Stavros, the good-hearted pizza man? He seemed sympathetic, but would he be willing to close up shop on short notice to confront Laskaris? Doubtful.

So who else? Clumping footfalls overhead suggested enlisting Penelope, but unable to forget her housemate had informed on her, Anna cancelled the temptation. Leafing through her address book turned up an entry for Portia, her web guru at Prótos, someone she felt she could trust. But thinking she might say something about it to their boss, Irene, Anna figured she'd better inform Irene first. With no known police connections but plenty in the media, Irene could grow one stout tree limb. She placed a call.

Waiting with unformed words for Irene to answer, a notification popped up. Anna happily aborted the call to read the message. It was Fotini, saying she'd forwarded to six people but not how many had responded, asking if something was happening she should know about. Not so far, Anna shot back. Just be prepared.

After responses stopped dribbling in, she tallied what they reported on her fingers, coming up with fifteen responders overall, of whom she figured at most half would bother to rouse themselves. Not good enough. She wanted twenty or more bodies at the scene. Time to try Irene again. It went to voicemail: "Hi Irene, it's Anna. Give me a call when you have a chance."

She was hungry but her scanty pantry had little to offer. Realizing she had less than two hours before retrieving Ramadi from school at Katia's place, she headed down to the avenue with a shopping bag to collect some edibles and grab a quick bite to tide her over. Tonight, she decided, they would have stew.

#

Anna dashed down to Dimokritias Boulevard, managing to round up a head of cabbage and some desiccating root vegetables at the greengrocer's, a gimpy stew hen from the butcher, and followed her growling stomach to the anarchist café for a spot of spanakopita. The barista informed her they were out of it, so she settled for a cheesy panini.

Five long minutes later it came, delivered by Chris, the shift coordinator who last month had ejected Laskaris for being a bigoted asshole. She and Chris had worked together to rehab a branch library into a social center during her first year in town, but nowadays only intersected here.

She invited him to sit down.

"Remember that nationalist toad you threw out who taunted my son and insulted me?"

Chris nodded. He'd always been a man of few words.

"Well, thanks for that. Has he come around here again?"

Chris shook his head. "Not on my watch. What about him?"

"A lot you don't know," she said in a lower register. "I'll let you in on something, but you need to promise not blab it around. Okay?" His chin bobbed a bit, which she took to signify assent.

"What would you say if I told you he's a child trafficker?"

Chris rubbed his chin. "How do you know?"

"Because I caught his partner doing it and have other evidence. These kids get sexually abused and sold into slavery. It has to stop."

He leaned toward her. "You don't say. And you're going to stop them?"

"Me and a bunch of others who are sick of this sordid trade. You wanna know how?"

Chris offered that he was all ears, which she proceeded to fill up, ending with an invitation to join a flash mob to out them on short notice, along with as many friends, associates, and possibly customers as he could muster.

Chris wasn't sure, and wanted to know how she could be sure a kidnapping was in progress. To assuage his skepticism, she opened a phone app that showed a city map.

"I'll know it's going down when this app shows me a certain vehicle heading to Nikaia, thanks to a GPS tracker that lets me follow it."

Chris squinted at the map. "And that thing's the vehicle?"

She turned the phone around to find a blue dot blinking at her from a side street near Monastiraki Square. "Omigod! Ottovio did it! He installed the tracker! See, there's where it is. In a parking lot on Athinaidos Street."

To his further bewilderment, she let on that a surveillance camera had captured that vehicle at the house in Nikaia where the traffickers lived, and then showed pictures of it there and in that parking lot.

While expressing admiration of her research skills, Chris asked why she wouldn't inform the police and let them handle the matter.

"I'll turn over my evidence after we expose these creeps." And in almost a whisper: "Confidentially, the thing is, we think a police detective is protecting them. That's why we need a street action."

"A corrupt cop wouldn't surprise me, but aren't there special Hellenic Police units that handle such crimes? Why not call them?"

"So I'm told, but I can't take a chance on what they might do. Besides, I've got a human rights agency's rescue squad for backup."

Chris leaned back, tenting his fingers. "I still can't believe you did all this or if it could work, but there it is. And it all depends on you."

"*No*," she said, loudly enough for heads to turn. "It depends on regular people caring enough to get off their asses to save a child and put exploiters behind bars. Good people like you." The fierceness of her delivery surprised even her.

"So please. Spread the word to your comrades in the collective and some of your regulars and speed to the scene, even if you need to shutter the café for the duration. Think of it as community service."

After suffering further choice words about the civic responsibilities of anarchists, Chris said he would pitch in, and consented to be on speed dial. They exchanged phone numbers with him promising to rally his collective, as best he could.

She dug out money to pay her bill. He pushed it back. "Food's on the house for the work you're doing, whatever comes of it."

"Why thank you. I'm sure something will. Just can't say exactly where or when."

She hoisted her shopping bag. "Last I recall, you people had an old school bus sitting around somewhere. Still got it?"

An affirmative nod. "Parked over at the social center," he said. "Are you asking to use it?"

"I might hitch a ride if I'm nearby when time comes. In any case, you'll get directions by text that you should pass on to your contacts. Relay the message, gather up the willing, and race to wherever it says to go. You'll have a map. A busload would be awesome."

"We'll see," he said as he picked up her plate. "You know how anarchists operate. Consensus and all that …"

"Well," she said as they walked to the front, "bet there's consensus that child trafficking is evil. Tell them all they need to do to put these creeps out of business is show up and shout out."

#

Late as usual, Anna was bustling down Katia's block to retrieve Ramadi when Irene rang back saying hi, long time no see, to which Anna replied she's been super busy "pursuing an urgency."

"What agency are you pursuing and why?"

Anna slowed her pace. "No agency. An urgent matter that's only going to get more so, something you might be able to help with."

"Oh. I thought you were calling back about the redesign of the Prótos home page. You got my email, right?"

Anna pretended to have read it. "Yes, that's exciting. I can't wait to check it out. But the reason I called, actually, was to see if you would, umm, help us collar some kidnappers."

"Tell me more."

Anna leaned against a lamppost to give an abridged rundown of her recent crime-stopping efforts, visualizing her boss's elegant eyebrows arching in sync with her intonation. "I see … you're collecting activists … shadowing criminals … Preparing to confront them … Have you been doing this on Altogether?"

"Not really. Our network includes people from the League plus a bunch more, and I thought you might want to help us by alerting media outlets to cover our confrontation of a kidnapping in progress."

Hearing "media," "confrontation," and "kidnapping," juxtaposed seemed either to intrigue or confound Irene. "I need to know more about this," she said after a few beats. "Do you have time to scoot up here so we can bring each other up to date?"

Even though she would much rather fetch Ramadi and run him home to feed him chicken stew, Anna told her boss sure, but her son would have to come along.

"You've told me so much about him I'd love to meet him. When can you be here?"

Within the hour, Anna guessed, and they clicked off. She hoped Ramadi would be up for an excursion on the Metro to see where Mutti worked, which turned out to be fine with him.

#

Anna found Irene outfitted in a beige suit accessorized with a retro pearls and quite perky for late afternoon. Irene greeted Ramadi warmly and chatted him up almost as if he were a new intern. He didn't request a job, but awed by the super-sized computer monitor on her meeting table, wanted to know if it showed movies. She obligingly pulled up a swivel chair, fired it up, and found a *Sponge Bob* video to entertain him.

They huddled at Irene's gleaming desk for a demo. "Take a look. I've redone the Prótos front page to spotlight Altogether groups," Irene said as a gallery of featured websites paraded across the page. Only four of them, including the League's home page, but that seemed plenty for Irene.

"Nice presentation," Anna said. "But I can see the League's needs work. I'll get to it, but I've been sort of preoccupied this past week."

"So you said. It's the kidnapper Servopoulos and his shady partner, I presume."

"We know they're still at it and not only do the police not care, this detective in Nikaia seems to be helping them."

"Shameful if true, and must put you in a tough spot. But how do you know that?"

"I've seen them palling around on two occasions. Have a video to prove it. And photos. And that's why we need to throw them a surprise party."

Before Irene could respond, Anna was leafing through her photo gallery. "Here we go. This is their back door in Nikaia, early morning.

219

See Servopoulos and this guy we've identified loading a carpet into that van? See how it sags? There's a small human being inside it. That's what they do, where they do it, and how they do it."

Unbidden words filled Anna's head. *That was masterful, kiddo! Keep it up!*

"My goodness! Did you take those pictures?"

"Not me. We put up a robot camera to keep tabs on that house. Then we found where that van parks and put a tracker on it. Take a look."

Irene settled back in her chair, nibbling an arm of her rose-tinted specs. "That's okay," she said. "As incredible as this seems, I believe you. But why are you telling me? Am I supposed to do something about it?"

"I wouldn't expect you to rush over to demonstrate with us. But might you be willing to tip off the news media when something happens? You know how to do that. I don't."

"And tell them what? To show up with camera crews?"

"Exactly. To cover the confrontation and document a kidnapping in progress. To make sure the cops can't cover it up."

Irene exhaled through pursed lips. "I can see how that would help. But if anything goes wrong—say someone gets hurt—there would be an investigation that Prótos might get dragged into."

"I suppose, but couldn't you tip them anonymously? Anyway, aren't reporters supposed to protect their sources?"

Ramadi's video was over. "Mutti, can we go home now?"

"Just a little while longer, sweetheart. Here, I'll give you something to do." She grabbed a little book of puzzles and a pencil from his backpack and told him to connect some dots to find the animals while Mutti finished up.

"There are discreet ways to handle such things," Irene said, still tilted back and gazing into the middle distance. "And if all ends well, we could credit a Prótos employee for saving a child."

"And if it doesn't?"

"Guilt by association. You know something about that, I believe."

"Well, I'm willing to risk that and want to believe you would too. A child's whole future could be at stake, if not his life. I'm not asking for much, Irene. Just to get on the horn when a text comes saying there's been an abduction and here are the details."

"I don't know. Let me think," Irene said, eyes arcing upward, hopefully gathering resolve.

Having concluded her thought process, Irene came from behind her desk and clasped Anna by her shoulders. "Well, if you catch these guys in the act, you'll have done a great public service. But if it's a false alarm, we'll lose credibility and you might end up in jail."

"Or in somebody's crosshairs," Anna said, recalling an equally hesitant Peter Mavridis saying: "It better be the real deal or there will be hell to pay." A surprise party with a missing guest of honor wouldn't go down well with the celebrants.

Anna shuffled Ramadi out the door and shuttled him home. There, she set to fixing supper. As she distractedly sliced vegetables, a hen wasn't the only thing stewing. Like a jigsaw puzzle with pieces missing—particularly watchbird number one—a plan was taking shape, but what kind of scene would it make when it comes together?

221

PART FOUR

STRONGER TOGETHER

The second night has fallen since I began hovering around the Piraeus Metro portal. Not much to see here beside a vagrant sleeping on a bench under a filthy towel. I doubt Akhmed will show up in his taxicab, not at this hour. Earlier today I tried getting into a cab with a passenger just to see what would happen, but something like air pressure repelled my attempt. My plan is to enter Akhmed's car and go where he goes, but that may not be possible. Let me visit Katrina, then.

No, wait—a little sedan is pulling up to the taxi stand. It might be his, but I can't tell in this orange light. A man with a shopping bag emerges from the rear and enters the Metro. The driver gets out and scans the scene, then leans against the door and puts his hands to his face. The flare of his cigarette torch reflects from his eyeglasses and etches familiar features. My brother, dragging on a cigarette! AKHMED! YOU SHOULDN'T BE SMOKING!

A strange look comes across him as he exhales, peering left and right. AKHMED! THROW IT AWAY! He takes another puff, tosses his smoke down, and opens the door. From under his seat he grabs a sweatshirt and pulls it over his polo shirt. Looks like he shops at the bazaar too.

Here goes. I will my way into the passenger side. It worked this time!

He seats himself, regards his phone for a while, and then starts the car just as a woman emerges from the portal with a hat and a satchel. She starts running toward a bus idling at the bus stop, waves frantically as it pulls away, and stamps her foot. Akhmed gets out and waves to her. They talk briefly and he opens the back door for her, but she heads for the front seat. Modesty dictates that I scoot to the rear.

He pulls away and doubles back. I cannot believe this is happening! I am riding in my brother's car! It has been seven years since we were last together in Mosul. I feel the joy I felt in Farida's kitchen upon seeing his letter. He might feel something too, judging from his wide-eyed alertness looking through me from his mirror. I will stay with him until he goes home, wherever that is, because if I don't know where he sleeps I may never find him again.

Akhmed is following the same route as the bus I have taken between the Metro and Keratsini. He and the woman in the front seat are exchanging words. She is not young or old, wearing jeans, a blue work shirt, a leather jacket, and a motorcycle cap. She takes it off, places on the center console *and smooths her tangle of reddish hair. She is doing most of the talking and talks fast. I am not sure how much of what she says he understands.*

It is dark, but I see a familiar landmark, a cinema not far from Andreas. After it, at the top of a hill, Akhmed takes a right and the car glides down to the middle of a block that is very familiar to me. When he stops the car, in front of a little house I know why. This is where Katrina lives!

Now I remember. I have met this woman. She lives upstairs from Katrina. I only met her once, coming back to the house, in the alley. A Greek woman, an artist. Also an activist like Katrina and a bit of a busybody, I was told.

Akhmed says something as he takes her money and presents his card to her. She accepts it and replies. He smiles in his lopsided way and they both get out. Akhmed kindly conducts her down the dark alley to the back door I know so well. I go too, wondering if she might invite him in. Apparently not, because when she unlocks the door Akhmed gives her a slight bow and walks away.

Katrina's kitchen light is on. Should I stay or should I go with Akhmed? I choose him, because he is my brother and I do not want to lose him again. AKHMED! WAIT FOR ME! I silently cry as he hastens up the alley.

We settle into his car. He consults a map on his phone and drives off. I am stunned by what just happened, also frustrated. Akhmed had no idea how close he came to his only nephew, and I have no way to tell him.

Chapter Twenty-Five

THE ATHENIAN ANARCHIST STRONGHOLD of Exarcheia, a twenty-minute hike down from the Acropolis, was in the news again—not for clashes with Golden Dawn hooligans or for rowdy protests against Greece's supplication to foreign bankers and bureaucrats, but for housing foreign refugees in "liberated" tenements. Sometime in the wee hours, Hellenic Police in battle gear stormed the neighborhood. They battered their way into several squats and rounded up the sleepy residents before shoving them into buses destined for one of the migrant detention centers scattered across Attica. Those who resisted being uprooted were beaten and hauled to the busses. With customary insouciance, newscasters likened the raid to a response to a rat infestation and praised the officers for selflessly staying up past their bedtimes.

Soberly taking credit for the official brutalities was the recently elected right-wing New Democracy Party, having swept to victory in national elections several months earlier in a stunning rebuke to the discredited Syriza coalition of the left. The best Anna and her friends could say about their socially conservative and economically neoliberal new rulers was that at least they weren't neofascist thugs.

"It will be the worst of both worlds," the President of the Transport Workers Union had predicted after the midsummer election in which fewer than half of Greeks voted. "With its absolute majority in Parliament, New Democracy will double down on the privatization and colonization agenda that began under Syriza, and surely make good on its pledges to criminalize migrants and refugees."

The predicted backlash had come to pass, Anna thought as she watched morning news with pictures of riot police bringing truncheons down on protestors' shoulders amid clouds of tear gas, and herding frightened residents away at gunpoint. She fumed over the media's glib references to the "Peoples' Republic of Anarchia," as they tended to label the secessionist district with scarcely concealed contempt.

Also watching was her five-year-old. "Why they do they chase people? Did they do something bad?"

Anna switched off the telly. "Not really, Ramadi. They were just living here. They came from far away and have no place to go. Now they will have to live in tents out in the open. Isn't that sad?"

"Tents. I like tents," he said, probably recalling attending an outdoor day camp the previous summer. "Can we go too?"

"I don't think you'd like it. You wouldn't have your books or bike or TV programs. They would only let you bring your clothing and toothbrush. Believe me, you are much better off here."

Taking his mutti's words under advisement, Ramadi did not reply. But news of the raids worried Anna. Fatma and her Irmak lived in an Exarcheian squat, and might have been forcibly evicted and consigned to a makeshift tent city. Worried for them, Anna called her Turkish friend.

She was relieved to reach Fatma at the Piraeus community clinic, just seven blocks away. Irmak was safely with her. They had fled there after being informed that police were ominously massing, and had spent the rest of a restless night on examination tables under emergency blankets.

"Did your building get raided?"

She said not. "*Hayir*. A friend who stayed behind told me it wasn't. Maybe because we have agreement with landlord to pay rent and utilities and do repairs."

"So what are you going to do?"

"I don't know yet. Tomorrow we see."

"You can come here if you want. Take the bedroom. I can tent the kitchen table and camp under it with Ramadi. He would love that."

"*Çok tessekurler*, thank you. You are kind but we are okay here."

Anna demurred, suggesting that Fatma might pack up some first aid supplies from the clinic for when she went back, something Fatma said she'd already done. Anna again urged her to come, saying if Exarcheia had quieted down by the morning they could all go up there as planned, check out the aftermath and see if they could help. That made sense, Fatma said, and told Anna to expect them but not to sacrifice her bed.

Thus came to pass an impromptu pajama party with borrowed nightshirts, preceded by a supper of leftover stewed chicken and a rice pilaf that Fatma insisted on fixing. Irmak was a slim, sloe-eyed sweetie, her olive-skin completed by braided auburn tresses. Despite their six-year gap in age, she and Ramadi took to one another. While the mothers cleaned up, in the next room Irmak told stories to Ramadi in Greek with occasional lapses into Turkish as Anna revealed certain matters to Fatma in hushed tones.

She exposed Fatma to her spycam's photos from the kidnappers' alley where she intended to rally her volunteers. Fatma doubted she would be able to quit her post on short notice but would gladly spread word. She'd seen many posters around her district and posts on social media begging for information about missing kids, she told Anna, and applauded her for taking action.

They were taking tea at the kitchen table when Fatma's phone tingled, a text from a neighbor wishing her to pass on word of an assembly in People's Park tomorrow at noon in response to the evictions. Telephone trees, Anna observed, were nothing new to Fatma.

Fatma forwarded the message, prompting Anna to consider alerting her network about the rally, but fear of a fracas with police and of sidetracking her followers put that thought to rest. But she would go, indeed they all would, taking Fatma's medical supplies, water bottles, and their bicycle helmets. Anna retrieved the backpack she'd taken to previous demonstrations. She rummaged through it, finding only a towel, two bandanas usable as face masks, a bottle of eyewash, and a canister of defensive pepper spray.

As expected, Ramadi cheered her suggestion that they transform the table into a tent for a sleep-in, so that Irmak could use his bed. Up went table leaves to receive two blankets, and out from storage came two air cushions that Anna had purchased for use by radicals on the run. As the moms pumped, Ramadi brightly informed them that he'd rather camp out with Irmak, an arrangement that Irmak found agreeable as long as they were provided with separate sleeping bags and a flashlight. "He's going to be quite the ladies' man," Fatma said as Anna prepared tea.

"Might be. He's already much less shy than his papa was when I met him. At first he slept in the kitchen, but I managed to fix that."

"My family would have banished me or worse if I had done something like that. But these things are almost normal in Europe. Knowing you, I'm sure you knew what you were doing."

Anna paused from draping blankets, faintly smiling. "Not really, Fatma. But it's nice of you to think so."

They'd just arranged their campsite when three dull thuds sounded from the back door. Fatma's eyes widened. "Listen! Are you expecting anyone?"

Anna shook her head as three more thumps followed. "Just you two. Hold on."

From a drawer Anna extracted a rolling pin and stole to the door, motioning Fatma to take up the other side. She twisted the latch and peeked past the security chain into the vestibule.

A muffled voice through the door said "Hello? Is me, cab driver."

"Maybe it's someone looking for Penelope," Anna whispered.

"Who's that?"

"My housemate upstairs. I'm gonna see. Stay here." Anna handed off the rolling pin, slid open the chain, and switched on the light in the vestibule. Taking a step forward she asked who was there.

"You lady I give ride to?"

"Who wants to know?"

"I cab driver. I bring hat left in cab."

"Just a minute," Anna said. She dug a key ring out of her pocket and unlatched the outside door to find a man holding a motorcycle cap. He was young, with a mop of wavy black hair, a dark shadow of a beard, and thick tinted glasses. His otherwise pleasant face was marred by pinkish scars and pitted by acne or possibly something more life-threatening.

"I am sorry for disturb," he said in halting Greek. "This is house I take another lady to."

"It's okay, Fatma," Anna said over her shoulder. "Just a cab driver. He must have driven Penelope home."

~

AKHMED! Here is your nephew! KATRINA! Invite him inside!

~

"Come in," Anna said. "She lives upstairs. I will give the hat to her. It was very kind of you to return it."

He stepped into the kitchen, magnified brown eyes blinking. Seeing Fatma, he bowed and apologized again for troubling them. Irmak came to the bedroom door to warily regard the intruder with Ramadi clutching her leg, gaping at the young man's disfigured face.

For five seconds they stood as statues until Anna extended her hand to accept the cap, saying "We were about to have tea. Would you like some?"

Together at last! AKHMED! MEET KATRINA AND MY SON! KATRINA! THIS IS MY BROTHER!

Alas, no signs of recognition, but somehow the event I wished for has happened. Though I cannot take any credit, and even though they fail to perceive me, they sometimes seem to heed my will.

My unbidden admonitions erupt like sneezes, briefly banishing vision and thought, as if to expel some of my shame. For that instant I forget to pity myself for my wretched condition. Perhaps that points to a way out of my detention.

Akhmed seems uncomfortable. He presents his card to Katrina and waves good night. I better stick with him for now.

For a Sunday breakfast, Anna emptied her egg carton to make a frittata. Afterward, Fatma washed as Anna dried, remarking on the dutiful young taxi driver and speculating on where he might be from. Declining refreshment, he had handed Anna his card and invited her to call anytime she needed a ride. Instead of the expected *Uber*, the card said *Ur-Taxi* in English, Greek, and Arabic, with a phone number but no name. She stuffed it in her jeans.

After a latish start and a longish wait for a bus to the Metro, around eleven the four of them emerged from the Omonia Square Station with Fatma and Irmak in headscarves and Anna and Ramadi in bike helmets. Propelled by the disapproving eyes of a nearby knot of well-equipped Hellenic policemen, they picked up their pace. First stop was the ADYA free walk-in clinic hosted by OpenBox, for Fatma to deliver the supplies she'd looted from her clinic and get a rundown on injuries sustained overnight.

The clinic disagreeably announced itself with a skunk-like odor. It seemed that after assaulting squatters last night, to make sure Exarcheians knew who was boss, police had tossed canisters of tear gas into the unoccupied OpenBox lobby, and its acrid stench still lingered.

"E-euw, this place stinks!" Ramadi said.

Irmak sighed. "You get used to it."

The head nurse told Fatma that most of the previous night's intake suffered from exposure to tear gas. The rest were mostly victims of beatings, one requiring hospitalization, and a distraught grandmother who'd suffered a heart attack. Sensing there was little she could do there, Fatma escorted them across Exarchion Square to her flat for the promised *böreks*. Along the way, Anna rang up Imogene, who said she still wanted to come and looked forward to meeting Anna's friends.

Background music was provided by loudspeakers rasping out a muezzin's plaintive call to prayer from a minaret two blocks away. Anna clicked off and blotted her eyes on her sleeve.

"Is everything okay?" Fatma asked.

"Just had a flashback to a funeral in a mosque. Some things are hard get used to."

Knowing the outline of Anna's story, Fatma could empathize. "I understand," she said as they joined their children at the curb. "We have both suffered, but not without compensation."

#

An hour later the two women had arranged themselves on a bench at Parko Navarinou facing a playground where Irmak and Ramadi—but mostly Irmak—propelled a see-saw.

"I see what you meant about compensation," Anna said, watching the children play. "When Ramadi was born, I didn't know what to do with him. Now I don't know what I'd do without him."

"We wanted many children," Fatma said. "Irmak was two when we lived in Diyarbakır, in Eastern Turkey. Yilmaz was running for city council. Someone bombed a campaign rally. Yilmaz was killed."

"Oh, no! How horrible! Did they catch the bomber?"

"The bomber blew himself up and police didn't pursue the matter. Nobody was ever arrested. We were sure the government was behind it. And then I started getting death threats. Me, a nurse at the hospital! That's when I knew we had to leave Diyarbakır."

"You had no relatives or friends to take you in?"

"My parents are dead and my only brother disappeared. I have cousins but didn't want to impose on them because they were struggling too. One of my schoolmates who had come here told me there were jobs for nurses. She helped us get visas, just before all the Syrians started coming."

Anna nodded as she processed Fatma's eerily resonant story. "I know what you mean. Something like that happened to me. The threats from nationalists shook me up so much I fled to Turkey, just the other way around."

"Threats? To you?"

Anna was considering how to avoid exposing the roots of her sorrows when she spied Imogene entering the playground with Viktor skipping ahead. Thankful not to explain, she waved and called out. "Hey, it's great to see you."

After hasty introductions, Imogene warned them to beware. Police were gathering, likely in anticipation of the coming assembly in the park. "They're like killer bees," she said. "They can swarm at any time and sting like crazy. Let's keep our kids close." Instinctively, Anna reached for their bike helmets, only to realize she'd left them at Fatma's.

Residents were filtering into the park to congregate in a dusty clearing for the event. A bed sheet strung between two trees spelled out "RESIST FASCISM! HANDS OFF REFUGEES!" in Greek, English, and Arabic. Soon a man and a woman who co-chaired the collective that ran the park mounted inverted trash containers to call the meeting to order through a bullhorn. The community had resolved, they announced, to protect immigrants from another raid by allocating them to safe houses that they urged the community to provide. They asked for a show of hands of those willing to board at-risk foreigners, which Imogene did, followed by Fatma. Unable to visualize housing a family of desperate refugees in her compact quarters, Anna didn't volunteer.

The bullhorn blared that word was being spread on social media bearing certain hashtags alerting at-risk migrants to pack their essentials and find their way to the park to pair up with volunteer hosts. Anna could see a bed sheet being torn into armbands and passed out those willing to accept boarders, hopefully temporarily.

Anna told Imogene and Fatma she would watch the kids while they went to procure their armbands. After they waded into the crowd, Anna escorted the boys through a row of sparse shrubbery to a small playground that featured a sandbox with toy cars and trucks that had seen better days.

The boys seized upon the vehicles to fashion a race track and make motor noises as they pushed their jalopies around it. Anna asked Irmak how much space they had in their apartment.

"We have two bedrooms and a living area with a kitchen. Not a lot. I can sleep with my mother and give my room to the migrants. I hope it will just be the two of them."

"As you saw, my place is even smaller and pretty far away. But if you get overloaded let me know."

Irmak nodded, just as Fatma and Imogene returned wearing white armbands, accompanied by a girl who looked more adolescent than Irmak but stood half a head shorter. "This is Naila," Fatma said, "from Syria. She and her mother will be staying with us."

Like Irmak, Naila was slender and had a nice smile, but with darker hair and complexion. She seemed to be at ease with them, having lived in a strange land for a year, Fatma told them.

"Is Naila's mom here?" Anna asked.

"She's at home, close to here," Fatma said, "gathering some things to take to our house." She introduced Anna to Naila in Arabic, explaining the girl spoke only a little Greek. Anna smiled, pointed to her chest and said "Anna," and then to Ramadi in the sandbox. "My son, Ramadi. Arabic name. His father came from Iraq."

Fatma translated but Naila seemed to have understood and smiled at the boys racing their cars. Fatma said something to Naila in Arabic and handed her a slip of paper on which she'd written her address and phone number. "I told Naila we would wait for her and her mom here." She translated Naila's reply: "It is very close. I can be back with her in fifteen or twenty minutes."

Naila set off on the curving path leading to Trikoupi Street. Anna turned to Imogene to ask if she had been assigned boarders.

"Not yet. An organizer said someone will text me. I hope they can speak Greek."

As the women chatted, a pigeon alighted in the sandbox to stupidly stab at a candy wrapper, catching Ramadi's eye. He crept toward it, only for it to flutter off down the path to score a seed pod and bob away with Ramadi in stealthy pursuit. When the pigeon stopped to regard its prize at the bend in the path, Ramadi hunkered down and sprang upon it like a cat, but the bird just flicked its tail and squeaked up and away, leaving him stretched out in the dirt. Imogene took note and told Viktor to help his playmate up.

Viktor ran to Ramadi, urging him to get up and come back. As Ramadi came to his knees, Viktor pointed ahead. "Look!" he said. "See her with those men?"

"You mean that new girl?" They could see Naila standing on the sidewalk, arms at her side, fists clenched. Two men, one tall and curly-headed, the shorter one in a watch cap, stood stretching out a carpet they seemed to be selling. The girl shook her head and turned around to leave, just as the man on the right deftly circled to encase her in the carpet as the other one plastered a cloth over her face. One more turn of the carpet and the men lifted it off the ground, shouldered the squirming cylinder, and tossed it into the back of a van parked at the curb. The taller man clambered aboard and swung the doors shut. His partner vaulted into the driver's seat to bull the van into the line of cars creeping toward the end of the block.

The entire encounter had lasted about a minute. Onlookers would only have seen a couple of men rolling up a carpet and loading it into their truck. The boys mutely gaped after it before beelining back, one screaming "*Mutti!*", the other "*Mamá!*"

Chapter Twenty-Six

Akhmed stirs in his cot in the storeroom of a sporting goods store. He seems to serve as night watchman, though he's not especially watchful. Every morning the owner comes to open the store, allowing Akhmed to roam for the rest of the day in his taxi. The man seems to be an Arab, which does not surprise me. Today he did not come. Perhaps it is Sunday.

Watching Akhmed sleep is a snooze in itself, but I keep close hoping he reconnects with Katrina. When I urged him to go back to her house he paid no attention. This could take a while.

Sunday or not, Akhmed dresses and pushes through the rear door to a lot where his car is parked. He is lucky to have a safe place to keep it. We get in and he drives to a small café on a street corner marked by street signs in Greek I cannot decipher. I follow him in and watch him take his morning meal.

He picks up his phone from the counter, wolfs down his food, gulps his tea, and we take our leave. I am hoping his rider is someone I know but it turns out to be a package he delivers somewhere on the other side of the Acropolis.

Heading toward the city center, he spots a couple on the sidewalk looking at a map and pulls over. They appear to be tourists. They eye him with suspicion as he hands the man his card. Now they show him their map and point to a place marked National Library of Greece in English. After some give-and-take in sign language, they get into his car, appearing to disapprove of its shabby interior. I make an invisible face at them.

Anna heard the boys shouting and turned to look as the boys galloped up, shrieking, to attach like burrs to their respective mother's legs.

Anna and Imogene hoisted their sons to their chests. "What's wrong?" Anna asked.

The boys panted in counterpoint. "Some men" … "carpet" … "wrapped up" … "truck."

"Back up," Imogene said. "Viktor, are you saying Naila was hit by a truck?"

"No, Mamá, she was p-put into one and t-taken away!"

"Two men stopped her," Ramadi said through tears. "They had a carpet."

"Oh no!" Anna said. "Did they wrap up her up in it?"

Ramadi nodded, sniffling. Wailing in Turkish, Fatma streaked down the path to the street. Irmak ran after her, followed by Anna and Imogene, still clutching their boys.

At the sidewalk, Viktor said, "She was right here." He pointed to an empty parking space. "And the truck was over there."

Anna peered right and then left to see two lanes of cars inching toward an intersection. She hoisted Ramadi, pointing down the street. "Is that the truck, that white van near the corner?"

"I … I think so," he said.

She turned to face the others. Imogene had deposited Viktor and was embracing Fatma, who wept on her shoulder. Anna planted Ramadi. "Omigod! It's the kidnappers I've been watching! They got the Syrian girl!"

The event she'd been expecting had happened, but of all the places and times and people it could have been, it was here, now, and Naila. Paralyzed by urgency, she recalled Chris telling her at the café: "It all depends on you." No, she'd objected, saving a child takes a caring community, as if she could manufacture one with a text message. But what else could she do? She gulped down air and found her phone. Her hands shook as she opened her tracking app.

"What do you mean, watching kidnappers?" Imogene asked.

"She showed me," Fatma said, "pictures of men putting carpet in truck with someone inside." She peered down the street. "But I see no truck like that."

"It cleared the intersection. Turned left. See?" Anna said, offering her phone.

The women squinted at the screen, a street map displaying a yellow line running down Trikoupi, turning left, and ending at a blue dot.

"What the hell?" Imogene said. "How is this possible?"

"My friend ID'd the driver, found where he parks his van, and planted a GPS unit on it the other night. No time to explain it all, Imogene." She fished out a business card from her jeans. "While they're stuck in traffic, let's call a cab. I'll see if what's-his-name from last night is available."

Anna dialed and put the phone to her ear. "Ur Taxi? This is Anna. You came to my flat last night, Remember?"

A pause. "We're at Parko Navarinou in Exarcheia on Trikoupi. How soon can you get here? … I see." And to Imogene, "He says he's about to drop off at the National Library. Is that close to here?"

"A ten-minute walk or a five-minute run," Imogene replied, pointing down toward Panepistimiou Boulevard. "And from there, where, may I ask?"

"Nikaia, probably," Anna said. And to her phone: "Wait for us at the library. Again, my name's Anna. We're three women and three kids. See you there, Ur Taxi."

When Anna ended the call, Imogene said: "Nikaia? Why not call 112? Tell police where to find them. What could we possibly do to free Naila? These men are dangerous!"

"That's their home base, and here's the thing with police," Anna started to say, but stopped when shouts swelled from within the park. They turned to see people scattering, some scrambling towards them, fleeing a swarm of men in blue with shields and batons advancing toward the assembly area. They were met by angry shouts and chants of "POLICE OUT OF EXARCHEIA! HANDS OFF IMMIGRANTS!" Flashes erupted near those standing their ground, followed by fumes, A few of the grenades got hurled back. Undeterred, the centurions waded into the crowd, batons raised.

"I'll tell you," Anna said, "but cops are heading our way and I expect your white armbands could spell trouble. Let's get our kids out of here. Come on!"

Fatma nodded and sniffed. A yellowish grey mist was wafting toward them, the kind Irmak had told Ramadi you get used to.

"All right," Imogene said as people ran toward them. "Viktor, let's go."

They strode down Trikoupi forming a phalanx of their own, with a determined Anna on one end, a dubious Imogene on the other, Fatma and Irmak taking up the middle, with two disconcerted boys in between, holding hands, marching to an uncertain destiny.

#

They trooped five abreast, faster than the boys said they enjoyed. For their sake, every few meters the mothers crooked their elbows to let the boys dangle before setting their feet in motion again.

"My heart aches for Naila," Fatma said, staring blankly ahead. "And now that the police have scattered the organizers, I have no way to reach her mother."

"You know," Anna said, "if we can save Naila, not knowing might spare her mother some grief."

Fatma grimly nodded. Looking back to her phone, Anna issued an update. "It made it past Exarchion. Now it's on Stournari, heading west. So, if they turn left on Oktovriou, it means they're probably trying to get on Panepistimiou, not far from where we're supposed to meet our cab."

At the library, as if covering a marathon, Anna said: "They're half way down Oktovriou. Bet they're heading for Pireos Avenue, but we'll see."

Shortly a faded turquoise Toyota Corolla decorated with blotches of primer pulled up, faintly squeaking like a dove taking flight. An older couple clambered out and shuffled through the plaza. The driver rolled down his window, leaned out, and squinted at them through dusty spectacles.

"I remember," he said in weak Greek. "From house in Keratsini. Please to get in."

Imogene and Fatma slid into the back seat to sandwich the boys. Irmak squeezed onto her mom's lap. Anna rode shotgun, device in hand.

~

Even though I don't take up space, it's gotten crowded in here. But Allah najni! Look who just got in! It's Katrina, right next to

Akhmed! As at their first encounter at her flat, I see no sense of recognition. What it will take to discover their connection I do not know, but somehow it seems fated.

In the confines of the taxicab, time seems to dilate. Akhmed says to the five people in the rear: "Do seat belts please. Children also." And to Anna: "Where you go?"

"Don't go anywhere yet," Anna replies. "I'll let you know. Probably Nikaia."

"How long you want wait?"

"Not long. Your car is making a funny noise. Is it okay?"

"Is water pump. Need new one. But we get there. Please enjoy its music."

"I'll try. What's your name?"

"Akhmed"

"Where you from, Akhmed?"

"Escape Syria, come here from Turkey. You?"

"Escaped Switzerland. Anyway, we're following some folks, so I'll tell you where to turn as we go, okay?" She checks her phone. "Let's move out. Stay on Panepistimiou for now."

Akhmed pushes up his glasses to peer at her screen. A blue dot flashes near the Omonia roundabout about 500 meters ahead, inching toward Saint Constantine Street.

"You want follow that?"

"Yes, please. That's our friends' car. We're following them home."

"Okay," Akhmed says, stepping on the gas. "We catch up."

The Corolla hurtles forward, passing several cars. In the back, Fatma winces, the boys make faces. Imogene's thumbs orbit above woven fingers. "No need for speed, Akhmed," Anna cautions. "Our friends need time to settle in before we show up."

A zig and a zag and both vehicles are on Pireos, heading southeast, a good kilometer apart. Relieved to have a navigator, Akhmed inserts his earbuds to enjoy some music. Currently he favors derivative Turkish heavy metal, if only to spite his puritanical former captors.

"Once I'm sure they're heading home to Nikaia," Anna says over her shoulder, "I'll activate the network."

Fatma is hunched over as in prayer. Imogene is not; "Network? You need to tell me what you're getting us into," as if Anna had a ready answer.

"Call it a demo, uprising, citizen's arrest," Anna tells Imogene, bypassing Akhmed's plugged-in ears. "One of theses creeps kidnapped a boy named Sami right off the street six weeks ago. I was there and got pictures of it. Sami was saved and the guy was arrested, but the judge let him off. So Sami's mom and I and some of our friends decided to do something about it."

"And what was that?"

"We organized an anti-trafficking league. Made a website to publicize it. Set up a phone tree to broadcast emergency alerts to supporters, which I'm about to do."

"And what are *they* supposed to do?"

"Show up, surround their house, yell at them until an NGO's rescue squad arrives to back us up. By the time they arrive, the corrupt police will have no choice but to arrest these creeps."

Imogene stiffens. "Anna, they have the girl, and now Viktor and I could be hostages too."

"You could've stayed behind, Imogene. Why did you get in the taxi?"

"I was afraid to go home. But now that I know what you're up to I feel even more unsafe."

"Forgive me, Imogene. I never intended to put you through this. We can let you out and you can hail a ride back home, if that's what you want."

Suddenly, a polyrhythmic thumping fills the cabin. Akhmed scowls. Anna grouses, "*Scheisse*, not a flat tire!"

"We should be so lucky," Imogene replies, and tells the boys to stop kicking the front seats. They comply, giggling at the success of their tomfoolery.

Approaching a large intersection, Akhmed slows and peels off an earbud. "Which way, Anna?"

"Sorry," Anna answers. "Been talking." She stabs at her phone to adjust her map. "Destination still seems to be Nikaia. It's straight ahead, but please pull over there," she tells him, gesturing beyond the intersection.

Akhmed shrugs and pulls to the curb, beating his steering wheel in time to a rock anthem only he can hear.

"You and Viktor can get out here," Anna tells Imogene. "Just cross the street, get on a bus or hail a cab. I'll let you know how it went."

Akhmed idles, Imogene deliberates, Fatma frets. Anna intercedes: "Okay Fatma, time to alert our contacts. Here comes a text with the details to pass on." She opens a draft message addressed to her first responders with attached picture of their destination in Nikaia and a link to a map marking the spot.

YOU ARE URGENTLY NEEDED RIGHT NOW TO STOP A KIDNAPPING, reads the Greek text. THIS IS NOT A TEST. DROP EVERYTHING, PASS THIS ON, AND GET TO THE ADDRESS ON THE MAP ASAP! DO NOT CALL POLICE. BE PREPARED TO DO SOME SHOUTING. A CHILD'S LIFE IS AT STAKE.

Having triggered an incident, Anna sucks in her breath and dials Peter Mavridis, begging his voicemail to read her message and activate his team of guardian angels on the double.

Fatma says text received, dutifully passes it on, and buries her face in her hands again.

You are motivated," Imogene says, "Fatma is motivated, but how many others are?"

"I can only hope," Anna replies. "I spent weeks signing up people who might care, lined up first responders and hopefully some news outlets. Are you sure you don't want to be part of that?"

"Right. Have you arranged childcare too?"

Anna ignores the sarcasm. "Expect other moms will show up, probably some with kids. Maybe you can help with that."

Seeking his mother's eye, Viktor asks "Are we going to another demo?"

Imogene squeezes his knee. "I think we'll sit this one out, sweetie."

Grabbing his other knee, Ramadi urges, "Don't go, Viktor!"

As confused as ever, Akhmed says "So, Anna, we go or no go?"

Anna studies her screen. "They left Pireos and are now on Petrou Ralli, heading straight for Nikaia, about two kilometers ahead of us."

She turns to Imogene. "We should get going. Shall we part?"

Imogene's eyes search the mottled roof liner for an answer. Anna's eyes do too, wanting to know if she was crazy or not to send non-combatants into enemy territory. *What would Mahmoud want me do? What AM I doing?*

Everyone looks worried except for Akhmed. I sense desperation in Katrina's eyes. Whoever they are following must be bad people. I can only send her and the others love and courage to face what lies ahead.

"All right," Imogene says, sighing. "I'll attend this freak show, but nobody better get hurt, especially any of the children, or you'll never hear the end of it."

"Freak show," Ramadi says, assimilating the phrase into his lexicon.

"Appreciate that, Imogene, very much," Anna says. "I doubt you'll be at risk, certainly not to the extent I am. These characters are evil, but they aren't homicidal maniacs, and there's strength in numbers. So, is there anyone you can call who would come to help?"

"My husband."

"Then send him these directions." Anna forwards her alert.

Imogene passes it on, urging her mate to make haste from Analipsi with his crew of painters. "Michael says map received and he'll come quick as he can."

Anna is focused on her phone. "Thanks." That's great. Some of my people say they're already on their way."

"Sounds like big party!" Akhmed says, grinning.

Inside Anna's head, a familiar voice. *Right. Did you remember to bring balloons? Got liability insurance?*

Very funny and not so funny, Anna thought back. *Sure, something bad could happen. I would feel terrible if someone got hurt. But there's both strength and safety in numbers.*

Someone could still be roughed up.

Peter will bring medics. Police will come. You want me to hand out liability waivers? Nobody's gonna hand me one.

No reply. Anna shakes her head and tells Akhmed to step on it.

No idea where we are or where they're headed, but Katrina has a map on her phone that shows a moving dot that they seem to be following. The women are texting. Akhmed is smiling but they are not. The one in a headscarf weeps now and then, the other looks cross, but our son and that other boy seem okay. I sense grief, anxiety, tension. What in Allah's name is going on?

Magnisias Street was deserted when the Corolla squeaked up to the kidnappers' cottage, fifteen minutes after their "hosts" had settled in. Anna instructed Akhmed to circle around the block and stop at the alley. She peered in expecting to see the white van parked behind the house, but instead found the silver Mercedes wagon in its place.

"That's Laskaris' car," she said. "But where's the van?" She brought up her tracker to find it on Petrou Ralli, vectoring toward Central Athens.

"What if Naila is still in it?" Fatma said.

"She must be here. Why else would they have come?" Anna said. "We can find the van later."

They circled the block. Anna told Akhmed to drive past the house and park. She handed him twenty euros. "Please hang around in case we need you. You're welcome to join us if you wish."

"Maybe. If they want me. I no have party clothes."

"No problem, Akhmed, all are equally welcome here."

A utility van was approaching from behind. Anna's neck tingled as the unmarked vehicle loafed past and pulled in not far ahead of them. Mindful that the police used such vehicles to deploy gendarmes behind enemy lines, as it were, she was relieved to see its rear doors swing open to disgorge a diverse group of civilians.

Descending first was a substantial close-cropped woman in aviator sunglasses and a t-shirt that warned: *No, I will not fix your computer.* She lent a hand to Ottovio in coveralls with a black satchel slung over his shoulder. Then a man whom Anna didn't recognize jumped out, followed by someone she did, Kosta's exotic customer Marcos Hexadecimos, outfitted in an orchid-print mu-mu. Next came a man in work clothes vaguely resembling Andreas, and then Andreas himself, accompanied by Kosta and his domestic partner Thomàs. They gathered in a knot, murmuring, warily absorbing the scene through shifting eyes.

Telling the others to wait in the car, Anna jumped out and ran to hug Andreas. "I'm so glad to see you. But let's keep it quiet until others arrive."

"How many are you expecting?" Andreas asked, still in her embrace.

"No idea."

Anna beckoned to the bewildered passengers. "Gather 'round and I'll tell you what's going down here."

Taking it in, Akhmed turned to the two moms in the back seat. "Look like she has many friends."

Beatrice and Gyro unfolded a drop cloth. "Gyro made this," Ottovio said. "Can't have a demo without banner." Emblazoned across it in chunky red letters was ΣΤΑΜΑΤΉΣΤΕ ΤΗΝ ΠΑΙΔΙΚΉ ΔΕΣΜΌΣ ΤΩΡΑ! — END CHILD BONDAGE NOW!

Anna complimented their handiwork just as a battered yellow VW Samba bus rattled to a stop next to her. Its front door creaked open. "Where do you want us to go?" the driver asked. It was Shift Coordinator Chris piloting his anarchist café collective's all-purpose school bus with a half dozen conscripts fogging its windows with puzzled faces.

"No way! Chris, boy am I glad to see you!" Anna whooped before remembering to lower her voice. "Umm, tell your people to wait here until that guy gives you the nod." She pointed at Andreas, who acknowledged her presumption by sticking out his tongue.

As the Samba lurched up the block to park, she implored Andreas to marshal the group. Pointing past the house, she said, "I'll go down there to wait for others to show up. Stay put and keep quiet until I signal. Then we'll all march to that blue door, chanting our hearts out."

"Chanting what?" Andreas asked, as Chris and his perplexed passengers joined them.

"Chant the banner, let 'em know they're busted. Release the girl and give themselves up. See what you can come up with to captivate the media."

"Media? What media?"

"Whatever news hounds my boss at Altogether can round up. Stand tall and shout it out. You've done this before."

"What if those guys try to shoot their way out?"

"They won't. Anyway, that's what the police are for."

"I thought you didn't trust the police."

"I don't, but they'll show up, and whose side do you think they'll take if that happens?"

"Look, Anna. They have a hostage."

"A lot of good that will do them. Even if they get away, they won't get far, not with all this attention."

"Have it your way, Anna," he said. "It's your show. But if something like that goes down you'll have a lot of explaining to do." A refrain she by now knew by heart.

"I know, I know," she said, just as Kosta tapped her shoulder, telling her to turn around. Two blocks down Magnisias Street, a small clump of people, women mostly, several with children, were approaching on foot. The closest one had stopped walking and was looking over her shoulder, possibly sensing a hostile presence. It turned out to be a taxicab, from which two women and a man alighted to join the group. More than a squad but less than a platoon, a company was forming.

Chapter Twenty-Seven

REMINDING ANDREAS THAT HE'D marshaled bigger street actions in the past, Anna wished him luck, blew a kiss, and sprinted down the block. Akhmed waved her down as she approached.

"What I do? Stay here? Go?"

"You're welcome to join us. This isn't a party, though." She nodded at Fatma. "The party we were following kidnapped a girl, and we're here to get her back. A rescue squad is coming, so please stick around."

"*Allah yahfuzuhrum wayahfizuhum aminin!*" Akhmed cried, uncharacteristically wishing them God's protection. "But I stay with car, wait for you. Is not my business and I am not legal here."

"I understand," Anna said. "Thanks for hanging in." Then to his distraught passengers: "Maybe you should stay here with Akhmed until we see how things go."

"I-I don't know," Fatma said. "Maybe yes, to watch over children."

"Viktor and I will wait here," Imogene said, "at least until Michael arrives."

"That's fine," Anna said. "Ramadi, you stay with Fatma and Imogene. Do what they tell you. I'll be back to get you as soon as I can."

"I wanna come!"

She leaned in and squeezed his chin. "Look, sweetie, I can't watch you in the middle of all these people. Stay in the car where you will be safe."

Before Ramadi could protest, she was gone, running down the street waving her arms over her head. He watched her recede through the rear window and then swiveled back to see a knot of people gathered around Andreas. Then he was squirming into the empty passenger seat and opening the door.

Imogene reached for him and missed. "Ramadi!" she said, gripping Viktor's arm. "Get back here! Do as your mother said!"

Unheeding, Ramadi jumped out and bounded up to Andreas to clutch his leg.

"Ramadi, what are you doing here!"

"Mutti say I stay with you. Please," he said with arms extended.

Sighing, Andreas stooped to hoist Ramadi onto his shoulders and told him to hang on to his pony tail. "Quiet, everybody," he told his squad. "We wait here, and when the signal to advance comes, we hoist the banner and start chanting and move toward that blue door along with Anna's group."

"Chanting what?" asked salon customer Clyde asked, having suffered the misfortune of being coiffed at the wrong time.

Beatrice pointed to Gyro's END CHILD BONDAGE NOW banner. "Well, here's a start. Anyone have any other slogans?"

"How about 'PEDERASTS ARE CRIMINALS'?" one of Chris's crew said.

"That's sort of general," Marcos said. "How about 'RELEASE WHAT'S-THEIR-NAME NOW!' Isn't that why we're here?"

"That's good, Marcos" Andreas said. "But what is the victim's name?"

"Nyla," Ramadi said. "I think her name is Nyla."

"Thanks, Ramadi," Andreas said. "So our chorus will be 'END CHILD BONDAGE! RELEASE NYLA NOW!' Shout it out, but keep it for when we move out."

"There's Mutti!" Ramadi said from his perch, tugging on his steed's tail.

Andreas peered down the block, where Anna was gesticulating to a knot of people. He turned back to inventory his troops. Someone was missing. Last time he'd looked, Ottovio had been holding up the middle of Gyro's banner, but now the geek was gone.

#

Half way down the block Anna stopped to catch her breath. Volunteers were arriving and clustering around her, about eight so far. She turned toward Andreas, to count his contingent. When her eyes fell on the faces peering at her from the back of the Corolla, its back doors swung open to disgorge Fatma and Irmak, who ran up to join her.

"I couldn't just stay in car with all this going on," Fatma said.

"Where's Ramadi?" Anna asked.

"He jumped out and ran over to your friend," Fatma said. "We couldn't stop him. See him on that man's shoulders?"

"Don't like that," Anna said. "You should have gone after him."

When Fatma didn't answer, Anna shook her head and pivoted to her responders. "See that house with the blue door? Inside are two men and the teenage girl they abducted in Exarcheia an hour ago."

Murmurs arose, followed by questions. She waved for quiet. "Pipe down, everyone! Keep quiet until we move out; When I clap my hands above my head we'll march on the house chanting, shouting, demanding they free her. Are you with me?"

A few fists, followed by more, rose in solidarity, just as her phone pealed. Ottovio was calling. "I'm at the end of the alley. The Benz is parked off to the side with nobody around. How many people you got?"

"Almost a dozen," Anna said, "plus another around Andreas."

"Tell some of them to break off," he said. "Go to either end of the alley to block escape."

"Good thinking. Reminds me. Your spycam, did you reboot it?"

"Still outta juice. Can't do everything, fearless leader."

"*Scheisse.* So, whatever happens back there, make sure to get pictures."

"No problem. I show you. Look at their house. Okay? Now look straight up. See anything?"

Anna craned her neck to scan the sky. "Is that a drone? Yours, I hope."

"Don't tell anyone. I'm keeping it fifteen meters up so people won't notice it."

"So I'm on video right now?"

"You and bunch of others. Whatever happens, you'll have proof. I gotta go."

The line went dead. Anna glanced up. The quadcopter was now right above her. Sensing people were getting restless and feeling more than a little exposed, she punched up Peter Mavridis again. This time he answered.

"Peter! I'm glad I reached you. Did you get my messages? We're all set on Magnisias Street. Are you on your way?"

"Got them. What's the situation?"

"Two men are inside a bungalow with a blue door at number 34 after abducting a girl in Exarcheia. My kid witnessed it. We followed them here and have several dozen people standing by to disturb their peace. I had hoped you guys would be among them."

"I see. On the assumption this wasn't a fire drill, I mobilized a team of six with two vehicles and we're headed your way. Don't try anything before we arrive. Should be in ten minutes. And now that there's a hostage situation, I'll notify Hellenic Police."

"I'll hold off, Peter, but please wait to do that. I want police to be the last to get there. I told you why that's important!"

Uttering a Greek explicative Anna was happy not to understand, he lit into her. "Who knows what these men might do, Anna! I'll call police whether you like it or not! Now that you've put all those people in danger this is a public safety issue!"

"Okay, okay. Maybe it's time to alert the Nikaia Precinct. Tell them you're here to rescue a child and want backup, but not storm troopers. I'm so glad you're coming, but will you do that for me, *please*?"

"Okay," he said, sighing. "I'll call Nikaia. Now what's the situation there?"

"Open the street map I texted. Pull up the street view. Visualize two masses of protesters some ten meters away from that house in either direction."

She was describing the alley where Laskaris's wagon sat when Kosta ran up, telling her Andreas wanted marching orders. With Peter still on the line, Anna said: "Have the banner people and half the others stand by to march on the house. The rest should break off and run back up the block and around to the back alley."

She asked Peter if he'd copied that, but he seemed to have hung up. She pocketed her phone, yanked a bandana from her jacket, mopped her brow, and was tying it around her head as Kosta asked: "To do what?"

"Another group will head to the other end. When you see them, start to converge on a Mercedes wagon that's parked there. Try not to let it get away."

"When? Now?"

"Hold on. I'm waiting for reinforcements, professional humanitarians. When they come I'll clap my hands over my head, like this," she said, demonstrating, "and we'll converge on the house making noise."

"Got it. This is so exciting!" Kosta said, and scurried off.

Taking Anna's inadvertent semaphore for a call to action, the people around her moved forward. Chanting and ululation echoed through the street. The clamor brought out curious onlookers, a few of whom traipsed after the throng. Anna saw Kosta address Andreas with Ramadi riding high, and soon they and four others broke away and started trotting up the block. Having uncorked her genies, all Anna could do was to call out: "Surround the house! Those with children, stand back!"

~

The street we are on is a blur slowly coming into focus. Whenever I visit a new place, a fog surrounds me. After a while it starts to retreat and I can see farther and more clearly. Now I see Katrina in the street, leading people this way. They seem to be shouting.

First she had Akhmed follow a car to this place. Now I sense she is leading a protest against whoever lives here. It worries me. She is in the thick of the action and our boy seems vulnerable sitting on Andreas's shoulders. Should I follow Katrina or mind our son or stay with Akhmed in his car? I will wait here to see what happens, then decide.

~

To the left of the blue door was a picture window behind a sun blind. As demonstrators converged on it from two directions, Anna cringed when its slats creaked open just long enough to reveal a dark countenance. Someone yelled: "WE KNOW YOU'RE IN THERE. RELEASE THE GIRL!" The blind snapped shut and several women started pounding on it with their fists until the thin metal dented.

"DON'T LET THEM ESCAPE!" Anna shouted. "You six, stay here to block the front! Reinforcements are coming! The rest follow me around the block to the alley behind the house! They have a car back there."

Ignoring questioners, she sprinted off with Fatma, Irmak, and six others in pursuit. At the corner, Anna froze as a white SUV, emergency lights flashing, bore down on her. The cavalry had come.

Anna's phone chimed. "We're here," said Peter said. "Where are you?"

"Right in front of you. In a black bandanna. Almost run over. Some of us are heading around back."

A man in a yellow slicker leapt out from the passenger seat, phone to his ear. "Here come the medics," he said. "Don't go anywhere." He closed the connection just as a yellow ambulance flashing blue rolled to a stop. Anna waved her companions on. "Run! Block the alley! I'll come soon!"

She approached the swarm of yellow jackets around Mavridis, gulped air, and plunged into his circle, trying not to think about what might ensue should Naila not be inside the cottage.

"Hi Peter, I'm Anna," she said, extending her hand.

In response to her gesture, Peter folded his arms. "May I ask what your plan is for all these people?"

"We're here to expose their sordid racket and rescue Naila, and won't leave until she's safe."

He lifted a hand to cup his chin. "It seems you're acquainted with the victim. How so?"

"My friend Fatma was planning to shelter Naila and her mom from a police raid on immigrants. They're Syrian refugees. When Naila left to bring back her mother, two men confronted her on the sidewalk, blocking her way with a carpet they held up. Then they wrapped her up in it and tossed her into a van that we followed here."

"That's rather incredible. Where were you?"

"Exarcheia. Parko Navarinou. Riot police were lobbing tear gas to break up a people's assembly. I suspect the kidnappers had gotten word about it and were looking for kids who got separated from their parents and found poor Naila."

"I believe you, but that doesn't change things for us. We're not supposed to go in without clear evidence that a victim is inside. And even then, law enforcement ought to lead the way. How can you be sure the girl is present?"

"Our spy camera's battery died, so no photos. But our kids witnessed the abduction and we tracked their van all the way from Exarcheia. They didn't stop anywhere along the way."

She brandished her tracking app and followed its yellow brick road with her index finger. "See, it stopped in the alley behind that house for a few minutes and then headed back toward central Athens. Good enough evidence?"

"I'm not going to ask how you pulled that off." He raised his eyes to appraise the festivities. "So what's your plan now?"

Anna gestured at the protestors clustered around the front door. "Besides these people, two groups are blocking the back alley in case they try to drive off."

"With or without the victim?"

"Umm … good question … What would you expect?"

"Best case, they give themselves up. Worst case, they bring her out at gunpoint. What would you do then?"

Unable to answer a question she should have anticipated, Anna said: "I think its time to call the cops."

"They're on their way. So hold your horses."

His advice was met by an echoing chorus of shouts and jeers.

"That would be our people in the alley," Anna said. "Something's going down there." She took off, shouting over her shoulder. "This way!" Rounding the corner, she noticed the drone stealthily drifting down in pursuit.

"Wait!" Peter yelled, then cursed when she didn't. He summoned his teammates and instructed them to deploy at each end of the alley and wait for the police.

Over the hubbub, a police siren warbled, coming their way.

Chapter Twenty-Eight

RUNNING DOWN THE SIDE street, Anna watched the drone overtake her, turn right at the alley, and pass behind a building. Short of breath, she came up behind a clutch of people at the end of the alley to piercing shrieks of "LET HER GO! LET HER GO!" Rising on her toes, she spotted the wagon. Behind it, Andreas led half a dozen chanting supporters forward with Ramadi on his shoulders. In between, Ottovio stood, working his controller.

"What's happening here?" she asked the tall woman who obscured her view.

"Just as we all got here, two men carried a sagging rolled-up carpet to the car and shoved it in. Now they're getting in. Was that the girl?" Before Anna could answer, the wagon's Diesel engine chuffed and growled.

Anna plunged to the fore to see the wagon creeping toward them. Laskaris was at the wheel, mouth drawn under his mustache, eyes darting between her and his mirrors as Andreas's group gained ground. Then Servopoulos was leaning from the passenger window brandishing a pistol, bellowing: "MAKE WAY OR BE ROADKILL!" Protestors scrambled and Anna ducked as his gun swung toward her. Close by, sirens stuttered to a halt.

"STAND YOUR GROUND! DON'T LET THEM PASS!" she cried. Soon, the big wagon was upon her and she was grasping its grill, then clawing at the hood ornament, shrieking: "*Hör auf, du Arschloch.*" Undeterred by the scatological insult, Laskaris grinned as her footing gave way.

Her feet had slipped under the bumper when a bearded man darted up, grasped a flailing arm, and began dragging her away. Better late to the party than never, taxi driver Akhmed was tugging his passenger back from eternity, muttering: "You some crazy woman!"

Just shy of deliverance, a loose cobblestone undermined his footing, sprawling them onto the pavement. Both would have been mauled but for a brilliant spot of ruby light sweeping across the wagon's windshield to rest on Servopoulos's cheek, emitted from a sidearm in the two-fisted grip of a uniformed policewoman planted behind them.

"DROP YOUR GUN!" Sergeant Melina Cristopoulos said, as protestors ducked, dove, and flattened themselves against walls. "HALT! DROP WEAPON! EXIT CAR WITH HANDS UP!" Servopoulos spat and let his gun fall. Melina's laser slid over to illuminate Laskaris, who stopped the vehicle just shy of the fallen couple.

Just as he'd sheltered a comrade in battle, Akhmed sprawled on top of Anna, apologizing for the intimacy. A woman set to hurl a cobblestone let it fall. Hyperventilating protesters scrambled to their feet.

A policeman bulled forward to cover Servopoulos as Melina approached Laskaris. "TURN OFF CAR! GET OUT! SHOW ME YOUR HANDS!"

As Laskaris complied, Andreas and Kosta raced to the car. Kosta raised the tailgate and was reaching for the rolled-up carpet when a man shouted from behind: "YOU, AT THE CAR, STEP BACK! ALL OF YOU, STAND ASIDE!"

They looked back to see a man in a grey suit sprinting toward them wielding a pistol. The men complied, backing away, arms raised. Neither recognized him as Lieutenant Antonio Nicolaides, but the uniformed officers and medics behind him underscored his imperative. They brushed past the demonstrators, not noticing Ottovio jockeying his eye in the sky.

At the tailgate, Nicolaides waved his weapon at the protestors and again ordered them to move away. "There's a girl inside," Andreas said from the side of the alley, hands clasped behind his neck. "Be careful!"

Three meters away, spread-eagled with hands on hood, Laskaris and Servopoulos were being patted down by Melina and her fellow officer. "Cuff them!" Nicolaides said. "Take them to the squad car!"

"I think you can get up now," Anna said from under Akhmed's torso.

He rose on his haunches and helped her to an unsteady footing. She took some steps to test her aching right ankle and decided it was useable. As the two cops marched their suspects away, Fatma streaked to the wagon shrieking, "Oh Naila! Get her out of that *kilim*!"

Fatma reached into the tailgate for the carpet, but the detective pinioned her wrist. "Please let us do this, Ma'am," he said. "She'll be free soon enough. We need to preserve evidence."

Fatma stepped back as the officers slowly unrolled Naila, who lay still for a moment, then put her hands to her face, crying. After checking for wounds, Nicolaides told her she was safe.

"She doesn't speak Greek," Fatma told him, and spoke to Naila in Arabic as medics helped her to her feet. As some of the evidence sought was rather personal, a female first responder conducted her and Fatma to an ambulance for a more thorough inspection.

~

Now I get the picture. Katrina led a rescue effort that involved many people that seems to have worked. I am stunned. I cannot believe how brave she was and am so proud of my brother. After all this, I feel they will surely get to know one another. But now, where is our son? He was with Andreas, but not any more.

~

Watching policemen lead the kidnappers away, Anna squeezed Akhmed's shoulders and kissed him on both cheeks.

"Thank you!" she said, and hugged him again. "That was very brave. If not for you, Ramadi would be an orphan. "

A tear traced a ragged crescent down his scarred cheek. Almost as if in a trance, staring through her to some harrowing time past, he said: "Ramadi. Orphan …"

"Thankfully he's not. But where is he?"

She scanned the scene. No son. Noticing Andreas, Kosta, and Thomás loitering nearby, she excused herself from Akhmed and ran to them.

"Where's Ramadi?"

Andreas' eyes danced about the alley. "Don't know. When the police came he slid off me and I guess I lost track. Did he come to you?"

"Are you kidding? He could have been in the line of fire, Andreas. He must've gotten scared and run away. We've got to find him."

Kosta said, "Just as the cops came, I saw him dash away."

"In what direction?"

He pointed across the alley. "That way, toward the house."

"Omigod!" Anna said, soiled hands at cheeks. "Look! Isn't the back door open?"

"Seems so," Andreas said. "You don't suppose …"

"I do suppose! We have to see if he's inside!"

Andreas rubbed his chin. "I don't know … Shouldn't the police …"

"Come ON!" Anna urged him, latching onto his arm and tugging him like a hound on a leash. As they passed by Inspector Nicolaides inspecting the wagon's hatch he looked up to see, striking his occiput on the transom. Through a swarm of sparks, he shouted: "Hey! You can't go in there. That's a crime scene!"

Anna shook her head, and scurried through the doorway, pulling Andreas after her.

"*Skata!*" Nicolaides said, and charged after them, gripping his head. "Damn her idiot ass! I'm gonna cuff them both."

Anna and Andreas found themselves in a kitchen updated with granite countertops and coldly gleaming appliances. On a breakfast island, a box of corn flakes and a carton of milk sat next to a bowl of sodden cereal with a spoon sticking out.

"RAMADI! It's Mutti. Are you in here?" Anna cried.

Hearing no response, Andreas suggested they head up front.

"RAMADI! Where are you?" she said, just as Nicolaides burst in.

"Get out of here now! This is a—"

"Shush! My son is in here! RAMADI!"

"—crime scene. And don't touch anything on your way out."

Ignoring the edict, she approached an open door with steps going down.

"RAMADI! ARE YOU DOWN THERE?"

A muted "Mutti?" wafted up the stairs.

"I'M COMING!" Anna yelled.

"DON'T!" Nicolaides said, rushing over and pushing her aside. "Who knows who's down there."

Andreas came up behind them to shout: "RAMADI! It's Onkle! Are you alone down there?"

"Mutti! Onkle! Come see what I found!"

"He sounds okay," Andreas said. "I think it's safe to go down."

"Stay here," Nicolaides growled. He hunched down the stairs, gripping his pistol in both hands, training it left and right before attaining the concrete floor without incident. Over his shoulder he instructed them to turn on the light. Andreas flipped a switch inside the doorway and a fluorescent fixture flickered on. Anna stood before him, gaping, fingers pressed to cheeks.

Facing the detective were three doorways. The middle door was recessed behind the other two and stood ajar with light shining out. Those on either side were hinged plywood panels with padlocks hanging from hasps. With flicks of his muzzle, he nudged open first door, then the other, revealing windowless closets with chicken wire ceilings and circus motif wallpaper. In each, a foam pad with a thin blanket lay on the floor next to a chamber pot. Hugging the wall, he edged toward the center door, gun poised. Atop the stairway, Anna bit her lip as she clutched Andreas' arm.

At least the detective lowered his weapon when Ramadi popped into the doorway holding out a plastic replica of a fighter jet with American insignia. "Onkle, see?" he said brightly before freezing, eyes wide. He let his prize fall to the carpet, perhaps sensing that this what happens to kids who take other people's toys.

Nicolaides abruptly grabbed the boy's arm and yanked him out. "Go! Run upstairs!" he urged before springing into the room and dramatically sweeping it with his pistol.

"Come Ramadi!" Anna said as he ascended to her eager arms. "Everything's okay. That policeman won't hurt you."

Andreas brushed past them and inside found Nicolaides surveying the room, an oblong windowless chamber with walls of unpainted sheet rock and a beige shag carpet. A grey futon on a tubular steel frame occupied the wall to their left. Behind it, a green paper backdrop, like TV studios use to chroma-key weathermen, covered the entire wall. Nearby, a jumble of toys in a carton— dolls, toy soldiers, plastic cars and trucks, and oddly, a stethoscope. Beside it, a second box overflowed with small garments, costumes, and play hats.

"Party time in the children's house of detention?" Andreas suggested.

Not replying, Nicolaides approached the other end of the room, partly obscured by a folding screen. Behind it, a table with a computer, two monitors, and an audio mixer. A nearby cardboard box held assorted cables and cords, a microphone, and some DVDs. A pair of movie lights with diffusers mounted on tripods bracketed a tripod holding as video camera abjectly pointing downward.

"A production studio," Andreas said. "Hate to think of what got produced here."

Nicolaides sniffed. The room was dank, redolent of sweat, stale cigarette smoke, mold. Dark splotches on the beige carpet hopefully had come from a wine bottle lying nearby. When Andreas reached to right it, Nicolaides intercepted his hand. "Touch nothing!"

Anna and Ramadi crouched in the stairwell clutching one another as Nicolaides withdrew a handkerchief from his breast pocket, grasped the coveted fighter jet, and deposited it in the toy box. "Sorry, lad, but the plane stays here." He shooed them upstairs. "Okay, folks, porno party's over. Time to go."

Anna hauled Ramadi up the stairs in her arms.

"Mutti, what's porno?" he asked.

"Ugly pictures that turn men into stone," she said.

#

Anna emerged onto the patio trailed by Andreas and Nicolaides, deposited Ramadi and stood blinking in the sunlight as people vied for her attention. Waving her over were Katia and Daria and Imogene and Fatma. Peter Mavridis, his team mates clustered about him, also beckoned. Taking Peter's gesture personally, the detective headed toward him, but halted in mid-stride. He cupped his hand to his forehead and squinted skyward at a flying machine faintly buzzing ten meters overhead. As if sensing Antonio's antipathy, the drone scooted down the alley and around the corner.

Ottovio hovered the drone out of sight and made a phone call. On Magnisias Street, Gyro watched the drone flutter down beside his truck. When its rotors stopped, he folded them, stashed the drone in the cargo bay, and shut the doors.

Ignoring her friends, Anna squatted before her son with a piercing gaze.

"Ramadi, that was stupid," she said, grasping his hands. "Why did you go in that house?"

"There was a lot of shouting," he said, avoiding her eyes. "Then I saw policemen with guns. It scared me."

"So you ran into the house. Weren't you scared to do that?"

"It … it looked like a place to hide."

"And why did you go downstairs?"

"I … I thought it would be more safer. Please, Mutti, can I have that jet plane?"

"No, sweetheart, it belongs to someone else. I'll buy you a Jay-Jay. Is that okay?"

She released his hand and pulled him to her, stroking and squeezing his back. "Please, promise me you'll never go into a strange house alone again."

"I promise, Mutti," he said, just as a shadow fell over them. Collectively eclipsing the sun were Fatma, Irmak, Imogene, and Viktor. Akhmed was with them, and they all started praising her at once.

Anna released Ramadi and arose. She brushed off her jeans, along with their compliments. "How is Naila? Where is she?"

"She is still in ambulance," Fatma said. "I was there. She said she really scared but not harmed, and the medics couldn't find any signs of injury or abuse beyond bruises and scrapes."

"Will they let her go, then?" Anna asked.

"No. Police are with her now listening to her story. I wanted to take her home, but was told that the Children's Advocacy Center people will do that. They have protocol."

Anna removed her bandanna and ran her fingers through her air. "How strange. I might never see her again."

"Sure, you will," Fatma said. "I still expect to shelter her and her mother. I will call you to come over."

Akhmed broke in. "Anna, I take you home for free."

"Thanks, Akhmed. You're a sweetheart, but no need. I can get a ride with my friends. Why don't you take Fatma and Irmak back to Exarcheia instead."

"Okay," he said. "But please to call anytime you need ride."

"Deal," she said and hugged him "Can't say how grateful I am for saving me. Than you again, that was very brave."

"You welcome. Hope it will be only time."

From the corner of her eye, Anna saw Melina break off from Nicolaides to approach them. Excusing herself, she went to her, unsure of what to expect. It turned out to be an unexpected embrace.

"You know, Anna," Melina said. "I sensed you were up to something you weren't talking about, but never imagined how elaborate it was. But people could have gotten hurt in all that commotion. You were nearly killed."

"I know. It was a close call. I'm so grateful you showed up and took charge."

"I tell you, I surprised myself. This was first time to pull my weapon since joining the force."

"Guess your training paid off. You were great. I owe you, and I'm sorry for being secretive. I had to because I didn't trust your detective friend, and I figured you would tell him whatever I let you in on."

"Why couldn't you trust Antonio? He's one of the best men we've got."

"Well, he could have arrested them earlier but he didn't. Anyway, we all saw it and you have more than enough evidence in that basement to put them away."

"Perhaps, but we need to talk. There's a lot you don't know, Anna."

Failing to bore into Melina's brain through her eyes, Anna said "Same goes for you, but maybe not now."

"Sure," Melina said. "Let me take you to lunch and we'll talk."

Anna blinked a few times, and then told Melina that she'd be happy to get together but needed time to decompress.

"Sure, but it's kind of important, so how about tomorrow?"

At that awkward moment came a tap on her shoulder. Ottovio was informing her that Gyro was packing it in, and did she and Ramadi need a ride. They sure did, she told him, and bade an eager good-bye to Melina.

"See you," Melina said. "Get some rest. I'll call you about lunch."

Not relishing the prospect, and wishing she could sleep for three days, she clasped Ramadi's hand and loped after Ottovio. She hoped what Melina knew that she didn't wouldn't hurt her.

#

As Anna's goals tended to be, a three-day sleep was unrealistic. Even one night's seemed unattainable as Anna squeezed into bed beside her sleeping child, her mind turning over the events of the day. While she felt she'd played it well, she sensed the game wasn't over. And so, instead of counting sheep, to summon sleep she played mental solitaire, hoping the deck wasn't stacked against her.

For her figurative hand she first drew the Ace of Spades, long thought a symbol of bad luck. That had to be the unfortunate Naila, thankfully now safe and sound and barely touched by inhumane hands.

Then came Fatma, Queen of Spades, who had risen to see Naila through it, reminding Anna that Queen of Diamonds Fotini had failed to show her royal face.

Turning up next, the cunning Jack of Spades, Ottovio, who had devoted himself to her chimeric cause. Thanks to his dark arts, she held evidence that could keep those knaves out of circulation, unless King of Clubs Nicolaides trumped her hand. She hoped the detective would fold instead.

Then, as grateful as Anna was for Melina's life-saving intervention, that Queen of Clubs likely had some cards up her sleeve to play at tomorrow's *tête-à-tête*.

For herself, she drew Queen of Hearts. Despite doubting her claim to the throne, had not Her Highness run a successful campaign? But she would have died in battle except for the gallantry of the Jack of Diamonds, that sweet young man with the thick glasses and a bad complexion who seemed oddly transfixed by her.

As her Five of Hearts slept at her side, the Jack of their suit turned up, rendered with a ponytail and a Tyrolean hat, the Austrian prince she'd courted half-expecting a royal wedding.

Gazing into the middle distance, she could almost see her cherished King of Hearts striding in. What would he think of her now, want her to do, want for their son?

She collapsed her hand and replayed her day. It had started and now was ending right here, via Exarcheia and Nikaia. Naila had been snatched at around one in the afternoon and been recovered by three.

She couldn't believe all that frenzy had lasted but two hours, a hurried climax to two long months of foreplay but, all in all, more satisfying than some she'd had.

Thinking she was tired of thinking, thankful that her inner critic had given it a rest, Anna followed suit. She punched down her eiderdown pillow and rolled onto her side to embrace her child, still unsure of what the stakes were, but prepared to let her cards play out as they may.

Chapter Twenty-Nine

MONDAY DAWNED AND KEPT dawning before Anna stumbled from bed. Her late start left barely enough time to shovel breakfast into Ramadi and escort him to Daria's to do his letters and numbers, affording her time alone to entertain her anxieties about lunching with Melina. In the jolting sanctuary of a homeward-bound bus she ransacked her phone's data to assemble recent events into a narrative for the policewoman who knew things she didn't.

One thing Melina didn't know, she reflected, concerned the van's driver, currently an un-indicted co-conspirator. As passengers jostled by, she opened her tracking app to see what had become of the vehicle. From Nikaia it had laid down the yellow brick road straightaway to its home base at Meteor Imports/Exports. And after one brief foray this morning to somewhere nearby and back, it had slept in its parking lot. Thumbing through imagery from the parking lot camera confirmed that Leander Eugenides had piloted the van when it went for that outing, all by himself. Solid evidence, but did it prove that Eugenides was part of their team?

Trudging up the hill to her flat she figured it would be best to clue in Melina about her devices and let the cops handle Eugenides. Laying her cards on the table would help keep her story straight in the pre-trial inquisitions she assumed she would inevitably undergo.

Turning onto her street she spotted a double-parked yellow-and-white sedan with a TV station logo, no doubt related to the young woman standing at her building's unanswerable front door. Anna's stride slackened and stopped as she recognized her as the reporter in the frisky blue dress who'd interrogated her at the courthouse at Servopoulos' mockery of a trial. Today she sported grey trousers and a blue blazer, and mercifully wasn't accompanied by her gnomish videographer.

In no mood for media fame and sure she'd be hounded if she made a dash to her alleyway, Anna loitered in a doorway waiting for the reporter to give up and go away. As the front flat was vacant, the woman's knocks and hullos would be in vain and she would move on. Anna turned her back and pretended to fumble for her keys, pondering who had pointed the correspondent to her house. Perhaps she'd wrung it out of Fatma, possibly Irene, or from court records. Whatever, the media now knew where to find her.

You might as well stop being so furtive and face the music, her inner voice asserted with customary abrasiveness.

And let the whole world know what kind of snoop I've been? What will that get me beside a place in the Voyeurs Hall of Fame?

Respect, I suspect, and a chance to shine your light. You're a leader now, so act like one.

Easy enough for you to say. Got a flashlight?

Very funny, but do yourself a favor and tell a good story. Take the credit you deserve for saving that girl from a life of vile servitude. Then savor the appreciation you seem to feel you don't deserve.

The reporter did give up, but as she opened her car door, she spotted Anna skulking across the way and sauntered over. "Excuse me, but do you know the person who lives in that little house over there?"

Before Anna could prevaricate, the visitor said, "Wait! It's you … Anna Burmeister! I interviewed you at that kidnapper's trial. It's me, Zoe Karaoúli from Alpha TV. I'm glad I caught up with you. Do you have a few minutes to talk?"

Anna nodded vertically, then horizontally. "I need to prepare for an appointment. Can it wait?"

"I'll be brief then," the reporter replied, going on to describe a demonstration and police raid at a house in Nikaia the previous day that Anna might know something about. "Just a few quick questions, if you don't mind." She extracted an audio recorder from its case.

Placing her hand over the device, Anna stuck out her jaw. "I sort of do if this is on the record."

"Fine. I won't quote you. Just for background."

"So put this thing away and I'll see what I know."

The reporter tucked away her gizmo and opened her notebook. "Tell me what you know about the abduction and what happened next."

Anna inhaled and expelled: "The kidnapped girl was an immigrant being helped by a friend of mine. We were with our kids at a community meeting in a park in Exarcheia and when she left to go home she was abducted and then the police attacked the meeting."

"You saw the abduction?"

"Our kids saw two men roll her up in a carpet and toss it into a van. We saw the van pull away and hailed a cab and followed it all the way to Nikaia."

"And the demonstration—how did that happen?"

"Well, after that travesty of a trial, some moms I know decided if we heard of a kidnapping we should count our kids and alert one another, and created a child protection network. I told you about that, and perhaps your own reporting from the trial inspired other moms to get involved, because a lot more people came together than I ever expected."

"That's amazing. That you happened to be on the scene of a kidnapping by the same fellow, twice."

Anna shifted her handbag to her other shoulder. "Call it kismet. Look, I gotta go."

"Sorry to keep you," Zoe said, plucking her phone from her blazer. "Just one more thing, if you don't mind." She stroked the screen and presented an aerial photo. "Is that you in front of that wagon? Someone claimed it to be."

A black bandanna and khaki-clad sleeves were all that identified the person with palms defiantly pressed to the hood of the Benz in front of a small crowd.

Anna bit her lip as Zoe zoomed in. "Must be," she said. "Hard to tell from overhead. Where did you get it?"

"Someone who flew a drone at the scene wants to sell his movie to the station. He sent a couple stills and a clip."

Why didn't I see this coming? Anna asked herself.

That milk is already spilled, her innerlocutor interjected. *The question should be 'How can I make the most of this?'*

Unconsciously miming Andreas, Anna stroked her chin in thought. "Are you buying the movie?"

"I hope so, but it's not up to me. Seeing it unfold from above would top off an inspiring story."

"One that just might ruin my life if these creeps have creepy friends. Guess I can't stop you from running it, but please don't use my name."

"We won't if that's what you want," Zoe said, and pocketed her phone. "You know, you're much more than a source to me. At the courthouse you told me you were 'just a mom.' I think you're that and a lot more. You took on a situation that would have daunted most moms. You should be damn proud of what you did."

Unaccustomed to unsolicited validation, all Anna could say was: "Thanks. Might be, if there's justice this time." And after a pause: "Now you tell me, please. How did you find out about this incident and who told you to contact me?"

"A tip came in. I'm on the crime beat."

"From whom, may I ask?"

"Can't say. Confidential sources and all that."

"Well then," Anna said over her shoulder, "count me as one of them. Sorry, I'm late. Bye."

She strode across the street, wishing she was just a mom again.

#

Though her plan had been to go home to prepare for her lunch date, Anna decided instead to duck over to the salon to thank Andreas and Kosta for being the vanguard of her first responders.

Part of her didn't buy it: *Is this how you prepare to meet Melina, by running to Andreas?*

Stop the accusations, already. For all anyone knows, you're responsible for at least half of what I've gotten into.

Her counter-accusation led Anna to question the concept of free will, at least as it applied to her. Who had kidnapped part of her mind?

She inquired within. *Who are you? And don't try to tell me you're my subconscious.*

Wouldn't dream of it, dear, whatever Doctor Freud might say. Think of me as your 'sub-conscience' if you like, helping you to do the right thing by yourself and others.

Anna chewed on that. *The right thing. Hmmm. Why should I listen to you?*

Not that you often do. You want I should leave you alone?

Great idea. Why not do that.

I would, but I can't leave without breaking my contract.

Contract?

That's all I can say. Check with Max.

Max? Do I know a Max?

Sure you do. Max the editor. Max, who signed you on to this project.

That snoopy writer's project? I forgot about that. Are you kidding?

When no answer came, Anna shook her head vigorously until her temples ached, and with a great sigh, headed to the salon.

#

Anna crossed Radical Chic's threshold to find Kosta at his station trimming a middle-aged client with an unruly fringe of hair as best he could with what little he had to work with.

"Salut, Kosta," she said into the big mirror. "I dropped by to thank you guys for your support yesterday. You were awesome."

"Wasn't that *something*!" he said, dimpling his cheek with an index finger for emphasis. "I was so excited to have been part of it. You *must* let us know when there's another kidnapping!"

"Unlikely, but thanks for asking and for coming. So where's your ex?"

Kosta nodded toward the back door. "Your paramour is upstairs, powdering his nose or something. Be my guest."

With *paramour* ringing in her ears, Anna stalked to the rear door and shut it behind her. On her way to the back stairway, her gizzard brain broke its short-lived silence. *You go girl! Make him give you what you want!*

Didn't I tell you to fermez votre bouche? she told her virtual traveling companion.

Not in so many words, but I get the point.

Finding the upstairs door unlocked, she let herself in. Everything in his cozy kitchen was neatly in place except for him.

"An-Andreas?" she said, her voice quavering. "Mind if I come in?"

The parlor was also unoccupied. She peeked into the bedroom. "It's Anna. You here?"

"In here," came a muffled reply. "Shaving. Be right out."

She sat on the corner of the big bed staring at the mauve wall, nervous, impatient, apprehensive, listening to the faint tinkle of tap water. She checked her phone. Two hours to get downtown.

He emerged from the bathroom in his elegant thrift shop dressing gown. "Well, *here* is my heroine." He plopped down beside her to peck her forehead. "You must be *exhausted* after all that. How *are* you?"

She laid a hand on his thigh. "Just a little scraped up and tired. Didn't sleep well last night."

"Bad dreams?"

She kicked off her shoes and reclined. "No dreams. More like instant replays of a game that isn't over. Call it PTSD-Plus"

"I'm not surprised. Plus what?"

"Getting dragged into another trial, for one thing, having to tell all."

"You don't seem so pleased with your accomplishment."

"If only I knew what it was. See, there's Nicolaides. I'm sure whatever game he was playing with these guys will get covered up. They may get off and then I'll be fair game."

"So maybe keep a low profile for a while."

"Fat chance. You saw how pissed-off Nicolaides was. Then this morning a TV reporter showed up at my door. Pegged me as the organizer. Asked me how it happened. Showed a frame of me from Ottovio's damn drone. Can't wait to have it spread over the airwaves."

Andreas lay on his side next to her, tentatively cupping her shoulder. "I'm sure you handled it well. If it makes you feel any better, I admire you more than anyone I know, maybe ever knew."

"Really? Pushy, neurotic me?"

"Really. I guess I haven't been good at expressing it, but it goes back years, to when we took to the streets. You organized demos, handled logistics, motivated the community. And then, after the police grabbed George, your energy kept us going. Without you, we would couldn't have put together an operation."

She rolled over to face him. Her arms found his back. "Basically, I was just following your lead."

"Come on. You did *a lot* more than that."

She blotted an eye on his bathrobe lapel. "And what good did it do? I lost Mahmoud. Pasha is still in power in Turkey. How foolish we were to think we could incite revolution by getting rid of him."

"Losing Mahmoud after almost succeeding was *unbearable*, but it was an *accident*. My point is—

"That I could have damn well prevented it."

She was crying now, gulping air between sobs. "Look at me. I killed the man I loved trying to kill someone else. It wasn't an accident. It was negligent homicide and I'll never forgive myself."

He reached to the bedstand for a tissue and wiped streaks from her face. Propped on his elbow, he met her glimmering eyes and gently shook her shoulder. "Stop *berating* yourself! You have *nothing left* to atone for! Mahmoud *lives*! He lives in you, he lives in *me*, and especially in *Ramadi*! He would be *proud* to see how you are raising him. I know I am."

She kissed his smooth cheek redolent of bay rum. "You've been a great onkle for him and I'll be forever grateful, but it's my cross to bear and it sometimes feels like I'm about to topple over."

"Then impale George with it. Did he not instruct you to stab Mahmoud if he couldn't elude capture?"

She bit her lip. "I could never have done that. I never should have listened to the bastard. Anyway, if they saw me do it they would have taken me too. It would have been pointless."

He held her close until his shoulder was damp with tears and then gently let go. "You're a wreck," he said. "Let me make some tea for you."

She rolled onto her back and unbuttoned her blouse. "Not now. What I need is something more intimate." She sat up, unclenched her bra and wiggled out of her jeans. When she wore only her socks, she untied his bathrobe and stroked the fine curls of his chest, and then worked her way down to something furrier. "I need to lose myself. I need you."

If Andreas had a mind to object, he didn't say so, and if she heard a small voice saying *Am I right?* she paid no heed.

Chapter Thirty

EVEN THOUGH MELINA HAD likely saved her life at the tempestuous demo at the kidnapper's house, Anna felt uneasy meeting the policewoman for lunch. But, following the precept that a good offense is the best defense, Anna arranged to meet up at Taverna Kalógeros, saying the food and some confidential information would be well worth the trip. She would show the selfie of the three partners in crime taken right there at the taverna, run down what she knew about Leander Eugenides, and after lunch stroll over to Meteor Import-Export Ltd., where with any luck they would find his white van. These were the cards she would play. Melina, no doubt, had some of her own, hopefully not one reading Go Directly to Jail.

On the Metro heading downtown, she dreamily reflected on how sweet the morning sex had been, Gizzard-Brain be damned, remembering how Andreas had tenderly massaged her back while giving her a pep talk. But, as it were a lollipop, she dared not savor the moment too much, lest it melt away.

She forced herself to refocus on what to make of the crooked detective. While he had been perfectly procedural yesterday, he clearly resented her unexpected intervention. Maybe lay out her evidence and ask Melina for her take on Nicolaides' lucrative little sideline, should she dare.

Why not? she heard someone say. *Unless of course you think Officer Melina is in on the take.*

Anna startled and swiveled her head, but just one somnolent graybeard was seated nearby. *Oh, it's you again*, she told her contentious innerloper. *Maybe I just will.*

The subway's P.A. lady blared "Monastiraki Square." Ascending the escalator, Anna decided to ring up Andreas to thank him for her lingering glow. At the top she stood aside to let others pass and dialed from her address book.

"Hello. This Anna? You need ride?"

"Oh hi, Akhmed," she said. "I was trying to reach someone else and dialed you by mistake. How are you?"

"Okay, good, how you?"

"Not bad, but I'm on my way to meet someone for lunch so can't talk now."

"You need ride after lunch?"

"No, that's okay," she replied, but then rewound. "Well, maybe. I'm up at Monastiraki. After I'm through, I need to pick up my son in Drapetsona and then take him home to Keratsini. That's a lot of running around, so maybe you should pick me up."

"Sure. What time?"

"Around two, maybe. I'll call you when I know, okay?"

"No problem, Anna. I take you anywhere, crazy lady."

"Umm, thanks Akhmed. I appreciate it. Talk to you later."

Forgetting about Andreas, she clicked off and stepped from the portal into gusty winds coursing through the big plaza that nearly blew away her beret. Pages of newspapers and plastic wrappers swirled about her as she made her way to Aeolus Street, home to the taverna and, by all accounts, the God of Wind, bucking her way down the pedestrian alley to the eatery's brownstone portico. Having cleared the outdoor tables of diners, Aeolus graciously held the door when she yanked it open before slamming it shut behind her.

Among the startled diners was Melina, whose crisp blue uniform made her immediately recognizable. Equally unmistakable was the man in a grey suit sitting across from her who noted Anna's entrance with an air of detachment before turning away. None other than her favorite cop in the whole wide world, Inspector Antonio Nicolaides.

#

Nicolaides arose to offer Anna a chair. "*Charismata*, Anna. I hope you don't mind me being here."

She let him lodge her between them, noting a hint of a smile on the policewoman's typically dispassionate lips.

"Hello Antonio," she replied as he took his seat. "Guess I don't, but it is a bit of a surprise. What brings you here, may I ask?"

"To haul you in for interfering with an investigation with that bit of street theater on Magnisias."

Anna glanced in alarm at Melina, now definitely smirking.

Her gaze returned to Antonio. He too was cracking a smile, a rare event in her ken.

"Just kidding," he said. "But there were times I wanted to do that. Look, what happened on Sunday wasn't in my plan but we did grab those guys in the act. I don't know how you managed that, but it worked … well, sort of."

"So it was a good thing?" Anna asked, unsure where this was going.

"Yes and no. The good part is that we're sure to convict these guys and put an end to their sordid business. But your intervention also aborted a sting operation and left important questions unanswered."

The waiter came by to take their orders. Anna ordered the first thing that came to mind as she pondered whether he'd really been working undercover, or was this a ruse to cover his complicity. But Melina, who must have known something about the sting, could have told her— unless she too was on the take, but that was almost unthinkable.

"Okay, I'll clue you in," Antonio said, dipping a wedge of pita in olive oil and watching it drip, "as long as you keep it to yourself and tell us what you were up to."

Anna's head bobbed as she tried to frame a response that was thankfully interrupted by strains of *le Marseillaise* issuing from under the table.

"Is that yours?" Melina asked.

Anna dug out her phone. "I better take this" she said, inspecting the incoming ID. Melina cocked her head as a faint female voice wafted from Anna's right ear. Anna let her have her say. "Afraid not, Irene. Tell that reporter I can't comment on an ongoing investigation. Anyway, I'm in a meeting and tied up after that. I'll call you tomorrow."

Congratulating herself for stonewalling Irene to intimate to the cops she could be trusted, Anna signed off. She laid the phone on the table and folded her arms. "Sorry about that," she said. "Now, what we were talking about? Oh yeah, the investigation you claim I impeded. Care to fill me in?"

An inaudible and atypically positive response came from within: *Perfect! You turned the table!*

In slow motion, Antonio uncrossed his legs, crossed his arms, and leaned in. Speaking from the side of his mouth, he disclosed that he'd questioned Laskaris in a missing child case based on an anonymous tip. Sensing that Laskaris knew more than he was telling, he decided to call his bluff, hinting that trouble could easily come his way. To keep the heat off, Laskaris agreed to give Antonio a piece of the action by way of a monthly stipend. The hush money, he attested, was dutifully placed in escrow.

Anna leaned back and asked what happened next.

"Not much. But I expected financial pressures would prompt him to act. Then I could pressure him to cough up his trafficking connections in return for a reduced sentence."

"So you were after bigger fish," Anna said. "Catch any?"

"I might have," the detective replied, "had the not woman sitting next to me stolen my bait—twice, in fact."

"Sorry for that," Anna said. She turned to Melina: "You knew all this?"

"Not the details, but enough to warn you off. Even so, you decided you were the better detective. But yesterday, why didn't you simply call the police when the girl was abducted?"

"Simply because I personally observed Antonio consorting with those guys on two separate occasions. Did not exactly instill confidence in him."

"Wait. Consorting?" Nicolaides said, forefinger tapping the table.

"After that so-called trial, Fotini and I saw Laskaris pick up Servopoulos. We followed them in her car to Nikaia. We were parked near their house when you showed up with a bottle of wine to celebrate that miscarriage of justice. Then, a couple of weeks later, I saw you hoofing around with Laskaris in Papandreou Park. Remember?"

"Don't you understand? I was building a relationship."

"What was I supposed to think was going on?" She turned to Melina. "I assumed Antonio was protecting them and you were doing his bidding. So I kept an eye out for what I was sure would happen and tried to round up some civilian first responders."

"Including the Children's Advocacy Center, it seems," Melina said. "How did you arrange that?"

"Might you know someone there named Nikki Troia?" Anna asked.

"The name rings a bell."

"Well, she rang me up. Said 'a friend' suggested it, never said who. Anyway, nice woman. Introduced me to Chief of Rescue Peter Mavridis. Told him I expected an abduction to go down at some point, and wanted his team to back us up when it did. It was a hard sell, but he came through."

Melina nodded. "Good man. It was he who alerted us, and fortunately for you just in the nick of time."

"Guess I cut that a little too close. Thanks for showing up when you did and controlling the situation. But were it not for me, Naila would still be caged up and you wouldn't have a clue."

Nicolaides again tilted toward her on crossed arms. Across the table, Melina crossed hers and sat back.

"Look," he said, "what you did was foolhardy and dangerous. And thanks to your little surprise party we were forced to act before we learned who they do business with."

Anna stiffened. "Hate to think how many kids they might have taken before your 'relationship' panned out," she replied, and then leaned back. "Maybe I can help you with that."

"Maybe you should," the detective said, tapping the table.

She thumbed through her gallery to the photo Ottovio had dredged up. "This is why I wanted to come here. This Facebook photo was taken in this room last spring. See the guy in the middle? He calls himself Leander Eugenides. You might want to check him out."

"Any particular reason other than guilt by association?" Nicolaides said.

"Well, for one thing, he works at an import-export firm not far from here, where he keeps the van that carried Naila off."

"Is that so. Did you witness him driving it?"

"Not then, but I'd previously spotted Servopoulos and someone who looked like Eugenides tossing some other victim into the van, rolled up in a rug like Irmak was."

"Where was that?"

"In the alley behind the house where you captured them. It was around 6 AM five or six days ago."

"And you just happened to be there?"

"Not me. A watchbird taking photos."

"Watchbird?"

Anna showed them another photo. "You were probably too busy enforcing the law yesterday to notice a little birdhouse on a tree while you were back there. Inside is a camera trained on the alley. See two guys lugging that bulging carpet? The one facing you is Servopoulos. It's hard to make out the other one, but it has to be Eugenides."

The officers leaned in, squinting, as Anna pinched and scrolled. "You had a surveillance camera?" Nicolaides asked. "Where did you get it?"

"A friend made it from a cell phone. Worked pretty well until the battery ran out."

"Is that picture all the evidence you have from it?"

"Out of hundreds of photos, pretty much. I can show you Laskaris at the back door having a smoke, but that's about it. By the time they delivered Naila, the camera had run out of juice. But I have other evidence."

"Like what?"

"Eye-witnesses. We were in Parko Navarinou in Exarcheia when my son and another boy saw them waylay the girl on Trikoupi Street. They told us two men rolled a carpet around her and threw it into a white van."

"Who is 'us'?"

"My friend Fatma, her daughter Irmak, and Imogene, the other boy's mom."

"So what did you do?"

"We caught a cab and followed them to Nikaia. On the way I texted my network to hurry over there. You know the rest. Oh, and Melina, thanks for suggesting setting up a phone tree."

Antonio shot Melina a raised eyebrow. Anna made a show of checking her phone and pushed back her chair. "Sorry, but I have to pick up my son soon. Let's walk over to where Eugenides works so you can check out that van. Can we go now?"

#

They had all wisely agreed, Anna believed, to split the tab for lunch. Wouldn't look good for her to be paying off cops or them buying a witness's testimony. On the street, the officers strolled behind Anna in a hush of discussion she wished she could overhear. She rubbed forefingers and thumbs to summon the van to its usual spot and to distract her from the tension inching up her neck. Hoping to forestall any attempt to drag her to the station house, on Athinaidos Street she placed a quick call and then checked watchbird #2. To her relief, the white van was lounging in its accustomed location.

At the shabby office building, she pointed to the corroded nameplate by the front door. "That's Eugenides' company, Meteor Import-Export, on the first floor. There's a fire door back along the side that they probably prefer using."

Nicolaides stuffed his hands in his jacket pockets as he surveyed the scene. "You seem to have spent a lot of time here," he said, pivoting to face her.

"Not much," she said as they strolled into the parking lot. "This is only my second visit, but I have a … reliable source."

Antonio and Melina traced her steps along the wall exchanging wordless glances.

"Anyway," Anna said, pointing ahead, "here's the guilty vehicle."

Hands still in pockets, Nicolaides peered through the windshield and circled around the van. "I can see a carpet inside," he said. "Could be circumstantial. What makes you believe they transported the victim in this vehicle?"

"I'll tell you," Anna said. "In fact, I'll show you. Hold on." She knelt down and peered under the bumper, got up, and stooped again along the side. "Aha! There it is!" she said, flattening herself and worming under the van until just sneakers and grunts protruded.

"Magnet's strong," she said crawling out with a small black plastic box a little heftier than a cell phone. "Almost couldn't pry it off."

She handed it to Melina, patted dust from her jeans, and tapped her phone with grimy fingers as the officers examined the oblong object.

"This is a tracking device, is it not?" Melina asked.

"Correct," Anna said, turning her phone at them. "And now it's tracking you." On her screen was a map of the neighborhood where they stood. It showed no yellow trail, though, just a blinking blue dot.

"That's you," Anna said, "and it seems the van hasn't gone anywhere today. So let's look at yesterday." She backspaced in time, zoomed out the map, and followed the van's itinerary from the parking lot with her little finger. The yellow trail meandered toward Exarcheia, coming to rest on Trikoupi. From there it circled past the police riot in People's Park around to Pireos Boulevard and from there to Petrou Ralli to make a beeline to Nikaia, arriving in the alley at 1:37 PM.

"That's where they offloaded Naila. And then Eugenides drove straight back here, see?"

The officers regarded the screen without comment.

"If you'd like," Anna said, "I can put the thing back and let you know when Eugenides goes somewhere so you can intercept him."

Antonio shook his head.

"Please don't," Melina said. "While I appreciate the trouble you've gone to, I doubt that your maps are admissible evidence. You had no authority to track that vehicle."

Anna threw up her hands in mock surrender. "Okay, arrest me for it. But you caught those guys fair and square. You don't need my inadmissible maps."

Nicolaides looked at the transponder and then at the van. He cleared his throat, and spat into his handkerchief. "Impound the thing for the duration. She can have it back when this is over."

"Be my guest," Anna said. "But leave it on so I'll know where to find it."

Both cops smiled, just as a metallic squeak from behind turned their attention to the fire door being pushed open. Upon stepping out, the pusher, a man in coveralls with glasses and receding hair, couldn't help but notice Melina's blue uniform as the door clanged shut.

"And here's the guy you wanted to track down." Anna said, eying Eugenides and then Antonio. "Go say hello."

The man patted his pocket as if he'd forgotten his phone and pulled a keyring from his trousers. As he started to unlock the door, the detective waved his badge at him. "Hi there. Hellenic Police. Might I have a word with you?"

Anna noticed a faded blue Corolla pull to the curb across the street and gave it a wave. "Looks like you don't need me in the way. My taxi is here. May I go now?"

Glancing after Nicolaides, still clutching Anna's tracker, Melina stammered: "I ... I guess so. I'll call you later."

Anna took two steps and turned back. "Oh yeah. Did you know Laskaris was passing himself off as a police warden?"

With a conspiratorial wink, Melina said, "Antonio gave him a fake badge and had some precinct cards printed up. He thinks he is but of course he isn't."

"All that and no get-out-of-jail card," Anna said, winking back.

"You know," Melina said, "I heard there's an opening for a real warden over in Keratsini. You seem to have a knack for police work. I'd love to see you on the force."

For a frozen moment Anna gaped at Melina as if her soul were being solicited. *Before you kiss her off,* her inner extrovert advised, *think about it. Get paid for doing good. Benefits. Advancement, even. And inside info about police corruption.*

Preferring not to get into an argument with herself at this particular moment, she told Melina: "Dunno what to say. I gotta go." She strode toward the street. Along the way she blew a kiss to her parking lot watchbird, thinking, *Okay, okay, I'll think about it. Enough already. Didn't I tell you get lost yesterday?*

Her advisor's response was unexpectedly contrite and oddly unsettling. *Sorry. Guess I've worn out my welcome. Have a nice life. You're on your own, sis.*

Somehow I doubt that.

Chapter Thirty-One

A CHEERY "*MARHABAAN*, ANNA," ushered her into Akhmed's sagging passenger seat. "Nice to see you. Where you go today? We have another adventure?"

"*Scheisse*, I hope not! Like I said, it's to Drapetsona to pick up Ramadi." Glancing back at the officers, she said: "Get going before I implode."

"You mean explode?" He looked her up and down. "You suicide bomber?"

"In a way, I guess. I blew away my credibility. I'm such a donkey-ass!"

"You no donkey. I see you save that girl. You hero. Wish someone had saved me like that. Why you feel bad?"

"Because I was wrong all along about that detective over there being crooked. He was after those guys too."

Akhmed peered past her at the cops interviewing Eugenides. "He not do good job?"

"You don't understand. I got in his way. If they ever find out, all the people who came out for me will think I'm a fool. I'm completely mortified."

"You not dead yet, Anna. You full of life."

"Thanks, Akhmed," she said, patting his arm. She plucked a string of wooden beads dangling from the rear-view mirror and started thumbing through them. "Anyway, let's go get my son. It's getting late."

Akhmed smiled benevolently. "Nice boy, but sometimes makes trouble. Like his '*um*.'"

He got underway and piloted the car through congested streets to the E56 expressway that arced around the Acropolis before plunging toward Moschato and Piraeus, where traffic was even more bogged down. As they inched along to the chirping rhythm of the Toyota's water pump, Anna sighed and slumped back, winding the wooden beads around her fingers.

"Guess it wasn't all bad," she said. "At least lots of people showed up and those guys are out of business. And thanks to you I wasn't crushed to death. I really owe you. Ramadi too."

"You call boy Ramadi. Funny. Why you pick Ramadi?"

"Was his father's family name. Why is that funny?"

"Mine too. Akhmed Al Ramadi. What was father's given name?"

"Mahmoud, Mahmoud Al Ramadi. He was Iraqi. But you said you are from Syria. Must be a coincidence."

Without signaling, Akhmed weaved across the right lane to the angry blare of a truck, pulled to the curb, and killed the engine.

"Why did you stop?" Anna asked. "Please keep going. This makes me nervous."

Akhmed wiped his eyes with his sleeve. Half swallowing, half crying, he said: "I am Iraqi. My big brother name was Mahmoud. Daesh kidnapped me, took me to Syria from Mosul. Never saw Mahmoud again. I had fight for them almost two years. See my face? All burned from bomb blast."

Anna's teeth clamped on her lower lip. Her eyes bulged. "And then?"

He sniffled, cleared his throat. "We were in Raqqa. Kurdish and American soldiers came. They find me after bomb, treat my wounds. Daesh melt away and I escape, cross over to Turkey, then get ride to Antalya."

"How strange. Mahmoud went to Syria too, up north, and then hitched through Turkey. Was in a battalion that fought Daesh. Said he killed one."

Akhmed leaned back, eyes closed, lips curling up. "Good for him. Lucky it was not me."

"So what brought you here?"

"In Antalya I get work as tea boy. Hear customer say Greek cruise ship look for workers. It take me on and I clean cabins. We dock here and they pay me. That night I slide down rope, climb fence, and get away."

Gripping his knee with an unsteady hand, Anna said: "Please tell me this awful story is true: Daesh came to your house in Mosul and killed your parents and took you with them. Your older brother was at university. You never saw him again. Am I right?"

Akhmed was quivering, bent over the steering wheel. "*Naem!* Yes! *Hafizna Allah!* God save us!" He wiped his red-rimmed eyes to see Anna also weeping. "Mahmoud, your husband, where he go?"

"I'm sorry ... to have to tell you this ...," she said between sobs. "He died ... In Turkey ... We buried him in Izmir. He never got to see his son."

Akhmed expelled three great sighs. His hand went to the prayer beads Anna held. "Me no religious now. Not after Daesh. This *masbaha* was his. I take when they came to house and hold up to show them I praise Allah and they let me live. I keep for Mahmoud if ever I see him again."

"I know," she said between gulps of air. "It's like a rosary, used to count your prayers. I have one that belonged to my grandmother."

Anna solemnly hung the beads back on the mirror, wiped away Akhmed's tears, and then pulled a quivering shoulder to her in a delicate embrace.

A stream of impatient drivers crept past the Corolla gawking at its occupants clutching one another, tinging their shirts with tears of grief and recognition. Akhmed straightened up, started the car, and merged it into the lazy metal stream. Unconcerned with the halting traffic, they took turns weaving their stories into a fabric something like muslin. Gazing at his profile, thinking how much he resembled Mahmoud under his scarred complexion and heavy glasses, she asked him how old he was. Twenty-three, he said. Same as Mahmoud when she first met him, she replied, remembering Mahmoud telling her how nearsighted his little brother was and what a poor fighter Daesh would find him to be and found herself wondering if he had ever killed anyone.

When Akhmed asked her what Mahmoud was doing in Turkey, she didn't hedge, laying out their mission to assassinate the president with a poison dart launched from a tube he carried disguised as a blind man's cane. She was surprised he found their covert action if not admirable, then at least understandable. But she held back when he asked her how Mahmoud had died, only saying that he'd accidentally touched some of his weapon's poison. The truth of her complicity could wait until she got to know him better.

#

When at last they reached Daria's place, Anna asked Akhmed to wait while she retrieved Ramadi.

"Sure, Anna. I wait for you until Prophet returns."

She was half an hour late for her pickup. Letting her in, Daria remarked on Anna's red-rimmed eyes and asked if she was all right. More or less, Anna told her. She'd been through a couple of tough days, topped off by an intense emotional encounter—of the good kind, she hastened to say.

At the sound of her voice, Ramadi launched himself into the front room flapping a sheet of paper and into her open arms. "Mutti," he said, beaming, "Daria taught me to write Arabic. See?"

"That's fabulous," Anna said. "I'm so proud of you! Thank you, Daria." She perused Ramadi's ragged calligraphy. "Good job! I want to learn it too. And now we know someone who can help us."

She grabbed Ramadi's backpack, kissed Daria and Yasmin goodbye, and followed Ramadi downstairs, not bounding as he did, but absently, dazed with wonder and expectance. Her lot in life might never be the same after this, and that might not be such a bad thing.

As they approached the taxi, Anna extended her palm toward Akhmed's jalopy and told Ramadi that today they didn't need to take all those buses. They had a ride, the best they could ever have.

"Do you remember this car?" she asked him, pointing to the piebald Corolla. "And our driver Akhmed from yesterday?"

"I do. He took us to that house with the model plane and all the people outside."

"*Marhabaan*, Ramadi," Akhmed said as they tumbled into the rear seat. "You fine-looking boy." And to Anna, "Like you when you smile."

At that moment, all that had mattered to her—capturing the venal kidnappers, outwitting the police, even her tug-of-love with Andreas—somehow felt resolved, receding like Daria's front door in Akhmed's rear-view mirror. Her disused dimples in full display, she said: "Ramadi, I have a big surprise for you. This is your *real* onkle from Iraq, your papi's brother. What do you think of that?"

He looked at her quizzically and then studied Akhmed before turning to her again.

"He doesn't *look* like Onkle Andreas," he said. "You mean I have two of them?"

And then, before she could even begin to explain, his head pivoted back to Akhmed to ask an even simpler question.

"Onkle, can we go get ice cream?"

After I rode with Akhmed to take the woman and daughter home I felt tired, maybe from all that excitement. And a sense of lightness that draws me back to wherever that misty place is.

I must have slept. How strange. I awake wondering if things have changed for better or worse. So I visit Katrina. It is late at night and she and our boy are not home. I check at Andreas's house. He sleeps there alone. I visit the taverna and the café. They are closed. Nor is Akhmed at his sleeping-place. Where are they? Are they together? In trouble?

Where else have I been that they might be? I check the Metro station near the ferry terminal where I found Akhmed—deserted by all but a destitute man, homeless like me.

I am close to where I first met Andreas the day I landed in Piraeus. Something moves me to retrace my route from where I landed. I do it in reverse, following the boulevard along the harbor. I come to a familiar street corner across from a cruise terminal where a church sits. It was here that Andreas saved me from arrest by a policeman wanting to see my papers and I was petrified. Now I follow the cross-street up the hill I walked down, to a square with a café where I took my morning meal, the first food I had tasted since coming ashore from two days at sea. Even without benefit of body, that refreshment is still vivid to me.

From which of the five streets meeting at this square did I enter that morning? In the dark they look so alike and so different traveling the other way. One will take me to where I slept that first night, a cove where the fisherman dropped me. When dawn came, I climbed an embankment to start my trek to meet my new comrades, also the path to my demise.

I choose a street and suddenly I am there, by dark lapping water. I drift down to where I stumbled ashore all wet. Nearby sits a boulder with small rocks stacked on top. It looks like the kind of way-post piled up to guide travelers. No hikers pass by here, so why would someone do that?

I drift back up to the roadway. Under a street-lamp down the road a small car is parked, the only one along the long promenade. Is it not Akhmed's old sedan? Through its fogged windows I see two persons huddled in back, asleep, their heads bowed over a little one straddling their laps with a jacket thrown over him. It is my family, together at last!

On the pavement I see a shimmering puddle, water perhaps, oozing out from under the car. Do they sleep here because his car will not start? And why have they come to this lonely place shadowed by apartment towers at a cusp of the sea where I made landfall? I recall pointing out this place to her on a map. Perhaps she remembered and directed Akhmed here in my honor. I am overwhelmed. There is no god but God.

Chapter Thirty-Two

Several Weeks Later

AKHMED DROVE INTO THE small parking lot at Andreas Papandreou Park and turned to his passenger. "This is where your *um* tell me to take you. She say you know the way."

He got out and opened the back door to retrieve a kite with the head of an eagle attached to a spool of string as Ramadi opened the passenger door and stepped onto the pavement. Slinging the kite over his shoulder, Akhmed took the boy's hand and they trudged through the gate to follow one of a grid of footpaths that delineated several dozen square plots, each with something different to do: playgrounds; picnic and performance pavilions; a privet-hedge maze; a giant sundial to race around; gardens with ponds. Something for everyone.

A five-minute walk found them at a field of patchy grass alongside an oversized chessboard, where elderly men kibitzed as two of them shuffled chess pieces half their height between squares. Akhmed handed the reel to Ramadi and commenced walking backwards. When they were about five meters apart, with a leap, he released the kite. The string tensed as a breeze wafted the paper bird of prey aloft. Ramadi dodged and tugged as he let out more line, his body language miming his tethered eagle's gyrations, urging: "Fly, *aetós*, fly!"

Retreating to drag *aetós* higher, Ramadi stumbled on a stone, losing the spool as he fell. As it slithered away, the kite plummeted to earth behind a hedge, out of sight.

"You okay?" Akhmed asked, helping him up.

Sniffling, Ramadi asked, "Where is my kite, *Onkle* Akhmed?"

"Not *onkle*, Ramadi. That's German. Call me *eamm*. I am not just *any* uncle, I am your father's only brother! Your *E-am-m*. When will you learn, my brother's son?"

"I am sorry ... Eamm. Please find my kite."

Akhmed pointed. "It is over there, Ramadi."

The boy followed his finger to spot the kite's tail slung across the shrubbery. He retrieved his reel and ran to it, trailing string that kept getting caught in tall grass. The hedge fronted a living maze of blind passages within which, his mother had told him, a monster was said to lurk, and then played Minotaur to his Theseus. There had been trouble that day a month ago, he recalled.

He was standing by the hedge with a wrinkled brow when Akhmed came to him. "This … this is the lab-ee-rint," Ramadi said. "Can you go in and get the kite?"

"Sure. We both go. Come."

Ramadi wasn't so sure. "I don't wanna. I was scared in there."

"You were here? You get lost inside?"

"With my mutti. She saw bad men and we had to hide."

"You mean those kidnappers we follow to their house and police come?"

Ramadi nodded.

"Well, they not here now," Akhmed said, taking Ramadi's hand. "Come, we get kite."

They entered the maze and found the captive kite. Akhmed extricated it and hauled in string until it resisted, snagged somewhere. Handing the kite to Ramadi, he chomped on the string until its fibers parted.

They retraced their steps out of the labyrinth and walked back, Ramadi reeling in string. Next to the empty field, a king lay toppled on the now-deserted chessboard. Akhmed retied the string, but after several attempts at launching *aetós* into flaccid air ended in failure, the two headed home, soaring aborted.

In the alley behind the house Akhmed kicked at a cobblestone and knelt down to retrieve a house key. He unlocked the back door, and then the inner one painted saffron to let them into the kitchen.

"Mutti! We're home!" Ramadi said.

Akhmed said he was thirsty and poured water for them from a bottle in the fridge.

"Mutti! We're home! Where are you?"

"Maybe her work keep her," Akhmed said. He sipped some water and held out a glass to Ramadi.

"Eamm Akhmed," Ramadi said, ignoring the offering, "will you stay here till she comes?"

"Sure, '*iibn aliakht*," he said. "Please drink this. Maybe we make evening meal. Let me text her."

Ramadi refreshed himself while Akhmed's thumbs twiddled and then laid his phone on the table. "We wait for her to say." Then he patted the kite's eagle head. "Sorry. You fly next time." His Greek was improving but still needed work. Ramadi's Arabic encompassed just a few nouns, honorifics, and family names, but Akhmed was working on that.

Shortly, Akhmed's phone sounded from the table. Ramadi stabbed at it. "Mutti?"

"Hi Love," his mother's voice said. "Sorry I'm late. How are you?"

"We went to park to fly *aetós*. I fell and it fell into that lab-ee-rint."

"Are you hurt, *schatz*?"

"I guess not. But *aetós* wouldn't fly after that."

"I'm sorry. Glad you're okay. Now, let me talk to Onkle Akhmed, please."

"It's *Eamm* Akhmed," he said and passed the phone.

She told Akhmed, "I'm on the Metro to Piraeus, approaching Moscato. Then I take the bus home."

"Where you come from?"

"Way up in Chalandri, with officials, for a child protection task force meeting. I was impressed to see humanitarians and police working together. How they do things will take some getting used to, but I think I will like this job. I'll tell you more later. There's leftover stew in the fridge you can heat up. Cook some rice. See you then."

Akhmed told her he would stay for supper and then go back to the sporting goods store in Athens where he and his taxicab slept for free.

He put the phone down and went to parse the fridge for yesterday's remains. As he rummaged, Ramadi asked, "Eamm, how did you get here?"

"On big ship, Ramadi. Full of tourists. Party ship. I get off when it come here."

"That sounds fun. Why did you get off?"

"Not fun for me. I work cleaning cabins. But got paid, tips sometimes. Enough to buy old car, start over here."

"You come here to see me and Mutti?"

"Did not know about you. Just trying to get by."

"So how did you find us?"

"Was miracle. Only Allah knows. I tell you what I think someday."

Ramadi came over to Akhmed and tugged at his jeans. "Tell me now. Tell me about my *papi*."

"You mean your *al'ab*, Ramadi?"

"No *Eamm*," the boy insisted, not understanding father in Arabic. "I mean my *papi*! Who died."

"That would be your *al'ab*. Remember that," Akhmed said gently, motioning Ramadi to sit with him at the table. His thick glasses started to fog. "War all around Mosul. Militia men come to house, take me prisoner. Mahmoud was not home. I never see him after that."

"Where was Papi then?"

"He was student at engineering campus. Wanted to rebuild our country after war."

"Did he finish school?"

A tear trickled down Akhmed's pockmarked face. Blinking it away, he removed his glasses. "I do not think so," he said, and coughed. "Anna say he escape to Syria, fought in war there. Militia take me to Syria and made to fight, but on other side. Lucky we not meet there."

Leaving much sorrow unsaid, he arose, wiped his eyes with a napkin, and pushed on his glasses. "Ask your *um*. Maybe she know more. Now I show you how we cook rice. But first we wash hands so we start off clean."

⁓

Providence has brought Akhmed and Katrina together. It cannot be me, as I have no influence on earthly events. Though I witnessed their first encounter, it was Katrina who must have drawn him to her as she did me. Let them know one another, share good days, and guide my boy to a more peaceful and purposeful manhood than my own. I pray for good times to come to them.

And just as for them, something has changed for me. The voices of that heavenly chorus are more distinct than before. The obscuring mist above me has thinned to reveal swirling shadows beyond. As in an airplane ascending through heavy clouds, the sky brightens and the Earth falls away.

I go with it. Farewell, my loved ones! I pray that we shall reunite, but only in due time. Certainly, after all that has happened and may yet to come, I can wait.

But before I go, I must tell one last thing. AKHMED! STOP SMOKING!

THE END

Disclaimer

First thing you should know, I didn't write this book and take no responsibility (well, maybe some) for its content. Second thing is stop reading now until you've read the whole book or you'll be sorry. Maybe it'll make more sense to you than it did to me.

I'd almost forgotten about that writer who was supposed to be shadowing me when Max the editor checked in the other day with some news. The manuscript is finished, he said, and he'd been polishing it. He thanked me for my patience and for being a good sport and asked if I might like to read it. Sure, I said. He sent me a link to a doc and a password to open it. He said I could comment but it couldn't be altered, copied, or downloaded—intellectual property, copyright, pre-publication security, blah blah blah.

Thirty-two chapters, mostly about me, that took a while to get through. I fell asleep reading it in bed and woke up after vivid dreams with my head spinning and my laptop out of juice.

Once I got over being creeped out, I found things mostly as I remembered them and some I hadn't. Some got left out I thought he should have kept, like how Zoe and I got to be friends or how Mahmoud kept popping in on my dreams. Max apologized for the omissions. He blamed them on Page Count, whoever that is.

The telling of some scenes, especially the tenser ones, felt pretty true to life. I know I should feel flattered and grateful for how things turned out, but I came across as sort of obnoxious, obsessive, and oblivious to what Nicolaides was up to. If only Melina had leveled with me about him being undercover, my life would've been a whole lot simpler.

And when Max and I met for an audio chat, he pointed out that at least some characters warned me of my folly. I suppose Andreas and Irene and Peter did, even Ottovio, but only Melina knew the detective's game plan while I thought he was corrupt.

Yet, he reminded me, did I not get some appreciation along the way, a lot of which I seemed to dismiss? Sure, but only at the end did it start to feel deserved.

Then he asked why I'd put myself through all those exertions. I said he should know—to get those guys, put them in jail, keep them from ever snatching another kid. True, he said, but maybe it was more than that. Besides my obsession, what did I want, really want, he asked like some kind of therapist.

I couldn't pin it down. On one hand, I wanted to make a difference and have people come with me. On the other, I don't like being singled out as the leader. I thought back, all the way back to Africa where sleazy men were always hitting on me. I tried to avoid them by keeping to myself but it kept happening. And when I got here, I blogged and organized under an assumed name. I didn't want to show up in police records or on some nationalist's enemies list, but that happened anyway. So much for keeping my head down.

Best I could tell him it a sense of purposefully belonging. Community and solidarity, surrounded by a second family looking out for me and vice versa.

It seems I'd experienced some of that, Max kindly pointed out, didn't I agree? Guess I found closeness with Andreas, and with the moms I got to know. Penelope and I are on better terms. Zoe's been very supportive. So has my Swiss family, at least over Zoom.

Anyone else with ties that bind? he asked. The guy is a bulldog.

One part or another of my stupid brain finally coughed up an answer. Besides Ramadi and Andreas, Akhmed of course. He's a sweetheart—not that I love him or anything. He must have suffered a lot but he's not bitter the way Mahmoud was. And he has relatives back home who Ramadi should get to know. Me too, but first we need to learn Arabic.

He started on another question but I shushed him. Turned it around and asked him point blank did the writer make me want all those things or did I?

He took a long time to answer. At last, he said everything that happened did so "on its own accord" or from choices I made. For his part, all the writer could do, he claimed, was to try to "temper my impetuosity."

Then it hit me: Was that Gizzard Brain? To think that the writer put something like a ventriloquist's dummy inside my head makes me crazy. I hope it's gone for good. At least we parted on good terms.

"But you didn't bail this time, did you?" he said. "And in the end, wasn't your embarrassment worth the admiration you've gotten for your commitment, perseverance, and strength of character?"

Well, I must admit the experience left me more trusting in people. After all, a bunch of them I didn't even know showed up in Nikaia. I better text my phone tree a thankyou.

Right, he said. They hauled ass for you. So maybe don't doubt yourself so much from now on. Play to your strengths and challenge your weaknesses. Then he said he had to go, but I wasn't done with him.

I had to know about all those coincidences. Like witnessing two kidnappings by the same man, one a girl I'd just met.

To which he claimed I'd "put myself there." Seemed to think I had a choice.

But what about running into Akhmed? I asked. Of all the taxi drivers out there. Max put it this way: "Not all twists of fate have rational explanations. Perhaps a higher power was at work."

Higher power? I don't believe in that stuff.

That's why he'd stripped out certain parts from the copy he let me read, Max said. For my own good. Details I had no need to know and probably wouldn't believe anyway.

No idea what he was talking about. "Explain," I said.

He cleared his throat and kind of dribbled out: "Let's just say … that your support system is … bigger than you know."

I assumed he was slyly referring to the writer. It made me want to hug Max for all the love and care they put into this thing, which after all is all about me. But since we were talking over the Internet, I just thanked him with all my heart, blew a virtual kiss, and we signed off.

Would I do it again? I dunno. Is the third time a charm or a comeuppance? But since I can always say no, as we say in German, *Lass die Puppe tanzen*—let the doll dance."

My limbs are twitching. I gotta go.

Anna

Acknowledgements

Over the course of writing this novel, Aygül and I purchased and moved into our first house, bought a new car and put 40,000 miles on it, saw our daughter graduate from high school, go on to college, and then to graduate school. Just as does *Her Own Devices*, our lives had many moving parts that took a while to work out. Throughout, Aygül kept me on the ball and juggled ones I let fall. I can't say how much I love you.

To all who selflessly volunteered to help me birth this book, my everlasting gratitude. You know who you are, but readers don't: Jay Alexander, San Cassimally, Nick Chrisman, Linda Chuss, Daniel Gover, William Oppenheimer, and beta readers Max and Christina of Quiet House Editing. Valuable feedback came from members of the Metrowest Writers Guild, and especially from several dozen members of the Columbia Fiction Foundry, who have patiently collectively vetted the book over almost two years. Many thanks to Publisher Sandra Fluck, who boosted my spirits by hosting online excerpts from the novel at TheWriteLaunch.com and essays about it at BooksCover2Cover.com. I am even grateful to Google, without whose maps, views, and images my settings could not have come to life. Hats off to designer Errol Richardson and artist Deniz Dutton for their evocative cover art. And, of course, had Guernica World Editions' Publisher Michael Mirolla not believed in and patiently shepherded the work from draft to print, you would not be reading this now.

I also want to thank my characters, especially intrepid Anna and long-suffering Mahmoud, for putting up with my intrusions. Thank you all for your kind contributions.

Credits

Actors, principal

Those you're expected to care about. All but Ramadi are from the prequel, Turkey Shoot.

Akhmed: Iraqi Mahmoud's long-lost younger brother, somewhat worse the wear for two years of Isis captivity in Syria, whom Mahmoud discovers driving a decrepit gypsy cab in Athens

Andreas: Peaceable Austrian radical-turned-hairdresser, formerly Anna's co-conspirator, now reluctant helpmeet and conflicted bisexual lover.

Anna: Insecure Swiss expat who, after a tragedy, stopped calling herself Katrina. She de-politicized to raise Ramadi, but kept her commitment to anarchism alive. She continues to bite off more than she can chew, as her skeptical inner voice repeatedly warns her.

Mahmoud: Iraqi freedom fighter who died trying to topple a despot, now in limbo halfway to Paradise. From there, he visits the earthly plane, surveilling his loved ones without benefit of ears, hoping Akhmed and Anna will meet.

Ottovio: Greek uber-geek who repurposes cell phones and hacks into databases for just causes, in this case Anna's. Will hack for food and future considerations.

Ramadi: Affable love-child of Mahmoud and Anna (then Katrina), now five, fascinated by flight; moored by *Mueti* Anna, *Onkle* Andreas, and the moms of Anna's unlicensed preschool collective.

Actors, support

Thirty other characters with speaking parts; unless noted, they're Greek. Those marked "+" first appeared in Turkey Shoot.

Antonio Nicolaides: Inspector, Nikaia precinct, whom Anna finds of dubious probity

+ Beatrice: Ottovio's equally geeky paramour

Cassie: Kiddie Cloud daycare co-op co-founder
+ Chris: friend of Anna, shift manager at the anarchist-run No Name Café
Damon: manager of Taverna Omphalos, where Anna briefly worked
Daria: Persian, single mom and Kinder Cloud co-founder
+ Evangeline Vyros: Estate Agent, friend of Andreas who researches property for him
Fatma: Turkish, nurse at the Keratsini Free Clinic whom Anna befriends
Fotini Evangelatos of Piraiki: kidnapped boy Sami's mom, wife of banker Ilias
Gizzard-Brain: Anna's intrusive inner critic whom she argues with and rarely obeys
Gyro: itinerant handyman, friend of Ottovio
Imogene: Exarcheian mom Anna meets in Parko Navarinou with her son Viktor
Irene: Market Manager at Prótos, Anna's supervisor at Altogether
Irmak: Turkish, 11, daughter of Fatma
Katia: Kiddie Cloud co-founder
+ Kosta: Andreas' ex-domestic partner, owner of Radically Chic hair salon
Leander Eugenides: possible bagman for Servopoulos and Laskaris
Marcos Hexadecimos: cross-dressing client of Radically Chic Salon
Marten Piperal: Estonian, CTO of Olympus InterConnect and architect of Altogether
Max: the novel's helpful editor, dialoging in Anna's prologue and epilogue
Melina Cristopoulos: Desk Sergeant in Nicolaides' Nikaia precinct, mom in Anna's orbit
Naila: a misfortunate Syrian immigrant teenage girl
Nikki Troia: social worker, Child Advocacy Center
+ Orhan Demirci: Turkish, CEO of Olympos InterConnect telecom who befriended Anna
+ Penelope: Artist living upstairs from Anna
Peter Mavridis: Chief of search & rescue, Child Advocacy Center
Theodoros Servopoulos: kidnapper whom Anna outs as he snatches a child

Various legal professionals in a Piraeus courtroom

Vasilios Laskari: Greek nationalist child trafficker and Servopoulos' partner

Viktor: 8, Ramadi's playmate, son of Imogene from Exarcheia

Zoe Karaoúli: reporter for Alpha TV, who takes interest in Anna's exploits

Organizations

Altogether, Orhan Demirci's social media platform, run by Protos with Anna as webmaster

Child Advocacy Center, Greater Athens; provides social services to children and families; rescues and shelters abused and abandoned children

Child Protection League of Greater Athens, organized by Anna and other moms after one of their kids is kidnapped, online at *Altogether*

Kinder Cloud, a floating daycare collective of five moms, instigated by Anna

Prótos, Greek ISP hosting Orhan Demirci's *Altogether* social network

Olympos InterConnect, Demirci's Anatolian ISP, partnering with Prótos

Radically Chic, Kosta's gay hair salon where Andreas works and Anna visits

Locations

Cities

    Athens, Greece

        Exarcheia

        Monastiraki

    Mosul, Iraq

    Piraeus, Greece

        Drapetsona

        Keratsini

        Nikaia

        Piraiki

Tampouria
Ramadi, Iraq
Eateries
East Asia, Chinese, Athens
Golden House of Pizza, Greek, Keratsini
Monks Taverna, Greek, Athens
No Name Café, Counter/Multicultural, Keratsini
Omphalos Taverna, Greek, Keratsini
Parks
Andreas Papandreou, Keratsini
Parko Navarinou, Exarcheia

About the Writer

Geoffrey Dutton wasn't always a novelist. There was a time when all he wrote were scientific papers and reports about software he and his colleagues coded. Their innovative techniques for processing and visualizing geospatial data were esoteric at the time, but led the way to digital way-finding and Web mapping tools that everyone now takes for granted. Had these far-reaching geo-technologies never come about, Geoff could not have written his novels. Not only did he rely on the Web to research them, he used digital maps and views to get acquainted with places he'd never visited, and had his fictional characters do the same.

Belatedly realizing that even with fifty published academic papers he would still need to work for food, Geoff set his sights on high tech. The new millennium found him writing a newsletter for an IT research firm, and then slid into technical writing, anonymously documenting other people's code.

Eventually, when the financial software startup where he worked was bought by a public company that in turn was gobbled up by private equity, he bailed. Weary of enabling capitalist tools, Geoff struck out to write whatever suited his fancy, starting with things that didn't, like electronic surveillance, kabuki politics, and military adventurism. Soon, he branched into memoir, short fiction, and satire, littering the Web with several hundred pieces of prose before building a blog and beginning work on a novel motivated by his country's needless and heedless impositions in the Middle East that ruined so many innocent lives. As one might expect, it adopted the victims' radicalized perspectives.

Publishing that novel, an international conspiracy thriller called *Turkey Shoot*, released on 9/11/2018, failed to satisfy both Geoff and his characters, especially his female lead. Having left her bereaved and in a family way, Geoff felt a moral obligation to rehabilitate both her and her late lover in this book. How well that worked is up to you to say, but at least they seem satisfied.

You can usually find Geoff, Aygül, and a pampered pussycat in an old mill town west of Boston. When he's not writing, revising, blogging, and pitching his prose, he's typically engaged in feeding his family. He particularly enjoys preparing wild mushrooms he forages around the area. Everyone's fine, so far.

Online Publications

Bookstore:
https://bookshop.org/shop/perfidy-press
Publishing Website & Blog:
https://perfidy.press
News & Opinion Blog:
https://progressivepilgrim.review
Articles for CounterPunch:
https://www.counterpunch.org/author/geoff-dutton/
Content on Medium:
https://medium.com/@gdutton
Draft Novel Excerpts:
https://thewritelaunch.com/author/geoffrey-dutton/
Essays and Reviews:
https://bookscover2cover.com/author/geoffrey-dutton/
Monthly Newsletter:
https://perfidy.press/subscribe/
Twitter (X):
https://twitter.com/PerfidyPress
Linked In:
https://www.linkedin.com/in/duttongeoffrey/
Email:
geoff@perfidy.press

Printed by Imprimerie Gauvin
Gatineau, Québec